CATHERINE RYAN HYDE

What if the only way
to save your mother…
is to leave her?

Don't Let Me Go

Catherine Ryan Hyde is the author of several highly acclaimed novels including the award-winning *Pay It Forward* (which was made into a feature film starring Kevin Spacey and Helen Hunt), *Love in the Present Tense* (a Richard & Judy Book Club bestseller), *Chasing Windmills, When I Found You, Second Hand Heart* and *The Hardest Part of Love*.

PRAISE FOR CATHERINE RYAN HYDE

'This gritty love story is compelling reading'
Sun

'Surprisingly wonderful'
Mirror

'A remarkable story of the magic of love'
Daily Express

'This novel has a steely core of gritty reality beneath its optimism' Amazon.com

'A quick read, told with lean sentences and an edge'
Los Angeles Times

'A sweet and honest look at the pains and pleasures of love' Jane Green

'A work of art . . . enchanting'
San Francisco Chronicle

www.**transworldbooks**.co.uk

DON'T LET ME GO

Catherine Ryan Hyde

BLACK SWAN

TRANSWORLD PUBLISHERS
61–63 Uxbridge Road, London W5 5SA
A Random House Group Company
www.transworldbooks.co.uk

DON'T LET ME GO
A BLACK SWAN BOOK: 9780552776677

First publication in Great Britain
Black Swan edition published 2011

A CIP catalogue record for this book
is available from the British Library.

Addresses for Random House Group Ltd companies outside the UK
can be found at: www.randomhouse.co.uk
The Random House Group Ltd Reg. No. 954009

The Random House Group Limited supports The Forest Stewardship Council®
(FSC®), the leading international forest certification organisation. All our titles
that are printed on Greenpeace approved FSC® certified paper carry the FSC®
logo. Our paper procurement policy can be found at
www.randomhouse.co.uk/environment

Typeset in 11/13.5pt Giovanni Book by
Falcon Oast Graphic Art Ltd.
Printed and bound by CPI Group (UK) Ltd, Croydon, CR0 4YY

2 4 6 8 10 9 7 5 3 1

In memory of Pat, who got me into my first writers'
workshop . . . somehow.

Billy

Every time Billy looked out his front sliding-glass door, he saw the ugly, gray LA winter afternoon move that much closer to dark. A noticeable difference each time. Then he laughed, and chastised himself out loud, saying, 'What did we think, Billy Boy, that sunset would change its mind and break with tradition just this one night?'

He looked out again, hiding behind his curtain and wrapping it around himself as he leaned in front of the glass.

The little girl was still there.

'We know what this means,' he said. 'Don't we?'

But he didn't answer himself. Because he *did* know. So there was really no need to belabor the conversation.

He pulled his old flannel bathrobe over his pajamas, wrapping it too tightly around his stick-thin frame, then tying it with a rope that had replaced the robe's sash some half-dozen years earlier.

Yes.

Billy Shine was about to go outside.

Not out the apartment door and on to the street. Nothing that insanely radical. But out on to his little first-floor patio, or balcony, or whatever you might properly call that postage-stamp-sized piece of real estate adorned with two rusty lawn chairs.

He looked out again first, as though he might see a storm or a war or an alien invasion brewing. Some act of God that might justify his failure to follow through. But it was only a tiny bit closer to dark, which was hardly unexpected.

He unwedged the broomstick – the improvised burglar-proof lock for his sliding-glass patio door – coating his fingers with dust and lint as he did so. It hadn't been moved in ages. And it shamed him, because he prided himself on cleanliness.

'Note to self,' he said out loud. 'Clean everything. Even if it's something we think we won't use anytime soon. On principle, if for no other reason.'

Then he slid the door open just the tiniest bit, sucking in his breath, loudly, at the feel of the chill outdoor air.

The little girl glanced up, then down at her feet again.

Her hair looked almost comically disheveled, as if no one had brushed it for a week. Her blue cardigan sweater had been buttoned incorrectly. She could not have been more than nine or ten. She was sitting on a step, her arms wrapped around her own knees, rocking and staring at her shoes.

He'd expected something more from her, some more dramatic reaction to his presence, yet couldn't put his finger on exactly what he'd thought that might be.

He sat gingerly on the very edge of one rusty chair,

leaning over the railing, looking down at the little girl's head from maybe three feet above her.

'A gracious good evening to you,' he said.

'Hi,' she said, in a voice like a soprano foghorn.

It made him jump. He almost upended the chair.

Though hardly an expert on children, Billy reasoned that a girl who looked that depressed should speak in a barely audible voice. Not that he hadn't heard this little girl's voice through the walls many times before. She lived in the basement apartment with her mother, so he heard her often. Too often. And she'd never sounded only barely audible. Yet, somehow, he'd expected her to make an exception on maybe just this one occasion.

'Are you my neighbor?' she asked, in the same startling voice.

This time he was ready for it.

'It would seem that way,' he said.

'Then how come I never met you?'

'You're meeting me now. Take what you can get from this life.'

'You talk funny.'

'You talk loud.'

'Yeah, that's what everybody says. Do other people say you talk funny?'

'Not that I can recall,' Billy said. 'Then again, I don't talk to enough people to gather a genuine consensus.'

'Well, take my word for it. It's a weird way to talk, especially to a kid. What's your name?'

'Billy Shine. What's yours?'

'Shine? Like the stars, or like your floor shines if you wax it?'

'Yes. Like that.'

'Where did you get a name like Billy Shine?'

'Where did you get *your* name? Which, by the way, you still haven't told me.'

'Oh. It's Grace. And I got it from my mother.'

'Well, I didn't get the name Billy Shine from my mother. From my mother I got Donald Feldman. So I changed it.'

'Why?'

'Because I was in show business. I needed a dancer's name.'

'Donald Feldman isn't a dancer's name?'

'Not even a little bit.'

'How do you find out what is and what isn't?'

'You just know it in your heart. So, look. We could sit out here all night and continue this charming exchange. But I actually came out here to ask you why you're sitting outside all by yourself.'

'I'm not, really,' she said. 'I'm really out here with you.'

'It's almost dark.'

She moved for the first time since he'd come outside, looking up as if to fact-check his sentence.

'Yeah,' she said. 'It is. So, you're not in show business any more?'

'No. Not at all. Not in any way. I'm not in any business now.'

'Didn't you like being a dancer?'

'I loved it. I adored it. It was my world. I sang, too. And acted.'

'So why'd you stop?'

'I wasn't cut out for it.'

'You weren't good?'

'I was very good.'

'Then what weren't you cut out for?'

Billy sighed. He had come out here to ask questions, not to answer them. And yet it had seemed so natural, so inevitable, when the roles reversed on him. In fact, he wondered why he'd ever thought he could be the grown-up in this – or, for that matter, any other – conversation. Just good acting skills, maybe. But who even knew where those skills had gone off to these days? What you don't use, you lose.

'Everything,' he said. 'I wasn't cut out for anything. Life. Life is something I'm just not cut out for.'

'But you're alive.'

'Marginally so, yes.'

'So you're doing it.'

'Not well, though. I am not turning in a suitable performance. Thank God the critics have moved on to more promising pastures, and not a moment too soon. Could you go inside if you tried? I mean, if you needed to?'

'Sure. I got the key right here.'

She held it up in the fading light. Held it for him to see. A shiny, new-looking key dangling on a cord around her neck. It caught and reflected a beam of light from the streetlamp, which had just come on. A miniature flash for Billy's eyes.

Shine, Billy thought. I *do* remember the concept.

'I'm having a little trouble,' he said, 'understanding why anyone would be outside when they could just as easily be in.'

'Don't you ever go outside?'

Oh, good God, Billy thought. Here we go again. There was just no way to stay on top of the conversation.

'Not if I can help it. Aren't you scared?'

'Not if I stay this close to home.'

'Well, *I'm* scared. I look out and see you out here all by yourself, and *I'm* scared. Even if you're not. So maybe I could talk you into doing me a favor. Maybe you could go back inside so I don't have to be scared any more.'

The little girl sighed grandly. Theatrically. A girl after Billy's own heart.

'*Oh, OK.* I was really only going to stay out till the street-lights came on, anyway.'

And she trudged up the stairs and disappeared inside.

'Great,' Billy said out loud, to himself, and to the dusk. 'If I'd known that, I could have saved myself a whole lot of honesty.'

Billy didn't sleep well that night. Not at all. He wasn't able to prove definitively that the massive, unspeakable act of going outdoors had caused the upset and the bad night, but it seemed reasonable to think it had. It was a place to which he could direct blame, at least, which was better than nothing.

When he did drift off, usually for just a few minutes at a time, he experienced the flapping of the wings. A recurrent dream, or half-dream, or illusion. Or hallucination. The more disturbed by life he felt on any given day, the more the wings would beat in his sleep by night.

They tended to startle him awake again.

He did finally, eventually, get to sleep for real, but not until an hour or two after the sun came up. And by the time he finally woke, stretched, and rose – for it didn't pay to hurry these delicate issues – it was well after three thirty in the afternoon.

He rose, and tied back his hair in the usual manner – a

long, narrow ponytail down the middle of his back. Then he leaned over the bathroom sink and shaved by feel, sometimes keeping his eyes closed, sometimes gazing into the plain wood of his medicine cabinet as if it contained a mirror, as it probably had at one time, and as most medicine cabinets did.

He made coffee, still halfway hearing the rustling of those wings in his head. A kind of non-macabre haunting. But a haunting, nonetheless.

He opened the refrigerator, only to remember, just as he did, that he was out of cream. And groceries would not be delivered again until Thursday.

He dumped three spoonfuls of sugar into his sad black coffee, stirred without enthusiasm, then carried the mug to his big sliding-glass door. He pulled back the curtains in order to peek at the spot where he'd seen the little girl the previous evening. Maybe she'd only been a dream or a vision, like the beating of wings, only louder.

She was still there. So apparently not.

Well. Not *still*, he told himself. Inwardly, silently, he corrected his own thinking. She had slept inside. Of course. She must be out there *again*. Yes, *again*. That felt at least slightly less disturbing.

He looked up to see old Mrs Hinman, the woman who lived in the attic apartment of his building, make her way down the sidewalk toward home.

'Good,' Billy said, out loud but in a whisper. 'Tell her to go inside.'

The old woman moved in a slow but determined waddle, paper shopping-bag clutched tight, the neck of her single bottle of red wine protruding over the top of the bag. There was always a bottle, Billy had noticed, and it always protruded. Only one bottle, so it wasn't that she drank all that much. Was she advertising? Or, as seemed more likely to Billy, keeping it close at hand in case it should be needed as a weapon?

This had been a decent working-class neighborhood once, even as recently as twelve years ago, and Billy could not forget that. He could not release the observation. Some inner part of him always felt he should have grown accustomed to the situation, but it was a habit. And the breaking of habits was not Billy Shine's strong suit.

Wanting to know what, if anything, Mrs Hinman would do regarding the girl's situation, Billy cracked open the sliding-glass door, as quietly as possible. Then he secured a post behind the curtain, still holding his pathetic black coffee, and watched and listened.

His heart pounded, but he wasn't sure why. Then again, in what situation was he sure of . . . really . . . anything?

The old woman stopped at the bottom of the gray concrete stairs and looked up at the child, who was playing with a cheap-looking hand-held electronic game. She didn't earn Grace's attention immediately. But in time the girl grimaced, as if she had just lost the game anyway, and looked down to meet Mrs Hinman's eyes.

'Hello,' Mrs Hinman said.

'Hi,' the girl said in return. That voice again. She had a voice that seemed capable of doubling as a glass-cutting device.

'Where's your mother?'

'Inside.'

'Why are you out here all by yourself?'

'Because my mother's inside.'

'Don't you think it's dangerous? This isn't a very good

neighborhood, you know. What if some bad man came?'

'Then I would run inside and lock the door.'

'But maybe he will run faster than you can.'

'But I'm closer to the door than he is.'

'I suppose that's true. But it still troubles me. What's your mother doing in there that's so important?'

'She's asleep.'

'At four o'clock in the afternoon?'

'I don't know,' the little girl said. 'What time is it?'

'It's four o'clock in the afternoon.'

'Then, yes.'

Mrs Hinman sighed. Shook her head a few times. Then she made her way up the stairs, one apparently difficult step at a time, as though climbing an alp, and disappeared from Billy's view. He heard her come through the outer door and into the foyer.

And still the little girl stayed.

A few moments later he was washing his coffee cup in the sink, having poured most of the nasty stuff down the drain.

'Only a barbarian drinks coffee with no cream,' he said out loud, 'and we may be many things, and we deny none of them, but we are not a barbarian.'

Perhaps he'd make himself a cup of tea later, to replace the caffeine his body had come to expect. But when he checked the refrigerator again, he found he had no lemon. And only a barbarian drinks tea with no lemon.

He heard a pounding on the door of the basement apartment, just underneath his. It was the apartment where the little girl lived with her mother.

He waited, still and silent, wanting to hear if the mother would answer. But nothing and no one moved below him – at least, not that he was able to hear.

Then a much larger pounding startled him, and made him jump, and set his heart to hammering again. It was the sort of pounding a policeman will exact on a door just before breaking it down and entering without the occupant's permission.

Silence.

Maybe the mother wasn't even home. Maybe the little girl had been instructed in the art of making excuses for her mother while she worked, or ran around with men. It seemed incomprehensible, but Billy knew it happened as a matter of course these days. Motherhood was nothing like what it had used to be.

Then again, what was?

One more unusual thing transpired on that day.

It was only a few minutes later. Billy had been hearing the murmuring of voices in the hall, near the mailboxes. But that was nothing unusual, so he didn't make a point of listening.

It sounded like Mrs Hinman and Rayleen, that tall, pretty African-American woman who lived right across the hall from him. The one Billy sometimes envied through the glass, because she had style, and presented herself well. She always seemed sad, Rayleen. But Billy reasoned that to add happiness to your wish list would be to put the whole list of requests out of feasible reach. In the real world, style and appearance would have to do.

'Take what you can get from this life,' as he had told the little girl. As he would tell other people, if he knew any.

But then, suddenly, voices were being raised.

He heard Rayleen say – shout – with an agitation that seemed unlike her, 'Do not call Child Protective Services on that poor little girl! Promise me you won't! Promise!'

And Mrs Hinman, obviously alarmed by being shouted at, raised her voice and said, 'Well, what would be so wrong about that? It's what they're there for.'

Billy slunk to the door and pressed his ear against it.

'If you really hate that poor little girl so much,' Rayleen said, still distraught, 'you might as well just shoot her. I swear it would be a million times more humane than putting her in foster care.'

'Now why on earth would you say a thing like that?' Mrs Hinman replied.

And Rayleen said, 'Because I know. Because I know things. Things you don't know. Things you'll never have to know, and just be grateful for that.'

'Are you a social worker?' Mrs Hinman asked.

Rayleen snorted, and then said, 'No, I'm not a social worker. I'm a manicurist. You know that. I work at that hair and nail salon down on the boulevard.'

'Oh. Yes, of course. Of course you do. I'd just forgotten.'

And then, frustratingly, they moved off in the direction of the stairs to Mrs Hinman's apartment. And, though they continued to converse, their voices now came through Billy's door as nothing more than a muffled buzz.

Nearly two hours later, Billy looked out his glass door on to the gray winter day. Looked down on to the porch to see if the girl was still there.

She was.

He could have looked sooner. He'd thought of looking

sooner. But he knew she would be, and he knew it would frighten him to see that she was.

He made a mental note to ask, for a second time – that is, if he ever got up the nerve to talk to her again – why she didn't sit inside.

Grace

There was just no getting around it. Curtis Schoenfeld was a giant stinkhead. Grace had known it for a long time, and so she wasn't quite sure why she'd listened to him, and why she'd let it hurt her feelings, what he'd said.

Why had she even believed him?

She sort of had, though, and that was just the problem.

You know how sometimes the nicest person in the world will yell at you and hurt your feelings because you're doing something like talking too much when they're trying to think or worry (or both)? Well, stinkheads are just the opposite of that, Grace supposed, because every now and then they will open their stinky mouths and say something horrible that might even possibly be true.

It was at the Saturday night meeting, the one in the church. Except not the church part of the church, not the religious part. It was the room where they did quilting lessons and had potlucks and stuff, and Sunday school, except this was only Saturday.

Some people even called that meeting the kid meeting, because lots of the people there were new in the program, and babysitters cost money. So people just brought their kids along. And it was a very big, very long room, so that the meeting people could sit on one side and have their meeting, and the kids could sit on the other side and be kids.

The kids had to be quiet. The meeting people didn't have to be quiet.

That F-word guy was sharing. One of the guys Grace didn't like. He seemed mad at everything, so that when he met you, he was already mad at you, and he didn't even know you yet. And every other word that came out of his mouth was that one Grace would not be likely to mention (but it started with an F).

'I mean, really,' she'd said once, complaining about him to her mom. 'Every other word. Get a dictionary.'

It's not like she exactly cared. She knew the word. She'd heard it before. It just seemed rude.

So Grace was on the other side of the room with Curtis Schoenfeld and Anna and River Lee. Anna and River Lee were playing pick-up sticks, but Curtis couldn't play, because he was in a wheelchair, and he couldn't reach down that far. He had that spinal thing, that spinal-something. He always said spina-something, but Grace knew he was just being lazy or stupid and leaving off the 'l' at the end, because everybody knows it's spinal, with an 'l' at the end. He was older than Grace, maybe even twelve, which is why she thought he should know these things.

So Grace wasn't playing pick-up sticks, either, because Curtis couldn't. How nice is that? Which is why Grace thought, after the fact, that it was a particularly bad time for Curtis to go and be a poophead to her.

And she wasn't shy – also after the fact – about sharing that opinion.

So, anyway, he leaned his big head over to her (he had a big head and a red face, that Curtis) and said, 'I heard your mom went out.'

Grace said, 'Curtis, you big moron, she did not go out. She's sitting right there.' And she pointed to the meeting side of the room.

He laughed, but it wasn't like a real laugh. It was more of a fake laugh, like an idiot laugh. First it just squeaked out of his stinky lips like a balloon when you stretch the end (the end you just blew into, that is) and let air back out. But then later he changed it on purpose, and then it sounded like a donkey making that donkey noise.

Grace usually tried not to talk about Curtis like he was a total poophead, because you're supposed to be extra nice to someone who's in a wheelchair, but Curtis Schoenfeld just kept pushing it too far. Sometimes you just have to call a poophead a poophead, she firmly believed, no matter what he's sitting on.

'Not out of the *room*,' he said, 'out of the program. She's out. She's using. I can't believe you didn't know.'

Then the room got kind of spinny for just a second, and she could hear all those F-words firing off like little pops from a toy gun, like little firecrackers, and Grace remembered thinking how she *had* been extra-sleepy lately, her mom. That was in the one second before Grace decided to decide it wasn't true in any way.

So she gathered herself up big and she said, 'Curtis Schoenfeld, you are a total boogerhead!'

The F-words stopped. Everything stopped. It got real quiet in that big room, and Grace thought, Ooooops. I think that might have been just a little tiny bit too loud.

Grace always had trouble with that. Loud came naturally to her, and quiet took a lot of work, and if she let down her guard for even one tiny little second the loud would come marching right back in again.

Grace's mom got up from the table and came back to the kid part of the room, and all three of the other kids gave Grace that look. You know. That 'you're gonna get it now' look.

She took hold of Grace's arm and walked her outside.

It was dark out there, and kind of cold. People always think it doesn't get cold in LA, but it gets plenty cold sometimes. And, also, they were in a neighborhood where it's not so smart to be outside, but Grace figured her mom must've thought they were close enough to the people inside to be OK. Well. She didn't know what her mom thought, really, she just knew what *she* thought, which is that she would yell like the devil if anybody came up to them, and run inside for help. And she knew her mom must've felt safe enough, because she lit a cigarette and then sat down on the cold street with her back up against the church.

She ran a hand through her hair and sighed real big, and Grace could see a sort of embarrassing rip in her jeans.

'Grace, Grace, Grace,' she said. She seemed too calm, and Grace wondered why she wasn't getting mad. 'Can't you ever just be quiet?'

'I try,' Grace said. 'I try to be quiet, really I do.'

Her mom sighed another time, and puffed on her cigarette, and she seemed to be moving kind of slow.

So then Grace gathered up everything she had that was brave, and she said, 'Are you on drugs again?'

She braced for her mom to get mad, but nothing happened.

Her mom just blew out a long stream of smoke, and stared at it all the way out, like maybe if she watched closely enough it might sing and dance or something, and Grace remembered thinking she was pretty sure her mom used to do everything faster.

When her mom finally said something, this is what she said: 'I'm going to meetings. I'm at a meeting right now. I still call Yolanda every day. I'm working my ass off here, kiddo. I don't know what more you want from me.'

'Nothing,' Grace said. 'I'm sorry, I don't want anything more from you, that's fine. I'm sorry I was too loud. I was trying to be quiet, really I was, but then Curtis Schoenfeld was a boogerhead to me. And when I was trying to be extra-nice to him, too. He's such a liar. I wish I didn't have to go to meetings with him. Couldn't we go to different meetings, with no Curtis?'

A really, *really* long wait while her mom decided to answer.

'Like which ones? They don't all allow kids, you know.'

'Like that nice AA meeting at the rec center.'

'Right now I need the NA ones more.'

'Oh.'

'Just play with Anna. And . . . you know . . . the one with the weird name.'

'River Lee.'

'Right.'

'I wasn't *playing* with Curtis. You don't have to *play* with Curtis for him to be a boogerhead to you. He just *is*. There's no staying away from it.'

Grace's mom stomped out her cigarette and peered at

her watch, extra-close in the dark, as if it had to touch her nose before she could see it.

Then she said, 'Deal with it for another twenty-five minutes, 'K?'

Grace sighed loud enough for her mom to hear. 'OK,' she said. But it came out sounding like the F-word guy trying to say 'pleased to meet you' and not sounding very pleased.

All three of the kids were staring at her when she went back in.

River Lee said, 'Did she yell at you?' in a sort of almost-whisper.

And Grace said, 'No. Not at all. Not even a little bit.'

She was being kind of snooty-proud in front of Curtis, and she knew it.

Nobody went back to playing right away, which was weird, because then they pretty much had no choice but to listen to the meeting. This ratty-looking woman, the kind of person you see sleeping on the street, shared how her kids got taken away when she went to jail for helping her boyfriend rob a bank. All behind drugs. They gave up the kids because they wanted more drugs, and that seemed like a good trade at the time.

Really depressing.

Then some other people shared, and they were sort of medium-depressing.

Some meetings weren't depressing. That nice AA meeting at the rec center was much better, Grace felt, because the people there had more time in the program, and usually it didn't make you want to kill yourself.

After the meeting Yolanda came up to Grace, and smiled down from way up above her, and Grace smiled back.

'Hey, Grace,' she said. 'Do you have my phone number?'

Grace shook her head and said, 'No, why would I have your phone number? It's my mom who's supposed to call you, not me.'

'I just thought you might want to have it.'

She handed Grace down a piece of paper with the numbers on it, and Grace read them off to herself, though she wasn't sure why. Maybe because it felt like school, like homework, as if Yolanda were saying, 'Look at these numbers and see if you know what they all are.' Grace knew her numbers really well, but did it anyway.

'OK. Um. Why would I want to have it again?'

'Just in case.'

'Just in case what?'

'Just in case you ever needed anything.'

'Then I would ask my mom.'

'Well, just in case she wasn't around, or you couldn't ask her for some reason.'

'Like what reason?'

'I don't know, Grace. Anything. If you were alone or something. Or if you were having trouble getting her to wake up. If you got scared about anything, you could call.'

That was when Grace decided not to ask any more questions. Not even one more.

'OK, thanks,' she said. And she stuck the phone number in her pocket.

'Don't tell your mom.'

'OK.'

Stop talking, she was thinking, but she didn't say it.

Then Yolanda gave them a ride home, which was good, because it's scary riding the bus home in the dark, and Grace was already scared.

Billy

Billy woke suddenly, hearing someone shout outside. It had come from the sidewalk in front of the apartment house.

Just one word.

'Hey!'

He squeezed his eyes closed again, mourning the sudden loss of his expectation for the new day: simply that it would be suitably quiet, and without conflict.

Then, being a realist at heart, he jumped up and slunk to his front lookout place, the big sliding-glass patio door, and peered around the curtain.

The girl was still there. No, not still. Again. Again, he meant.

Felipe Alvarez, one of his upstairs neighbors, was squatted down next to her, apparently engaging her in conversation. And Jake Lafferty, his other upstairs neighbor, was trotting up the walk to intervene, as if he found the scene quite unsatisfactory.

Then again, from what little he had been able to hear and observe over the years, Billy gathered that his gruff neighbor Lafferty found precious few situations to his liking. In fact, Lafferty even took it a step further by wearing that dissatisfaction on his sleeve, a misguided badge of . . . well, something. Billy tried to decide what, but found he couldn't imagine.

Now Lafferty trotted to the base of the stairs and called out, 'Hey! José! What are you doing with that little girl?'

Felipe rose to his feet. Not combative, so much – well, not quite, Billy gathered – but ruffled, and on guard. It made Billy's poor tired heart hammer again, because it smacked of conflict, his least-favorite life element.

If only that little girl would go inside! Her presence there on the stairs, day in and day out, was like a wild card thrown into Billy's day, dealing him terrifyingly unpredictable hands.

But, terror or no, he wanted to hear what came next. So, ever so quietly, he slid open the patio door about six inches, the better to watch and listen.

'First off,' Felipe said in his fluent but heavily accented English, 'my name is not José.'

'Well, I didn't mean that it was,' Lafferty said. 'It's just an expression. A nickname. You know.'

'I *don't* know,' Felipe said. 'I don't know at all. Here's what I know. I know I've told you my name prob'ly ten times. And I know you told me your name once, and I don't never forget it. It's Jake. Right? So how bout I just call you Joe instead? I mean, most white American guys are named Joe, right? So that'll be close enough, don't you think?'

Billy glanced down at the little girl, to see if she looked afraid. But she gazed back up at the two men with an open, almost eager face. As if what happened next could only be entertaining and fun.

She was plump, that little girl. What was it these days with kids and extra weight? In Billy's day, kids ran around. There was barely such a thing as a fat kid. If there was, it was a rarity.

Then again, he'd spent nearly his entire childhood in dance class, which is hardly the land in which you'd find a plump kid – if there was such a phenomenon. Oh, he'd gone to school, of course. What choice would he have had? But he'd blocked those memories as best he could.

'I know his name!' Grace said. Well, shrieked.

But Felipe held up one hand to her and said, 'No, wait. Let's just wait and see if *he* knows it.'

'Listen you—' Lafferty said, signaling that he'd had quite enough.

Billy's heart hammered faster, wondering if one of the men would strike the other. But Lafferty never even managed to finish his sentence. Because, no matter how firmly you corked the mouth on that little girl, it didn't stay corked any longer than just that moment.

'It's Felipe!' she shouted, obviously proud of herself.

'Fine,' Lafferty said. 'Felipe. How about you answer my question now, Felipe?'

'Oh, yeah, and that's the other thing,' Felipe said. 'I was just asking Grace how come she's not in school, and that's *all* I was doing, and I don't appreciate your suggesting otherwise.'

'You really are always looking for a fight, aren't you?'

'Me? *Me?* I'm not the one looking for a fight, *compañero*. Every time I see you, you got that same chip on your shoulder. I don't fight with nobody. You ask anybody who knows me. You just carry that same fight with you every place you go, and then dress it up to look like the other guy's fight. You musta had that chip on your shoulder so long you don't even see it no more. I bet you don't even know what the world would look like without that great big chip blocking your view.'

Lafferty swelled his chest and opened his mouth to speak, but the noisy girl beat him to it.

'Do you guys have to fight?' she asked, at full volume.

Billy smiled, inwardly admiring her. From where on earth did that brand of courage emerge? Then again, she was a kid. A kid could get away with just about anything.

Lafferty looked down at the girl disapprovingly.

'Why *aren't* you in school?'

'Her name is Grace,' Felipe said.

'I know that,' Lafferty said, but it came off as unconvincing, and Billy was not sure, from the sound of it, whether Lafferty had known that at all. 'Why aren't you in school, Grace?'

'Cause I'm not allowed to walk all that way by myself. My mom has to take me. And she's asleep.'

'At nine o'clock in the morning?'

'Is it nine o'clock?'

'It is. Five after.'

'Then, yeah. At nine o'clock.'

'That doesn't sound right.'

'You're the one with the watch,' Grace said.

Lafferty sighed miserably. 'Do you have a key?'

Yes, Billy thought. She does. It's very new. It sparkles. It has shine. That wonderful, indefinable quality. Shine.

'Yep.' She held the key up so Lafferty could see it. It still dangled on the long cord around her neck.

'Go inside and see if you can wake her up.'

'I already tried.'

'Try again. Will ya?'

The girl blew out her breath, loud and dramatic. Then she rose to her feet and tromped inside.

The minute she did, Felipe made his way down the stairs. Lafferty moved closer, stood nearly chest to chest with the younger man, and they stared each other down.

Billy leaned on the edge of the sliding door, feeling mildly faint.

'I'm not your *compañero*,' Lafferty said.

'You don't even know what it means.'

'No, I don't, and that's just the trouble.'

'It's not an insult.'

'Well, how am I to know? When I was your age, I was taught to respect my elders. My father taught me that.'

'You know what *my* father taught *me*? That if I wanted respect I better plan on earning it. All I did was get down and ask that little girl how come she wasn't in school, and then here you come out of nowhere, treating me like I'm some kind of child-molester or something.'

'You shouldn't even ask her *that* much. It's a crazy world. Everybody's suspicious about everything. Guy your age shouldn't even get that near a little girl to ask anything at all. It could be taken the wrong way.'

'A guy *my age*? You sure my age is the problem here? What about you? You asked her.'

'That's different. I'm older.'

'Oh. Right. I forgot. Guys in their fifties are never child-molesters.'

'You got a mouth on you, son.'

'I'm not your son.'

'You're sure as hell not. If you were my son you'd treat me with respect.'

Just then Grace appeared again, and the two men jumped back, as if the little girl were their parent or their teacher, and they'd been caught fighting. It seemed ludicrous to Billy from the outside, from the observer's stance, but in another way he could imagine how such a thing could happen in the confusion of the moment.

'She won't wake up,' Grace said.

Lafferty looked at Felipe, who looked back.

'That doesn't seem right,' Lafferty said to Felipe. Then, to the girl, 'Did you see any bottles lying around?'

'No. What kind of bottles?'

'Like the kind of bottles you drink from.'

'She wasn't drinking.'

'Is she OK? Should somebody call a doctor?'

'She's not sick. You just can't wake her up when she's sleeping.'

She sat back down on the stairs, as if planning on staying a while.

Lafferty looked back at Felipe again. Then he took the young man by the sleeve and pulled him across the weedy grass and out of the earshot of the little girl.

And that, unfortunately, put them squarely out of the range of Billy's ears as well.

But they weren't fighting now. That much Billy could tell from their body language. They had their heads together, conferring about something, deciding something. Occasionally Lafferty would glance over his shoulder toward Grace.

'Have a wonderful solution,' Billy said, out loud, but quietly enough so as not to give himself away to Grace, who was still quite close by on the stairs. 'Because this is certainly a problem.'

But a moment later Felipe peeled away and strode down the sloping lawn, out on to the sidewalk, and down the street.

Lafferty came up the stairs, and Billy waited hopefully, still thinking his neighbor might have a perfect idea up his sleeve. But he walked right by Grace, as if some alien force field had suddenly rendered her invisible.

Just as his foot touched the top step, he looked up and saw Billy watching – caught his eye – which was as close as possible to the only part of Billy peeking around the curtain. He stopped in his tracks.

'What're *you* looking at?' he bellowed.

Billy leaped backwards into his own apartment, folded over himself and sank to the rug, his heart fluttering in panic. He remained in this highly protective posture until he'd heard his neighbor come through the front apartment house door, close it behind him, and move along the hall and up the stairs.

Then he jumped up and slammed the glass patio door closed, quickly and gingerly, as if the door itself had been the source of all this upset.

He did not look out again at any time that morning.

He knew the girl must still be out there, but he could not bring himself to check.

It was almost dusk when he began to debate the issue with himself. Out loud.

'We don't want to know *that* badly,' he said.

Then, upon some reflection, 'We do want to know. Of course. Of course we do. Just not *that* badly.'

'Besides,' he added a moment later, 'it's not dark enough.'

He glanced out his sliding-glass door again.

'Then again, when the streetlights come on, it will be too late. Won't it? And then we'll have to wonder all night. And wondering tends to keep us awake.'

He sighed deeply, and tied on his old robe. But not really because he wanted to ask the question so badly as to brave the outdoors for his answer. More because there was simply no other way to end the utter exhaustion of wrestling with himself on the issue.

The little girl looked up when he slid the patio door open.

Billy did not initially step out.

It was a little earlier, a little lighter, than it had been the last time he'd gone outside. A shocking thought, he suddenly realized. Had he, really? He'd really gone outside? Maybe that had only been a dream.

He shook such thinking away again, forcing his mind to focus. Back to the issue at hand: that it was not as dark this time. And darkness served, if need be, as a rudimentary form of cover.

He wanted to step backwards, into his safe home, and slide the door closed again. But the little girl was watching him, waiting for him to come out. How insane would she think he was, if he backed up now? How much of the truth was he willing to let her see?

He took one step out into the cool late afternoon, then immediately dropped to his knees. He moved on his hands and knees for a step or two, then hit his belly and slithered to the edge of the patio. It had not been a move thought out in advance. Yes, he knew it was much weirder than just going back inside. But it happened that way. And it was too late to either fix it or mourn it by then.

He looked over the edge of the patio at Grace.

'Why are you crawling on your belly?' she asked, in her famous voice.

'Shhhhh,' he said, instinctively.

'Sorry,' she said, with only the tiniest bit less volume. 'I always have trouble with that.'

'It's a long story.'

'Tell it.'

'Maybe some other time. I came out here to ask you a question.'

'OK.'

'Why are you sitting outside?'

'You asked me that the last time.'

'I know I did. But you didn't answer me.'

And, at least for the first few moments, she didn't answer this time, either.

'I mean, I know your mom is somehow doing something other than looking after you. That much is clear. But you have a key. You could still sit inside.'

'Right.'

'So, why?'

'Maybe you should tell me the story about crawling on your belly first.'

'I don't think so. I think we do my question tonight.'

'Why yours?'

'Because I asked first.'

'No, you didn't. I asked first.'

'I asked the other night. You said so yourself.'

'Oh, that's right,' Grace said, solemnly, as if accepting that the rules were quite clear on that. 'You did. Well, it's like this. If I sit inside, then nobody will know I'm in trouble. And so then nobody will help me.'

Billy's heart fell. Literally, from the feel of it. He felt physically aware of the sensation of it falling, hitting the organs in his poor lower belly. None of which could have happened, of course. But all of which carried a felt sense of itself all the same.

'Oh, you're in trouble, huh?'

'You didn't know?'

'I guess I knew.'

'See, it has to be somebody who lives *here*. Because that way I can still stay with my mom.'

A silence. Billy could see and feel where this train was headed, which is why he offered no reply.

'Can you help me?'

Another long silence fell, during which Billy was aware of the pebbly nature of the patio surface against the front of his chest and legs.

'Baby girl, I can't even help myself.'

'Yeah. That's what I figured.'

It was a low and very dark moment, even by Billy standards. Not only had it just been firmly established that he was utterly useless, but clearly this little girl had been fully able to see for herself how useless he was, even in advance of being told.

'Sorry,' he said. 'I'm sorry I'm useless. I wasn't always. But now I am.'

'OK,' she replied.

'Well, goodnight,' he said.

'It's not very late,' she said.

'But I won't see you again before bed. So that's why the goodnight.'

'Goodnight,' she said. Rather flatly.

Billy slithered back inside for the night.

Grace

Grace missed one day of school, but then the next day Yolanda came and got her, and took her to school in a car. It was too bad, in Grace's view, because, really, she could miss every single day of school from now until the end of time and it wouldn't hurt her feelings even one tiny little bit.

'How am I supposed to get home?' Grace asked Yolanda. 'I'm not allowed to walk by myself.'

'Your mom'll come and get you.'

'Are you sure?'

'Positive.'

'How can you be so sure?'

'Because I had a long talk with your mom, and she promised me.'

'What if she breaks her promise? It happened before.'

'I'll keep an eye out. But this time I'm pretty sure. She told me she's ready to pull herself together.'

'That would be nice,' Grace said.

But it was just a thing you say. Maybe it would happen, and that would be nice, but maybe it wouldn't. And Grace knew it would be extra-hard if she spent all day thinking how nice it was going to be, and then it wasn't. Grace hated that worse than anything.

So she tried hard not to think too much about it all day, but she thought about it a lot while she was waiting for the bell to ring. It made her feel nervous and weird. It made her want to eat the very last chocolate bar she had hiding in her backpack; but she didn't, because she figured the teacher would catch her, and if the teacher caught her, she'd take the candy away. And that was Grace's last one. If she'd had more money she'd have spent it on more chocolate, but that was her allowance, and it was all gone for the week. Grace always said she'd make the candy last, but then she never did.

When the bell rang, it made her jump.

She ran out into the hall, dug out the chocolate, and unwrapped it while she was running. Well, walking fast. She ate it on the way to the back door, where her mom always met her.

She was there. Her mom was there! Grace was surprised. At least, a little bit surprised.

'What are you eating?' Grace's mom asked. She didn't sound too slow, and she seemed pretty much awake, at least, as best Grace could tell.

'Nothing.'

'Now don't lie to me, Grace Eileen Ferguson. You still have some of it on your lip. It looks like chocolate.'

'Oh. Yeah. That. We had that last period.'

'I'm going to talk to your teacher, then, about not giving you junk food. You know I don't like it when people give you junk food.'

'Please don't. This is the first time I've seen you in days.

I mean, not seen you, but seen you. I mean . . . you know what I mean. I mean, I wish we didn't have to fight.'

Grace knew her mom felt guilty, so she was pushing on that guilt button just a little bit.

'OK, you're right,' Grace's mom said. 'Let's just go home.'

While they were walking home, Grace was thinking, Wow, she's all pulled together, and that's nice. But she didn't say so, because she didn't want her mom to know that she'd only just then started believing in it.

Her mom made Grace macaroni and cheese and hot dogs, which was the favorite of all her mom's dinners. Sometimes when her mom was guilty . . . well, it was not always such a bad deal. While they were eating, Grace's mom asked if she wanted to go to that nice AA meeting at the rec center, and Grace said, 'Definitely, yeah.'

So, after dinner, they rode there on the bus.

There was this weird guy on the bus who kept staring at them. He was sitting right across from their seats. He didn't look weird on the outside, Grace noticed. He had on a nice coat and a wedding ring, and his hair was clean and all, but she could tell he was weird on the inside because of how he was staring.

Her mom didn't seem like she noticed.

Grace's mom had this little plastic bottle of water between her knees, and after a while she put her head back and dropped something in her mouth and washed it down with a slug of the water, but Grace couldn't see what it was she dropped in.

So she said, 'What was that?'

'It's nothing,' her mom said. 'I have a headache, that's all. Don't forget who's the mom and who's the kid.'

'Right,' Grace said. 'Got it.'

'I'm trusting you to stay out of the candy basket tonight, OK?'

'I can have one piece of licorice, right?'

'You can have one piece of anything you want. But one is enough.'

Grace's mom said that every time, but she couldn't really watch the candy basket every minute, so usually Grace ended up with more.

But this time the way it played itself out was all different. It was good, in a way, but not so good, all at the same time.

The candy basket situation worked like this: the basket was passed around the table, and everybody took one piece (unless you didn't want a piece, which some people didn't, and Grace always found that impossible to understand), and then it made the rounds again so people could take one piece of whatever was left over. But Grace was not sitting at the table with them. Grace walked around wherever she wanted, just being quiet so they could have their meeting. So she could pop up wherever the basket was, and just keep getting more candy. And the only thing that could stop her was her mom.

Only, that night, Grace's mom wasn't stopping her. So that's why it was good and not so good at the same time. Good, because Grace snagged a record amount of candy; but not so good, because her mom was getting sleepy again, and that's why she didn't put a stop to the situation.

So then Grace started to get mad, because she was beginning to know that her mom took drugs for the headache, real drugs, big drugs, and it made her mad because when other mothers got a headache they just took aspirin. At least, all the mothers of all the kids she knew from school. And the more Grace saw her mom leaning on her hand and then falling asleep and falling off it again, the more Grace decided to eat candy.

So she popped up where the basket was, and reached in front of a lady, and just grabbed every single piece of the red licorice. She could get her hand around all of it at once.

Then she went and sat in the corner, with her back up against the wall, and ate licorice and felt mad.

Then the meeting was over, and people were putting on their jackets to go, and some of them kept smiling at Grace like they were feeling sorry for her, which Grace hated more than anything.

After a while a tall man came over, and he had a gray mustache, and he squatted down to be the same tallness as Grace, and then he said, 'That's your mom, huh?'

By now Grace's mom was resting with her head down on the table.

'Yep,' Grace said, like she wasn't too happy about it, but then she reminded herself to be careful about things like that, because her mom was still the only mom she had.

'She's in no shape to drive you two home,' the man said.

'We don't even have a car,' Grace said. 'We came here on the bus.'

'Oh. Maybe Mary Jo can drive you home. Mary Jo?'

This woman came up to them, pretty short and little, with gray hair and a wrinkled face, and the tall man got Grace's mom on her feet and sort of steered her out to this lady Mary Jo's car. It was a very small car, the kind with only two seats, and they belted her mom into the passenger seat up front, and Grace had to fold herself up small in that space behind the seat-backs.

While they were driving home, Grace had to tell the lady

which way to go to get to their apartment house, and also she had to answer a lot of questions, all at the same time.

Like, the lady asked her, 'Do you know who your mom's sponsor is?'

And she said, 'Yeah, it's Yolanda.'

And the lady said, 'I don't know a Yolanda.'

And Grace said, 'She's from the other program.'

The lady looked surprised, and said, 'She only has an Al-Anon sponsor?'

And Grace said, 'No, not *that* other program, the *other* other program. The narcotic instead of alcoholic one. That one.'

'Oh, right,' the lady said, after a minute. 'That explains why she doesn't smell like she's been drinking.'

And then all of a sudden Grace minded the lady, and the questions, and the whole night, and the everything. She just suddenly minded everything in the whole world, and wouldn't talk to the lady any more, and was in a bad mood. She wanted more licorice, but she'd already eaten it all.

She had to help get her mom into the house, and it wasn't easy. Then she thought that would be the last worst thing to happen that night, but it wasn't, because the lady wouldn't leave. She made Grace find Yolanda's phone number, and she called Yolanda and told her she wasn't going to leave until Yolanda came over there, because she couldn't see fit to leave a child alone like that. That's how she said it. She couldn't see fit. Grace had no idea what that meant, but it made her mad. But, at that point, pretty much everything would have.

After a while Yolanda showed up, and Mary Jo went away, which was a relief. Grace was supposed to say goodbye to her, and thank her for the ride, but she didn't want to, and she was feeling extra-stubborn, so she wouldn't.

After she left, Yolanda looked down at Grace with that pity look Grace hated so much. She hated that look more than anything.

And Yolanda said, 'Well, kid. Looks like we have ourselves a situation here.'

Yolanda stayed the night, and took Grace to school the following morning. Grace didn't think about it too much during the school day, because if Yolanda wanted to . . . sort of . . . add herself to the situation . . . that was OK. That certainly wasn't the end of the world. Yolanda was a little scary-bossy on a few rare occasions, usually when dealing with Grace's mom, but mostly she was pretty OK.

So, it was after last bell, and Grace was walking down the hall toward the door, slowly, eating a candy bar that she'd traded most of her lunch for, and the candy was so completely taking her attention that she walked right into another student – not once but twice. When she stepped outside, she finally looked up, scanning around for Yolanda or her mom. But neither were there, and her face fell.

A woman waved.

'It's me,' the woman said. 'Your neighbor. Rayleen. Remember me?'

'Yeah,' Grace said.

Then she looked around some more.

'I'm here to pick you up.'

'You?'

'Me.'

'Why you?'

'Why not me?'

'Where's Yolanda?'

'She needs to be at work.'

'She said she'd take off work to pick me up.'

'But she can only do that once. Or so. She can't do it every day. So we thought, since I could do it just this one day, maybe we should save her taking off work until tomorrow. I'm surprised she didn't tell you.'

'She might've told me something, I think, like maybe that somebody else would be here. I don't think she said who, though. Or maybe I guess I might've forgot.'

They began the long walk home together, through the gray neighborhood. A car drove by, projecting rap music at earsplitting volume, and Rayleen winced. Grace could feel the bass notes in every muscle of her belly, but she didn't wince.

When they could hear again, Grace said, 'So you can only do it this once, huh?'

'Usually I'm at work. I went in early today. I had a client who changed her appointment from the last appointment in the afternoon to early.'

'If Yolanda can only get off work once or so, who's going to pick me up day after tomorrow?'

'I thought maybe when we got home we could talk to Mrs Hinman. She's retired. I was thinking maybe she would.'

'What if she says no?'

'Well, then . . . I guess we'll cross that bridge when we come to it.'

'Oh. Whatever that means. How do you know Yolanda?'

'I don't, really.'

'Then how did she ask you to pick me up?'

'I saw her in the hall this morning, when she was waiting for you to come up the stairs. I just talked to her a little about your situation, is all.'

'Oh,' Grace said.

She didn't ask any more questions, at least, not until they got home.

When they got home, Grace asked, 'Are we going upstairs to see Mrs Hinman now?'

But Rayleen said, 'Don't you want to go in and put your backpack down first?'

'Not really.'

'I think you should,' Rayleen said.

Not having much in the way of a strong opinion on the subject, Grace answered with a blank shrug.

Rayleen followed Grace inside.

Rayleen paused briefly at Grace's mom's open bedroom doorway, and stood looking in at Grace's mom, asleep on the bed. Rayleen seemed all prepared for something to happen, but Grace's mom never moved, never flicked an eyelid, never made a sound. The shades were drawn, in this case a set of dusty blinds covering the high basement windows. Grace could see her mom in the little glow of afternoon that leaked through the blinds. Her hair had tumbled all around her face, covering it. It made Grace a little uncomfortable for Rayleen to see her mom that way, but she wasn't sure exactly why.

'Are we going?' she asked. The minute it came out of her mouth, Grace knew, with that familiar guilty feeling, that she'd been too loud.

Rayleen jumped, and then she froze there in the doorway, as if expecting Grace's mom to open her eyes or something. Actually, Grace also thought – just for a minute – that her mom might wake up. They both waited for it, but it never happened.

'Yeah,' Rayleen said quietly. 'Yeah, we're going to see Mrs Hinman now. Let's go.'

But she didn't go. Not right away. Instead she wandered back into the kitchen, where she opened a few cupboards. Grace wasn't sure why the insides of the cupboards would seem interesting to Rayleen – or to anybody else, for that matter. Rayleen opened the refrigerator and stared into it for a time.

'There's nothing here for you to eat.'

'I think there's some cereal at the back of that cupboard. And I know how to boil eggs.'

'But there's only one egg left.'

'Oh.'

'Maybe we should order a pizza.'

Grace sprang to life as if someone had suddenly plugged her into a power supply. She jumped up and down, literally, screaming with delight.

'I love you, I love you, I love you, that's the best idea anybody ever had, you're my best friend, I love you, I love you, I love you!' she shrieked, among many other things, all along those same lines.

'OK, my eardrum,' Rayleen said, pressing one palm to her Grace-facing ear. 'That's my eardrum.'

Grace's mom still did not wake up.

The phone jangled suddenly, and Rayleen jumped again. A second ring, and then Grace ran to it, and picked it up.

'Hello?' she said. Well. Screeched.

A woman on the line asked if she was Grace Ferguson.

'Yeah, this is Grace.'

The woman then asked to speak to her mom.

'She can't come to the phone right now,' Grace said.

The woman asked if she was alone.

'No,' she said. 'Rayleen is here.'

The woman asked to speak to Rayleen.

Grace held the phone out to Rayleen. 'She wants to talk to you.'

Rayleen took the phone, but hesitantly, as if it might be more dangerous than anybody else's phone.

'Hello?' Pause. 'My name is Rayleen Johnson.' Pause. 'I'm her neighbor. And . . . actually, if you don't mind my asking, I'd like to know who *I'm* speaking to, as well.' Pause. 'Oh. Well, right. There hasn't been anybody home all day, so that's why you just now got somebody. Grace was at school. I just now picked her up from school.' Pause. 'Yes, ma'am, I'm looking after her.' Long pause. 'It's like this, ma'am.' Rayleen was half whispering now, but Grace could still hear her just fine. 'I think that report you got might be all my fault. Not Grace's mother's fault at all. My fault. Who was it that called you, anyway?' Pause. 'Oh. Right. Sorry. Of course you can't. I'm sorry for asking. I just wasn't thinking for a minute, there. Anyway. Here's the thing. Grace's mom hurt her back. And so she's been on some heavy meds. You know, painkillers and those muscle relaxers that make you all sleepy. So that's why she's paying me to look after Grace. But . . . Well, I hate like hell to even admit this, because I just feel so terrible about it, but there was one day I messed up on my schedule and I wasn't there when I was supposed to be, and Grace was alone for a while. But I swear to you, I promise, with my hand on a stack of Bibles if you want, nothing like that is ever going to happen again. Anybody can make a mistake, right? One mistake. But I'm a good babysitter. I'm responsible. Really, I am. Grace will be OK with me until her mom gets better.'

Long pause.

Then Rayleen gave her name again. And she spelled it – well, spelled her first name, as any idiot can spell Johnson, even fourth-grade Grace (or, at least, so she thought until she learned there was an 'h' in it) – and explained how her address was the same as Grace's, only apartment D instead of F. Then she read off her phone number.

Grace noticed that Rayleen's hands were shaking, but wasn't sure what to make of that. Maybe they always did. She'd never thought to check.

'But she's kind of—' Pause. 'Right. I'll make sure she calls. Give me the number, I'll write it down.'

After she hung up, Grace waited for Rayleen to explain who that had been on the phone, and why. But she never did.

She just took Grace by the hand and walked out the door with her, saying, 'Let's go talk to Mrs Hinman now.'

'Who is it?' Grace heard Mrs Hinman call through the door of her attic apartment. She sounded scared, like she was already sure it was a robber or some other kind of bad man, and was just trying to think how to stay safe against him. Like it hadn't even occurred to her yet that it might be somebody nice.

'It's your neighbor Rayleen,' Rayleen said. 'And Grace.'

'Oh,' Mrs Hinman said through the door, sounding only

the tiniest bit happier. 'I'm coming. I'll be right with you. Just this one bar lock tends to stick a bit. This will just take me a moment.'

Grace said to Rayleen, 'And then we can order the pizza?'

But just then Mrs Hinman opened the door wide.

'Oh, my,' she said. 'Rayleen. What's wrong? You look very upset.'

'I have to talk to you,' Rayleen said. 'It's really important.'

Still holding Grace's hand, Rayleen marched them into the apartment and stopped at the kitchen table, staring at a game of solitaire – actual solitaire with actual cards, not the kind you play on your computer. Grace had only ever seen the kind you play on your computer.

Rayleen said, 'I didn't know anybody played solitaire any more.'

Grace said, 'People play it on their computer.'

Rayleen said, 'Yeah. Computer solitaire. But not with real cards.'

Mrs Hinman, who was still busy fussing with the re-doing of all those locks on her door, said, 'Well, if that isn't the silliest thing I've ever heard. Computers cost thousands of dollars, and a pack of cards costs about ninety-nine cents.'

'No, computers don't cost that much,' Grace said. 'And, besides, you can do lots of things with a computer, but with cards you can only play cards.'

'What did you want to talk to me about?'

'Right. Sorry,' Rayleen said. 'We want to know if you'll pick Grace up from school for a few days. Just until her mom is . . . feeling better.'

'You can't be serious.'

'Why wouldn't I be serious?'

'Do you know how far away the grammar school is?'

'Yeah. I was just there. It's about ten blocks.'

'*Each way*. It's about ten blocks *each way*. I'm an older woman, in case you hadn't noticed. I can't walk twenty blocks a day. My knees would swell. They come up sore just from walking to the market, and that's only a four-block round trip.'

Rayleen sat down hard on Mrs Hinman's couch. Very hard. It made her bounce once, just a little bit.

'I'm in trouble,' she said. 'I did something. Just now. I won't say something bad, because I don't know that it was bad. But something I could get in trouble for. I lied to a social worker from the county. Told her I was Grace's babysitter. So now I am. Now I have to be. Because they could send somebody out. Any time. Somebody could show up at the door, and then not only could they take Grace away if nobody's watching her, I could get in trouble because I was supposed to be in charge.'

'Oh, my,' Mrs Hinman said. 'I can't imagine why you would do a thing like that.'

'I just didn't want to see them put this poor little girl in the system.'

Then Mrs Hinman looked at Grace, who was just standing there, near Rayleen's legs, and said, 'Maybe we should talk about this some other time.'

But Rayleen said, 'No. I don't see it that way. I think people do too much of that. Keeping things from kids because it might upset them. This is her life we're talking about. I think she has a right to hear. Anyway. I can take her to school before I have to be at work in the morning, but I need somebody to pick her up.'

'Why don't you ask Mr Lafferty?'

Rayleen snorted. Really. Snorted. Grace thought it sounded funny, but it was clear that this was not a funny situation in any other way besides the snort, so she was careful not to laugh.

'That nasty man? I don't want a guy like that anywhere near Grace. He's mean and he's rude and he's bigoted, and I don't like him one bit.'

Mrs Hinman leaned in and whispered, 'He wouldn't be bigoted against *her.*'

'That's not the point. The point is, she shouldn't have to be around somebody like that.' Then, to Grace, Rayleen said, 'I'm not so sure about Mr Lafferty. Do you know him?'

'I think so. He's the one who doesn't like Felipe, right?'

'That sounds about right. See, I'm not sure he's the right person.'

'Why don't you ask Felipe? Or Billy?' Grace asked cheerfully.

'Billy? Who's Billy?'

'You know. Billy. Our other neighbor. On the first floor.'

'Across the hall from me? You know him?'

'Yeah. Why?'

'Well, nobody knows him. I've never even seen him. I've lived here for six years, and I've never once seen him. I've never seen him go out, and I've never seen anybody go in. I heard he even has his groceries delivered. How do you know him?'

'I just do. We just talk.'

'Felipe might be a good idea,' Rayleen said. 'Yeah. Maybe we should ask Felipe.'

'But who will look after her until you come home?' Mrs Hinman asked.

Rayleen's face went soft, like she was sad and scared all at the same time, like she was about to have to beg for something very important.

'I was hoping *you* would.'

'Oh, well. I don't know about *that*.'

And Grace, sensing the importance of the moment, jumped in and said, '*Please*, Mrs Hinman, *please*? I'll be really good, and I'll even try to be quiet, and it's only for a little while anyway, until my mom gets better.'

'I'm sure you would be very good, honey,' Mrs Hinman said, 'but I'm afraid that's not the point. I'm just not the right person to watch you. I'm too old, and I haven't got enough energy.'

Just before Rayleen got up from the couch, Mrs Hinman took her by one sleeve, pulled her closer and whispered something in her ear. But Grace could hear it just fine. Why did people always do that? Did they think she was deaf? Grace had very good ears, but nobody seemed to know that about her.

What Mrs Hinman said was this: 'It's not your problem. And you're only going to make it worse. And you're just postponing the inevitable, anyway.'

Rayleen yanked her arm away, pulling her sleeve out of Mrs Hinman's fingers. She never answered. She took Grace's hand, and left without saying anything more.

Just at the door Grace said, 'Now can we order the pizza?'

But it turned out that first they had to talk to Felipe.

There's always one more thing you have to do, Grace thought, downhearted now, before they let you order the pizza.

* * *

The minute he opened up the door, Rayleen said, 'Felipe. Are you OK?'

And Felipe said, 'Sure. Why?'

'You look terrible. Are you sure you're OK?'

'You look sad,' Grace added in that big voice of hers.

And then, suddenly, just when Grace said that, it looked as though Felipe was trying to hold back from crying. Grace was pretty sure of what she saw, but at the same time figured she might be wrong, because he was a big grown-up man, and big grown-up men didn't cry. Well, probably didn't. Actually, Grace wasn't sure. She just knew she'd never seen such a thing. Big grown-up ladies did, every now and then, but not so much men; at least, not so far as she knew. But it seemed to be happening that way now, so it was worth thinking some more about it.

Felipe swiped at his eyes with one hand, then squeezed them shut, hard, like they were hurting him, and rubbed them.

'Damn allergies,' he said. 'Drives me crazy. Come in, come in. Gotta talk fast, though, because I'm just getting ready for work.'

But Rayleen didn't go in, and so Grace didn't, either. Grace thought maybe it was because of what Felipe had said about needing to go to work, or maybe because he was sad, but she wasn't sure. So she just did the safe thing, which of course was simply to do what the grown-up in charge seemed to be doing.

'We came to ask you a favor,' Grace called out, rather cheerfully.

'We did,' Rayleen said. 'So, you don't work construction in the day any more?'

'No. No, I got a better job. In a restaurant. Actually doesn't pay as well, but it's steady. I needed something steady. What's the favor?'

'I was hoping you'd pick Grace up at school for a few days.'

'Oh. Sure. I could do that.' Then his face changed, as if he had only just thought of something troublesome. 'Oh. No. No. I take it back. I couldn't. I'm sorry. Wish I could. I'd help if I could. But it's that guy across the hall. He'd make trouble for me. I know he would. Few days ago, I got down on one knee and asked Grace why she wasn't in school – that's all I did – and he practically had me on a prison bus to the state pen over it.'

'Shit. Damn it. That guy is such an asshole,' Rayleen said. Then she looked down at Grace suddenly, as if only just remembering that Grace was standing right there. 'Oh. Sorry, Grace.'

'I've heard those words before, you know,' Grace said.

After all, it's not like she was a baby.

'Well, I'm sorry you heard them from me. Listen. Felipe. What if I could smooth things out with Lafferty?'

'Um . . .'

'Just let me try, OK? If you were really sure he wouldn't interfere, then you'd do it?'

'Sure, I don't mind getting her from school for a few days. But then who's gonna take care of her until you get home? I mean, what do I do with her then, just leave her in her own apartment? Because I gotta get ready for work pretty soon after that.'

Rayleen's forehead furrowed, even more than it had been furrowed all along, or, at least, all along since that phone call.

'We're working on that,' she said. 'The only thing I know right now is that she can't be alone. Which includes being in her apartment with just her mom. She's got to be with somebody all the time.'

'Billy!' Grace chimed in. 'Let's ask Billy!'

'Who's Billy?' Felipe asked.

'Our other neighbor!'

Then Rayleen took over and said, 'Grace claims she knows the guy who lives across from me downstairs.'

'You're kidding. Nobody knows that guy. I didn't even know it was a guy. I've lived here three years, and I've never seen nobody come or go from there. I thought maybe it was just an empty apartment.'

'It's not,' Grace said. 'Billy lives there.'

'How do you know him?'

'I just do. We just talk. I know all kinds of things about him. He used to be a dancer. And a singer and an actor, but now he's not. And his name is Billy Shine, but his mother didn't give him that name. She gave him the first name – I think Ronald or Douglas – and his last name was Fleinsteen, but he changed it because Fleinsteen wasn't a dancer's name. I have no idea how he knows what is and what isn't – a dancer's name, I mean – but he says you can just know stuff like that. He's very nice.'

Felipe looked at Rayleen, and Rayleen looked at Felipe, and Grace looked at both of them. She could tell they were trying to decide whether to believe her or not, though she had no idea what was so hard to believe about knowing Billy.

'I think Grace has a very active imagination,' Rayleen said.

'I do!' Grace said. 'I definitely do. I know so, because everybody tells me so. Everybody says that.'

'Anyway,' Rayleen said, this time to Felipe. 'We just haven't worked all the bugs out of that after school thing. But Lafferty . . . you just let me take care of Lafferty, OK?'

'Yeah. Sure. Let me know how that goes. But . . . sorry, but . . . I should prob'ly get ready for work.'

'Oh. Right. Of course. I'm sorry. We'll leave you alone to get ready, now.'

''Bye, Felipe!' Grace shouted.

''Bye, Felipe,' Rayleen added, more downbeat.

Then he closed the door.

When they'd started walking down the hall together, Grace said, 'I don't think Felipe has allergies. I mean, maybe he does. I'm not saying he doesn't, because how would I know? I'm saying I'm pretty sure he was sad, and I think he was crying, and I think maybe he just said allergies so we wouldn't know.'

'Maybe,' Rayleen said, but she sounded like she was thinking about something else entirely.

'I don't really like it when people see me cry, either, except maybe my mom, because I've been crying in front of her since I was a baby. But, like, at school, I hate that worse than anything. If I started to cry over something at school, and some of the other kids saw me, I'd do what Felipe did and lie about it. I know I would. I'm gonna have to remember that, actually. Allergies. That's a good one.'

And Rayleen said, 'I have to think where you can be while I talk to that Lafferty guy.'

'Jake,' Grace said. 'I think his name is Jake, and also, why can't I come?'

'Because it might get ugly.'

'So? I've seen things get ugly before, you know.'

Grace knew Rayleen wasn't paying very good attention,

but instead was all caught up in something she was thinking in her head, the way grown-ups almost always are. Usually they're not listening at all, especially not to kids.

'And I have to think who'll take care of you after school,' she said.

So Grace said, 'Let's ask Billy,' because, no matter how many times she said that, she couldn't seem to get it to stick in Rayleen's head.

'I'm not so sure about that,' Rayleen said.

'But he's really nice. And we know he'll be home. Because he's always home.'

'Well, that's a hard point to argue.'

'I know why Mrs Hinman and Felipe don't want to look after me,' Grace said. 'I know what they told us, but I also know the real reason why not. It's because they don't like me.'

They were all the way downstairs when Grace said it, walking down the hall towards Rayleen's apartment, because that seemed to be where they were going to stay for a while, at least until Rayleen figured out if Grace got to go along on this Mr Lafferty thing. But when Grace said what she said, Rayleen stopped.

She was still holding Grace's hand, except Grace wasn't sure why, because it's not like they were crossing the street or something. There's not too much trouble you can get into walking down a hall, at least, not that she knew of. Grace thought it was because Rayleen was upset and figured Grace must be upset, too, only Grace wasn't very upset. Or maybe Rayleen just wanted somebody to hold her hand, and Grace was the only one around to do it.

Anyway, whatever the reason, Rayleen stopped, and she looked down, shocked, like Grace had just said something terrible. Like she'd said a bad word or something, but Grace went over everything she'd said, really fast in her head, and there were no bad words in it.

'Why would you say a thing like that, Grace?'

'Because it's the truth.'

'Why wouldn't they like you?'

'Well, I'm not really sure, but I know some people don't. I think maybe they don't like me because they think I'm too loud, because people tell me all the time that I'm too loud, and they say it like it's a thing they don't like. And maybe, I think, sometimes people like kids because they don't have to spend too much time with them, and can just say a few things to the kid and then send them right back to their mom. So I think maybe people don't like me as much now that my mom isn't such an easy person to send me back to.'

She kept looking at Rayleen's face while she was saying all this, and Rayleen's face still had that terrible look, like Grace was breaking her heart, but she didn't really know why, because it was just the truth.

'I'm sure everybody likes you.'

And Grace said, 'No, not everybody.' But Rayleen looked so miserable that Grace decided to change the subject, because she didn't like making people miserable, at least, not if she could help it. So she said, 'Do *you* like me?' And then, as soon as she'd said it, she realized it wasn't really as far from the subject as she thought it ought to be.

'Of course I do.'

'What do you like about me?'

But, you know what? Rayleen couldn't think of anything.

'Well, I don't really know you very well. Yet. Later I'll get to know you better, and then I'm sure I'll be able to tell you lots of things I like about you. Tons. I'm sure.'

'So you really *don't* like me. Yet. You just don't exactly *not* like me.'

'No, I do. I definitely do. I just need more time knowing you before I can give you all the reasons why.'

'I like *you*. And I know why, too. It's because you're letting me order pizza.' Grace thought it might be wise to bring up the pizza, just to make extra-sure it hadn't been forgotten. 'And because, out of all the people who saw me sitting on the stairs, you're the only one who decided to help me.'

Grace waited. But Rayleen didn't say anything. She didn't even start walking again. They were still just standing there, in the middle of the hall, holding hands. It was almost as though some big wind came along and stole all Rayleen's words or something.

So, since somebody had to say something, Grace said, 'Let's go talk to Billy.'

And Rayleen got unstuck then, and she said, 'OK. Yeah. Let's do that. I'd like to meet this friend of yours.'

'And then pizza,' Grace said.

'Yes,' Rayleen said. 'And then pizza.'

'Oh, dear,' Billy said. Then he froze for a long moment, as if a simple 'Oh, dear' might be enough to heal the situation.

But the person on the other side of the door knocked again.

'There seems to be someone at our door,' he said.

He spoke the words quietly, and in a reasonable tone, then took a moment to congratulate himself on his ability to stay calm.

People knocked on his door. It wasn't an entirely unknown phenomenon. It happened. But *that* was always on grocery delivery days. And *this* was not.

'Oh, dear,' he said again, in response to the third knock.

It was a polite knock. Did robbers and muggers, and other sorts of miscreants, knock politely? Probably. Probably they did. They *would* do that sort of thing. Just to lull one into a false sense of security.

He slipped over to the door as if darting through sniper fire without benefit of cover, and stood with his back to the heavy wood.

'Who's there?' Billy called out, careful to monitor his voice for steadiness. Unfortunately, the effort was a complete and utter failure, and his voice broke as if in the process of changing with puberty.

'It's your neighbor from across the hall. Rayleen. And Grace. You know Grace, right? She says she knows you.'

'Yes, we – I know Grace,' he said, a bit more steadily. Then he lowered his voice. 'But we don't know *you*,' he muttered, much more quietly. 'Seeing you out the window, and thinking you present yourself well, is hardly knowing.'

'I'm sorry,' Rayleen said through the door. 'Is there someone there with you right now? Should we come back another time?'

Good question. Should he make them come back another time? But if he told them to, they surely would. And then he'd have to live for days in the knowledge that the same axe was about to fall on him again. The prospect seemed unpalatable. No, the least painful time to deal with this situation would definitely be now.

Billy undid two locks and opened the door a few inches, the safety chain still in place.

He looked down at Grace, who waved at him. He could definitely see the middle part of Rayleen, the part that hovered at about Grace-level, but he couldn't bring himself to look up at her face. She might try to look into his eyes, or commit some other unbearable act of human relations.

'Hi, Billy!' Grace shouted. Well. It wasn't shouting by Grace standards. But for anyone else it certainly would have been.

'Hey, Grace.'

'We came to ask you a favor!' Grace made favors sound

fun, like ice cream cakes, or being the one who gets to whack the piñata with the stick.

Billy bent down to Grace's level, hands on his knees, and, through the crack of the open door, addressed her in what could only be called a stage whisper.

'Grace, I thought we talked about this,' he said.

'Right. I know. But this is different.' Grace imitated his stage whisper, landing at just about the volume most people would use in normal conversation.

'How is it different?'

'Because Rayleen is really the one helping. You'd just be helping her help. Which is so much easier.'

'I'm right here,' Rayleen said, causing Billy to jump. 'I can hear all of this.'

'I know,' Grace said. 'I hate that, too. People do that to me all the time, like I don't have good ears or something, but I can always hear them. *You* even did that to me, Rayleen, just today, and Mrs Hinman did it, too. It's silly, I think. I have very good ears. I hear just about everything. I mean, unless it's so far away that nobody could hear it. I bet I even hear as good as a dog, but I don't know for sure, though, because we've never had a dog. My mom says it's hard enough just taking care of *me*.'

Rayleen sighed, and then said, to Billy, 'May we come in?'

Billy sucked in a deep breath and tried to calm his heart.

'It's a bit of a mess. I haven't had time to do much with the place.'

'Sure,' Rayleen said. 'Yeah. I can relate. My housekeeping staff has been on vacation for days, and I'm very unhappy with my current interior designer. So I know just how you feel. Let's get real, OK? These apartments are all just about the same level of dump. And this is a little on the life-or-death side, or I wouldn't be asking. We're really not going to be doing much in the way of judging. I promise.'

Billy straightened, and, unable to think of any graceful way out, pressed the door closed, undid the safety chain, and opened his door to them.

'Do come in,' he said, his hands and voice shaking.

He perched on the very edge of his couch, working at the nail on his index finger with his teeth. Rayleen didn't sit, just walked into the center of his living room and stood. And spoke.

'Grace needs a place to be for about two hours in the afternoon. Just until I can get home from work. And it's probably just for a little while. I hope. But, look . . . it's a big deal. Huge. The county opened a file on her. So if somebody comes by to check . . . well, she has to be supervised. I'll just leave it at that.'

Meanwhile Grace was walking around his apartment, looking at the framed photos of Billy's younger years. She didn't appear to be listening, but Billy sensed that she was, anyway.

He tore more deeply than intended at the nail on his index finger, ripping it below the quick and drawing blood.

Grace walked up to where he sat on the couch and stood alarmingly close. Just inches from him. He froze in that closeness, pressing a finger over his torn nail to hold back the bleeding.

'What are you doing to your nails?' she asked.

'Biting them,' Billy said.

'Why?'

'It's what I do when I'm nervous. What do you do when you're nervous?'

'Nothing. Just be nervous, I guess.'

'Everybody has something.'

'Sometimes I eat candy when I'm nervous.'

'Aha! Classic case.'

'But sometimes I eat candy when I'm not nervous, too. So I'm not sure if that counts.'

Then she peeled away again, as if fresh out of interest, and headed in the direction of Billy's kitchen.

Still not wanting to make eye contact with his adult visitor, Billy lit into a thumbnail.

Not a second later, Grace was back in his face, almost literally, shaking one finger at his forehead and chastising him.

'Billy Shine, you stop that biting your nails this very minute!'

Time stood still. Billy breathed in once, aware of the girl's nose almost close enough to touch his. Then, without advance notice, he burst out laughing. To his further surprise, Grace launched into spontaneous giggles, as if his own laugh had infected her.

'Don't spit on me or anything,' Grace said, wiping off her face.

Then Billy burst into another round of laughter, and Grace caught the giggles again, immediately. A stubborn case, this particular giggle fit. She had a hard time pulling herself together.

'OK,' Billy said, rising to his feet, a slight hint that the visit could be over now, or at least soon.

'OK?' Grace asked.

'OK what?' Rayleen asked.

'OK, Grace can stay here for a couple of hours a day for a little while,' Billy said. Then, unexpectedly, the next thing he said was, 'Oof.'

Because Grace hit him full in the stomach with her whole self, throwing her arms around his waist.

He put one hand on her head, marveling at the slight warmth of her scalp. An actual live human being. How long had it been since he had touched another person, or been touched in any way? A dozen years? Fifteen?

He felt as though the sensation was melting him. Almost literally.

He sank to his knees, which made him just her height, and hugged her back. From the outside, he figured – hoped – it appeared as a deliberate move. In truth, his knees had simply melted.

'You said *yes*,' Grace said, in something bizarrely akin to a whisper. 'Everybody else said no. That must mean you like me.'

'I do, actually,' Billy said, learning the information the exact moment he imparted it.

'What do you like about me?'

'You're brave,' he said, pulling back from the embrace and holding her at arms' length by her shoulders. Enough of any type of closeness was enough, especially for one day.

'How am I brave?'

'Well. You go outside.'

'Duh. Yeah, me and everybody else on the planet.'

'How about when you stopped those two big men fighting?'

'What two big men?'

'Jake Lafferty and Felipe Alvarez.'

Grace's face lit up. She did not ask how he happened to come by that information, or even how he knew the names of all the neighbors he'd never met.

'Yeah. Wow. I guess I *am* brave, huh?'

She hit him again, another projectile hug.

'I knew you weren't useless,' she whispered into his ear. Then, more loudly, 'Well, see you tomorrow, Billy.'

And, with that, she marched out the door.

'Thank you,' Rayleen said, just before letting herself out.

She closed the door behind her, leaving Billy to ponder what he'd just gotten himself into. But there was really no dissecting it from the point of view of the present. Tomorrow would tell. Right at the moment there wasn't much to be done about it. He'd said it, and that was that.

He decided to take a nap. He was feeling wrung out, and needed the rest.

Billy woke to a banging on his door.

He lay in bed for an extended moment, pulling the covers up tightly under his chin. But the banging repeated itself, startling him, even though this time he'd known to expect it.

He took a deep breath and accepted that there was only one way to make it stop.

He rose, delicately, and tiptoed through the living room to the door.

'Who's there?'

'It's Jake Lafferty, from upstairs.'

'Oh,' Billy said.

If he'd said more, the shaking in his voice would have come through too strongly, too obviously. It would have given him away, in a potentially dangerous manner, like a prey animal showing blood or a broken leg to its predator.

'I want to ask you one question. Before you start looking after that little girl.'

'OK,' Billy said, betraying his trembling, in spite of the brevity of his answer.

'Are you going to open the door, or what?'

'Probably not.'

'Any special reason why not?'

'I find you a little . . . threatening.'

'Ah, geez,' Lafferty said. 'Which brings me back to my question. Are you a homosexual?'

'Excuse me?'

'Is it really that you didn't hear the question?'

'No, not really. It's more that I'm having trouble believing it.'

'Look. I got a right to ask, in this case. Because you're going to be looking after that little girl. Right? And everybody knows homosexuals are more likely to be child-molesters. Otherwise it would just be your business. But that's why I have to ask. Because everybody knows that.'

The room spun slightly around Billy's head. He reminded himself to breathe, quickly, before he passed out.

'Um. No. Not really. Everybody doesn't know that. Because it's nowhere even close to the truth.'

'Are you kidding me? Then who do you figure is molesting all those little boys?'

'Um. A bunch of married guys about your age.'

'What are you suggesting?'

'Just that you're wrong. About pretty much everything.'

'I notice you still haven't answered my question.'

'Let's just say, for the sake of the argument,' Billy said, still openly trembling, 'that you were right about everything. You're not. But just for a second, let's imagine a world where you were. Have you met Grace?'

'Of course I've met her.'

'Is she . . . *a boy child*? Or a *girl child*?'

'Oh,' Lafferty said. 'Yeah, OK.'

Billy heard the first few of Lafferty's footsteps as he headed down the hall, and then one word muttered under Lafferty's breath. The word was, 'Fruitcake.'

Billy went back to bed, in spite of his knowledge that the chance for more napping had long ago evaded him.

He lay awake for all but maybe forty-five minutes of that night. And, within that forty-five minutes, he felt himself surrounded, swallowed, by the beating of wings. Longer, whiter, more passionate than usual. A cacophony of wings.

'Who brought you home from school?' he asked Grace.

He sat perched on the very edge of his sofa, watching her look around his apartment. Watching her peer at all of his photos again, as if she hadn't just examined them the previous day.

He couldn't focus away from his lack of sleep. It left his nerves raw, and feeling as though they'd been recently sandpapered.

'Felipe did,' she said. 'That way Yolanda wouldn't have to take off from work. Because they don't pay Yolanda when she takes off from work. She can take off. But then she just loses the money.'

'And Yolanda is . . .'

'My mom's sponsor.'

'Sponsor? What kind of sponsor? What does she sponsor her to do?'

'In the program. You know. Like an AA sponsor, except Yolanda is NA.'

'Oh, good Lord, that explains a lot,' Billy said, wishing after the fact he hadn't said it out loud.

'What does it explain?'

'Forget I mentioned it. Oh – that's me in an Equity waiver production of *The Iceman Cometh*.'

'I understood the photo better before you told me that.'

'So how did Jake Lafferty find out I was going to be taking care of you?'

'Oh, that's easy. Rayleen had to go talk to him. Because Felipe didn't want to come pick me up at school, because he figured Mr Lafferty would give him a hard time about it. So Rayleen had to go talk to Mr Lafferty, and I had to go, because otherwise I would have been alone with just my mom, who was asleep, and then if the county came to check on me, that would be bad. So I went along. And, wow, he was really mad. But Rayleen didn't act like she was one bit scared of him. She just told him Felipe was gonna pick me up from school, and he better just stay out of it. He didn't like it much, but he just sort of said, "Why should I care? Do whatever you want." But then he wanted to know where I'd be after Felipe went to work, which seemed weird to me, because, a minute before that, he'd just said he didn't care. I told him a lot about you.'

'Oh. OK. That explains a lot.'

'You say that a bunch, did you know that? What does it explain?'

'It explains why he came down here and asked personal questions.'

'What kind of personal questions?'

'Well . . . how can I tell you . . . if they're *personal?*'

'Right,' Grace said. 'Duh. Sorry.'

'What did you tell him about me?'

'That you used to be a dancer and an actor and a singer . . .'

That explains a lot, Billy thought, but he kept it to himself.

'. . . and that your name was Billy Shine, but that your first name used to be Rodney or Dennis or something . . .'

'Donald. Actually.'

'Oh, Right. Donald. Sorry. And I told him your last name used to be Fleinsteen, but you changed it to Shine, because Fleinsteen wasn't a dancer's name.'

'Feldman,' Billy said, suddenly even more tired.

'Oh. Feldman. Where did I get Fleinsteen?'

'I wouldn't venture to guess.'

'There you go talking weird again. I guess I told him wrong. What's this one? Is this you dancing?'

She held up a framed photo that had been sitting on the end table near the couch. It was indeed a photo of Billy dancing.

'Yes. In fact, it's me dancing on Broadway.'

'What's Broadway?'

'It's a street. In New York.'

'It doesn't look like a street. It looks like you're dancing inside.'

'Right. In a theater. On Broadway.'

'Oh. Is that good?'

'That's about as good as it gets.'

'Too bad you don't do this any more. I mean, since you loved it so much.'

'Well, look at it this way, Grace. If I were still dancing, I'd be on Broadway right now, and then who would look after you?'

'True. But that's another thing I was thinking we could talk about, because if you were still a dancer—'

'Maybe we should play the quiet game,' Billy interjected.

'What's the quiet game?'

'You know. The one where we try to see who can go the longest without talking.'

'Ugh,' Grace said, putting the Broadway photo back in the right place, but at the wrong angle. 'Sounds really boring.'

'I'm just so tired, though,' Billy said, leaning over and fixing the angle of the Broadway photo. 'I didn't sleep last night. I'm just not sure how much more energy I have for talking.'

Grace appeared suddenly in front of him, bouncing up and down on her toes, her hands on his knees.

'Will you teach me to dance?'

'That takes energy, too.'

'*Please*, Billy? Please, please, please? Please, please, please? *Pleeeeease?*'

Billy sighed deeply. Wearily.

'OK,' he said. 'I guess it takes less energy than listening to that.'

The next day, Felipe came and got Grace at school, but he didn't take her home. Instead, he walked her down to Rayleen's hair and nail salon, on the boulevard. It wasn't called that, and she didn't own it or anything, but that was where she worked.

'Why there?' she asked Felipe while they were walking together.

'I don't know,' Felipe said. 'She just said to bring you down there. She said she told you about it.'

'Oh,' Grace said. 'Maybe. Maybe she said something and I forgot.'

'Do you mind going down there?'

'I don't think so. Not really. I was just looking forward to going to Billy's, because he's teaching me to dance. He's teaching me this dance called the time step. He says it's the first, most basic thing I gotta learn. Except I don't know why they call it the time step, because it's not a step. It's a whole dance. It's like, *tons* of steps. I have trouble keeping track of them all. But I only had one lesson so far. It's *tap*. Do you know what that is? Tap?'

'Sure,' Felipe said. 'I've seen tap dancing.'

'I have to wear these special shoes, that are tap shoes. And I don't have tap shoes, of course. I mean, why would I have tap shoes? So Billy let me wear this really special pair of his, from when he was young. They're really special because they were his very first pair. From when he was about my age. But, you know what? They're still too big for me. Even when Billy was my age, his feet were bigger than mine. I guess because he's a boy. Anyway, I had to put on three pairs of socks, and then they fit me. I can't take them home, though, because they're too special, but I can wear them at his house. And I have to dance in the kitchen, because you can't tap dance on a rug. Anyway, I was just sort of looking forward to getting my second lesson, but I guess I can do that tomorrow. You're not listening to me, are you, Felipe?'

'Oh, sorry,' Felipe said. 'Yeah. Mostly. I was mostly listening.'

'Were you thinking about the thing you're sad about?' Grace asked, because he looked sad.

'A little bit. I guess I was, a little bit.'

'Do you want to tell me? Sometimes that helps.'

'Maybe not today,' Felipe said. 'Maybe someday, but maybe not today. It might be hard for you to understand, anyway, because it's grown-up stuff. You know. Man – woman stuff.'

'Oh,' Grace said. 'Yeah. That stuff *is* hard to understand.'

They walked in silence for a block or so, and then Grace asked, 'Felipe? Do you speak Spanish?'

'Oh, yeah. I speak Spanish better than I speak English.'

'I think your English is good.'

'Thank you.'

'Will you teach me to speak Spanish?'

'Well,' Felipe said, scratching his head. 'I guess so. I guess I could teach you a little bit. Here's a good thing to know how to say. "*Cómo se dice en Español . . . ?*" That means, "How do you say in Spanish . . . ?" And then you could just point to the thing you wanted to know how to say. Or tell me the word in English. And then we could add a word every day.'

'*Cómo se dice* in *Español*,' Grace said. 'Why is there an English word in there?'

'There isn't.'

'In.'

'*En*,' Felipe said. 'E-N.'

'Oh. *Cómo se dice en Español.*'

'Very good.'

'But you have to tell me how to say something. Today. That's not enough for today, just learning the question. I think I should have an answer for today, too.'

'OK. What do you want to know how to say?'

'Tap dancing. Teach me how to say tap dancing, OK?'

'You have to ask it right, though.'

'Oh. Right. Sorry. *Cómo se dice en Español* . . . tap dancing?'

'*Baile zapateado.*'

'Whoa. That sounds hard.'

'Maybe we should do an easier one today.'

An old man walked by with a bulldog on a leash, so Grace said, '*Cómo se dice en Español* . . . dog?'

'*Perro.*'

'*Perro*,' Grace said.

'Good.'

'Felipe? Do you like me?'

'Sure, I like you.'

'What do you like about me?'

'Lots of things.'

'Name one.'

'Well. You asked me to teach you a little Spanish. Nobody *ever* asks me that. Everybody just figures Spanish-speaking people should learn English. It never occurs to anybody to learn a few words of Spanish. That shows a lot of respect for me. You know. And for my language. That you asked.'

'I liked my Spanish lesson,' she said. 'I guess if I had to miss my tap dance lesson, it's good that at least I got a Spanish lesson. I wonder why Rayleen wants me to come down to her salon.'

'I think she wants to do something with your hair,' Felipe said.

'Oh. My hair. Right,' Grace said. 'That explains a lot.'

'Good Lord in heaven,' this lady named Bella said, holding up the back of Grace's hair.

Bella was a big, heavy African lady. Not African-American, like Rayleen, but really African-African, from Nigeria (this is what Rayleen told Grace), with that nice accent that people have sometimes when they're from Africa. And dreadlocks. She wore her hair in dreadlocks.

She was one of the hair-stylist people at Rayleen's salon, and friends with Rayleen, who stood close by, shaking her head and clucking her tongue.

Grace could see them both in the mirror.

'Can you brush it out?' Rayleen asked.

'Oh, honey, that would hurt like the devil. And she

would lose a lot. I think we should cut it.'

Grace watched Rayleen in the mirror. Watched Rayleen furrow her brow.

'I'm not sure what her mother would think about that.'

'What do you care what her mother thinks? Where is her mother when this decision needs to be made? Something needs doing, and somebody needs to decide to do it, so let that somebody be you.'

The more Bella talked, the more Grace liked her accent. Even though she wasn't sure she liked what Bella was saying about her mom. Still, it would be nice to get a haircut, instead of having all those knots pulled out, which was vicious. Grace hated that more than anything. So it would be nice to just have them decide. Right here and now.

'I'll end up being the one who has to hear it from her, though,' Rayleen said.

She was thin, and pretty, Rayleen. Grace looked at her as though she'd never seen her before, because it was different, seeing her in the mirror and all, and because of the way Bella was standing right beside her. Not that Bella wasn't pretty. Grace thought she was. But she wasn't thin. And she wasn't as pretty as Rayleen.

Grace felt Bella's long fingernails raking lightly through her hair – at least the part that could still be raked through – and along her scalp, and it felt good, like a massage.

'You sure she'll even get up from her bed long enough that you'll have to hear about it? Have you even gotten her to call the county yet?'

'She says she did,' Rayleen said, like she wasn't very sure.

'She did!' Grace piped up. 'I know she did, because I was right there.'

'Oh. Good. Did she say what she was supposed to say?'

'Yeah. That you were my babysitter and all. Yeah.'

Rayleen furrowed her brow even more deeply. 'Was she . . . did she seem . . . pretty . . . awake?'

'Medium,' Grace said.

Rayleen and Bella looked at each other's eyes in the mirror, and Bella rolled hers a little bit, so Grace could see the whites of them.

'I guess we just keep our fingers crossed,' Rayleen said.

And Bella said, 'So, let's focus, girls. What about the hair?'

'I think we should let Grace decide. It's her hair. Grace?'

'Hmm,' Grace said. 'I think probably we should cut it. Because I hate that thing where somebody brushes out my hair when it's knotty. It pulls. But . . . I don't know. Will it look OK?'

'*Will it look OK?*' Bella howled. 'Oh, my goodness! Little girl! You don't know who you're talking to! If I cut it, it will look superb!'

'I don't know what superb means,' Grace said.

'Like good,' Rayleen said, 'only better.'

'Oh. OK, then.'

So Bella put one of those drapes around Grace, and snapped it tightly at her neck, and Grace made a mostly pretend noise like being strangled.

'You don't want to get the hair down there under your collar, though,' Bella said. 'That'll itch like crazy.'

'Right, I hate that,' Grace said. 'I hate that worse than anything.'

'We should teach her how to brush her own hair,' Rayleen said.

'I know how to brush my hair,' Grace said, a little too loudly.

She was distracted, looking at the image in the mirror of a woman customer in the chair behind hers, because the woman held a little tan chihuahua dog on her lap.

'*Perro*,' Grace said, but nobody was paying much attention.

'Then why didn't you?'

'We only have one brush, and it's up on top of the dresser in my mom's bedroom, and I can't reach it. When I was a little kid, I tried pulling out the drawers and using them like steps, so I could climb up there. Not to get the brush. To get something else, but I don't remember what the something else was any more. I forget now. It was so important at the time that I climbed up there, but now I don't even remember. Isn't that funny? Anyway, the whole thing fell down on top of me, and I was screaming and crying, and my mom had to run get one of the neighbors to help get it off me. That was before we lived here. That was back when we lived right off Alvarado Street. Anyway, I wasn't about to try that again.'

'I can't really wash it properly until I get these knots out,' Bella said, as though she hadn't even been listening. She pulled out a long, sleek, pointy pair of scissors and held them, paused, over Grace's head.

Bye-bye hair, Grace thought. But it was better than all that brushing and pulling.

'I'm surprised no one noticed at her school,' Rayleen said. 'Wouldn't you think her teacher would notice that nobody brushed her hair for weeks?'

'Maybe she did,' Bella said, still holding the scissors paused. 'After all, you still don't know who called the county.'

'Hmm,' Rayleen said. 'Right. I hadn't thought of that.'

* * *

Walking home with Rayleen, Grace couldn't stop looking at her fingernails. She held them out in front of her, both hands at once, and admired them. It made her trip over a crack in the sidewalk twice. Well. Three times.

'You might want to look where you're going.'

'But they're so beautiful!'

After the haircut (which looked funny, in a way, probably just because it was something Grace wasn't used to, but also kind of stylish and nice at the same time), Rayleen had given Grace nails. They were the kind you paste on, and they were a really pretty shade of pink, and they had sparkles and other little charm things pasted on. Like, one little paste-on charm was on her middle finger, and it was silver, and shaped like a tiny flying horse. She couldn't stop looking at the flying horse.

'I'm glad you like them,' Rayleen said.

'I know how to speak Spanish,' Grace said, still looking at the nails.

'Since when?'

'Just since today.'

'You learned Spanish just today?'

'Some. I know *cómo* you *dice en Español* . . . dog. It's *perro*. You *dice* "dog" in *Español* by saying *"perro"*.'

'OK, I stand corrected. That's a lot of Spanish to learn in one day. I'm impressed. Oops. Look out, Grace. Look where you're going.'

Grace looked up just in time to zig-zag around two young women walking toward them on the sidewalk.

'Sorry,' she said to them. Then, to Rayleen, 'Maybe when we get home we can order a pizza.'

'Maybe,' Rayleen said. 'But it's not going to be like the

last pizza. I could barely carry that thing into the house. I didn't know a pizza could even cost that much. When the guy told me the bill, I thought he was kidding. Who orders pepperoni *and* sausage *and* Canadian bacon *and* meatballs all on one pizza?'

'Me.'

'And triple cheese? I mean, I've heard of double cheese, but . . .'

'I'm sorry if it was too much money. But you said to order what I wanted.'

'Right,' Rayleen said. 'I did. So, live and learn. But this time I'm making the call. And this time I'm telling you in advance that you want cheese and pepperoni. Period.'

Grace smiled to herself. Because it was still pizza. And it was still a million times more pizza than she was about to get from anybody else besides Rayleen.

'Have you thought of what you like about me yet?'

'Yes,' Rayleen said. 'As a matter of fact, I have. You're a survivor. And you don't complain. Now, that's just off the top of my head, and it's just so far. Like I said before, I'm sure when I get to know you better, there'll be tons more.'

'It's good for now,' Grace said, sneaking a quick look at her nails again. One had a little crescent moon charm stuck on – her right pinky one. 'That and a pizza's plenty good enough for today.'

Billy swung his apartment door wide and leaped out into the hallway, landing right in front of Rayleen and Grace.

'Why did you not tell me Grace wasn't coming today?' he bellowed, alarmed by the sound of his own anger. 'I was beside myself with worry. I mean it. I had a miserable afternoon. Absolutely abysmal. I thought something had happened to her. I was a mess. My fingernails are bitten right down to the quick. And beyond. Every single one of them. Look at this.'

But he didn't literally offer them for inspection.

Rayleen stood a moment – her mouth open wide – while he spoke. Then she looked down at Grace.

'Grace,' she said. 'You didn't tell him. You promised you'd tell him.'

Grace looked up into Rayleen's face. 'Oooooops,' she said.

Then all Billy could do was stand there like a fool, all the passion and fire drained out of him, because you can't very well stay mad at a kid Grace's age for forgetting something.

'I'm sorry,' Rayleen said. 'It's all my fault. I take total responsibility. I shouldn't have put it all on Grace. Next time I'll tell you myself if we change the plan.'

'I'm sorry, too, Billy,' Grace said. 'I didn't mean to make you bite your quicks.'

Billy sighed deeply, pushing out a whole afternoon of abject panic.

'Can I still get a dancing lesson?' Grace asked.

'Oh, no. No, not today. I'm afraid not. That was just too exhausting an afternoon. I couldn't— Oh, my God! Would you look at you! Look at your hair!'

'Do you like it?'

'*Like it?* Girlfriend, you are a changed woman! I mean, girl. You are a new girl. You are *styling*! I am *very* impressed!'

'And look at the nails.'

She held her fingers out, proudly, for Billy to see.

'Amazing,' he said. 'Absolutely amazing. You have been reborn.'

She smiled up at him for a moment.

Then Billy's spell broke, unexpectedly, like a bubble popping.

'Oh, my God, I'm out in the hall,' he said, and scrambled back inside.

'Yeah, and in your pajamas,' Grace said.

He closed the door most of the way, peering out through an inch of crack.

'We sort of figured you knew,' Grace said.

Grace said to Billy, 'I'm still really sorry about yesterday.'

She was standing in his kitchen – because there was no place to *sit* in his kitchen – leaning her back against the washer-dryer, and trying to pull Billy's special tap shoes over three pairs of socks without bunching up the socks.

'You don't still have to be sorry about that.'

'But look at your poor nails. They're so sad.'

'No, don't look at my poor nails,' Billy said, shoving his hands deep into the pockets of his old bathrobe. It hurt, because all of his fingers were still sore.

'Why not look at them?'

'Because they're sad.'

'I just feel like it's my fault,' she said, getting the first shoe in place at long last.

'Look. Baby girl. It's not your fault if I'm such a freak that I can't handle a little mild tension.'

'Don't call yourself that,' she said, frowning as if for the cameras. Dramatically. A girl after Billy's own heart. 'I don't like that.'

'Besides,' he said. 'It was an honest mistake. The past is the past. It's gone, thank God.'

'I thought you liked your past.'

'Some of it, yes. Some of it, no.'

'But you have all those pictures around to remind you of it.'

She set her one shod foot down on Billy's kitchen linoleum. The tapping sound drove clean through every one of Billy's defenses and found a feeling place. A little like bumping into an ex-lover, suddenly and without warning, someone who'd hurt you beyond repair, but whom you still loved.

How much of his life had he devoted to that tiny, but absolutely singular, sound?

'I like to remember the good parts and forget the rest.'

'I don't think that works,' Grace said.

'You don't think what works?'

She tested the sound of her taps once, on purpose, doing a slow flap step, remembered from her first lesson. Then she set about to pull on the other shoe.

'It's like people who want to feel only happy but not sad,' she said. 'It never works. You either feel things or you don't. You don't get to pick and choose. At least, I don't think so.'

Billy didn't answer straight off. He just stood, his shoulder leaned on the door frame, and watched her work on the second shoe, admiring her intense concentration.

After a few seconds, she looked up at him.

'You got quiet.'

'Kids your age shouldn't say things like that.'

'Why? Was it stupid?'

'No. It was smart. Too smart.'

'No such thing as too smart. Aha! Got it!'

She laced up the second shoe and strode out into the middle of the kitchen floor, tapping her way through the time step routine Billy had taught her, and managing to get every single step in the wrong order. But it was danced with good feeling, at least in the lower half of her body.

The sound, though not perfect against kitchen linoleum, again filled Billy's stunted gut with memories. They could not, he noticed, be sorted out into two groups, those to be kept and those to be discarded. They came as a package deal.

'Wait, wait, wait,' Billy said, focusing back on the dance performance itself. 'You forgot a few things.'

'Well, I didn't have a lesson yesterday.'

'Let's not work on the time step right now.'

'But I want to learn it!'

'You will. I promise. But I want you to have arms. Remember when I told you I want you to have arms?'

'I have arms,' she said, holding them up as proof.

'I told you what that means. Remember? When I say I want you to have arms?'

'Oh! Yeah! Um. Let me think. Nope. Sorry. I don't remember.'

'It means you're concentrating so hard on getting the steps right that you're only thinking about your feet. Which I understand, because the time step involves some remembering, especially after just one lesson. But I want you to get off on the right foot, no pun intended.'

'You did so intend that.'

'Actually, I really didn't. Here's what I'm saying. I don't want you getting into a bad habit of moving your feet correctly but holding the rest of your body stiff, like a statue. This is not Riverdance, you know. Not that there's anything wrong with Riverdance. Only that this isn't it.'

'I don't know what that river thing is.'

'Right. I might have predicted that. Let's do something really basic with your feet. Let's do a series of stamps and stomps, and when you get into a simple rhythm with that, you can start to focus on your torso and arms.'

'What's a torso?'

'Upper body.'

'Oh. Why didn't you just say so?'

'No talking. No giving the teacher a hard time. Especially not at these prices. Now. With your right foot. Stamp.'

Grace brought her right foot down with a satisfying

sound, then raised it again, looking up at him and smiling.

'That's not a stamp. That's a stomp.'

'Darn it,' she said, smile fading. 'I always get those two confused.'

'I told you how to remember the difference. Remember what I taught you about that?'

'Not really.'

'Like a stamp on a letter?'

'Right! I remember! When you stamp a letter, the stamp stays down. Right. So a stamp is when I stamp down, with both taps at the same time, heel tap and ball tap, and then I leave my weight on that foot.'

'Right. Stamp with your right, shift your weight right, lift up your left, stamp with your left, shift your weight left, repeat.'

'This is easy,' Grace said, after the third or fourth stamp cycle. 'Too easy.'

'That's why now you're supposed to think about the rest of your body.'

'Oh, right. My arms,' she said, still stamping. 'What should they do?'

'Ask them.'

'That's dumb.'

'Try it before you say it's dumb.'

Grace's arms came up to about waist level and began to shift in rhythm with the stamps. Billy smiled inwardly.

'Good thing nobody lives downstairs except us,' Grace said.

'Indeed a good thing,' Billy replied.

Except, just at that moment, someone knocked on the door. All motion froze in the kitchen, and they waited there in silence for a beat or two, staring through the open kitchen entryway to Billy's front door.

'Damn it to hell!' Billy said, under his breath. 'Why do people keep knocking on my door? Nobody ever knocked on my door except delivery guys. For years. And now all of a sudden this is like a daily occurrence.'

'It's my fault,' Grace said, in a surprisingly restrained whisper.

'Not really.'

'It started when you said you'd look after me, though.'

'True enough.' Then more loudly, Billy called out, 'Who's there?'

'It's Eileen Ferguson. Your downstairs neighbor.'

Billy exchanged a look with Grace.

'Is she supposed to know you're here?'

'I'm not sure.'

Billy took a deep breath, walked to the door, undid all of the locks except the safety chain, and opened the door several inches, hoping he was the only one able to hear the pounding of his heart.

'I'm sorry,' he said. 'Too loud?'

'Yeah, kind of. I'm trying to take a nap, and whatever you're doing up here sounds like that dance company that does the stomp dancing with trash cans on their feet.'

'Sorry. Didn't realize anybody would be trying to sleep at this hour.'

If she caught the mild dig, she chose not to let on.

She looked bad. Billy knew he was a fine one to judge, yet he couldn't surgically remove the judging from his nature. It was simply too much a part of him now. Sure, he probably looked like hell, too. Then again, he hadn't gone out to knock on a neighbor's door. If he had, he would certainly have freshened up a bit first.

Well, he wouldn't have gone in the first place. Let's be real. But theoretically.

'Well, I was. Have you seen my daughter? Grace? Do you know Grace?'

'Everybody in the building knows Grace.'

'Do you know where she is?'

'I . . . know she's OK.'

She shot him a skeptical look.

'If you don't know where she is, how do you know she's OK?'

'Because we have something of a schedule,' Billy said, wondering if he'd just revealed too much. 'Grace is at school, and then somebody picks her up, and then somebody takes care of her until Rayleen gets home, and then she's with Rayleen. So she's either at school, or with Felipe, or with me, or with Rayleen.'

'But if she was with you, you'd know it.'

'So true!' Billy said, jokingly, making light of the gaffe as best he could.

'Hmm. I didn't know about that schedule thing. I thought it was all just Rayleen. But that's nice, I guess. That's good. For Grace. I guess. Well, if you see her, will you tell her to come home?'

'I will. If I see her I will.'

'Thanks,' she said, and peeled away down the hall.

Billy closed and locked the door again, then stood with his back leaned against it, breathing out the excess stress.

He rejoined Grace in the kitchen. The girl was still halfway practicing stamps, but without ever lifting her feet.

Just shifting her weight and bending her knees. And having arms.

'Good arms,' he said.

'Thank you. It sucks that now I can't dance. Why did it have to wake her up? Nothing ever wakes her up except maybe an hour a day. And it has to be now.'

'She wants you home.'

Grace sighed.

'OK,' she said. 'This shouldn't take very long.'

She unlaced and pulled off Billy's tap shoes as if saying goodbye to an old friend.

Not two minutes later, she was back.

'She was already out again. I bet it wouldn't wake her up this time.'

'Not willing to risk it,' Billy said.

'We could go outside.'

'*You* could go outside.'

'Oh, right. I forgot. Maybe we could just go out on your patio. Your patio isn't right over my house.'

'It's broad daylight, baby girl.'

'So?'

She waited for him to answer. For a surprising length of time. Billy was amazed by her patience. But, of course, she did give up eventually.

'You can't even go out on the *patio*?'

'Let's just say I choose not to.'

'But I saw you out there twice.'

'But the first time it was nearly dark. And the other time it was dusky. And I was slithering on my stomach, if you'll recall.'

Once again, Grace didn't say anything for a long time.

So long, in fact, that Billy began wishing she would. Almost anything she could say at that point would be better than nothing at all.

Finally Billy couldn't stand it any more, and filled the silence.

'I never claimed to be normal,' he said.

'I guess that's true,' she said. 'Well. Whatever. I like you anyway. How bout if I go out on the patio, and you stand right here and watch me through the glass, and if I do something wrong you open the door and tell me so?'

'That could work,' Billy said.

By the time Rayleen got off work and came to get her, Grace had put in a solid hour of dancing with no break of more than a minute or two. Her face glowed red, her short hair dripped, but still she danced.

She not only had arms, but she returned to practicing her time step, slowly, and in proper order, and when she memorized it and brought it up to normal speed, she somehow managed to bring her arms along.

She could be a dancer, Billy thought. If she cared enough, and took the time, and didn't get distracted by boys or ego or the world, or all of the above, she could. If she didn't get beaten down by the savagery of the life, maybe. It made Billy ache – a fine line of pain through his solar plexus – just to think of it, but he couldn't tell if the ache meant he was proud of her, jealous of her, or scared for her.

Probably all of the above.

When Rayleen showed up, Grace pulled her into Billy's apartment and over to the sliding-glass door, and made her watch while she performed her time step out on the patio. Rayleen stood shoulder to shoulder with Billy, playing her role in their audience of two.

'Impressive,' Rayleen said. 'You know she's learning Spanish, now, too.'

'Good for her. I wish I knew more Spanish. So useful in LA. Although . . . probably more utilitarian for people who go out of the house.'

Rayleen glanced over at him, then back at Grace before Grace could notice the shift in her attention.

'I owe you an apology, I guess,' she said. 'I didn't say it straight out, but . . . I had my doubts about leaving her here.'

'Sounds like normal thinking,' Billy said.

She glanced over again, eyebrows raised.

'Hey,' Billy said. 'Just because I don't think normally doesn't mean I don't know normal thinking when I hear it.'

She placed one hand on his shoulder. And just left it there. And so it happened again. The melting. Only this time it wasn't appropriate to fall to his knees, and there would be no way to cover for himself if he did. So he worked hard at keeping his knees solid and unmelted.

A moment later Grace finished her dance with a broad flourish, and bowed at the waist. Rayleen took her hand back to applaud, and Billy was both relieved and disappointed to feel it go.

Then Grace launched into an encore of stamps and stomps, proving she knew the difference between the two, and could alternate smoothly.

'Her mom came by,' Billy said. 'I didn't let her know Grace was here. I wasn't sure if she was supposed to know.'

Rayleen pulled a couple of deep, audible breaths.

'Yes,' she said. As if deciding and speaking at the same time. 'She can know. It's OK for her to know. I just decided. Grace is thriving here, and I dare anybody to challenge that. Anybody who has a problem with that can come take it up with me.'

'Thank God,' Billy said. 'Because I really hate it when people come take things up with *me*.'

Grace

It was about seven in the evening, two days later, when Grace and Rayleen heard Grace's mother calling her from the basement stairs.

'Where are you, Grace?' her mom shouted, like she was already madder than hell not to be able to find Grace, even though she'd only just barely started looking.

'You better go tell her where you are,' Rayleen said.

'But my eggrolls will get cold.'

'Tell her where you are, and then come back and finish your eggrolls.'

'It'll be kind of hard to walk.'

'Just don't smoosh the cotton down too much. And keep your toes spread. Whatever you do. That way you won't smear the polish.'

'I thought the cotton was supposed to keep my toes spread.'

'Keep them spread even more than that.'

'OK, I'll try.'

Grace slid down from the hard wood chair and waddled to the door, one eggroll in each hand. Then she had to shove one of the eggrolls in her mouth so she could open the door. But she still had a little eggroll grease on her hand, and so couldn't get the door open until she got smart and used her shirt tail.

During all this, Grace's mom called a second time, sounding even madder.

By the time she waddled out into the hall, to a spot where her mother could see her, she'd launched into the process of chewing the eggroll she'd been holding in her mouth, which made it hard to have a conversation.

'There you are,' her mom said. 'Come home now.'

Her mom's hair looked rumpled up, the way Grace's had until just recently. She had dark circles under her eyes. She looked bad. But, of course, Grace didn't say so. Wouldn't have, even if she could've talked properly.

Some things you just don't say.

'Can't,' she said, but it just came out as a big noise, too rounded at the edges of the sounds.

'What did you say?'

Grace pointed at her mouth with the other eggroll, asking in pantomime for her mom to wait while she chewed.

'What are you eating?' her mom asked, not quite taking the pantomime hint, or maybe just pretending she didn't.

Grace pointed and chewed a while longer, then said, 'Eggroll. Which is not junk food.'

'Come home now.'

'Can't. I'm eating eggrolls. And getting a footicure.'

'*Pedicure.* Who's giving you eggrolls and a pedicure?'

'Rayleen. You know. My babysitter.'

'Right. Rayleen. She knows I'm not actually *paying* her to be your babysitter, right?'

'I don't know. I think so. I'll ask. But I gotta go now.'

'But I want you home. I had no idea where you were.'

Grace placed both hands firmly on her hips. Even the hand with the eggroll.

'Mom. You haven't known where I am for *days and days*. It's really more like you didn't even wonder till just now. I don't see why I have to give up my eggrolls and my foot manicure just because you finally woke up and figured out about how you don't know where I am.'

'I was asking where you were just yesterday.'

'Yeah, but then you were asleep about a minute later, before I could even come tell you.'

These were all brave things to say, and Grace knew it. They came from some mad place, some leftover bad stuff. They were bundles of words wrapped around criticism, and a few hurt feelings.

She waited to see what her mom would do. In the old days, her mom would've gotten mad. That's all Grace knew for sure.

'OK, fine,' Grace's mom said, 'but when you're done eating and . . . well, when you're done, come right home.'

''K,' Grace said, and stuck the other eggroll in her mouth.

Then she waddled inside and slid back up on to the chair so Rayleen could work on her toenails some more. (Even though the only part left was checking the polish for dryness and taking the cotton out from between Grace's toes.)

When she'd finished chewing, Grace said, 'Do you think I was too snotty to my mom?'

And Rayleen said, 'No. Frankly, I don't. I think you were perfect. Just exactly snotty enough.'

*   *   *

Grace padded, barefoot, shoes in her hand, down the basement stairs, looking forward to the idea of spending some time with her mom. For a change. She tried the door to her own apartment, but it was locked.

She knocked loudly, and called through the door, 'It's me, Mom. Let me in, OK?'

The door swung wide, and Grace's mom stood in the open doorway, her mouth gaping open, jaw hanging.

'Oh, my God!' her mom whispered on an exhale of breath. 'Grace Eileen Ferguson, what have you done to your hair? Did you cut it all off with scissors?'

Grace tried to answer, but never got that far. Her mom took Grace's chin in her hand and pushed her head sideways, first one direction and then another, looking at the haircut from all different angles.

'No. You didn't. You couldn't have. This is a professional haircut. This looks like a real haircut. An expensive one. Who cut your hair?'

'Bella,' she said, yanking her chin back.

'And who's Bella?'

'A friend of Rayleen's, at the salon where she works. Why? Don't you like it? Everybody else likes it.'

Grace's mom never answered. Instead she took Grace by the hand and marched upstairs and down the hall with her.

While they were marching, Grace said, 'You saw me already. Just before. You saw me standing out in the hall eating eggrolls with cotton between my toes. Why didn't you say about my hair then?'

'I didn't see it.'

'I was standing right in front of you!'

'You were way down the hall. I thought you just had it pulled back in a ponytail or something.'

'Don't you like it? Everybody else likes it.'

They stopped marching in front of Rayleen's door. Grace's mom banged hard on the door, so hard it sounded like somebody trying to beat down the door with a battering ram, like the police did on TV.

Out of the corner of her eye, Grace saw Billy's door open an inch or two, and she could see one of his eyes through the crack. She waved at him, but he put a finger to his lips, and Grace knew what he meant by that, so she started pretending she didn't see him there at all.

Rayleen opened the door, and, when she saw who was knocking, stood with her hands on her hips, like she was getting ready to fight with everything except her fists.

'Isn't this going a little too far?' Grace's mom said. She sounded pissed.

'I have no idea what you're referring to.'

'Don't you? Look, I appreciate the fact that you're letting Grace hang around. I do. Especially since I'm not paying you. You do know I'm not paying you, right?'

Rayleen didn't answer. Just stood there looking stony, and Grace could tell that anything Rayleen said from this point on was going to be something she'd thought out very carefully first.

'But this is a little weird. This is too much. Because, she's still my daughter. Not yours. You get that, right? I mean, I take a nap, and when I get up, you've decided to redesign her.'

A long silence. Stony. Grace was learning that, when Rayleen was mad, the madder she got, the quieter she got.

'Grace got her hair cut three days ago,' Rayleen said. 'That's one long-ass nap.'

A silence that made the little hairs stand up on the nape of Grace's neck.

'OK. Look. I'm grateful. I'm grateful for . . . most of this. I am. Really. But for you to decide suddenly Grace should have short hair instead of long hair, like that's yours to decide—'

Rayleen stopped her there. Cut her off.

'Is that how you think it was? Grace. Tell your mom how it was.'

'Oh. OK,' Grace said. 'It was like this, Mom. The hair-brush was up on the dresser and I couldn't reach it, and I sure wasn't climbing up there after what happened the last time. You remember that, right? So my hair got so knotted and tangled up that Rayleen had to take me to the hair salon and ask her friend Bella to try to unknot it, but Bella said it was so bad that it would hurt like the devil to brush it out, and I'd lose a bunch of it, too. So then they said it was up to me, and they asked what did I want to do? And you know how much I hate it when I have knots and it pulls, only this was like a hundred times worse, so I said to cut it. Don't you like it? Everybody else likes it.'

Grace waited through a long silence. While she waited, she watched her mom get smaller – not literally, but in a way – like she just kept taking up less and less room in the hall. But really it was the mad part of her that got small. Not the real part, the body part of her.

'It's actually a nice cut,' Grace's mom said.

Then she started to cry. Grace had only seen her mom cry two or three times before, so that was sort of upsetting.

'I'm sorry,' Grace's mom said to Rayleen, through the crying, which by now was getting pretty big.

Then she took Grace's hand and led her back down the

hall, and Grace waved goodbye to Billy, and he waved back. Then Grace got led down the stairs to her own apartment, and while she was being led, her mom kept saying over and over again how she was sorry.

Well, at least I still get to spend tonight with my mom, Grace thought, even if she *is* crying. And sorry.

But Grace was mostly wrong about that. She didn't end up spending much time with her mom at all.

Not an hour later, Grace was back at Rayleen's door, knocking. She knocked lightly, so it wouldn't sound like somebody who was mad.

Rayleen answered like she was expecting a tall person on the other side of the door. She had to look down before she saw Grace standing there.

'Can I come in?' Grace asked.

'Yeah. Sure you can. You OK?'

'I guess. Can I stay here tonight?'

'If it's OK with your mom. What happened with your mom?'

'She's loaded again.'

'Oh,' Rayleen said. 'Sorry. Sure, you can stay here.'

A little later, when Rayleen was pulling out a blanket to make Grace a bed on the couch, she said, 'That's interesting, how you said your mom was loaded. You used to always say she was asleep.'

'Yeah. I got tired of that,' Grace said. 'She's loaded.'

Billy

'You don't look very happy,' Billy said to her, the minute she walked through his door.

To further underscore her mood, she did not make a beeline for his special tap shoes. Just shook out her sad little umbrella and flopped on the couch.

'Unh,' Grace said.

'What's up?'

'Nothing.'

'Why, Grace Ferguson. I never pegged you as a liar.'

'I'm not a liar! What a mean thing to say! Why would you even . . . Oh. Right. That. Yeah. I guess maybe there's a *little* something up.'

He sat down beside her on the couch.

'Talk to me,' he said.

In a small and guilty way, he found himself grateful for the diversion. He'd expected her to come bounding through the door all ready to dance, forcing him to deliver bad news, in which case the only bucket of ice water to hit that childlike enthusiasm would have been him, and his neuroses.

It was raining. That was the problem. It was raining, and Billy was unwilling to risk letting her dance any place but the front balcony. The uncovered front balcony.

Maybe he would be lucky and it wouldn't even come up.

Grace sighed theatrically. 'It's just this thing Mr Lafferty said.'

Billy felt his small daily measure of peace slip away at the mention of that name.

'What did that horrible man say to you? When did you even see him?'

'Just now. Out in the hall. I was coming in the front door with Felipe, who was teaching me the Spanish word for door – which is *puerta*, by the way, just in case you didn't know that – I didn't know that, until just now, so I thought maybe you didn't know that, either. I don't know how much Spanish you—'

'Grace,' Billy said. 'Focus.'

'Right. Mr Lafferty was in the hall. And he looked at me, and he looked at Felipe, and he shook his head, and he said all we were doing with my mom was just enabling her.'

'Oh,' Billy said. 'I'm surprised you know that word well enough to get depressed over it.'

'Well, I didn't. Exactly. But he just kept talking. And then it was pretty easy to see what he meant. Like, he kept saying he's known a lot of people who have problems with alcohol and drugs, and he said they almost never get better, but when they do it's because they have to. When they're about to lose something they just can't stand to lose. He said even their house or their car or their job probably isn't enough, because some people'll just go live under a bridge so they don't have to get better. He said it's always when they're about to lose the person they're married to, or their kids. He said that before, when the county was about to come get me and take me away, she might've had a reason to clean up her act. But why should she now? He said that you and Rayleen and Felipe are taking over all her responsibilities for her, so why would she get better? She doesn't even have any reason to try. So I guess that's enabling.'

'Right,' Billy said, finding her depression contagious. 'That's enabling.'

'He's not right, though, is he?'

Billy didn't answer.

'I mean, he's a jerk, you said so yourself, right?'

'Not in so many words,' Billy said.

'But you don't like him.'

'Not even a little bit.'

'So he's wrong. Right?'

Billy looked at the rug and didn't answer.

'OK, never mind,' Grace said. 'Let's just get to the dancing lesson. That'll make me feel better.'

'Oh. The dancing lesson. OK. Prepare not to feel any better. I'm not really comfortable with letting you dance on my kitchen floor any more.'

'Why? Because of my mom?'

'Yes. Because of your mom. Because I don't take it well when people come to my door and yell at me.'

'She didn't exactly yell.'

'But she will the next time. Because the next time she'll figure she asked me nicely once already.'

'But she almost always sleeps through stuff like that,' Grace said, right on the fine razor's edge of whiney.

'Right. *Almost* always. We just have no way of knowing

when we'll hit the exception to the rule. And, frankly, that's the kind of suspense I'm just not cut out to live with.'

Grace sighed.

Billy noted her lack of resistance. He knew what it meant, too. She was getting to know him unfortunately well. Well enough to know there was no point trying to reason with his anxieties.

They sat, side by side, slumped on the couch, for a long time. Without talking. Maybe ten minutes. Maybe more. Just staring out at the sheeting rain.

'This day sucks,' Grace said.

He looked over to see Grace's hand clamped firmly over her own mouth.

'It's not that bad a word,' Billy said. 'I mean, as words go.'

'No, it's not that. It's that I complained.'

'So? Everybody complains.'

'Rayleen says I never do, and that's one of the things she likes about me.'

They fell back into silence, and the watching of the rain, for a moment or two.

Then Billy said, 'Your secret is safe with me.'

'Thanks. Maybe I'll just dance on the rug. It's better than nothing.'

'OK, go get your shoes on. I mean, go get *my* shoes on.'

He didn't even watch this time, as she plunged into the drawn-out process of trying to make his old tap shoes fit. He had been that completely sucked down into the darkness of the mood.

What seemed like too short a time later, he looked up to see her do a stomp, followed by a flap step, followed by falling on her butt.

'Ow,' Grace said.

'Careful,' Billy said, lifelessly. 'It'll be slippery on the rug.'

'Great time to tell me,' she said, pulling herself to her feet.

She flapped another time or two, testingly, still leaving her weight on her planted foot.

'This sucks,' she said. 'Oops. I complained again.'

'One more time and I'm telling Rayleen.'

Grace's face fell pathetically.

'Really?'

'No, not really. I was kidding you.'

'Oh. Don't kid. I'm not in the mood. This doesn't work at all. It's too slippy. And I miss the taps.'

'Me, too,' Billy said. 'Only I've been missing them since before you were born.'

She came back to the couch and sat again, slumped, staring out at the rain.

'I heard it was gonna rain all week,' she said.

'There *is* one thing we could do. But I have no idea how we'd accomplish it.'

'What?'

'Well. It's not hard to make a little dance floor to practice tapping. All we'd need is a big piece of plywood. Five feet square, six feet square. Whatever we could get. And we can put it right here on the living room rug, and the rug would muffle the sound. Keep it from sounding so sharp by the time it went through the floor. So if we had that, we'd be golden. But that's sort of like saying, all we need to do is route the freeway though my living room. Easy, right? I don't go out. You can't walk to a lumber yard by yourself . . .'

'I could ask Felipe!'

'Does he have a car?'

'I don't think so. But maybe he'd walk or take the bus.'

'Big thing to carry home.'

'I could ask him,' she said, already halfway to the door. 'If he hasn't left for work yet.'

'The shoes,' Billy said. 'My shoes.'

Grace looked down at her feet, crestfallen. 'But I have to hurry, though.'

A tough pause.

Then he said, 'Right. Go. Hurry.'

The minute she tapped out into the hall, he felt the deep pang of separation. As if he'd just let her leave the house wearing his dog, or his baby. That is, if he'd had one of either to lose. He stared at the rain for a few minutes, purposely breathing into the anxiety in his chest, trying to honor it without adding to it.

Then Grace slipped back in. Literally. Came through the door, slipped on the rug, and landed on her butt again.

'I'm getting tired of doing that,' she said, still down.

'Maybe you better take the shoes off for today.'

Grace sighed, and began to undo the laces.

'He says he can't. He says it's miles and miles to the closest lumber place. And he must know, because he used to work doing construction. He says it's way too far to carry something that big home. And it would be too big to go on the bus with it. He says Mr Lafferty has a pickup truck. But he said he doesn't talk to Mr Lafferty, which I can sort of understand why, because Mr Lafferty isn't very nice to him. Felipe says it's because he's from Mexico. Do you think it's because Felipe's from Mexico?'

'Probably so, yes.'

'That's not a very good reason.'

'I agree.'

She sat on the couch beside him, the tap shoes in her hand, and then set them down gently on the couch between them. As if she saw them as being like a baby or a dog, too.

'So he says he won't ask Mr Lafferty, but *I* can ask Mr Lafferty. If I want.'

'Does Rayleen have a car?'

'Yeah. Rayleen does.'

'Oh. Good.'

'But it's broken, and she doesn't have enough money to get it fixed.'

'Oh. Bad.'

'What do you think I should do?'

'I think you should wait and talk to Rayleen before you do anything. Especially before you talk to Lafferty.'

''K,' Grace said.

And they stared at the rain for several minutes more.

'This is really boring,' Grace said.

'I would tend to agree.'

'What do you do when I'm not here?'

'Pretty much this.'

'Let's play a game,' Grace said.

'I'm not sure I've got the energy.'

'It could just be a talking game. You know, like a truth or dare sort of a game.'

'Ooh,' Billy said. 'I don't know. Sounds dangerous.'

'It's just words. How can words be dangerous?'

'You have a lot to learn about the world, baby girl. Nothing is more dangerous than words.'

'That's stupid. What about a gun? A gun can kill you dead.'

'Only your body,' Billy said. 'It can't kill your soul. Words can kill your soul.'

'Well, maybe we could just stay away from *those* words. You know. The dangerous kind.'

'Which ones did you have in mind?'

'I had a friend once. Well, I have a couple of friends, but not anybody I see outside school or anything. But I had a really good friend, Janelle was her name, but then when I was in first grade, she moved with her family to San Antonio. That's in Texas.'

'So I hear,' Billy said.

'We used to play this game at sleepovers. Like she'd sleep over at my house or I'd sleep over at hers. This was when my mom was clean, and the house was clean, and there was food and everything, and it was OK to have people over. So we'd be in bed, under the covers. We'd pull the covers up over our heads like a tent, like this tent that we could both fit into—'

'We're not doing that part,' Billy said.

'Right, I know, stop talking. Don't interrupt.'

'Sorry.'

'So then the game was just two questions. What do you want more than anything? And what do you *not* want more than anything? Like, what scares you really bad, worse than anything else?'

Billy rose to object, but it felt like too much trouble.

'You go first,' he said.

'OK. What I want more than anything is for my mom to get better. And what scares me most is what Mr Lafferty said, about how people almost never do. Because then I got to thinking that maybe she never will.'

Silence. The rain fell harder, if such a thing were even

possible. Like water falling from a chute, all at once and not even separated out into drops.

'That was a fast turn,' he said.

'Your turn.'

'I know. That's what I was just complaining about. OK. Here goes. What I want the most is . . . nothing. That's the problem. Everything I ever cared about is behind me, and there's nothing left to want. And, by the way, that's also what scares me. No future. Nothing to want. That's no way to live, let me tell you, baby girl.'

They watched the rain in silence for a few minutes more.

'Usually the game makes me feel better,' Grace said.

'Don't say I didn't warn you.'

'This day sucks.'

'No more so than usual, if you ask me.'

'Next time I won't, then,' Grace said.

It didn't seem late enough for Rayleen to be home. But then he heard her knock. She had a special knock, Rayleen. With a rhythm to it. Four little taps. One, two three . . . pause . . . four. If it could go on long enough, you could almost dance to it. And the real beauty of the situation was that Billy hadn't had to tell her that a special knock would do wonders for his anxiety disorder. She'd figured it out on her own.

He tilted his head toward the still-silent Grace.

'Did you lock it?'

'Oh. No, I forgot. I slipped and fell, and then I had to take the shoes off, and then I forgot.'

But that was a natural enough turn of events, Billy thought. The truly bizarre angle of the situation was that he'd forgotten, too.

'It's open,' he called. 'Come in.'

The door swung wide and Rayleen looked in at them, questioningly.

'What the hell happened to you two?' she asked.

Billy sighed. 'Nobody thrives *every* day,' he said.

'Rayleen,' Grace said. 'Can I go ask Mr Lafferty if he'll go to the lumber store for us? I know you don't like him, and I know you don't really like for me to be around him, but it's just this one favor. Just so we can get a big piece of wood. Please can I go ask him?'

'A big piece of wood for what?'

'For a dance floor for my tap dancing. So we can put it over the rug, and then it won't wake up my mom, and so then she can't come up here and yell at Billy.'

'I don't know, Grace. He's such a rotten guy. I'd be surprised if he'd be willing to do you a favor.'

'I could ask, though.'

'Sure. You can ask.'

Grace ran out the door, still in her sock feet.

Billy looked up at Rayleen, who studied his face for a moment. Then he patted the couch beside his hip and she came over and sat with him.

'Question,' he said. 'Are we enabling Grace's mom by taking care of her kid?'

'Hmm,' Rayleen said. 'Never thought about it.'

'Too bad. I was hoping you'd say no. It's just that she does nothing but sleep twenty-three hours a day, and it seems to me she wouldn't be able to do that without us.'

'Or she just would anyway, and Grace would pay for it.'

'But this way she can do it guilt-free, and with no consequences.'

'What got you thinking about this?'

'Something Lafferty said to the kid.'

'Lafferty! That figures. Goddamn that man. I hate him so much. Maybe I should go after Grace before she even gets up there.'

'Too late. I'm sure she's talking to him by now.'

Rayleen sighed. Sat back. Gazed out Billy's big sliding-glass door. What was it about rain that made people want to gaze?

'Sure is coming down out there,' she said.

A long silence, during which Billy had no comment to offer about the rain. It simply rained. It wasn't one of those things you talked much about, he felt. It was one of those things that just *was*.

'OK,' Rayleen said. 'Honest answer: maybe. I don't know. I guess I'll have to give that some thought.'

'Don't you hate it when a guy like that is right?'

'On those rare occasions when it happens, yes.'

Grace

Grace stood in the hall in front of Mr Lafferty's door, balanced on one foot, and scratching the instep of her other foot through the three layers of socks. She'd put Billy's wool ones on the inside, because they were the ones that bunched up the most when you tried to pull tap shoes over them. But, on the inside, they itched.

The door opened, and Mr Lafferty looked over her head, frowning, but then he looked down, and the frown disappeared.

It seemed odd to Grace that he was ready with a frown for anybody tall. Only Grace didn't seem to bring that out in him.

'Oh, it's you,' he said, sounding like she was an OK person for it to be.

'Yeah, it's me, Mr Lafferty. I came to ask you a favor.'

'Are you OK? Are you in trouble?'

'No, not really. It's just that nobody else in the whole building has a car that works—'

'You need a ride someplace? Where do you need to go?'

'Just let me tell you,' she said, trying to hide her frustration.

If it had been Billy, or Rayleen, she wouldn't have tried to hide it. She would have just said, 'Stop it! Stop interrupting!' But this was Mr Lafferty, and you had to be a little more careful with him.

'Sorry,' he said, which surprised her.

'I need somebody to go to the lumber store and get a big piece of wood.'

'What kind of wood?'

'I'm not sure.'

'How big?'

'Billy said five feet. Or six feet. Either one.'

'That's not quite all I need to know, though. Five or six feet in which direction?'

'Hmm,' Grace said, probably because it's what Rayleen always said at times like this.

'I better go ask him.'

'No!' Grace said. Well, she'd meant to say it, but ended up shouting it. 'No, please don't go knock on Billy's door any more, please. He hates that.'

She watched Mr Lafferty's eyes narrow, and she wasn't sure what to make of that, but it seemed to have something to do with the look she'd seen on his face before he found out it was only somebody short knocking on his door.

Why did everybody hate it when their door got knocked on? Grace thought she would like that. A new person, maybe, or a good surprise. She wondered if she would outgrow that openness when she got older, since it seemed everybody else had.

Then Mr Lafferty said, 'Let's try this. Why don't you tell me what it's going to be used for, and maybe that'll help.'

'Oh. Sure. It's for a dance floor. Because I'm learning to tap dance.'

'Ah,' Mr Lafferty said. As if that explained a lot, as Billy would have put it. 'So you need a *sheet* of wood. Like plywood. Like a big plywood square.'

'Yeah!' Grace shouted, excited now. 'That's what he said! He said plywood, and he said either five feet square or six feet square!'

'Sure,' Mr Lafferty said. 'I could do that.'

'You could?'

'Sure.'

'Wow. I'm surprised.'

'If you didn't think I'd do it, why even come ask me?'

'Well, it never hurts to ask.'

'Where are your shoes?' he asked, with a little bit of an air of disapproving of things like that.

'I left them down at Billy's. I was wearing his tap shoes. I need to get my own tap shoes, though, because I can only use Billy's when I'm at his place. I can't take them home. And I really need to practice at home, and at Rayleen's, because I'm not getting enough practice, and besides, they don't really fit me right at all, but I don't have the money for tap shoes, and I don't think Billy or Rayleen do, either. And I *know* my mom doesn't, so I don't know what I'm supposed to do about that, but if I had the wood, at least I could go back to practicing *some*. You know. Like, *at all*.'

'Fine,' he said. As if that could be the end of the conversation.

Grace just stood there. She wanted to ask, '*When* are you going to get the wood?' But it seemed rude. After all, he'd said he would, which was shocking enough, and it didn't seem right to ask any more questions than that.

'OK, thanks,' she said.

Then she padded along the hall and down the stairs in her sock feet.

She got down to the first floor just as Rayleen was leaving Billy's. She ran into Rayleen out in the hall.

'He said yes!' she screeched.

'Really?'

'Really! He said yes!'

'Well, I'll be damned. When is he going?'

'I don't know. I didn't ask.'

'Am I supposed to give him some money for it or something?'

'I don't know. I didn't ask.'

'What exactly did you ask?'

'If he would do it. And he said yes!'

Rayleen put a hand on Grace's shoulder. She seemed to be feeling down, Grace noticed. She hadn't seemed down when she came home, but now she was. Maybe she had caught it from Billy. And Billy had caught it from Grace. So maybe it was all her fault.

'Come on inside,' Rayleen said to her. 'I have to think of something to make us for dinner. I had a client cancel on me today, and another was a no-show, so we can't afford to order out.'

'Oh. That's OK,' Grace said.

'I'm not sure what we've got to eat.'

'What about when Mr Lafferty comes back with the wood? Do we have enough money for that?'

'I have no idea,' Rayleen said. 'I don't even know what plywood costs.'

But Grace could tell she was getting lower and more depressed.

They went inside her apartment, and Rayleen rummaged around in the cupboard and the fridge.

'I think it's going to have to be cereal or eggs,' she said.

'Oh. That's OK,' Grace said.

But it made her think again about this day sucking worse than most days, even if Billy didn't think it sucked any more than any other. But then she reminded herself about the wood, and then she knew it wasn't fair to think about it sucking, because it isn't every day when somebody goes out and gets a dance floor for you.

'Can we have both?' Grace asked.

'Sure. Why not?'

Rayleen said it like she didn't have any energy. Then she put crunchy oat cereal and an almost-empty carton of milk in front of Grace, and started breaking eggs into a bowl to scramble them, and she did all of it in that same way, like she didn't have any energy.

Grace poured a huge bowl of cereal, because there was lots, a whole box, but she only used a little milk, because she wanted to save some for Rayleen.

Meanwhile Rayleen was standing at the stove, watching this over her shoulder.

'You want more milk than that, don't you?'

'What about *you*?'

'I'm just having scrambled eggs. But thank you. That was very nice.'

'I can finish it? Are you sure?'

'I'm sure,' Rayleen said.

And she didn't say one other thing until quite a bit after she sat down at the table with two plates of scrambled eggs.

'Is there any ketchup?' Grace asked.

Rayleen got up and got her a bottle of ketchup out of the fridge.

'Thanks,' Grace said, and started squeezing it over her eggs.

And Rayleen said, 'Whoa. That's a lot of ketchup.'

Then they just ate, and were quiet after that.

About fifteen minutes after they'd finished eating, right around the time Rayleen had the last of the dishes dried and put away, they heard a knock at the door.

Grace ran and opened it, but there was nobody there.

She stepped out into the hall, still in her three pairs of socks. She looked both ways, but the only thing she saw was a big piece of plywood. Very big. Taller than she was. It was leaning against the wall near Rayleen's door.

She turned to run inside, to tell Rayleen, but smacked right into her immediately.

'Well, that was fast,' Rayleen said.

'But a piece of wood can't knock on the door,' Grace said.

'I don't think the wood knocked on the door. I think Mr Lafferty knocked on the door and then left.'

'Oh. Yeah. That does make more sense. What was I thinking, huh?'

'I'm pretty sure you weren't. You know what this means, don't you?'

Grace didn't. But she knew by the tone of Rayleen's voice that it wasn't good. It seemed it must mean something very not good.

'No. What does it mean?'

'It means he did something nice for us. And so now we have to go tell him we appreciate it.'

'Oh, is that all?'

'Sounds bad enough to me.'

'Want me to go alone?'

'No. I'll come. It won't kill me to thank him, too. Besides, I probably need to pay him back for it.'

'What if it's more than you have?'

'Cross that bridge when we come to it.'

'Right,' Grace said. 'I still don't know what that means.'

But Rayleen just locked the door behind them, and then took Grace by the hand, and they walked upstairs together.

Rayleen knocked on Mr Lafferty's door.

He answered with that same frown on his face. Only this time he saw Rayleen, and he kept the frown. He leaned on his door frame and just looked at her, and not in a very happy way at all.

'We came to say thank you,' Rayleen said.

'I liked the idea of her learning tap,' Mr Lafferty said. 'She needs the exercise. That's a good hobby, too. Wholesome, you know? Not like the crap kids are into these days. It sounded like a step in the right direction for her.'

'It was a very nice thing to do,' Rayleen said. 'Especially so fast.'

'Yeah, it was really fast!' Grace said.

Mr Lafferty just stared at Rayleen a moment, still not looking very happy.

Then he said, 'I can be a nice guy.'

Rayleen took a big deep breath before she answered, like she needed to count to ten first. Then she said, 'Obviously so. Obviously you can. So, what do I owe you for that?'

'If I'd wanted my money back for it, I'd have taped the

receipt to it. And I wouldn't have just left it down there and come back up here. I would have come to your door and told you what you owed me.'

He sounded a little bit unhappy, like there was some kind of problem, but Grace couldn't see why, because everything seemed to be working out really well.

'Thank you very much,' Rayleen said, like she was all done talking.

And Grace said, 'Yeah, thank you very much.'

Then Rayleen took hold of her hand and walked her down the hall. But before they could get to the stairs, Mr Lafferty called after them.

He said, 'Did Grace tell you what I said about what you guys are doing? Did she tell you I said you're only enabling her mom to stay addicted?'

Rayleen stopped dead, and Grace kept walking until she hit the end of the reach of Rayleen's arm, and then she bounced back again. Rayleen was looking back at Mr Lafferty, but not saying anything.

Then after a second, Rayleen said, 'I heard about it, yes.'

'Did you lie to her and tell her I was wrong?'

Another long pause. It made Grace nervous. She kept wondering why Rayleen didn't talk faster. The way she usually did.

After much too long a time, Rayleen said, 'No.'

Then she took Grace by the hand and they went back downstairs.

Grace knocked on Billy's door and said, 'It's me, Grace,' all at the same time, so he wouldn't get nervous.

He opened the door. Really opened it. No chain or anything, because it was only Grace. Well, Grace with

Rayleen standing right behind her, but that was still OK by Billy standards. At least, these days it was.

His eyes went wide when he saw the wood.

'So that's what you guys were chattering about out there.'

'Help us bring it in, OK?'

Billy's eyes changed. They got darker, and more closed off.

'I know, I know,' Grace said. 'It's the hall. But it's just for a minute. It'll only take a minute.'

Billy looked up at Rayleen.

'I'll grab this side,' Rayleen said. 'If you'll just come out real quick and get the other side, we'll have it inside in just a couple of seconds.'

Billy stood. He breathed. A lot. Like he was under a blanket and couldn't get enough air. He counted to three. Out loud.

'OK,' he said. 'One. Two. Three!'

At the same time as he said three, he leaped out into the hall and grabbed the other side of the wood. Then he ran back inside with it so fast that Rayleen almost couldn't keep up with him. She nearly fell down trying.

'Close the door! Grace! Close the door!' he said, when they were all inside.

So she did.

'Now I can still dance today!' she said. Shrieked, actually.

'Oh, I don't know, baby girl. It's awfully late.'

'It's not late! It's only about six thirty.'

'But I only have you from three thirty to five thirty.'

'So? Today you have me a little later.'

'But I'm used to three thirty to five thirty.'

They stood looking at each other for a moment. Grace

knew what Billy meant. She was asking him to do something different, new, and he wasn't good at that, and when you ran into something Billy wasn't good at, it didn't seem to help to argue.

Grace looked at Billy, and Billy looked back at Grace, then up to Rayleen, then back to Grace.

'Oh. Baby girl,' he said. 'Don't look so crestfallen.'

'Can't help it,' she said.

'OK, fine,' he said. 'Dance.'

Billy

Billy was asleep. A deep, blessedly dreamless sleep, with no rustling of feathers. No flapping of wings.

Then, suddenly and without notice, he was standing on his feet, wide awake, gasping for breath, heart pounding, wondering if there had really been a gunshot, or if that had only been part of a dream.

'But we weren't dreaming,' he said out loud.

Still, when unexplained things happened in the night, they often happened as part of a dream, whether you'd thought you were dreaming at the time or not.

Then again, there really had been a drive-by on this block just a handful of months earlier. Ten bullets had sliced through the windows of a first-floor apartment two buildings down, thankfully killing no one. Hitting no one. But Jake Lafferty had run all through their building, pounding on doors at two in the morning, asking if everybody was OK. With a shotgun on his shoulder. Billy had seen it through the peephole, while refusing to open the door.

But this gunshot . . . this gunshot had sounded, if anything, louder than the drive-by gunshots had.

'Maybe because we dreamed it,' Billy said.

After all, Jake Lafferty wasn't doing his night-time messenger Paul Revere number. So it must have been a dream.

Except, just then, somebody knocked on his door.

'That's not so much a Jake Lafferty knock, though,' Billy said out loud. 'More than Rayleen Johnson but less than Jake Lafferty.'

He turned on the bedroom light and checked the clock. It was only barely past ten thirty.

'Billy, are you OK?' he heard Grace call through the door.

He hurried to the door and threw it open wide.

Rayleen was standing there in the hallway with Grace in her arms. The little girl looked sleepy and scared all at the same time. Well, they both did. Well, all three of them probably did, actually, but in the absence of mirrors – and he owned none – Billy could only guess about himself.

'What *was* that?' Rayleen asked. 'Are you OK?'

'Drive-by?'

'I don't know. I would think Lafferty would have been down here with his shotgun by now.'

And Billy smiled, just a little, in spite of himself.

'It's not funny,' Grace said, still clutching Rayleen, legs wrapped around her waist, head down on her shoulder. 'It's scary.'

'Sorry. You're right. You guys want to come in?'

'No,' Grace said. 'We have to check on my mom and Felipe and Mr Lafferty and Mrs Hinman and make sure they're OK. Oh, wait. Look. There's Felipe.'

Billy looked up to see Felipe pause on the bottom step, looking relieved to see them all in one piece, and all in one place.

'Felipe,' Grace yelled, much louder than necessary. 'Will you go and see if Mr Lafferty and Mrs Hinman are OK?'

Felipe turned and trotted back upstairs again.

'Let's go get your key,' Rayleen said to the girl, 'so we can go check on your mom.'

'I'll go,' Grace said, wriggling to get down. 'She's my mom, so I'll go check on her.'

Rayleen set the girl down with her bare feet on the wood floor of the hall, and she danced from one foot to the other because it was cold.

'Sure you don't want me to come?' Rayleen asked her.

'Positive.'

'Go get your key, then.'

But Grace just headed off toward the basement apartment. A cautious step or two later, she pulled it out from under her pajamas and held it up for them to see: the key, still dangling on its cord around her neck.

She disappeared down the stairs to the basement apartment.

'Who knew she slept with that thing on?' Rayleen asked Billy, who only shrugged and shook his head.

He was still standing in his open doorway, not wanting to come out – of course – and not quite ready to invite anyone in after bedtime. In fact, he was still not wholly awake.

'I should have gone with her,' Rayleen said. 'What if her mom—'

'Oh, good God,' Billy interjected, cutting her off. 'Don't even say it. Don't even think a thing like that.'

'Sorry.'

'What is that on your floor?'

Billy pointed to an envelope lying just inside Rayleen's

open doorway, looking starkly white against the worn and darkened rug.

'Hmm,' she said. 'Don't know. Didn't even see it.'

She walked back and picked it up. She opened it as she walked back to Billy's door. But it wasn't light enough in the hallway to read the printing on the small rectangle of card stuck inside. It looked colorful, though. It didn't look like a written note. It looked more like an advertisement of some sort.

'I guess you'd better come in,' Billy said.

And he turned on all three lights in his living room.

Just then, both Felipe and Grace arrived back.

Grace bounded in, shouting, 'She's OK! She's loaded, and I couldn't wake her up all the way, but she's not shot, because she grunted at me, so that's good.'

Billy looked up to see Felipe paused in the open doorway. He had never seen Felipe before, except through the glass, and he expected that Felipe had never seen him at all. They eyed each other in the tentative way strangers often do.

'OK if I come in?' Felipe asked.

'Oh. Um. Sure. Please do.'

But Felipe only advanced a step or two into Billy's living room.

'Mrs Hinman's fine,' Felipe said. 'Little scared. Lafferty wouldn't come to the door. But that's prob'ly just cause I told him it was me.'

'But he answered?' Rayleen asked. 'I mean, you heard he was OK?'

'No. He's either out, or he made like he didn't hear me.'

'What's that?' Grace asked, pointing to the envelope in

Rayleen's hand. The fear and confusion of events had raised her voice to a near-shriek.

'It's a gift certificate,' Rayleen said, as if only just figuring that out as she reported it. 'It's a seventy-five-dollar gift certificate to a store called Dancer's World. And it's made out to you.'

'*Me?*'

'Grace Ferguson. That's you. Right?'

Grace screamed. She jumped up and down. Ten, then fifteen, then twenty times. She shrieked, 'I can get tap shoes, I can get tap shoes!' Then she stopped jumping and shot Billy a worried look. 'Can I get tap shoes for seventy-five dollars?'

'I'm sure you can get something decent,' Billy said.

And, of course, that got Grace jumping again.

'That's the best present anybody ever gave me! Tell me who gave it to me, OK? Please? Tell me who gave me that, so I can go hug and kiss them for ever! Tell me right now? Please?'

Billy looked at Rayleen, who shook her head. Then Rayleen looked at Felipe, and he also shook his head no.

'We don't know,' Billy said. 'Somebody just slid it under Rayleen's door.'

'Maybe your mom,' Rayleen said. 'Yeah. Must have been your mom.'

'I don't think so,' Grace said. The mystery of the gift must have sunk in for her, because she stopped jumping and screaming, and her face took on a thoughtful expression. 'She doesn't even know I started tap dancing.'

'Who else knows, then?'

'Nobody. Just you guys. Oh, yeah, and I told my teacher. But if my teacher wanted to give me a gift thingy for tap shoes, I think she'd've given it to me at school. Right? And besides, I just told her I was learning to tap dance, and for all she knows maybe I have my own shoes already, because I didn't tell her I needed my own shoes. Only you guys know that. Oh, yeah. And Mr Lafferty. I told him about it when I was asking him to go get the wood.'

'Hmm,' Rayleen said.

'Well, we're all in one piece,' Felipe said. 'So I'm going back upstairs. If it was a drive-by, we'll hear sirens in a minute.'

'Goodnight, Felipe,' Grace shouted. Then, when he was gone, Grace said, only slightly more quietly, 'I'm going to go ask Mr Lafferty if he gave me this. Because then if he says yes I can say thank you.'

'It's ten thirty,' Rayleen said. 'That's a little late to go knocking on his door. Besides, Felipe said he wasn't home.'

'Or that he just wouldn't answer because it was Felipe. Besides, we know he's awake if he's home, because somebody just shot off a gun.'

'OK, you can try,' Rayleen said. 'But then come running right back down.'

''K,' Grace said, and flew away.

As soon as she did, Rayleen leveled Billy with a look reserved for the adults of the building.

'What do you make of all this?'

'No idea,' he said.

'You really think Lafferty would do something that nice?'

'Maybe. He might. When she asked him for the dance floor, he had it back here in under an hour. Maybe he hates other grown-ups and loves kids. Some people can only tolerate little kids or dogs. Or both. It happens.'

'You don't suppose these two things are connected?' she asked, holding up the gift certificate.

'What two things?'

But just then Grace came bounding down the stairs again.

'He must not be home,' she said, 'because I said through the door all about how it was me.'

'OK,' Rayleen said. 'Let's just start settling down again, so we can get you back to sleep.'

'Are you kidding me? I'll never get back to sleep thinking about my tap shoes!'

'Try.'

Grace sighed and slouched back into Rayleen's apartment.

Rayleen looked up at Billy again.

'No sirens,' she said.

'Yeah. Well. In this neighborhood, minutes might mean hundreds of minutes. Or maybe they won't come until morning. Maybe even the police don't want to be down here at night. I wouldn't put it past them to wait for a safer hour to investigate.'

Rayleen snorted. 'And we're so used to this shit, if nobody was hit, maybe nobody even bothered to phone it in. I'm going back to sleep.'

'What was that thing you were starting to ask me? Something about two things being connected.'

'Oh. Never mind. That was a crazy thought.'

'You know what I think is interesting?' he asked her.

'No, what?'

'I was thinking about the drive-by a few months ago. Lafferty was out in the hall, running around, checking on everybody, but that was almost . . . it's like he needed to take charge of it or something.'

'No "almost" about it,' Rayleen said. 'It was a power trip. Pure and simple.'

'But other than that, nobody checked on anybody else. We just stayed in our apartments.'

'We didn't know each other. That's the difference.'

Grace appeared at Rayleen's open door, across the hall, looking impatient.

'Are you *coming* already?' she asked.

Then she rolled her eyes and left again.

'I was thinking *that* was the difference,' Billy said.

Rayleen smiled just a little, and then let herself out without saying more, and Billy locked the door behind her.

He walked into his bedroom and sat down on the edge of the bed.

'Now we'll never get back to sleep,' he said.

But he was not entirely correct. Mostly. But not entirely.

For twenty minutes or so, well after the first light of dawn, he drifted off. And was nearly blown over by the wind currents of the beating of wings. Then they disappeared, suddenly, driven away, in a kind of evaporation, by a sharp sound.

He opened his eyes and blinked into the light.

'Don't tell me. Let me guess,' he said quietly. 'Someone is knocking at the door.'

A second knock.

'I want my old life back,' he said.

Grace's voice, through the door.

'Billy, it's me, Grace. Don't get up if you're in bed, I just want to tell you that I'll be really late today, because Felipe is taking me to Rayleen's salon, and then I'm waiting there till she gets off work, and then she's taking me on the bus to the Dancer's World store to get tap shoes.'

'Right,' Billy called out. 'I saw that one coming.'

'I wish you could be there with us, so I'd know I'd got the best ones.'

'You'll do fine. Trust the clerk and tell him how much money you have to spend. He'll help you.'

'What if it's a she?'

Billy sighed. 'The trust part still goes.'

Rayleen's voice now, through the door.

'Just wanted to let you know I'm right here to make sure you heard that, Billy.'

'Thank you,' he said.

'Go back to sleep now.'

'I will,' he said.

But of course he never did.

'Wait till I show you what I bought,' Grace said, the minute she bounded through his door. 'I think they're good, and I sure hope you think they're good. The guy at the dance store said they were *very* good. Well, he said they were very good *for the money*. They were on sale. They used to cost over a hundred dollars, so that must be good, right? Because I didn't even have that much to spend, but I could get them because they were on sale.' Then, before Billy could even answer, she said, 'I'm worried about Mr Lafferty. He wasn't there last night, and he wasn't there this morning before I went to school, and I just tried and he's not there now. Why would he be gone so long? Where do you think he would go?'

'Oh,' Billy said.

Then a silence hung while he tried on some vague

thoughts, all of which had been hanging around anyway, but none of which had yet been acknowledged.

'Billy,' she said. 'Wake up. You're not answering any of my questions.'

'Sorry,' he said. 'I was just thinking.'

'What were you thinking about?'

'Nothing,' he said. 'Nothing, really.'

'Why, Billy Shine! I never thought you would be a great big liar!'

'Right,' he said. 'Sorry. I guess I was a little bit worried about Mr Lafferty, too.'

'But you don't even like him.'

'So true. I'm sure he'll be fine,' Billy said, though he wasn't sure at all. 'Show me what you bought.'

'Guess who got me the gift certificate?'

'You found out?'

'Yup. Guess.'

'I can't guess. Tell me.'

'Mr Lafferty!'

'But you said you haven't seen him.'

'Right. I haven't.'

'So how do you know?'

'The guy at the dance store told me. You were right, it was a man. You said it would be a man I was supposed to trust at the dance store, and you were right. Anyway, he was the same guy who sold Mr Lafferty the gift certificate. He said he just sold it to him yesterday. He didn't say the name Mr Lafferty, but he said it was a guy, kind of older but not real old, and he said the guy was very grumpy and rude.'

'Yup. That's Mr Lafferty,' Billy said.

'Close your eyes and I'll show you.'

Billy closed his eyes. And, while they were closed, his

mind slid softly back to the previous night. He heard
Rayleen ask, 'You don't suppose these two things are
connected?' and he knew, now, what she had meant. She
had meant the gift certificate and the gunshot. Maybe part
of him had even known it at the time.

He smelled the new leather of the shoes, close to his
face.

'OK, open your eyes!'

He opened his eyes, and melted inside.

'They're black,' Grace said, as if he couldn't see that. 'Do
you think black is good?'

'It's perfect. It goes with everything.'

'That's what the man said. And he said they have a
forced toe box.'

'Forced?'

'Something like that.'

'Reinforced?'

'Maybe. He said it makes you more . . . I forget, but it's
good.'

'Stable?'

'Yeah, I think so. And he said you can even change the
sound – you know, bigger taps or smaller taps – but I'm
not sure how, but maybe you can show me. He had some
others, with more like bows, like ones with wide ties, but
yours are lace-up, so I thought I should get lace-up; and
besides, those weren't on sale, so they weren't worth a lot
more than I paid. Do you like them?'

'Very much.'

He took another deep breath, filling his sinuses and
lungs with their aroma. It made him feel the tiniest bit
dizzy, but in a pleasant way. In a melting way.

We learned something new today, he thought, but did

not say out loud. We learned that one's first pair of tap shoes are always magic, even if they aren't *our* first pair.

He looked up to see Rayleen standing in the doorway.

'Maybe we should call the landlord,' Billy said to Rayleen. 'And ask him to check on . . . things.'

'Right,' Rayleen said. 'Things. I've been a little worried about things, myself.'

Grace

The next time Grace walked upstairs to try to talk to Mr Lafferty, there was some man she didn't know standing out in the hall. He was very tall and fat, and he was wearing coveralls, and holding a cigar in his teeth, but it wasn't even burning. Thank God, Grace thought, because she hated the smell of burning cigars worse than anything. The man was talking to Felipe, who was leaning in the open doorway of his own apartment.

Grace could hear part of what he was telling Felipe as she walked down the hall.

'. . . and the floorboards might even have to come up, or maybe we could just cut out some of the boards and put in a patch, because we're gonna have to slap a new carpet over it anyway, so it doesn't really matter what it looks like. And one wall'll have to be professionally cleaned and then repainted.'

'Hi,' Grace said, now standing about two steps from the man's knee.

'Well, hello, little lady,' he said.

So, that was kind of weird, Grace thought. I mean, who talks like that?

'Who are you?' she asked.

'I'm the building super,' he said, which didn't sound like a thing that made sense in any way.

Felipe, who knew her well enough to know she needed help, said, 'Casper is the man who comes and fixes things in our building. The landlord sends him over when something needs fixing.'

Grace narrowed her eyes and looked up at Casper.

'Then how come I've never once seen you here?'

Casper laughed in one big, rude snort, and then said, 'Guess nothing needed fixing.'

'Are you kidding me? Everything in this place needs fixing.'

Casper stopped smiling.

That was the moment Grace noticed that Mr Lafferty's door was standing open just a crack.

'He's home! Mr Lafferty is finally home! I have to go tell him thank you.'

A split second later she found herself in Felipe's arms, her feet dangling and swinging two feet off the ground.

'No,' was all Felipe said.

'Get her,' the super said, though Felipe pretty much already had. 'Don't let her go in there. My God, she'll have nightmares for a month. Besides, it's not even sanitary. It's a biohazard. It'll have to be professionally cleaned by one of those bio teams that cost a fortune. Owner'll be pissed.'

Grace relaxed slightly into Felipe's arms.

'Why can't I go in?' Grace whispered in his ear.

'Because Mr Lafferty passed away,' Felipe said.

'Does that mean died?'

'Yeah.'

'Oh.'

Just at that moment Rayleen's voice came booming up

the stairs, calling for Grace, because Grace hadn't actually bothered to mention that she was going.

'Grace? Where'd you go, honey?'

'Yeah, come up and get the kid,' Casper shouted back, startling Grace. 'She's got no business up here. Take her downstairs.'

Grace looked up to see Rayleen standing at the end of the hall, looking uncomfortable.

'Oh,' Casper said. 'I thought it was her mother.'

Rayleen didn't seem to like that, and she didn't answer it, either. She just marched down the hall and took Grace from Felipe and held her tightly.

'It was just like you thought,' Casper said. 'The . . . situation . . . you know, with Lafferty. So thanks for phoning it in. Because, you know, if nobody had noticed for a week, it would've been an even bigger mess than it is now. Although, considering how much of a mess it is now, that's pretty hard to imagine.'

'Come on, Grace,' Rayleen said. 'Let's just go downstairs now.'

'So you knew,' Grace said.

She was sitting at Rayleen's kitchen table, drinking a glass of milk and occasionally glancing up at the ceiling.

'No,' Rayleen said. 'I didn't know. I wondered. There's a difference.'

'But you didn't tell me.'

'Because it might not have been true. And then I would've just been getting you all upset over nothing.'

'Well, I'm sure upset now,' Grace said.

'I know you are, honey. I know. We all are.'

'But you didn't even *like* him.'

'No. But I didn't wish anything like that for him.'

'Why did he do it?'

'I don't know. I really didn't know him very well.'

'Why do you think?'

Rayleen sighed. 'I guess he was unhappy. When people are mean, it usually tells you they're unhappy.'

'He wasn't mean to *me*,' Grace said.

But she never got an answer from Rayleen about that. Maybe no answer was even necessary. It was just true, and it was too late for anybody to explain it to her now. Or even to themselves.

'He was nice to me three times, all just in the last few days or so. So that's a lot of times, right?'

Rayleen seemed to be lost in thought, but then she came to, just a little bit, like something woke her up from a nap.

'Three?' she asked.

But Grace's train of thought had moved along by then. 'We need to have a meeting.'

'Who?'

'All of us. You and me and Billy and Felipe.'

'What kind of meeting? About what?'

'Well, that's why you have a meeting,' Grace said. 'To tell everybody what the meeting's about. I'll go get Felipe.'

She ran for the door, but Rayleen called after her, saying, 'Don't go up there, Grace. Just call him from the bottom of the stairs.'

'Right, right, I know,' Grace said, because it made her a little impatient to be treated like she wouldn't know a thing like that already.

'Wait,' Rayleen said. 'Before you go. You said Mr Lafferty did three nice things for you. But I only know about two.'

Grace sighed deeply, thinking it should be perfectly self-explanatory.

'The dance floor,' she said, holding up one finger. 'The tap shoes,' she said, adding a second. 'And he told me what we're doing wrong with my mom. So that's three. So now can I go get Felipe?'

But she didn't even wait for an answer.

She ran to the bottom of the stairs and called up in her very loudest voice, which was louder than anybody else's loudest voice – at least, anybody she knew. Most of the time Grace had to sit hard on her loud voice and feel shamed for it, but every now and then a loud voice was called for, and that was Grace's moment to shine.

'Felipe! Come down a minute, OK? We're having a meeting!'

Then she ran and knocked on Billy's door, saying, as she did, 'It's me, Grace.'

He answered right away. No safety chain, either.

'Did you hear about Mr Lafferty?' she asked him.

And he said, 'No, but I was worried about it.'

'You, too? How come nobody told me?'

'Because we weren't sure. Just worried.'

'Yeah, that's the same as Rayleen said. Anyway, we're having a meeting.'

'I know.'

'How do you know?'

'Grace. The way you just announced it, people walking by on the street know. Hell, people *driving* by on the street probably know. Are we supposed to have this meeting in my apartment? Without anybody asking my permission first?'

'I don't know. We can have it anywhere you want. Oh. Wait. Right. I forgot,' Rayleen said from across the hall.

'Right. You forgot. Have it anywhere you want. Unless you want yours truly in attendance, and then your options narrow.'

Grace said, 'Huh?'

Rayleen, now standing right behind Grace, said, 'It means if you want him to be there it has to be at his place.'

'Well, of course, we have to have *you* there.'

'Then I guess I'm the venue of choice,' he said. Grace rolled her eyes, so he added, 'That means it's my place or nothing.'

'Right. I already knew that when *she* said it.'

By that time Felipe had arrived, so Billy had to open the door wider and let everybody in. Well, almost everybody. Just as she was headed in the door, Grace turned to see Mrs Hinman standing in the hall, just a few steps away, watching them.

Grace said, 'Hi, Mrs Hinman,' and started to close the door.

But Mrs Hinman said, 'Wait. What's all this about a meeting?'

'Oh, no. Not a meeting for you, Mrs Hinman. This is a meeting for us. Just us. You know. The people who take care of me.'

'All those people take care of you?' Mrs Hinman asked, coming a step or two closer and peering through the door.

'Yeah. Everybody except you.'

Then Grace closed the door. But, as she did, she noticed that Mrs Hinman looked a little hurt. But she couldn't stop to think too much about it, at least, not right then, because this was a very important meeting.

Billy was sitting so close to the edge of the couch that it looked like he might be about to fall on his butt on the rug, and Felipe was standing near the door with his arms folded over his chest. Only Rayleen looked even the tiniest bit comfortable, sitting in Billy's big stuffed chair with her legs crossed, but with her face still plenty curious.

'OK,' Grace said, standing in the middle of the living room and feeling very grown-up and ready to take charge of things. 'This is why we're here. We're having a meeting to talk about how we can . . . not . . . oh, no . . . now I forgot the word. What's that word Mr Lafferty said? About what we're doing with my mom?'

'Enabling,' Billy said.

'Right! We're here to talk about how to stop enabling my mom, because, you know, she's not getting better. And I need her to get better. Don't get me wrong, you guys have been great and all, but, well, she's my mom.'

Billy and Rayleen and Felipe all looked at each other, one set of them at a time.

'I don't know,' Rayleen said. 'I mean, what *can* we do?'

'Well, why do you think we're having a *meeting*?' Grace said, not bothering to hide her exasperation.

'I think what Rayleen means,' Billy said, 'is that there may not be anything we *can* do.'

A long, bad silence hung around the room after that, but while it was hanging, Grace decided she'd just have to think harder, because, after all, this was her mom.

'But Mr Lafferty said if she was about to lose me, she might get better.'

Rayleen's face changed, in a scary sort of way. Like she'd just seen a big hairy monster standing right behind Grace with its teeth and claws out.

'Oh, my God, Grace,' she said, 'you can't want that. You

have no idea what that's like, when the county comes and takes a kid away.'

'No, of course I don't want *that*,' Grace said, though, truthfully, she hadn't specifically known what she'd meant when she'd said it. 'But why can't *we* take me away from her?'

More of that silence.

Billy said, 'We're not sure what you mean.'

'Why can't we just tell her that she never gets to see me again until she stops using all the drugs?'

More silence, this time punctuated by one clearing throat and a couple of uncomfortable sighs.

'There might be a couple of flaws in that plan,' Rayleen said.

'Like what?'

'Like she only sees you maybe an hour a day as it is, and that doesn't seem to be enough to motivate her to make a change, and, more to the point, the police might call it kidnapping.'

'I can't go to jail,' Billy said. 'Period. It's out of the question.'

'And I'm more likely to go to jail for a thing like that than the both of you two put together,' Felipe added.

'Yeah, like the cops just love *my* skin tone,' Rayleen shot back.

'Guys! Will you please just listen? It's my idea, not yours. You didn't take me away. You just took care of me because my mom wouldn't. She's not gonna call the cops, because they'd know she was on drugs. Before she could call the cops she'd have to get clean, and get rid of all her drugs, because she knows we'd tell the cops about the drugs she's been using, and if she gets clean, she doesn't have to call the cops at all, because then I could just go home.'

'Hmm,' Rayleen said.

'But what if she does anyway,' Billy asked, 'just because she's irrational?'

'Well, the cops'll ask *me*, right? They'll say, did these people take you away from your mom? And I'll say, no, not at all, I just can't stand to be around my mom when she's loaded, which she always is right now, because, really, that's true, you know. And I'll just say I asked you guys if I could stay with you, and you said I could for just a little while, until things got better at my home with my mom, and that's not against the law, right?'

'I don't know about this,' Billy said, chewing on the nail of his middle finger.

'Me neither,' Felipe said.

But Rayleen said, 'I think it's a great idea. I'm willing to risk it. I'm already on record as her babysitter, as far as the county is concerned. I'll leave you guys out of it completely. I'm willing to just go down there and tell Grace's mom she has three choices. Lose Grace to the county. Lose her to us. Or get her act together. If she goes to the cops, which she's in no position to do, I'll just say Grace refused to go home and I let her stay with me. And Grace will back me up.'

'Wow,' Billy said. 'I was never part of a kidnapping plot before.'

'It's not kidnapping,' Grace said, much too loudly. 'It was *my idea*!'

'OK, enough!' Rayleen snapped. 'Enough talking about this thing. I'm going down there.'

And she marched out.

Grace sat on the couch with Billy, who was biting his thumbnail, and she slapped his wrist.

'Ow!' he said.

'Stop biting your nails!'

'That hurt.'

'I didn't hurt you any worse than *you're* hurting you.'

They heard the knock on the door of Grace's apartment, and they went silent.

Nothing happened.

Another knock, louder this time.

Still nothing.

'Great,' Billy said. 'Her only daughter's been kidnapped, and she'll never even know it.'

Grace punched him on the arm, but not very hard at all, and said, 'She'll find out, Billy. She wakes up *a little bit* every day. Well. Most days.'

Then Rayleen let herself back into Billy's apartment, looking kind of worn out, and saying, 'I guess I'll just have to keep trying till I get her.'

After the meeting, Grace went upstairs to the attic apartment to talk to Mrs Hinman, because she still had a nagging feeling that Mrs Hinman was feeling hurt or left out or both.

She knocked on the door, saying, at the same time, 'It's only me, Mrs Hinman, Grace.'

She'd learned that you had to do that with all the grown-ups in this building, because they were all pretty much scared of everybody and everything, all the time. Grace wondered if that was just this building, or if it was all the grown-ups in all the buildings in the world, but she only lived in this one, so there was really no way to know.

'All right, dear. Just a minute.'

It always took Mrs Hinman a long time to undo the locks.

When she finally did, she opened the door, of course, but she still seemed a little worried, as if Grace might have brought a team of thugs and bandits along for the visit.

'Can I come in?'

'Well, of course, dear.'

Grace walked into Mrs Hinman's living room and watched her redo all those locks.

'Did you hear about Mr Lafferty?'

Mrs Hinman shook her head and made a disapproving sound with her tongue. A kind of 'tsk' noise.

'Such a tragedy. Such a shame. Only fifty-six years old. And he had no one. No one. Even his grown children wouldn't talk to him. Of course, everybody always feels sorry for the person who has no one, but usually it's for a reason. There's a reason why nobody talked to Mr Lafferty.'

'I talked to him.'

'Good. I'm glad you did. I'm glad he had that before he died. Now, me, I have nobody, but it really isn't my fault. It's just that I'm eighty-nine, and I've outlived my husband and all of my friends.'

Mrs Hinman had finished the locks by that time, so she waddled into the kitchen, saying, 'Can I fix you a glass of juice or something? I don't have any soda.'

'That's OK. I'm really not supposed to drink soda.'

She'd actually been about to say, 'That's OK, I can't stay.' But then she couldn't bring herself to say it. Because Mrs Hinman had nobody, just like Mr Lafferty, and it wasn't even her fault, because she wasn't even mean. Well, not mean compared to Mr Lafferty. Then again, nobody was mean compared to Mr Lafferty.

'Here, how about a glass of apple juice, then?'

So Grace said, 'Sure, OK,' and sat down at her kitchen table. 'I came to say I'm sorry if you felt left out when we had our meeting. I just never thought you'd want to come to it, because you're not one of the ones who take care of me. I didn't mean you *couldn't* be one of the ones who take care of me, you know, if you *wanted* to be. It's just that you said you didn't want to, and all.'

'It's not so much that I didn't want to,' Mrs Hinman said, setting a glass of juice on the table in front of Grace. 'It's more that I didn't think I was up to the task. But I was thinking . . . Oh, where did I put that? Wait, let me find that little catalogue, and I'll show you what I was thinking.'

Grace sipped the apple juice and was shocked by how good it was.

'Wow,' she said. 'I never get apple juice. I should drink this more.'

'Well, you can always come up here for juice,' Mrs Hinman said. 'Oh. Here it is. Let me just show you. I have an old Singer sewing machine. Haven't had it out in years. Not since my husband died. But I used to be very handy with it.'

She sat down at the table across from Grace.

Grace asked, 'What did you used to sew?'

'Clothes. I used to make my own clothes. And Marv's as well. Here, look at some of these patterns.'

'What's a pattern?' Grace asked, looking, but not sure how to interpret what she saw. It just looked like drawings of clothes, mostly ladies' dresses.

'A pattern is something you buy to help you make a

dress. You cut out the pattern and pin it to the fabric, and then you know where to cut, and where to stitch, and where the darts and zippers go.'

'Oh. OK. Why am I looking at this again?'

'I just thought you might want to look through it and pick out a couple of dresses, and then I could dust off my old sewing machine and make them for you.'

'Oh, I get it,' Grace said. 'So that way you won't feel left out any more.'

Mrs Hinman reddened, and she seemed flustered.

'I was just thinking you probably don't have a lot of nice clothes, and you're growing fast, and it might be a good thing for your situation to have a few nice dresses, that's all. It was you I was wanting to help, not myself.'

'I can pick my own dresses?'

'Of course.'

'What about pants?'

'I can do pants.'

'What about tops to go with jeans? Because I mostly wear jeans.'

'There are all kinds of clothes in there,' Mrs Hinman said. 'Why not just look through it?'

So Grace stayed through that glass of apple juice and one-and-a-half refills, and picked out some new clothes.

'Guess what?' Grace shouted to Rayleen as she hit the bottom of the stairs, because Rayleen was standing right out in the hall.

Then she saw the lady.

The lady was wearing a suit with a skirt, in a dark color, and she looked like a business lady, and definitely like she didn't belong in Grace's building.

Grace froze in her tracks.

Rayleen said, 'Grace, this is Ms Katz. She's a social worker, and she came by to see that you're OK.'

'On a Saturday?' Grace said, because she couldn't think of anything else to say.

'Sure, we make visits on Saturdays,' Ms Katz said, smiling in a way that didn't look real. 'Your babysitter tells me you were upstairs talking to the old woman who lives in the attic apartment.'

Grace took two steps closer, because it seemed safe enough, and she figured she should.

'Yeah. Mrs Hinman. I went up to visit her because I was worried she might feel left out. She has nobody, and it's not even her fault. It's just that she's eighty-nine, and she lived longer than all the other people she knew.'

'That was sweet of you,' Ms Katz said.

'And guess what? She *sews*! She let me go through this pattern book of all the different clothes I can have, and I picked a few out, and she's going to make them for me. Isn't that nice of her?'

'Very nice,' Ms Katz said. 'You're lucky to have such nice neighbors.'

'Oh, I have the best neighbors! Billy is teaching me to tap dance, and Felipe is teaching me Spanish, and Mr Lafferty bought me wood for a dance floor and new tap shoes – but then he passed away. And Rayleen got me this nice haircut, and look at my nails.' She held her hands out for the social worker lady to see. 'Oh, poop, I lost a nail already.'

'I can fix it,' Rayleen said.

'It's a lovely haircut,' Ms Katz said. 'So you're doing OK, then?'

'I'm fine,' Grace said, a little worried about what would happen if she didn't answer just right.

'That's good,' Ms Katz said. 'I'll be dropping by every now and then to check and see that you're still OK.'

'Like when?'

'Just here and there.'

'Oh,' Grace said.

She wanted to say, 'No, don't,' but was pretty sure that would be a wrong thing to say.

Then Ms Katz left, and not a moment too soon. Rayleen let out her breath like she hadn't breathed in an hour, so she must've felt the same way.

Billy's door opened a crack, and he peeked out.

'It's OK,' Rayleen said. 'She's gone.'

'Good thing Grace wasn't really in trouble,' Billy said. 'She could have died waiting for that woman to show up.'

'That's the county for you. They never do enough, except when they do too much.'

Grace couldn't help noticing that Rayleen's hands were shaking. And Grace was pretty sure they hadn't at any other times, at least since that first time when Rayleen was on the phone in her apartment. So there weren't too many things that could make Rayleen shake like that, and they were always from the county.

They went back inside Rayleen's apartment, and Rayleen turned on the TV and sat Grace in front of it. A minute later Grace looked around for Rayleen, and saw her slumped down on the floor in the corner of the kitchen. And she was crying.

Billy

On Monday, Grace came slouching into his apartment at the usual time, wearing her tap shoes. He could hear the clicks they made on the worn hardwood of the hallway, and when his carpet muffled the taps, he mourned the loss.

He expected her to go straight to her plywood dance floor. Instead she sat on the couch with him and sighed.

'I don't think I should dance today,' she said.

'Because . . .'

'Geez, Billy. Do I really have to tell you? Somebody died!'

'Right,' he said. 'Got it. How come you have your tap shoes on?'

' Cause I love them.'

'Ah.'

'Billy? Do you think I could be a dancer?'

'I think you already are.'

'How do you figure?'

'Well, you dance, don't you?'

'I meant like a real dancer.'

'So you figure you're just a fake dancer so far.'

'Stop it, Billy! You know what I mean!'

It was not a teasing tone on her part. It was a flash of genuine anger. He tried to shake it off, laugh it away in the silence of his own gut. But he was stung, and he couldn't get out from under it as easily as all that.

'Yes. I do know what you mean. So I'll give you an honest answer. Maybe. If you're willing to work incredibly hard. I mean, the kind of work you'd have to do, I'm guessing you probably didn't even know this much work existed in the world. You're not a natural. But you could still get there.'

'What's a natural?'

'Somebody who dances pretty much the way they breathe, like it's just what their body was built to do. It's almost as if they're not even learning it so much as just brushing up on it. But then there's a whole other group. The pluggers. They have to work a lot harder, but they can get there eventually, too.'

'Were you a natural or a plugger?'

'I was a natural.'

'Hmm,' Grace said. 'So I guess being a natural's not all you need to get there.'

'Ouch.'

'Sorry.'

'True, though. Painful, but true. The hard work is the lion's share of the battle. Hard work can sometimes substitute for natural ability, but natural ability almost never makes up for not being willing to do the work.'

'I didn't get the part about the lion, but never mind. I know how weird you talk. But you weren't lazy, though. Were you?'

'No.'

'You were scared.'

'Let's talk about something else. Did you ever stop to think that Mr Lafferty might want you to dance, even at a time like this? Or especially at a time like this?'

'Think so?'

'He gave you the tap floor and the shoes.'

'True. I'm just not sure I even *feel* like dancing after somebody just died like that. Oops. You know what? Never mind. Forget I even said that. I forgot, I'm a plugger. I better get to work.'

She shuffled carefully across the rug to her plywood tap floor and took her position. She raised one foot. But before she could even lower it again, they heard her mother calling for her in the hall.

'Grace? Where are you, Grace?'

They looked at each other, frozen, and a little scared. They'd both seen this moment coming, and they both knew what it meant. The first time Grace's mother got her head up, she was going to hear the news. It was all they'd been waiting for.

Grace said, in a broad stage whisper, 'Told you it wasn't a good day for dancing.'

'OK, I called Rayleen at work,' Grace said, letting herself back in and hanging the key to Rayleen's apartment around her neck again.

'Is she coming home?'

'Soon. As soon as she can. She's just finishing up her second-last manicure, and then she says her last client of the day is a friend, so she can call the woman on her cell phone and reschedule her. And then she'll be right home.'

The voice stopped their conversation – Grace's mom's voice, this time calling from the sidewalk out in front of the building.

'Grace! This isn't funny any more! Come home!'

Billy tried to ignore it as best he could, but it wasn't easy. In fact, it was nothing but an act. And Billy wasn't nearly the actor he used to be. He glanced over at Grace to see if she appeared as unhappy as he felt. She looked as though she might be about to cry.

Another shout from Grace's mom.

'Grace!'

Billy could feel the strain of the experience in his mid-section, like Grace's mom's voice was pulling all the aliveness out of his belly and leaving only staticky tension in its place. Suddenly it felt as if nothing but staticky tension had ever lived in him. That voice seemed to completely erase any and all of the comfort of his past. Such as it was.

It's official, he thought. We're kidnappers.

He thought about wings. Wide, white-feathered, flapping wings. Anticipated them, really. Might as well get used to them, he thought to himself. Come nightfall they'll be our only companions.

'So . . . what did you tell Rayleen?' Billy whispered, though Grace's mom was ten times too far away to overhear.

'Just that my mom was . . . awake . . . *very* awake . . . and this might be a good time to have that talk with her.'

'Grace!'

This time her mom's voice came through as even more shrill and shocking, though she was halfway down the block by then. It made them both jump.

'She's getting scared now,' Billy said.

'It's really weird to hear her and not answer. It feels weird. It feels . . .'

Billy waited, as patiently as it was in his nature to wait. Then he said, 'Can't find the word?'

'Wrong,' she said. 'It feels wrong. But I didn't want to say wrong, because we had a meeting and we decided this was right. But . . . are we sure this is right? I mean, what if we're not doing the right thing?'

'Here's all we really know for sure,' Billy said. 'What we've been doing up until now is wrong. We pretty much all agree on that, even the late Mr Lafferty, who didn't agree with much of anybody on much of anything. So, if we make a change, at least we have a chance of getting to right. We're just pretty sure we're not going to get there without a big change.'

'Right,' Grace said. 'Thanks for reminding me.'

But she still didn't sound all that sure. And she was beginning to look genuinely stressed.

'You OK, baby girl?'

'It just feels different. You know. Now that we're actually doing it.'

'Things always do,' Billy said.

Rayleen came striding down the sidewalk about twenty minutes later.

'Record time,' Billy said to Grace.

'Are you kidding? It's been a *century*.'

They lay on their bellies on the living room rug, side by side, watching out the very bottom of the sliding-glass door.

'It's like a fifteen-minute walk. You have no idea how fast she got here.'

'Felt like a year.'

'It was twenty minutes,' Billy said.

'Seriously? Twenty minutes? How do you know?'

'I can see the kitchen clock from here.'

'How come some twenty minutes are so much longer than others?'

'A question for the ages.'

'Does that mean you don't know?'

'Pretty much.'

'Now I don't even know where my mom went. Here Rayleen rushed all the way home to talk to her, and my mom's off looking for me someplace around the corner or something, and who knows when she'll be back.'

She said it as though she meant it to be a complaint, but a note of relief shone through in her voice.

Billy said, 'Look again, baby girl.'

He hated to drop it on her like that, but it needed to be said. Besides, she'd see it for herself soon enough.

Grace's mom was walking back down the sidewalk toward home, approaching from the opposite direction as Rayleen, and it looked as though they were destined to collide right about at the walkway to their building.

'Oh, shit,' Grace said, and then slapped a hand over her mouth.

'Special price today on swearing. It's marked way down.'

'You're so weird, Billy.'

Then they both fell silent and watched it happen.

On the outside of the situation, it didn't look like much. Rayleen stood with her hands on her hips, looking relaxed, even though Billy knew she wasn't. Grace's mom was a good head shorter, and she puffed up her chest and did everything a person can do with body language to look big. She had long hair, Grace's mom, and she brushed it back a lot as they talked. A nervous tic, maybe.

The two women stood just far enough away from Billy and Grace's perch that it was impossible to see their facial expressions.

'She's mad,' Grace whispered, reverently.

'Your mom?'

'Who else?'

'There are two people out there.'

'Right, but which one is being told something that'll make her mad?'

'Can you really see that she's mad? Or do you just figure she must be?'

'I can tell by the way she's standing. She has a lot of different ways to stand, and I know them all by heart, and that one means she's mad.'

Just at that moment, Grace's mom split away from Rayleen and came stomping up the walkway to the front apartment house door.

'Oooh, you're right,' Billy whispered. 'Mad.'

'Maybe we shouldn't do this.'

'I think the die is cast.'

'Talk normal, Billy.'

'It means it's too late.'

They heard the front apartment house door bang open, hitting the wall in the hallway with a crack that made them both jump.

'Grace!' Grace's mom screamed.

Literally. Screamed.

Grace started to cry. 'I don't like this,' she said.

Billy put his arm over her, and pulled her close, just as her mom screamed again.

'Grace! Don't do this, baby! You still love your mommy, right? You know Mommy still loves you. Right, Grace?'

Grace cried harder, but silently.

'Grace! You want to be with me, don't you, baby?'

'Tell me again,' Grace whispered. 'Tell me again why this is a good idea.'

'Grace! I can do better, baby! I'll do better now!'

'She'll do better now!' Grace whispered, desperately, sounding as though she knew she was grasping at straws.

'Fine. If she does, then things will be OK. But she has to do better *first*. She can't just promise to do better later.'

'Why not, again?'

'Because that never works.'

'Oh. You were going to tell me again why we're doing this.'

'Because it might be the one thing we can do that could maybe, just maybe, shock her back into getting sober.'

'You're supposed to call it clean, not sober,' Grace said between sniffles.

'Doesn't really matter what we call it. We want her to get better. That's why we're doing this.'

'Right,' Grace said. 'But this sucks. I didn't know this would suck so bad.'

'Grace!'

This one was a full-on bellow. The scream of a person fully devoid of options. It reminded Billy of Stanley Kowalski in a ripped tee-shirt, bellowing up to Stella in *A Streetcar Named Desire*. Because he'd bellowed that line every night for two months, on stage, when he was only twenty-two years old.

It sent a shockwave through both of them. Billy could feel it conduct, between himself and Grace, like emotional lightning.

Then they heard the door to the basement apartment slam.

Grace just kept crying.

Rayleen came over at five thirty, just as she would have done if she'd been at work all that time. Billy recognized her knock – her one, two, three . . . pause . . . four knock – even though he'd never heard it sound so quiet before.

He opened the door for her. Then he pointed to his couch, where Grace was sprawled, sleeping, snoring slightly and drooling quite a bit.

'Now that's a new one,' Rayleen said, quietly, as Billy closed and locked the door behind her.

'She cried herself to sleep,' Billy said. 'Literally. She just lay there and cried for more than an hour. Went through almost a whole box of tissues. And then, well . . . I guess it just took too much out of her.'

Rayleen sat on the couch beside Grace and stroked the sleeping girl's hair.

'Poor baby,' she said. 'Since she's asleep and all, I was wondering . . . well, I didn't know she was asleep until I got here, of course, but I was wondering anyway . . . can she stay here longer today? Not to freak you out or anything, but . . . you know.'

'Um. No. Not really, I don't. I don't know the end of that sentence, if that's what you mean.'

'Just in case Mom does call the cops.'

Billy sat next to Rayleen on the couch, his hip up against Grace's. The girl did not wake up. He hadn't so much

planned to do it. It was more that he suddenly lost the use
of his knees.

'Do you mean to tell me that if the cops showed up right
now you'd claim not to know where she is?'

'When you say it like that, it sounds bad.'

'It sounds like a jailable offense. I mean, as opposed to
just saying, "Yeah, here she is, I'm her babysitter and she
refused to go home."'

'Holy crap, Billy, don't say jailable offense. You're right,
though,' Rayleen said. 'You're absolutely right. I don't
know what I was thinking. I guess today took a toll on me,
too.'

'Lot of that going around,' Billy said.

Rayleen stood, reached down for Grace, and lifted her
off the couch, settling the girl into a fireman's carry over
her shoulder. Grace hung limp, still out.

'What did you say to her mom?' Billy asked, half wanting to know, half not wanting to.

'Just pretty much what we agreed on.'

'What did she say to you?'

'Oh, she had a few choice names for me. And she kept
saying she didn't believe it was really Grace's idea. But I
think she might be closer to believing it now.'

Rayleen began to move toward the door, and Billy ran
quickly to unlock it for her.

'Are we doing the right thing?' he asked.

'I don't know, Billy,' she said. 'Hope to God we are.'

She looked both ways before carrying the girl out into
the hall and then unlocking her own apartment.

Billy watched them go, then locked up tight himself.

'God,' he said out loud. 'A concept like shine. We
remember it, but it just seems so distant now.'

* * *

He sat up all night in front of the TV, watching old movies.
To avoid the beating of wings. But he drifted off about four
thirty in the morning, halfway through *Breakfast at
Tiffany's*, and so they caught him just the same.

Grace

It was the following Sunday, and Grace was on her way upstairs to go see Felipe, to give him a message from Rayleen. But when she got up close to his apartment door, she saw the door to Mr Lafferty's old place standing wide open.

She figured she should probably just ignore it, after all the yelling and grabbing that had happened last time she'd tried to get near there, but by that time she'd forgotten the message for Felipe anyway, so that left her with nothing much to do.

She held still for a long time, trying to hear whether or not there was anyone at home inside Mr Lafferty's apartment. Then she heard a big sneeze, and it made her jump.

She clicked over to the open doorway (she was wearing her tap shoes, because she loved them) carefully, ready for anything. A man in jeans and a red sweater was sitting on a little chair, like a kitchen chair, going through some papers in a filing cabinet.

He looked up right away and saw Grace there, even though she was being very quiet.

'Hello there,' he said.

'Hi,' Grace said, and it came out quiet. Probably because she was just a little bit scared.

'Do you live around here?'

'Yeah,' Grace said. 'I used to live in the basement apartment with my mom, but I can't live with her right now because she's . . . not feeling good, so I'm sort of mostly living downstairs with Rayleen in apartment D. Who are you?'

'Peter Lafferty,' he said. 'I flew in this morning to go through my father's things. Not that there's much here to go through. But, even so. I have arrangements to make, anyway.'

'What kind of arrangements?'

He looked right at Grace, like he was trying to decide something, but Grace wasn't sure what. His eyes were a nice color of green.

'I have to figure out if he left any instructions. For . . . Well, things like whether he wanted to be buried or cremated. That type of arrangements.'

'Oh,' Grace said.

'Did you know my father?'

'Yeah, I did. He was nice to me. He did three nice things for me, all in just a couple of days.'

He looked up at her again when she said that, and Grace could see he was suddenly more interested. She looked at his eyes, and decided that what she'd just said was more interesting to him than anything else.

'So you knew him well?'

'Not very well, no. But he was nice to me.'

'You didn't . . .'

But then it started to seem like he would never finish his thought.

'What?' Grace asked, when she had run out of patience.

'You didn't spend time alone with him or anything, right?'

'No, why?'

'I just wondered.'

Then he went back to looking through the folders in the filing cabinet.

'Everybody else thought he was mean, but he was nice to me, so I was thinking maybe it's that he didn't like people much, but he liked kids.'

'You can say that again,' Peter said, like there was some little joke in saying that, but Grace didn't get that joke.

Then she couldn't think of anything more to say, and Peter didn't say anything more, so it was quiet for a long time.

Grace looked around the apartment. She'd never seen inside Mr Lafferty's before. It looked very clean and well-organized, and the rug was brand new. All the other rugs in this building were years old, actually worn thin in the spots that got walked on the most.

'That's a very pretty new rug,' Grace said, thinking it would be a nice thing to say, but then the minute it came out of her mouth she remembered. She remembered what that awful building super, Casper, had said about pulling up the floorboards and putting down a new rug. And then she wished she hadn't said anything about it in the first place. 'Sorry,' she said. 'Never mind. Forget I ever mentioned it. I just remembered why.'

Peter didn't even look up during any of this, so she didn't know if she'd upset him or not. She leaned her shoulder on the doorway and watched him for a while, even though what he was doing didn't seem very interesting.

After a few minutes he sneezed another big, explosive sneeze.

'Bless you,' Grace said.

He looked up then, like he was a little surprised that she would say 'Bless you', even though it seemed to Grace like a normal enough thing to say.

'Thank you,' he said, pulling a big white cloth handkerchief out of his jeans pocket and wiping his nose with it.

'I'm sorry if you have a cold,' she said, feeling that she wanted to talk to him more, but not really knowing what to say next.

'Allergies,' he said.

'What are you allergic to?'

'Ragweed and pollen, but it's winter. Mold. Cats, but I can't imagine my father keeping a cat, so I guess there must be some mold in here.'

'Why do you think he did it?' Grace asked.

She hadn't known she was about to ask that, and she could feel how much the question surprised them both.

Peter looked straight into her eyes for a moment.

Then he said, 'Would you like to come in?'

'OK.'

She walked into the living room, carefully, as if there might be a special place not to step, and she had better know it, somehow, magically, in advance. She hoisted herself up on to Mr Lafferty's couch.

'I'm sorry if I wasn't supposed to ask that. Mrs Hinman said Mr Lafferty had grown-up kids, but she said none of them even talked to him.'

Peter Lafferty sighed, the way grown-ups do when they're trying to decide what to keep to themselves and what to say.

'Seems a little weird to talk about that,' he said.

'Sorry.'

'Not your fault. So . . . I guess . . . since you know that much anyway . . . I have three brothers and two sisters. So, six of us in all. And not a one of them talked to our father. Just like what you heard. Hadn't for more than ten years. I was the only one who would still call him now and again, but a couple of weeks ago he just went too far with me, so I broke off contact. So, there. Now you know.'

He sneezed another big sneeze.

'Mold,' Grace said.

'I don't know. This feels more like my cat sneeze.'

'I don't think Mr Lafferty had a cat.'

'No, I don't suppose so. What about the people across the hall? Do they have a cat?'

'It's not two people, it's just Felipe, but he doesn't have a cat. Nobody does. I don't think cats are even allowed in this building. So, do you think the reason he did what he did is because you said you wouldn't talk to him any more?'

Peter sighed, and he slid the file cabinet drawer closed.

'I guess it didn't help,' he said. 'It pretty much left him all alone.'

Then there was a silence, and, during it, Grace felt she suddenly had the answer to something that was very important, but that had been hiding just beyond her reach for a long time. It was the answer to what was wrong with everything and everybody, which is a lot to suddenly know.

'That's it!' she shouted.

'That's what?'

'Nothing. I just figured something out. Something really important. You just helped me figure something out.'

'I'd like to talk to you some more,' he said, 'especially about how you knew him. But . . . if you'll just hang on a second. I just have to use the bathroom. Excuse me.'

Grace waited while he walked through the bedroom and disappeared.

'Oh, my God,' she heard him say.

'What?'

'Guess what I just found?'

'I give up. What?'

He didn't answer. Instead he came walking out of the bedroom carrying what looked like a deep plastic tray. Like a storage box, but not as tall, and with no lid. It smelled funny. Bad funny. Like the sharp smell that insulted your nose when you passed by that doorway where some homeless guys peed on the bricks.

'What is that?' Grace asked.

'It's a litter box.'

'I don't know what a litter box is.'

'It's something you have to keep when you have a cat.'

'Kitty, kitty, kitty,' Grace cooed in her quietest voice.

She could see him under there, under the bed. He had pretty gold eyes and he was looking at her, but he wouldn't come out.

'You're pretty,' she said. 'I like the way the colors change in a line right down the middle of your face. It's cool.'

He had blotches of white and dark and an in-between

color that was sort of strawberry blond, and Grace could almost halfway remember what you call a cat that looks like that, but the word stayed just out of her reach.

'Are you scared?' she asked him. 'I bet you are, because you never even met me before, but you must be really hungry, too, because nobody fed you for days. Now, don't try to tell me you're not hungry, because I know nobody fed you for days, so you can't fool me. Peter? He must be really hungry. Will you look and see if there's anything for him to eat?'

'Then I'd have to come back in,' Peter said from out in the hallway.

'Please? It's important.'

While they were waiting, she whispered to the cat a little more, because her loud voice might scare him.

After what seemed like a long time, Peter came into the bedroom. He was holding his cloth handkerchief over his nose and mouth like a mask, and in his other hand he held an open can of salmon.

'Ooh, that'll be good,' Grace said. 'If anything'll get him out from under the bed, I bet that'll do it.'

About an hour later, Grace stood in front of Rayleen's door with the cat purring in her arms. Every now and then the cat rubbed the side of his face against Grace's jaw.

She knocked quietly, so she wouldn't startle him.

She heard Rayleen call through the door, asking who it was, but she was afraid to call back, because, after all, she had only just very recently gained the cat's trust. And you have to be careful with the trust of a scared animal, once you've finally got it.

After a minute Rayleen opened the door anyway. Cautiously.

'Oh, it's just— Oh, my God. Grace. What have you got there?'

'My new cat.'

'*Your* cat?'

'Yeah. Mine. Now.'

'Well, I don't know where you're planning on keeping him. Not in here, that's all I know. Not in this apartment.'

'But he—'

'Grace. I'm allergic to cats.'

'Oh, no! Not you, too!'

'What do you mean, not me, too? Who else is allergic to cats?'

'Peter. Mr Lafferty's son Peter. That's why I have to take him. That's why I have to keep him, because Peter is allergic, and also because he has to go home on a plane. You sure he can't stay here?'

'My throat will close up and I won't be able to breathe.'

'Oh. I guess I have to ask Billy, then.'

'What about Felipe?'

'What's wrong with asking Billy?'

'You know Billy's not big on change.'

'I heard that,' Billy said.

Grace turned to see him peeking out through the crack of his door, the safety chain blocking her view of part of his nose.

'Sorry,' Rayleen said, 'but . . . I mean . . . was I wrong?'

'That depends. What's the question in question?'

Grace said, 'Can my new cat stay at your place for now?'

'Hmm,' Billy's partially-hidden face said. 'Maybe you should ask Felipe.'

'Told you,' Rayleen said.

'But you're *home*,' Grace said, in her just-at-the-edge-of-whining voice. 'You're *home*, to take care of him. Felipe has to work. And Mr Lafferty will be lonely, and he'll be scared.'

Grace watched Billy glance up, over her head. She turned around to see Rayleen catching his eye. So they were doing that thing grown-ups do when the kid needs a talking-to, and they're trying to decide who has to take the job.

'Honey,' Rayleen said. 'Grace. Mr Lafferty is dead.'

'Not Mr Lafferty the man. Mr Lafferty the cat.'

Billy said, 'You named the cat Mr Lafferty?'

'Yeah,' Grace said, proudly.

'Won't that be a little weird?'

'What's weird about it?'

'Because it's the same name as . . . Mr Lafferty.'

'*But he's dead*,' Grace said, exasperated. 'Like you guys were just trying to tell me about half a second ago, as if I didn't know that already. So that still leaves only *one* Mr Lafferty.'

'I'm going back in,' Rayleen said. 'Before my throat closes up.'

Grace turned back to Billy. 'Can I come in? Please? I mean, *we*. Can *we* come in, please?'

Billy sighed a very noisy sigh. More noisy than any sigh really needed to be. The kind of noisy that's more to make a point. But then he took off the safety chain and let them in, which Grace was pretty sure he would. She'd pretty much known all along that he'd sigh that big sigh, but then he'd go ahead and let them in.

She sat on Billy's couch and put her ear to Mr Lafferty's side to listen to the purring.

'He just sort of purrs all the time. Ever since I got him to come out from under Mr Lafferty's bed, he hasn't stopped purring even once, and it's really cool when you put your ear right up against him. It sounds like he has a motor or something, and it makes you feel good all the way inside, like all the way down to your tummy. You should try it, you really should. I know you, and I just know you'd like it.'

Billy sat on the very end of the couch, acting like couches made him nervous all of a sudden, but Grace figured it was really the cat he was nervous about, even though he wasn't looking at the cat.

'He's a *pretty* cat,' Billy said. As if that was the only good thing he could think of to say about Mr Lafferty. 'I'm not much of a cat person – or a dog person, for that matter – but I always thought calico cats were pretty.'

'Calico! That's the kind I was trying to think of.'

'I still think he needs a better name,' Billy said.

'I think Mr Lafferty is a perfect name.'

'But it's confusing.'

'I don't think it's confusing.'

'Look. Think about what you said a minute ago. He's been purring ever since you got him to come out from under Mr Lafferty's bed. So, Mr Lafferty's been purring ever since Mr Lafferty came out from under Mr Lafferty's bed. Confusing.'

'But he won't be under the bed any more, and Peter has to take all Mr Lafferty's stuff and either take it home or get rid of it, so then Mr Lafferty won't have a bed any more.'

'Who, the cat?'

'No, Mr Lafferty. Pay attention.'

'But you said *the cat* was Mr Lafferty.'

'I know you're just doing that on purpose, Billy. I know you're not even confused for real.'

'Try this one on for size. You overhear someone talking about how Mr Lafferty died. And just for a minute, you think, Oh, no! My cat!'

'Hmm,' Grace said. She pressed her ear to the cat's side again, because she wanted that nice tummy feeling back. 'Maybe you're right. But I already told him his name was Mr Lafferty, and I don't want to go and break a promise to him first thing, so I guess his name is Mr Lafferty the Cat. Why are you looking at me that way?'

'It's kind of long.'

'Let me ask him if he minds.' She pressed her ear to his rumbling side again. 'He says he doesn't mind. So. Can he stay here?'

'I don't know, baby girl. I'm afraid of animals.'

'You're afraid of everything!' Grace blurted out, exasperated.

Then, as soon as it left her mouth, she could tell she'd hurt Billy's feelings, and she felt bad.

'That was cold,' he said.

'I'm sorry.'

She wanted to go on to say, 'I didn't mean it.' But she sort of had meant it. She still agreed with it. She just knew now that she shouldn't have said it out loud.

'Really, I'm sorry, Billy. I didn't mean to hurt your feelings. Can I just leave him here while I go upstairs to Mr Lafferty the Man's apartment, so I can get Mr Lafferty the Cat's litter box and look for cat food?'

Billy hadn't finished looking hurt yet.

'I guess so,' he said.

Grace let the cat down on to the couch, and Billy

jumped up and backed all the way over to the window, which seemed like overdoing it, even for Billy. After all, Mr Lafferty the Cat wasn't even a very big cat.

Grace ran to the door.

'I figured out something really important,' she said, her hand already on the knob. 'I can't tell you everything about it now because I'm in a hurry, but it's about how people should all have somebody, and about how nobody should have nobody, and about how, now that I figured it out, things are going to be a lot different around here. We'll have to have another meeting.'

Then she threw open the door and raced out into the hall, slamming the door behind her.

Not three steps later, a hand stopped her forward progress. The hand just came out of nowhere, and slapped over her mouth so she couldn't yell, and then another hand grabbed around her waist, and then she was on her way down to the basement apartment whether she wanted to go or not.

Which she didn't.

She squirmed, and she even kicked backwards, but the kick missed.

She wanted to yell. She tried to scream, to say, 'Help! I'm being stolen!' but the hand over her mouth was too tight.

It wasn't until she was inside her basement apartment that she found out she'd been stolen by her own mom.

Billy

'We're getting impatient,' Billy announced.

It didn't sound noticeably different from Billy's daily comments to himself. But, in this instance, he was talking to Mr Lafferty the Cat, who looked directly into Billy's eyes when he spoke, unnerving him.

Mr Lafferty the Cat was curled on Billy's couch, settled, but not asleep. Staring at Billy. For just a moment, Billy dared to stare back. He had interesting markings, that cat, with a line of color change right down the middle of his face. Like a mime, Billy decided. Like a showman in make-up.

Maybe we have something in common after all, Billy thought, but he did not say any of that out loud, for fear the cat would hear it as some type of invitation.

Billy had already tried to sit down once, in his big stuffed chair, because the couch was alarmingly . . . taken. But Mr Lafferty the Cat had been inexplicably drawn to that move, and he had frightened Billy by jumping on to the arm of the chair and then trying to sit on his lap. So now Billy just stood, his back against the sliding-glass door, which felt shockingly cool. From his vantage point, he could see the kitchen clock, which he'd been watching with even greater than usual compulsivity.

'How can it take her an hour to go get your litter box and food? Unless she has to rummage around in all the cupboards looking for cat food. But still. An hour. Do you think she got distracted by something?'

Unsurprisingly, Mr Lafferty the Cat appeared to have no answers. No opinions.

Exactly two hours and twenty-six minutes after Grace had left on her cat-food run, someone knocked on Billy's door.

'Grace?' he said, running to answer it.

Mr Lafferty the Cat jumped down and crouched on the rug, ready to run under the furniture if anything else alarmed him.

It had been Rayleen's signal knock, and Billy knew it. But he called Grace's name anyway, because he wanted it to be Grace. She could be imitating the knock. Kids imitated.

He undid the locks and threw the door open wide.

It was only Rayleen.

'Oh. It's only you,' he said.

'Nice to see you, too. I'm thinking I need Grace back now.'

'I haven't got her.'

'Don't make jokes.'

'I'm not making jokes. I don't have her. Last I saw her she ran out my door so she could go up to Mr Lafferty's – the man, not the cat – to get a litter box and food for Mr Lafferty – the cat, not the man.'

'Maybe she's at Felipe's,' she said.

'I hope so,' he said, with a dawning sense that panic, rather than irritation, might be in order.

'I'll go check.'

Billy uncharacteristically remained there in the doorway, waiting and viciously biting his nails, until she came back down again.

Rayleen shook her head. 'You don't suppose she went back to her mom?' she asked. 'She was pretty upset about not coming when her mom called her.'

'No,' Billy said. 'Oh, it's not outside the realm of possibility. But it just doesn't seem possible *now*. When it first happened, maybe. Or tomorrow. But she just got this new cat, and she was going to run upstairs extra-fast and get something to feed him. She's excited about the cat. She couldn't wait to get back to him. And she knew she only had my permission to leave the cat here for a matter of minutes. It just doesn't work timing-wise. The whole thing just doesn't add up.'

'OK, I'll keep looking,' Rayleen said.

'Wait! Um. Sorry to sound like a wimp, but . . .' Too late, Billy thought. You've been sounding like a wimp all your life. But he pushed the voices away again. Such nasty bastards, as always. 'Maybe the cat can stay with Felipe while we figure all this out.'

'Sorry. Felipe isn't home.'

'Oh. Well, then maybe he does have Grace. Maybe they went someplace together.'

Rayleen shook her head, as if wishing she didn't have to. 'He was home. I talked to him. But now he's not. I don't want to freak you out too much—'

'Then don't,' Billy said.

'You really don't want to hear this?'

'Well. I guess I have to. Now.'

'OK. Here goes. There was one stranger in the building today. Mr Lafferty's son. He was here going through his father's things.'

'Yeah. I overheard that. Wait. Shit. You don't think—'

'We just can't take any chances, that's all. Felipe was talking to him for a while today, and the guy happened to mention where he was staying, which I'm sure he wouldn't have done if he was up to no good. But, just to be on the safe side, Felipe is going to go down to his motel and check it out.'

'I feel sick,' Billy said.

And he meant it quite literally. Suddenly he felt flushed, feverish. Achy. The world's fastest onset of the flu.

'Just keep breathing,' Rayleen said.

'You checked old Mrs Hinman's?'

'I did. There's one possibility we haven't discussed yet. Maybe her mom snatched her back. You know. Against her will.'

'Oh, God. I hope it's just something like that. Not that a thing like that isn't bad enough. Should we be calling the police?'

'I don't see that we're in any position to,' Rayleen said. 'We're not her legal guardians. So we call them, and they come over, and let's say it turns out she's at home with her mom. And we say we called them – why? Because we stole the kid, and her mom stole her back?'

'But if—'

'Don't think I haven't thought it through, Billy. Don't think I haven't run every possibility in my brain, including the ones that are very bad for her . . . and us. I think I'm just going to have to pound on her mom's door and tell her Grace is missing, and if she doesn't know where her kid is, then she better call the police.'

'Which looks very bad to her mom regarding our babysitting capabilities.'

'If she doesn't have her. If she does, it looks bad for us if we *don't* go ask. Grace disappears, and we don't even bother to check and see if she's home. Besides, it can't be helped,' Rayleen said. 'This is just a bad situation either way. All around. I'm going.'

Billy's knees felt so mushy that he sank gently down on to them, on the rug close inside his doorway. He glanced over at Mr Lafferty the Cat, just to be sure he wasn't about to try to get out. But he'd curled up on the couch again, and was watching Billy with mild curiosity.

He heard the pounding on the basement apartment door, and each knock went through him like a gunshot.

'Ms Ferguson?' he heard Rayleen call. 'Do you have Grace? Because, if you don't, we need to know. We need to put our differences aside to find her. I mean it. This could be serious.'

Another series of pounds.

Then Billy saw Rayleen come up the stairs again. Her face twisted with curiosity when she saw him kneeling by his door, tearing at fingernails with his teeth, though he hardly had fingernails left to tear.

'Why are you on your knees?' she asked, standing over him now.

Apparently the second part of the observation was self-explanatory.

'Long story. Can I tell it some other time?'

'So, surprise, knocking didn't answer much,' Rayleen said. 'My throat is starting to tighten up.' She took a few steps back from his doorway, defensively. 'I'll let you know when I hear back from Felipe.'

'Wait!' he shouted, pulling himself to his feet, against odds. 'Maybe Mrs Hinman would take the cat. You know. Just for tonight.'

Rayleen stood still in the hallway for a time, looking disoriented. As if she couldn't pull her head around to such trivial considerations.

'I guess I could ask her,' she said, finally.

Billy sighed with relief.

More fingernails, barely grown out to the quick line as it stood, fell victim.

Rayleen came back downstairs not two minutes later. A long two minutes all the same.

'Sorry, no,' she said. 'Mrs Hinman hates cats.'

'So do I!' he wailed, much more pathetically than intended.

'Well. If Mrs Hinman had the cat right now and wanted you to take him, you might win with that argument. But you have him. So it's that possession thing. You know. Possession being . . . I forget. Most of the law.'

'Nine-tenths,' Billy said, miserably. 'Tell me as soon as you hear from Felipe.'

'I will.'

'I still need that litter box. And food.'

'Oh, yeah,' Rayleen said. 'I think Felipe has them. I'll look into that.'

Billy closed and locked the door, then looked at Mr Lafferty the Cat, who was still staring at him.

'Stop staring at me,' he said. 'I'm not that fascinating.'

Predictably, the cat continued to stare.

'This is all your fault,' he said.

Mr Lafferty the Cat flicked his ears back briefly, but didn't do much more.

Felipe fed him a progress report through the door about half an hour later.

'The Lafferty guy doesn't have her,' Felipe said. 'I really think he's OK. She must be with her mom . . . I hope.'

'Thank you,' Billy called through the door. 'I still need the litter box and the cat food.'

'Oh, yeah. I gave them to Rayleen. I'll tell her.'

'Thank you,' he called again.

Then he began to cry uncontrollably.

Mr Lafferty the Cat came closer to investigate his tears, but Billy shooed him away with a startling sound, and the cat ran and hid under the couch.

It was nearly halfway through the movie *Moonstruck*, on late-night TV, when Billy heard the series of taps. He picked up the remote, stinging his bloodied and swollen fingertips, and muted the sound. He leaned over the couch and listened carefully.

One, two, three . . . pause . . . four.

But it wasn't Rayleen knocking on Billy's door. It wasn't anyone knocking on Billy's door. This was someone knocking on Billy's floor. From underneath. From the basement apartment.

He released an enormous sound, somewhere between a breath and a shout, and Mr Lafferty the Cat, who had been sleeping on Billy's stuffed chair, ran and hid under the couch again.

Billy held still and listened. And he heard it again. One, two, three . . . pause . . . four.

He ran to his front door and undid the locks with sore and shaky fingers. Throwing the door open wide, he ran across the hall, planning to knock on Rayleen's door. Instead he ran into Rayleen, literally, in the middle of the hall between their apartments.

'Did you hear that?' he shouted, radiating joy and relief.

'I did!'

'She's downstairs.'

'She must have waited till her mom fell asleep. To signal us.'

'Smart girl,' Billy said.

'Such a smart girl!' Rayleen crowed. 'I'll tell Felipe.'

'Maybe I can even get some sleep now.'

Much to Billy's surprise, she threw her arms around him. And they held each other. For a remarkably long time.

'Careful, don't let the cat out,' Rayleen said as she let go.

'Oh. Right.'

'By the way . . . Billy . . . you do know you're out in the hall, right?'

'Oops,' he said, and scrambled back inside.

In the night, Billy felt the presence of someone or something in the bedroom with him. He opened his eyes, and found himself staring right into the face of Mr Lafferty the Cat, whose gold eyes gleamed in the glow from the kitchen night light.

He screamed.

The cat ran and hid under the bed.

'Shit,' Billy said.

He understood now that the proper move would have been to have closed his bedroom door with the cat still on the living room chair or couch. And it's not that he hadn't thought of it. More that he hadn't been sure about sleeping without the usual glow of light. And he hadn't anticipated quite such a rude awakening.

He turned on his bedside light and lay awake for several hours, feeling an exhaustion of emotion, in his gut, at a level that could only be described as pain.

In time, without meaning to, he fell back asleep.

When he woke, it was due to a strange, muffled sound in his right ear. A kind of vibration and noise, but also the feeling that something was blocking his hearing on that side.

It was light. He was sleeping on his back, which he never did. He always curled up on his side, in a fetal position, in preparation for sleep. But this had been a sleep for which he'd been unprepared.

When he tried to turn his head, only then did he understand that Mr Lafferty the Cat was curled against the right side of his face, purring vigorously.

He sat up.

But, oddly, he found himself missing the warmth and the vibration. It was something he'd been feeling all the way down into his gut. And, apparently, he'd been feeling it for much longer than he'd realized. Apparently he'd grown partially accustomed to the feeling before it had even wakened him.

Slowly, gingerly, he lay back down again. The cat did not move.

For the next hour or so, Billy just lay there and listened, and felt.

He thought about Grace, and worried about her. What if she never came over to his apartment again? What if there were no more dance lessons? What if Grace never again yelled at him for biting his nails, or for interrupting? What if they'd ruined that, for ever, with what they'd tried to do, with their little kidnapping plot?

There was no real answer to the questions, at least, nothing available. But the purring helped a little.

It wasn't until the end of the hour, when he finally rose from bed, that Billy realized he had slept without a visit from the wings.

At the usual time, around three thirty in the afternoon, Felipe came knocking on Billy's door.

He did not have Grace in tow.

Billy looked at Felipe and Felipe looked at Billy. It was something a little like having a mirror to look into, Billy thought. An emotional mirror, at least.

'She's definitely with her mom,' Felipe said.

'You saw her?'

'Yeah. I went to pick her up. But her mom was there to pick her up, too. So what was I supposed to do? Can't you just see this Hispanic guy taking off with somebody else's kid while her real mother's standing right there? That would have been a disaster, huh?'

'Did you even get to talk to her? How did she seem?'

'She tried to come over and talk to me, but her mom wouldn't let her. So I guess she seemed sort of . . . not free. Like she wants to do something or be somewhere, but there's no getting around her mom. But she did call out something to me.'

'Yeah? What did she say?'

'She said, "Tell Billy I'm sorry about the cat." So then that's why I came by here. I know you don't like it too much when people knock on your door, but I just wanted to let you know I'll take the cat. You know. If you need me to.'

'Oh,' Billy said. 'That's nice. How nice. But, you know what? We seem to be getting used to each other. We've actually been getting along OK. We're kind of . . . settling in.'

'Oh. OK. Good. Fine, then.'

'You realize,' Billy said, 'that if her mom stays clean we may never see her again.'

To his surprise, his lip quivered slightly with the words, as if they might make him cry. Which, in front of Felipe, would be quite humiliating.

'I thought of that, yeah,' Felipe replied, not tearful, but equally down.

'Would you like to come in?' Billy asked.

It was unusual behavior on Billy's part, and he questioned himself regarding the move, both at the time he said it, and later, after the fact. The simplest possible answer seemed to ring true: he was now used to having company at three thirty in the afternoon.

Felipe came in and sat on Billy's couch.

'Coffee?' Billy asked.

'Great, yeah,' Felipe said. 'I'll be awake when I get to work. That'll be good.'

Before Billy could even get into the kitchen to start a pot, the cat came walking in from the bedroom, headed straight for Felipe, and sniffed at the cuffs of his jeans.

'Well, well, well,' Billy said. 'Here's Mr Lafferty the Cat now.'

Felipe looked up quickly, as if to gauge whether Billy was joking or not.

'Are you kiddin' me? She named the cat Mr Lafferty?'

'I would not kid about a thing like that.'

'Geez. There's just no getting away from the guy.'

'At least *this* Mr Lafferty likes you,' Billy noted, just as the cat jumped into Felipe's lap.

'Yeah. Thank God, huh? Thank God there's no such thing as an animal bigot.'

Billy went off to make the coffee.

As he was measuring the grounds into the filter, he looked up to see Felipe leaning in the kitchen doorway, watching. Mr Lafferty the Cat circled back and forth, around and through legs – first Felipe's and then Billy's – rubbing and purring and arching his back.

'I guess you two *have* settled in,' Felipe said.

He indicated with a flip of his head the china cup of water and the saucer of dry cat food, neatly arranged on a cloth placemat on Billy's kitchen floor.

'Fine china, yet,' Felipe added.

'We all have to eat, and there's no need being a barbarian.'

'So, I used to have this neighbor,' Felipe said, 'years ago, before I lived here. She had this big dog, like a Doberman, I think, and she used to swear to me that this dog was prejudiced. It was such a crock. She told me this story once where she says she's walking down the street with the dog, and, heading right towards them on the sidewalk, she says, there comes this big black buck—'

'Buck?'

'Right. Exac'ly. I know. This is my point. So she says the dog right away starts growling at the guy. Long story short, turns out this woman is so stupid she doesn't get how the dog won't trust black people because it can tell *she* doesn't.'

'Wow. What do you even say to a story like that?'

'Well, I started making fun of her. Like laughing at her, in a way. I said, "You saw a deer on the street? Right here in LA?" And she's like, "No, it wasn't a deer, it was a man. A big man." And then, I'm like, "Well, you said it was a buck. And a buck's not a man. It's an animal." But she never did get it. She just thought I was confused. But this other neighbor of mine, she's overhearing all this, and she's laughing her ass off, kind of behind her hand, you know?'

'Except, really,' Billy said, 'much as I like a good joke at a small-minded person's expense, it's not all that funny.'

'No. I guess not,' Felipe said, picking up the cat and holding him, scratching gently behind Mr Lafferty the Cat's ears. 'But sometimes you gotta laugh. I mean, what else you gonna do?'

Billy turned on the coffee maker, and, careful to keep looking at it and not Felipe, said, 'You know, he came down here. And gave me a hard time, too. Right before the first time I took care of Grace.'

'Lafferty?'

'Lafferty.'

'About what?'

'He wanted to know if I was gay,' Billy said, still pretending the coffee pot required all of his visual attention. 'He said he had a right to ask because, as he put it, "Homosexuals are more likely to be child-molesters."'

He sneaked a quick look at Felipe, who didn't notice, because he was busy rolling his eyes skyward.

'*Oh . . . my . . . God!* I swear that guy had child-molesting on the brain! It's like he never thought about nothing else. What the hell's wrong with a guy like that?'

'We'll never know,' Billy said. 'Now we'll never know.'

'Just as well,' Felipe said. 'I don't think I even *want* to know. Less I know about the inside of that guy, the better.'

'Like I could possibly be anything-sexual,' Billy said, purposely regressing the conversation without knowing why. 'I mean, look at me. How could I be anything but asexual? There's nobody here. Just me and this drab little apartment, and a direct-deposit every month from my mother that's just barely enough to starve on.'

'Well, at least she squeezes you out something.'

Billy laughed.

'My parents are rolling in it,' he said. 'Filthy. Rich in the filthiest possible sense of the word.'

'Oh.'

The longest pause in the history of pauses, Billy thought. He did not fill it.

'So . . .'

'Don't tell me,' Billy said. 'I'll guess the question. If I come from money, what am I doing in a place like this?'

'None of my business, but yeah. That's what I was wondering.'

'I think they figure if they give me just barely enough to stave off my literal death, it'll motivate me.'

'They don't want to enable you,' Felipe said.

A brief silence, and then they both burst out laughing.

'You can see how well it's working out so far,' Billy said, taking a grand and flashy bow in his old red pajamas.

'Oops,' Felipe said. 'I got news for you.'

He was sitting on Billy's big stuffed chair, with Mr Lafferty the Cat upside down on his lap, stretched out on his back and purring. Felipe was drinking his coffee with one hand and rubbing the cat's tummy with the other.

'Bad news?'

'Just news news. We're going to have to change Mr Lafferty the Cat's name to Ms Lafferty the Cat.'

'Girl cat?'

'Girl cat.'

'Grace will be . . .'

Then, to his embarrassment, he had to stop talking. So he wouldn't cry.

A long silence.

Then Felipe said, 'I know. I miss her, too.'

'I feel like I'm supposed to be hoping her mom gets clean. You know, for Grace's sake. But what about us? What about our sakes? What about if she never lets us see her again?'

'I don't know,' Felipe said. 'It's messed up.' A pause. 'Time'll tell.' He glanced at his watch. 'I better get ready for work.' He slugged down the rest of his coffee in one extended gulp. 'Thanks for the coffee.'

Felipe slid the cat down on to the floor and headed for the door.

'Let me know if you see her again,' Billy said.

'I will. I mean, both. I'll see her again, and I'll let you know, both. I'm going to her school tomorrow, too. And every damn day after that. So if her mom ever screws up and doesn't come for her? There I'll be. So I'll see her. Even if I don't get to talk to her. And I'll let you know.'

Felipe let himself out without saying more.

Billy began the process of locking the door after him, but, before he had even finished, he was startled by a sudden knock.

'Yes?'

Felipe's voice echoed through the door.

'Don't even bother to unlock it, Billy, it's just me again. I just wanted to say one more thing. I just wanted to say I wouldn't care if you were. I'm not like Lafferty. I'm not a prejudiced guy. My father taught me not to look down on nobody, not to think bad about nobody. Except assholes. He said it's OK to be prejudiced against assholes, because nobody *has* to be an asshole. It's voluntary.'

Silence. Billy seemed to have lost the ability to communicate.

'But you're definitely not an asshole.'

'Thanks,' Billy said.

'Later, *mi amigo*.'

'Thanks,' Billy said.

If there were any other words in the universe, they were unavailable to him in that moment.

Grace

It was already last period at Grace's school, and getting closer and closer to the final bell. And the closer it got, the more Grace felt like maybe she was about to throw up. Her face felt hot, and it tingled, and her stomach was feeling rocky, like that time when she had the flu.

But she didn't have the flu, not this time, and she knew it.

What she had was one of those situations where you get more and more nervous and upset, and then after a while you're so upset that you think you might throw up.

But there was really nothing much worse than throwing up in class in the fourth grade, unless it was peeing your pants, but even peeing your pants might only have been more or less a tie with throwing up. It was that bad.

So Grace asked her teacher for a hall pass to go to the bathroom.

It took the teacher a long time to write it out.

'Oh my gosh, please hurry,' Grace said, 'because I think I'm about to throw up.'

'Oh, dear,' her teacher, Mrs Placer, said, handing her the pass. 'Go to the nurse as soon as you're done.'

Which was an odd thing to say, since it was last period, and almost time to go home, but Grace figured maybe Mrs Placer wasn't thinking clearly about that. Grown-ups say all kinds of odd things, all the time, so this was just one more to add to the ever-growing list.

'OK,' Grace said, and ran down the hall as fast as she could.

It's almost always better to just say OK. It's better than arguing with them, just about every time.

She stood in the girls' room for a while, right at the door of a stall, but now that she was in a place where she could throw up if she needed to, it seemed like maybe she wouldn't need to after all.

After a while some older girls came in, three of them, maybe from the sixth grade, and they stood close to each other and passed a cigarette around, and one of them looked at Grace over her shoulder, and it wasn't a friendly look.

Grace hoped they weren't about to rob her, because that can happen in the bathroom. Not that she had anything to steal. But kids got hurt, too, especially if they didn't have anything to steal.

'Flu,' she said, thinking if they knew she might be about to throw up on them, and if they thought what she had might be catching, they'd keep away.

Just then the bell rang.

Grace sprinted for the back door.

Her mom was there. And so was Felipe. Just like the day before.

Grace's mom took her by the hand, too hard, and

marched off toward home with her. Grace glanced over her shoulder at Felipe, but, the minute she did, her mom pulled her around by the arm so she faced forward again.

'I'm going to get to tap dance at my school,' she told her mom. 'It's for an assembly. I'll be dancing in front of almost the whole school. First through sixth grades.'

'When?' her mom asked, sounding like she was thinking about something else entirely, and glancing over her shoulder at Felipe.

Grace turned to see if he was still back there – which he was – but then her mom turned her back around again.

'It'll be in three months,' she said.

'Good. That's plenty of time to learn to tap dance, I guess.'

'I already know how to tap dance.'

'Since when?'

'You missed a lot of stuff, you know. You've been gone a while.'

'Hasn't been that long.'

'It's been *weeks*.'

'It's just been a few days.'

'Yeah, a few *weeks*' worth of days.'

She expected her mom to maybe yell at her for saying all that. But nothing happened. Her mom just looked back over her shoulder at Felipe again.

'I have to tell Billy about the dancing at school,' Grace said.

'You're not telling Billy anything.'

'But I have to.'

'But you can't.'

'But I have to!' Grace shouted, finding a place in herself

that just would not back down. Then she said something even braver. Possibly the bravest thing she'd ever said to her mom. 'And I will!'

But nobody was paying the slightest bit of attention.

Grace's mom stopped suddenly in the middle of the sidewalk and turned around and started yelling at Felipe.

'Why are you following us?' she yelled. 'Why don't you just leave us alone?'

Grace said, 'He's not, he just lives the same place we do,' and Felipe said, 'I'm not, I'm just going home,' and they both said it at almost exactly the same time.

'Why did you even come down to her school in the first place?' Grace's mom shouted.

And Felipe said, 'In case there was no one there to pick her up.'

'But I was there.'

'In case you weren't, though,' Felipe said.

Grace looked at Felipe, and he looked so sad and helpless, and it started making her mad, that her mom was being so snotty to him, and not for any really good reason at all. She decided to take matters into her own hands, Mom or no Mom.

She ripped her hand free and ran to Felipe and threw her arms around his waist, one side of her face pressed against his belly. He was wearing a green flannel shirt, and it had been washed a lot of times. Grace could tell, because it was so soft.

'*Te amo, Felipe,*' she said, purposely loud enough for her mom to hear.

'*Te amo también, mi amiga.*'

'*Billy y Rayleen? Dice para mi, "Grace te amo."*'

'*Sí, mi amiga. Sí, yo lo hare.*'

Then Grace ran back to her mom, who grabbed her arm and pulled her down the street again.

'Ow,' Grace said. 'Could you loosen up on my arm? And slow down?'

'Just hurry up and walk with me.'

But it hurt, and that made Grace feel extra-defiant again. She stopped dead on the sidewalk, wrenching her arm free.

'Felipe! Would you go ahead of us? Please? Because I'm tired from trying to keep up with my mom, and she's hurting me.'

Felipe crossed to the other side of the street, while Grace's mom just stood and watched him, and then he got ahead, and crossed back. But he didn't look over his shoulder or anything. He just kept walking.

Grace's mom set off toward home again, but she walked more slowly this time, and didn't grab on to any part of Grace, so that was an improvement.

'Since when do you speak Spanish?' her mom asked.

'Told you there's a lot you missed,' Grace said.

When they got down the stairs to their basement apartment, they found a brown paper grocery sack in front of the door. With a big marking pen, in writing Grace didn't recognize, someone had written on it, 'FOR GRACE.'

Her mom picked it up and tried to look inside, but Grace, who was still feeling defiant, grabbed it out of her mom's hands.

'It says for *Grace*, not for *Eileen*.'

'But I need to see what somebody's giving you.'

'OK, fine, just give me a second and I'll show you. Don't have a total fit.'

Grace reached inside and felt soft cloth. She pulled it out of the bag, and let it unfold. It was a dress. A brand-new dress. Grace held it up in front of her, and it looked like it would fit just right, which was not too surprising, because Mrs Hinman had measured all the different parts of Grace before she even ordered the pattern. It came down to just Grace's knees, and it was the most perfect color of blue ever.

'That came out nice!' Grace said.

'Who bought you a dress?'

'Nobody bought it.'

'It just appeared?'

'Mrs Hinman *made* it for me. I have to go tell her thank you.'

'Later,' her mom said.

'Why not now?'

'Because I have to go with you, and I'm tired, and I need to sit down for a minute.'

'You don't have to go with me.'

'Oh, yes, I do.'

Grace sighed.

'OK, fine. Whatever. I'll just practice my dancing and you tell me when you're ready.'

Grace's mom opened the door and let them both inside.

Grace ran straight to her tap shoes, thinking – for the twentieth time, at least – how lucky she was to have been wearing them when her mom stole her. She got them on in no time, too. It was easy with these tap shoes, because they fit. Just lace them up and dance.

But then she decided to take a minute to run into her

bedroom and put on the new blue dress. She'd never danced in a dress before, and she wanted to see how it would feel. She slid it over her head, liking the soft feel of the cloth.

Then she looked at herself in the mirror, and drew in a loud breath.

'I look pretty,' she said out loud.

It wasn't just the dress, but the dress definitely finished off the look. The dress took the newish haircut, and the nails (Rayleen had fixed the one she'd lost) and turned them into a package of . . . well . . . pretty. And there was another thing, but Grace was only just now noticing it. She'd lost weight, without even meaning to. Without even trying. Must have been all those hours of dance practice.

She smiled at herself in the mirror, which she had never done before, then ran into the kitchen to dance.

Grace's mom was sitting on the coffee table lighting a cigarette, and she made a face when Grace began tapping on the kitchen linoleum.

'Whatever happened to smoking outside?' Grace asked, making a similar face.

'I need to keep an eye on you every minute. Do you have to do that tapping thing? The noise is giving me a headache.'

'Yes, I have to do it,' Grace said, without missing a step. 'I have to do it for hours a day. I have a performing thingy coming up, and I want to be good.'

'It's giving me a headache.'

'You said that already. I have to go to Rayleen's and get my pajamas.'

'We've been through this.'

'I'm not sleeping in my clothes again tonight. I need my pajamas.'

'You can call her when she gets home and ask her to put them out in the hall. Since when do you need to dance for hours a day? You never did before.'

'A lot changed while you were gone.'

Grace's mom finally took the bait and yelled at her. 'I wasn't gone that long! Stop saying I was! I'm sick of it!'

Grace's feet stopped moving. She stood with her feet apart on the linoleum, as though she wanted to be sure nothing could knock her over. She looked right into her mom's eyes, but her mom looked away.

'Look at me, Mom.'

Her mom glanced, quickly, then looked back down at the rug again and took another puff of the cigarette.

'Well, it's all true,' Grace said, 'whether you look at it or not. I tap dance, and I speak Spanish, and I have a nice new haircut that would've cost a lot of money if you'd had to pay for it . . .' Grace could hear her voice rising, but didn't think she could stop that if she tried, and besides, she had no reason to try. '. . . and I have nice fingernails and a foot manicure, and I'm wearing a dress that was made just especially for me, *and I have a cat!*'

The part about the cat helped her finish off with a particularly convincing shriek. Because they'd been debating the issue of whether or not Grace had a cat ever since her mom had stolen her.

Grace wondered if Billy could hear her through her ceiling (his floor), and if it made him smile a little to hear her be brave and stand up to her mom, or if it worried him

to hear any kind of fighting. She didn't want to worry anybody, especially not Billy.

'And one of our neighbors shot himself and you don't
even know it!' she screamed. 'And that's how long you've
been gone!'

Grace's mom got quieter, instead of yelling back. She
did that sometimes, but only when she was really mad.

'You do not have a cat,' she said. 'And I'm having trouble
understanding why you're yelling as loud as you can after
I just told you I have a headache.'

'I do have a cat. He's a calico, and his name is Mr
Lafferty the Cat.'

'Maybe the cat exists,' her mom said, still in that scary-
quiet angry voice. 'I'm not saying there is no cat. I'm saying
he can't be *your* cat, because you can't get a cat without my
permission.'

'Well, you weren't there to give permission, and it's too
late! And I got him, and he's mine, and I'm going to go see
him right now, and you can't stop me!'

And, with that, Grace marched over to the door.

Her mom got there first, though, and put on the safety
chain, which was too high for Grace to reach.

Grace grabbed a chair and hauled it over to the door, but
Grace's mom just grabbed the chair back and started to
haul it away from the door again, but by that time Grace
had already started to climb up on it. It just all happened
so fast.

Grace hit the floor with her right hip and shoulder, and
it hurt, especially the part on her hip.

'Ow!' she said.

'Well, I'm sorry, but you shouldn't climb up on a chair
while I'm moving it.'

'Well, you shouldn't move a chair while I'm climbing up on it,' Grace said, still down on the rug.

'Why are you being so awful, Grace? You're not usually like this.'

'Because I want to see my friends, and I want to see my cat, and you won't let me.'

'They tried to take you away from me.'

'No, they didn't! They just took care of me! It was all my idea! I didn't want to be around you when you were loaded! I hate being around you when you're loaded!'

In that quick and very dark moment, Grace's mom stood over her, and just for a split second Grace thought her mom was about to haul her off and smack her. Which she had almost never done before. Then again, they'd never had a fight this bad. At least, not out loud. But it was almost as though Grace could see the urge move through her mom. Fortunately, it just kept going. A minute later Grace's mom was talking in her quiet voice again.

'You're giving me a headache. I have to go take some aspirin. Don't you dare go anywhere while I do.'

And she walked away, through her bedroom and into the bathroom.

Grace looked at the door. She rose to her feet, but her hip still hurt when she put her weight down on that side. She thought briefly about pulling the chair back to the door again and unlocking the safety chain, but she figured her mom would catch her fast enough that it wouldn't do a bit of good anyway.

So she just hobbled into the kitchen and went back to dancing. It hurt her hip to dance, but not enough to stop her. Nothing would have been enough to stop her. Instead she just winced a little on every step.

Her mom came back in a few seconds later.

'Did you take your aspirins?' she asked.

'Yeah,' her mom said. 'I did.'

'You sure that's all you took?' Grace asked, still dancing.

'Don't push your luck with me, kiddo.'

'Do you even still have all those drugs in the house? Because, if you do, you'll probably take them. Sooner or later.'

'New subject,' her mom said, without much of any kind of energy at all.

'That's not just my opinion. Yolanda always says that to you.'

'More dancing,' her mom said. 'Less talking.'

So for the next twenty minutes or so, Grace danced, and watched her mom to see what she had really taken. It shouldn't take long to find out, she figured, because if she'd only taken aspirin, she'd stay awake. No real need to argue, she figured, when you can just wait and watch.

When her mom nodded off on the couch, with her head tipped back and her mouth open, Grace slid the chair over to the door again, climbed up on to it carefully (tap shoes were not ideal for this) and unlocked the door.

Her mom did not wake up.

She clicked her way up all three flights of stairs to Mrs Hinman's apartment and knocked on the door.

'It's only me, Mrs Hinman. Grace. I just wanted to show you how nice I look in my new dress and tell you thank you for it.'

She tried to talk like she had some energy, and like she was happy, so Mrs Hinman wouldn't think she didn't like the dress.

'We all thought you had to stay downstairs with your

mother now,' Mrs Hinman said through the door while she was undoing all those locks.

'Yeah,' Grace said, no longer bothering to hide her depression. 'I sort of did. It was sort of like you thought. But it didn't last very long.'

Billy

Knock. Knock. Knock. Pause. Knock.

Billy glanced into the kitchen to read the clock over his stove. Rayleen was home early. He scooted Ms Lafferty the Cat off his lap, and she ran into the bedroom.

He opened the door, and stared out into the hall, at no one. But of course it was not no one. With the possible exception of one plywood dance floor he'd overheard, it's quite rare for your door to be knocked upon by no one. He was just staring at the wrong level, the Rayleen level. He could see, in his peripheral vision, that someone was there. It was just someone lower. Someone closer to the floor.

He turned his gaze down to Grace's ruined face. She was crying, her nose slightly runny, her face streaked with tears. She was wearing a blue dress, one Billy had never seen before. In fact, he had never seen her in a dress of any kind. And this one was brand-new, and fit her perfectly.

He reached down and picked her up, and she wrapped her arms and legs around him and cried on his shoulder. Rather sloppily, but he really didn't mind. The warmth of her in his arms, and the impact of her emotion, made his knees feel runny and weak, so he took her to the couch, where they sat down as one.

She did not let go.

Her tears made Billy feel as if he might cry as well, even though he was not yet specifically sure what they were crying about.

'I'm sorry I couldn't let you know where I was,' she said in a blubbery voice.

'Well. You did. Sort of. You did that signal-knock on my floor.'

'But that was so long later. You must've been going crazy.'

'I felt better after you knocked.'

'Did you bite all your nails away?'

'I didn't really have much of any to begin with.'

'Does that mean yes?'

'Pretty much.'

'You know I would've let you know where I was. If I could. Right?'

'I never once doubted it. Where's your mom now?'

'Three guesses.'

'Oh.'

They stayed that way for a moment or two longer. Billy had passed the point of too much human contact, and felt the need to withdraw. But he didn't withdraw. He just sat still with the feeling.

Suddenly a shriek pieced his eardrum on the Grace side.

'My kitty! My kitty! My kitty!'

Grace launched off his lap, hurting his thigh and leaving one ear literally ringing.

Ms Lafferty the Cat had strolled into the room, and the cat was headed toward Grace, and Grace was headed toward the cat. But something was wrong, Billy noted. With Grace. Physically wrong. She wasn't walking correctly. She was favoring her right hip or leg. She was limping.

'Grace. What happened?'

'Nothing happened. I'm just saying hello to my cat.'

'You're limping.'

'Oh. That. That's nothing.'

'Did you have an accident?'

'Sort of. Hello, Mr Lafferty the Cat. I missed you. Did you tell Billy thanks for taking such good care of you?'

'What kind of accident? What happened?'

'Oh, it really wasn't anything. Well, I mean, it wasn't much. My mom and I just had this big fight.'

To his surprise, Billy found himself standing on his feet, with no memory of having risen from the couch.

'Your mother hurt you?'

'Well, yeah, sort of, but I don't think she . . .'

But Billy was out the door and down the hall before he could hear the end of the sentence. He trotted down the basement stairs and pounded on that awful woman's door.

Pounded!

As he did, a place in his gut began to tremble, the way it would if someone else had been angry, or creating a disturbance. But this wasn't someone else. This was Billy. It never had been before, not once in his life that he could recall, but now it was, and he was unable to stop the process. It felt as if he were being frightened by the angry behavior of someone else entirely.

'Mrs Ferguson!' he screamed. Screamed. He felt the strain in his throat from raising his voice so sharply. 'Mrs

Ferguson! I need you to come to the door! Now! I know you're not really awake but, frankly, I don't care! I wish to have a talk with you! Right now!'

He paused, still and trembling. For quite a long moment. He pressed his fingertips to the wood of her door to steady himself.

Apparently she was not going to answer.

But he had passed a point of no return in this horrifyingly new territory, and he needed to have his say. So he spoke his piece anyway, right through the door, hoping it would somehow enter her consciousness through a rear entry the way a person in a coma knows when you've been reading to her. And he said it in a loud and aggressive voice, which frightened him, even though the voice was his own.

'You may not hurt Grace. Do you hear me? You may not. Ever. Not ever again. I'm right here. Right upstairs from you. And I will not allow it. You hurt this girl again over my dead body. Do you understand me?'

No answer.

Billy turned to see Grace standing at the top of the stairs, holding her cat, her mouth gaping open, her eyes wide. A mirror of sorts. He turned back to face the door.

'I hope you're listening to me, Mrs Ferguson.'

'She's not really a Mrs,' Grace half whispered from the top of the stairs.

'It doesn't matter,' Billy said evenly. 'The rest applies.'

He pounded on the door one more time, three pounds, each one ricocheting like gunshot in his sore and shaky gut. The inside of him felt sandpapered, skinless, like a raw and open wound exposed to additional damage.

'Never again!' he screamed.

He felt a tug on the leg of his pajama pants, and it made him jump.

'Billy,' Grace whispered, in a voice quieter than a normal Grace whisper. It would have been whispering for anybody. 'Billy. You're out in the hall.'

The sandpapered expanse of his gut returned an exhausted pang.

'Actually,' he said, 'I knew. This time I knew.'

He felt both of her hands wrap around one of his.

'You better come back in,' she said. 'Come on. I'm taking you home.'

'I feel like a wet dishrag,' Billy said.

He sat slumped on his couch, Grace sitting next to him, cat on her lap. Both Grace and the cat stared at Billy constantly, as though he might be about to spontaneously combust.

'You *look* pretty bad, too. I can't believe you said all that stuff.'

'It needed saying.'

'All kinds of stuff needs saying, all the time. But it's not usually you saying it. Even Mr Lafferty the Cat was surprised. Weren't you, Mr Lafferty the Cat?'

'We changed the cat's name,' Billy said weakly.

'You can't change his name. And who's "we"?'

'Felipe and I.'

'You can't change his name. I promised him.'

'Well, see, the problem is, she's not a him. She's a her.'

'He's a girl?'

'*She* is. Yes. So we've been calling her *Ms* Lafferty the Cat.'

'You can't change his name. I mean *her* name. I

promised her that was her name. So her name is just going to have to be Mr Lafferty the Girl Cat.'

'Oh, I think not,' Billy said, feeling as though these simple words were exhausting his last crumb of energy.

'Why not?'

'Don't you think it's a bit long?'

'I'll ask him if he minds. I mean *her*. I'll ask *her* if *she* minds.' Grace held the cat up to her ear, pressing her face against the soft fur of the cat's side. 'She says she doesn't mind.' A long silence. Then Grace said, 'She couldn't even stay clean for three days.'

Billy said nothing, having no idea what to say.

'I meant my mom, not the cat.'

'I knew what you meant.'

'She knew I'd be gone again the minute she got loaded. And what did she do? She got loaded. I guess she loves drugs more than she loves me.'

'Addiction is a weird phenomenon,' Billy said, barely over a whisper.

'Have you ever been addicted to anything?'

'I'm addicted to staying inside my own apartment.'

'Oh. Right. But you just went out.'

'True.'

'Because my mom not hurting me was more important.'

'I guess so.'

'So why can't my own mom do that?'

'I wish I knew.'

'It sucks.'

'It does. Yes.'

'Don't tell Rayleen I complained.'

'I think she would agree that you're entitled in this case,' he said. 'Some things just require complaint.'

But, meanwhile, Billy was thinking, Sure, I broke my addiction for a minute or two. That doesn't mean I could do it from here on out. But he didn't say that out loud to Grace, because he didn't want to strip away her last shred of hope. If she had one.

Billy looked up sometime later to see Rayleen standing in his living room, holding and hugging Grace. Grace must have let her in. Had he fallen asleep, or just slipped into a coma of emotional exhaustion?

'What's wrong with Billy?' Rayleen asked Grace.

'He yelled at my mom, and now he's all wiped out from it.'

'Billy yelled at your mom?'

'Yeah, but I don't think she heard him or anything. But you should have seen him. He was plenty mad. I think even if she'd come to the door, I bet he would've yelled right into her face. And he knew he was out in the hall and everything.'

'Hmm,' Rayleen said, setting Grace down on her feet.

'Ow,' Grace said.

'You OK?'

'I hurt my hip. That's what Billy was so mad about.'

Billy looked up to see Rayleen towering over him, looking down with a soft look of concern in her eyes.

'Are you OK?' she asked. 'You look like you have the flu or something.'

'It just took a lot out of me,' he managed to say, the words mushy at their edges.

'Well, I would stay and tell you volumes about how proud I am of you. But my throat is starting to close up. So we'll have to do this some other time. Come on, Grace, let's go.'

'Don't take Grace,' Billy said, at a surprisingly strong volume.

It startled everyone.

'Why not?' Rayleen asked.

'Yeah, why not?' Grace asked.

'Couldn't you just leave her here for a while? I missed her. Oh, but that's selfish, isn't it? You probably missed her, too.'

'No, it's OK,' Rayleen said. Billy could hear an alarming wheeze growing behind her voice. 'I mean, yeah, I did. I missed her. Of course I did. But she can stay here for a while if you want.'

'Thanks,' Billy said.

'But aren't you worried about . . . what if her mother . . .'

'I don't care. I'm a kidnapper. Call the police.'

Rayleen stood a moment longer, looking down at him. He couldn't quite read the look on her face, but it didn't appear to be any type of insult.

'All righty, then,' she said, and turned to go.

'Don't forget the meeting,' Grace called as Rayleen let herself out. 'Tell everybody. We're having another meeting. Soon.'

'You never told me what—' Rayleen began.

'That's why you have a meeting,' Grace said. 'To tell everybody what the meeting's about. I told you that once already with the last meeting.'

'Yeah,' Rayleen said. 'I guess you did.'

Grace sat on the couch with Billy for a few more hours, watching cartoons on his tiny TV, her head leaned on his shoulder, Mr Lafferty the Girl Cat between them, where they could both pet her at any time.

'Oh, I forgot to tell you,' Grace said, without bothering to mute the volume on the cartoons. 'I'm going to dance at my school.'

Billy was too tired to listen to Grace and the cartoons at the same time. It was just too hard to separate out the sounds. But he was also too tired to say so, or to do anything to try to change it.

So he just asked, 'When?'

'Three months.'

'Good. Because we've got a lot of work to do.'

She didn't answer initially. In time Billy looked over to see that he had offended her, or hurt her feelings, or more likely both.

'I do a good time step,' she said, her bottom lip poking out a little farther than usual.

'Yes. You do. But I figured you'd want to do something more elaborate for a big school performance. A person's first public performance is no small thing. It's a defining moment. It's something you'll not soon forget, let me tell you. But it's up to you. It's your performance. Do you want to fall back on the time step because it's easy and safe and you know it best? Or do you want to really shine?'

Grace stroked the cat's back in silence for a moment or two. Billy felt as though he could look through her and watch the thoughts spinning in her brain. Tumblers waiting to fall into place.

'I want to shine,' she said at last.

'Good choice,' Billy said.

Grace

Grace stood at the bottom of the stairs, cupped her hands, and let loose with her best (or worst, depending on your prejudice in that area) Grace voice.

'Mrs Hinman! Hurry up! Don't be late to the meeting!'

She thought she heard a muffled cry from the stairs, and, in the silence that followed, something hard and noisy began bumping its way down the staircase, one thumpy step at a time.

Grace waited and watched until it came into view. It was a suitcase.

A moment later it was followed by a very spooked-looking girl. Well, lady. But a very young lady. Maybe twenty, or maybe only around eighteen. But definitely spooked. She had long blonde hair and big eyes, and she looked like a nervous horse listening for noises that would make her want to run away.

'You scared me,' the girl-lady said.

'Sorry,' Grace said, but apparently she said it too loud, because the lady jumped again. 'Who are you, anyway?'

'I'm moving in,' the girl-lady said. 'Upstairs.'

'Oh! You're moving into the apartment where Mr Lafferty killed himself!'

The lady's eyes got wider and more spooked. If such a thing were even possible.

'Somebody killed himself in there?'

'Yeah. Mr Lafferty,' Grace said, thinking it was weird that she should have to repeat herself so soon. Maybe scared people had trouble holding on to basic information.

'I didn't know that.'

'And now you do. So, what's your name?'

'Emily.'

'I'm Grace. Are you alone? Because if you're alone, you should come to our meeting.'

'I don't know what you mean . . . alone.'

'It's pretty simple,' Grace said. 'I thought everybody knew what it meant.'

'Alone . . . how?'

'Like, do you have a bunch of family and friends?'

'I have a family.'

'Oh. Good.'

'In Iowa.'

'Oh. Bad.'

'I have friends. Well. A couple. I guess.'

'In LA?'

'Not really, no.'

'You should come to our meeting.'

'I don't even know any of you.'

'Duh. That would be the point, wouldn't it?'

'I have to unpack.'

'Is that all your stuff?' Grace asked, pointing to the suitcase, still lying on the stairs at her feet.

'Pretty much, yeah.'

'So how long do you figure it'll take you to unpack it? We could wait for you. We don't mind.'

'I'm awfully tired.'

'Right,' Grace said, knowing by feel that it was time to give up. 'We're going to have a meeting every week. Maybe you could come to the next one.'

'Maybe, yeah.'

Just then Mrs Hinman appeared on the stairs, causing Emily to jump again. She picked up her suitcase and ran upstairs, brushing by Mrs Hinman before Grace could even introduce them.

Mrs Hinman eased her way down the stairs to the spot where Grace was standing, and the two of them very slowly walked along the hall to Rayleen's, because there was no point hurrying Mrs Hinman, and Grace knew it.

'Who was that?' Mrs Hinman asked.

'Her name is Emily,' Grace said. 'She's moving in upstairs, where Mr Lafferty used to live.'

'Oh. I see.'

'Why is everybody scared of everybody else?'

'Hmm. A good question. One of those mysterious aspects of the human condition, I guess.'

'You sound like Billy,' Grace said, making it clear by her tone that it was no compliment in this case. 'What did all that mean, what you just said?'

'I suppose it's a fancy way of saying some things just *are*.'

Grace sighed noisily, thinking that was a terrible answer, but not wanting to insult Mrs Hinman by pointing it out.

'I guess maybe we can talk more about that at our meeting,' she said.

*   *   *

'Who wants to go first?' Grace asked. Then, before anybody could answer, she added, 'Billy, can you hear us?'

Grace, Felipe, Mrs Hinman and Rayleen were gathered
in Rayleen's apartment, the door standing wide open. Billy
sat on a chair across the hall, just inside his open doorway.
Sitting on his hands. Probably to keep from biting his
nails, Grace figured. She'd already caught him at it once,
and put a stop to it.

Billy wouldn't come over to Rayleen's, for obvious
reasons, and Rayleen wouldn't go over to Billy's because of
the cat. So, silly as it seemed to Grace, this was the only
way to make a very important meeting happen.

'I'm fine,' Billy said.

'That doesn't answer the question, Billy.'

'Well, I heard you ask, didn't I? Or I wouldn't have
answered.'

'Oh. Right,' Grace said.

'Go first and say what?' Rayleen asked. 'We're still not
too sure what this meeting's all about.'

'It's about how people shouldn't be alone. Especially
when there are so many of us. Look at all of you. You're all
alone, and there are four of you, and that's really stupid,
because there are four of you. So why be alone?'

'So what are we supposed to say when it's our turn?'
Felipe asked.

'You're supposed to say why you're alone. All except Mrs
Hinman. She doesn't have to go, because she's only alone
because she lived longer than her husband and all her
friends.'

A silence fell, during which Mrs Hinman cleared her
throat and shifted uncomfortably on Rayleen's couch.

'Well, that's not entirely true,' Mrs Hinman said.

'But I heard that from *you*.'

'I know. Yes. I know you did. But what I'm saying is . . . really, if I were being completely honest, it's not entirely true.'

Another long silence. This was the other thing Grace had noticed about grown-ups. In addition to being afraid of each other, it was hard to wring any information out of them. At least, if it was information about *them*. If it was about what kids ought to do, then they were nothing but words.

'Marv and I were very close,' Mrs Hinman said, her voice quiet. Probably too quiet for Billy to hear. 'And, even though I don't suppose I would have seen it this way at the time, I might have used that as an excuse to let some of my friendships go. Some very old friends, too. I just let them drift away. Can't even say why, for a fact. It was just so much easier. Just me and Marv seemed like less trouble. Fewer arguments and hurt feelings and misunderstandings and whatnot, all the things people bring into our lives. But then, at the end, even Marv and I weren't as close as we used to be. Oh, I don't know. I guess in some ways we were. On the outside you wouldn't have seen that anything had changed. But there was something missing in there somewhere. Something hollow about it. I don't know how to explain it any better than that.'

The silence that followed seemed to make everybody uneasy except Grace. Rayleen looked at her fingernails, and Felipe bounced his knee up and down. Grace looked across the hall at Billy, and he had that anxious, stressed look on his face, even though Grace was pretty sure he hadn't heard most of Mrs Hinman's speech.

Mrs Hinman sat weirdly upright, hands clasped in her

lap, a shocked look on *her* face, as if someone else had said all those things, and she hadn't approved of any of them.

'This is a good meeting so far,' Grace said, to correct anyone who might be thinking otherwise. 'Who wants to go next?'

No one made a sound.

So it startled everyone, even Grace, when someone appeared in the open doorway and banged hard on the door, causing it to slam back against the wall.

Grace looked up to see that it was Yolanda, and that Yolanda was pissed.

Rayleen said, 'Oh, hi, Yolanda,' and stood up to greet her.

And Yolanda said, 'What's this I hear about you taking Grace away from her own mother?'

Grace got right between them, fast, so there couldn't be any trouble. Well, not too much, anyway. 'It was all my idea,' she said.

'*Yours?* You *wanted* to be taken away from your mother?'

'We wanted to . . . not . . . oh, crap, now I forgot the word again. Guys, what's that thing we wanted not to do with my mom?'

'Enable,' Rayleen said, still standing. Still looking aware of the fact that Yolanda was pissed. 'We wanted to stop enabling her.'

'OK. Now how 'bout you explain to me how letting her raise her own kid is enabling her.'

'*I* will!' Grace shouted. 'Please let me! I know this one real well! It's because she was doing nothing but sleep all day long, and all my nice neighbors here were taking care of me, but then we figured out that if they just kept taking care of me, she could take all the drugs she wanted and still know I'd be OK. And so we knew that was no good. So we figured sometimes people get better when they know they're about to lose something, if it's something they really, really don't want to lose. Like me. So we told her she couldn't see me again until she got clean.'

A brief pause, during which it was hard to guess what Yolanda was thinking. She wasn't giving anything away so far.

'Oh, my God,' Yolanda said. 'That's brilliant.'

'It is?' Grace asked, surprised that Yolanda liked it.

'Grace, you thought that up all by yourself?'

'Not really. I got a lot of advice from Mr Lafferty.'

'Actually, she put a lot of it together on her own,' Rayleen said.

'OK, tell you what,' Yolanda said. 'I'll go back down there right now and tell her she's shit out of luck, because I'm on your side. She'll be pissed, but oh, well. Life's like that sometimes. So, how long does she have to stay clean before she gets Grace back?'

Silence.

'Oh,' Rayleen said. 'We didn't set a time.'

'We should set a time,' Yolanda said. 'Because she keeps cleaning up for a day or two. Getting everybody's hopes up for nothing. I say we make her get thirty days. I'm right there with her at the meetings, and I'll know if it's the real deal.'

Everybody looked at everybody else.

'OK,' Rayleen said.

'Done,' Yolanda said, and rushed out.

'That was kind of weird,' Felipe said.

'Yeah, but it worked out OK,' Grace replied. 'And it doesn't get us out of having our meeting.'

'I think we should put off the meeting,' Rayleen said. 'In case your mom gets upset. I don't think we should be sitting here with the doors open after Yolanda has this little talk with her. Besides, we lost Billy again.'

Grace looked across the hall to see Billy's apartment door closed, apparently with Billy inside it. She sighed.

'I better go over there and talk to him,' she said.

'You know,' she said to Billy, who was sitting on the couch, looking shorter and more curled-up than usual, and hugging the cat, 'I need you to be at my school when I do my dance. You know. In the audience. Clapping for me and all.'

Billy snorted laughter. As if he really thought it was a joke. As if he hadn't seen this coming.

'No, seriously,' she said.

She watched the color drain out of his face, suddenly. At least, what little color he'd had to begin with.

'Grace. You know I can't do that.'

'No. I know you *can*.'

'Grace, I— '

'Look. Billy. Do you want to just do the easy thing, because it's what you always do? Or do you want to shine?'

He turned his eyes to her, looking bruised.

'That's not fair.'

'It was fair when you asked it to me.'

'That was different.'

'How was it different?'

'Because that was *me* asking *you*.'

'Just think about it. OK? Promise me you'll think about it. I know you'll come up with the right thing.'

'Overconfidence is a wonderful attribute of youth,' Billy said, quietly.

'I'm not even going to ask you what that means.'

'Probably just as well,' he said.

In the morning, Grace ran into the new lady, Emily – almost literally – in the hall on her way to school. Rayleen was walking behind Grace, half putting on her coat, and Grace was walking ahead, and nearly collided with the new lady at the bottom of the stairs.

She was carrying that same suitcase again.

'Where are you going?' Grace asked. 'To get more of your stuff?'

'Moving out,' Emily said, as if she didn't want to slow down to talk.

'But you just moved in.'

'I'm not spending one more night in that horrible place.'

'What's horrible about it? It has a very nice new carpet.'

'I can't explain it. There's something wrong with that place. With the energy in there. It's just a really bad vibe.'

Then she hurried out fast, too fast for Grace to keep up even if there had been more to say.

'Who was that?' Rayleen asked, when they met up at the front door.

'She was our neighbor,' Grace said. 'Just not for very long.'

'We should mark this day on our calendar,' Billy said, out loud, because he was changing out of his pajamas.

It was about a week later, a Saturday morning. He slid into his stretchy dance pants and then threw on a sweat-shirt, because dance pants and a pajama top was just too weird a combination, even for Billy. Even for Billy with no one around to witness the fashion faux pas.

Then he turned on the light inside his closet and worked his way back to the standing chest of drawers. He reached into the top drawer, identifying his tap shoes by feel. *His* tap shoes. Not the ancient, archival pair from his child-hood that he'd loaned to Grace. His regular adult tap shoes, the ones he'd worn at his most recent tap per-formance. Which, of course, had been none too recent. He pulled them out, and held them under his nose, remem-bering the subtle but distinctive smell of the old leather, and every memory that came along for the ride.

All the memories, as a package deal. No picking and choosing allowed.

He put them on in the living room, Mr Lafferty the Girl

Cat watching with uncharacteristic fascination, as if even she could smell the momentous atmosphere of this occasion.

Then he stretched. Got down on the worn-out old carpet and assumed familiar old positions, and cried out with unfamiliar pain when his muscles didn't yield to the acrobatics they had used to perform so easily.

In a moment balanced halfway between succeeding and deciding it was all pointless, Billy levered to his feet, walked carefully on the slippery taps to Grace's plywood dance floor, and began to choreograph a dance suitable for her school performance.

He would have done it sooner, but Grace had needed a full week to rest her injured hip.

'I guess she can at least *start* with a time step,' he said out loud. 'Just to work into the rhythm slowly.'

He knew from experience that it was best to start a big performance with something easy and familiar, because the first few seconds were the hardest. If you were going to freeze, or make a mistake, it would be on the first couple of steps. If your mind was going to go blank, it would be right up front. After the first few seconds of dancing, a sort of autopilot would kick in, and everything would fall into place.

So, he believed, if you're lucky enough to be in charge of your own fate on the subject, you start with a step you can almost literally perform in your sleep.

He began the strange process of slowly reminding his feet how that time step phenomenon had used to go. It was a weird feeling. His mind picked the step up again immediately. Everything from his brain through the nerve signals he sent to his muscles felt exactly the same. But the response from those muscles reminded him of a certain category of terrible dream, the one where you try to run from the monster, but your legs suddenly weigh hundreds of pounds or feel as though they're mired in warm tar.

He stopped, and stood still a moment in disheartenment, staring at the cat, who stared back.

'Relax, Billy,' he said after a time. 'We could get it back in a few months if we wanted to.'

Well, some of it, he could. But he was twelve years older now. And there was no getting that back. If there were, someone would have bottled it and sold it to the public years ago.

'She'll need turns,' he said, trying out a few. 'She could do some triple Buffalo turns, that would look flashy. Not too flashy. Just flashy enough.'

He slowly plotted them out on the six-foot-square dance floor, just to be sure they wouldn't send him flying off on to the rug. There was barely enough room to execute a series of turns, which he began slowly to move through.

Grace was smaller, and her legs were shorter, so if he could do it, so could she. She'd have to pay almost perfect attention, but that was good. The practice in discipline would serve her well. Then, on the school stage, she wouldn't lose track of her arc of turns and fall right into the orchestra pit. The six-foot dance floor would teach her to keep her turns tight and crisp. It would be the dancer's equivalent of swinging three bats around.

Billy stopped suddenly, struck, without warning, by an echo of something he had said out loud much earlier. He'd said, 'We could get it back in a few months if we wanted to.'

He stood nearly still, rhythmically tapping the toe tap of

his right shoe and hearing the question in his head as if for the first time.

Then he held completely still, not even tapping.

'Do we want to?' he asked out loud.

But no answer seemed to present itself, and there was more choreography to be done, and changing the subject again sounded attractive.

'Maybe something syncopated,' he said, trying out some wings, some traveling wing steps with toe hits, because they were more sophisticated.

He'd spent several minutes, and worked out quite a fancy routine, before realizing the flaw in his thinking. He stopped dead and thought it over more deeply.

'No,' he said out loud. 'Big mistake there, Billy Boy. You're visualizing *your* audience. Visualize *hers*. They don't want something that sophisticated. In fact, they might even think she was making mistakes, falling off her rhythm. No, they'll want something dependable. Balanced. User-friendly. Yet flashy! Everybody likes a little flash.

'I've got it,' he said, and moved into something different.

A series of trebles. Treble hops. Seven on one side, seven on the other, then bring it in tight, maybe down to four on each side, then two, then tighten up for a nice ending . . .

He counted it out as he danced it.

'One, two, three, four, five, six seven, hop . . . one, two, three, four, five, six seven, hop . . . one, two, three, four . . . one, two, three, four . . . one and a two, and a one and a two, and a one and a two, and a three and a stop.'

He ended suddenly with one foot smartly raised. A sudden burst of ending. The applause moment. He stood still, just for a split second expecting to hear it.

Instead he heard a signal knock at his door.

He walked carefully across the carpet to open it.

On the other side of the door was Grace, and a man Billy had never met. An African-American man with a shaved head and a full beard shot through with gray. He wasn't terribly old, though. Maybe mid-forties. He had eyes that Billy could only describe as sparkly. He had a single ruby stud-earring in his left lobe.

'Oh, my God, Billy!' Grace shrieked. 'Look at you! You're all dressed!'

'Don't make it sound like such a rare occasion,' he said, flipping his chin subtly in the direction of the stranger.

It was a hint that sailed well over Grace's head.

'It's only the very first time since I've known you, Billy, so that's pretty rare, don't you think?'

'Who's your friend?' Billy asked, hoping his face wasn't obviously red.

'This is Jesse. He's our new neighbor.'

Jesse looked right into Billy's eyes, causing him to look away. He wondered if Jesse was smart enough to sense that Billy did that with everyone. Equal opportunity evasion.

Then Jesse reached out a hand and Billy shook it, bearing up under the pressure of the nerve signals, which he felt as shards of glass in his brain and gut, warning him against skin contact with any stranger.

In fact, he suddenly wondered, should Grace be hanging around the building with a man none of them knew?

Billy took a deep breath. He'd always prided himself on being a good judge of character. Remembering this, he forced himself to look directly into the stranger's eyes for a fraction of a second. Then he looked away again, and let out a long breath of air.

It was OK. Jesse was OK.

'So,' Billy said, wanting to normalize the conversation, 'you moved in upstairs? Mr Lafferty's old place?'

'Yeah,' Grace said. 'He did. The apartment where Mr Lafferty shot himself. But it's OK. Because Jesse doesn't scare so easy. Not like our last new neighbor.'

'What last new neighbor?'

'Oh, right. You never even met her, did you? She was here for, like, one day. Then she said there was a creepy vibe in there and she moved out. I told Jesse but he didn't care. He said he had some . . . what did you say you had, Jesse?'

'Sage,' Jesse said. 'White sage.' It was the first time Billy had heard his voice. It was deep, smooth and reassuring.

'Yeah, sage,' Grace said. 'That's it. He said he was going to grunge the place with white sage.'

'Smudge,' Jesse said.

'Huh?'

'I said I was going to *smudge* the apartment with white sage.'

'Oh, right. Smudge. Where did I get grunge?'

'I'm not sure. Somewhere in your interesting and imaginative brain, I've no doubt.'

'Anyway,' Grace said, 'when you smudge with white sage it chases away evil spirits.'

'Actually,' Jesse said, 'I don't really believe there is such a thing as evil spirits, but if somebody left some bad energy hanging around, it might help. If I really thought there was some kind of spirit haunting the place, which I very much doubt, I wouldn't so much chase him away as make peace with him.'

'That would be a better tack to take with Mr Lafferty,' Billy said.

'It's a better tack to take with everybody,' Jesse replied.

Then they all stood awkwardly for a moment, and Billy realized he was being rude by not inviting them in. But he didn't do strangers in the apartment, especially not on short notice.

'I'm sorry,' he said, 'I'd ask you in, but—'

Grace interjected. Interrupted, really, though it was far from unwelcome.

'No, we gotta go,' she said. 'I gotta take him to meet Felipe and then Mrs Hinman.'

'He already met Rayleen?'

'Oh, yeah,' Grace said. There was something unusual hiding in the way she said it. A hint of subtext. But it was completely indecipherable based on the information Billy had to work with. 'Oh, my God!' she shrieked. 'Billy! You're wearing tap shoes!'

'I am.'

'I didn't even know you had those tap shoes. Those aren't the ones you used to loan me. Oh, right. Never mind. I just got it. These are ones for grown-ups. So why didn't you tell me you still had tap shoes?'

'I guess I thought it went without saying.'

'Wrong. Were you dancing just now?'

'I was choreographing some dance moves for you to learn for your big school performance.'

'Great!' she shouted. 'Yea, yea, yea! As soon as I introduce Jesse to everybody I'll come back down and we can get started. I think I feel better enough to start.'

'Nice meeting you, Billy,' Jesse said.

'Likewise,' Billy said, and made sure by his tone and

facial expression that his new neighbor would realize he meant it sincerely.

He watched Grace drag Jesse to the stairs, holding one of his hands in both of hers. It made him feel just a little tiny bit left out.

'Billy doesn't like people,' he heard Grace tell Jesse on their way up the stairs. 'He's . . . different. But he's a good guy.'

Grace arrived back about twenty minutes later, and grabbed up her cat before doing anything else.

'Before I start dancing,' she said, 'I have to tell you a secret.'

'How can you tell me if it's a secret?'

'It's not that kind of secret.'

'What kind is it?'

'The kind where you see something with your own eyes, and you know you want to tell somebody, but you know you don't want them to tell the whole world.'

'And you figure I'll be talking to the whole world in the near future?'

'Don't be weird, Billy. I mean, don't tell Felipe or Mrs Hinman – and definitely don't tell Rayleen.'

'OK, deal.'

They sat on the couch together, setting the stage for Grace's momentous secret.

'You ready?' she asked, still squeezing the cat.

'More than ready.'

'Jesse likes Rayleen.'

'Oh. How can you tell?'

'It was so easy. Right from the time I met him I was saying, "You should come to our meeting, we're having a meeting today and you should come." And he kept saying stuff like he had to unpack, and maybe everybody else would mind having him there because they didn't know him. And then I took him to meet Rayleen. And then the minute we walked out of there, he said, "So what time is that meeting?" '

'Oh, right. What time *is* that meeting?'

'I don't know. Whatever time I yell that the meeting is starting, I guess.'

'Well. Doesn't that just give *you* all the power?'

Grace punched him lightly on the arm. '*You* pick a time, then. I just figured I was the only one who really wanted the meeting.'

'You can say that again.'

'So what did you think of my big secret?'

'Well. It's not too surprising. Rayleen is a very attractive woman.'

'Yeah. She's pretty. And she's nice. But . . .'

'But what? There's something you don't like about Rayleen?'

'Oh, no. I like her all the way through. I was just gonna say that we don't really know her that well.'

'We don't?'

'I don't think so.'

'I thought we did.'

'I just know she works on people's nails at a salon, and that's sort of all I know. Not that I know a bunch more about Felipe or Mrs Hinman, but in another way I sort of do. It shows. With them it shows. But Rayleen doesn't show much. The only thing I know about her because it shows is what she's afraid of.'

Billy thought a moment, wondering if whatever Grace

had observed about Rayleen showed to him, too. After all, he'd just noted that he prided himself on being a good judge of character. But as far as he had ever known, or even sensed, Rayleen wasn't afraid of anything.

'And what's that?'

'The county.'

'The county?'

'You didn't hear me?'

'It doesn't really make sense. She's afraid of the county of Los Angeles?'

'Right.'

'What's she afraid it'll do?'

'Like, come and take a kid away.'

'Oh. Like that.'

'Yeah. Like that. Like maybe the county came and took her away when she was a kid.'

'Or maybe she had a kid and the county took the kid away. I guess if she wanted to tell us about it, she would.'

'That's why we're having the *meetings*,' Grace said. A little exasperated, as though it should be obvious. 'Nobody wants to tell somebody else bad stuff like that. You have to push a little harder to get that stuff out of people.'

'Are you ready to dance?'

He asked it quickly, in case she was about to push a little harder on him.

'Are you kidding? I've been ready for a *week*,' she said. 'I'll go get my tap shoes on. They're at Rayleen's. I'll be right back. You won't tell Rayleen my secret, right?'

'But she was there. She was there when you introduced her to Jesse. So, if he likes her, don't you think she knows?'

'I don't know. You never can tell with grown-ups.

They miss some really obvious stuff. Anyway, I sure wouldn't want her to know we were over here talking about it.'

'Talking about what?'

'About Jesse and Rayleen!' she shouted, fully exasperated, probably loud enough for Rayleen to hear across the hall.

'It's kind of a joke,' Billy said. 'It's a little signal. It means I already forgot there was anything to tell.'

'Why didn't you say so? How was I supposed to know that?'

'I thought everybody did. I thought it was a cultural thing. Like it was part of the collective unconscious by now.'

Grace rolled her eyes skyward.

'You're so weird, Billy.'

'Thank you,' he said, quietly, to her back, as she walked out his door.

He made his way carefully back to the dance floor and moved slowly through the routine one more time. He ended even more crisply than before, and stood, one foot raised, again thinking he was about to hear applause.

But not *his* applause. It was not about him this time. This was Grace's applause. Grace's first experience with the public ovation.

'Oh, good God,' Billy said, suddenly, and out loud. 'I really do need to be there. Shit.'

Grace

'*Please* somebody go first?' Grace whined.

She looked at every grown-up in the room, one at a time. Only Mrs Hinman looked back. Maybe because Mrs Hinman had already taken her turn, at the last meeting, and so wasn't feeling under the gun. Grown-ups always acted different when you put the tiniest little bit of pressure on them.

Everybody was gathered at Rayleen's. Everybody.

Even Billy was there. Dressed, yet. Standing with his back against the door, like his own apartment would save his life if he could just stay close to it. She caught him biting a thumbnail, but she figured if she yelled at him like she usually did, he might run home again, so she let it go by.

Rayleen was sitting cross-legged on the rug, her back up against the couch, where Jesse could only see her from behind. Grace wondered if Rayleen had figured that out on purpose.

Jesse sat looking around at all the faces like he was memorizing everything for later, and it was impossible for

Grace to tell what he was thinking, though she watched him and wondered about it a lot.

Felipe bounced one knee up and down and stared at the rug as if rugs hypnotized him.

'*Pleeeeease?*'

Then Rayleen opened her mouth to talk, which Grace took to be a good sign. But it didn't take long to realize her mistake.

'I don't know about anybody else,' Rayleen said, a sharpness in her voice that Grace had only heard Rayleen use when addressing Grace's mom, 'but I'm feeling pressured by this. I am *not* ready for this,' she added, glancing halfway over her shoulder in the general direction of Jesse.

Grace's face burned, and a line of ache radiated down into her belly. Rayleen had never spoken to her in an angry tone before, and to have it happen now, in front of all these people . . . including somebody new . . . well, it was nothing short of humiliating. Tears welled up behind her eyes, but she fought hard to hide them.

She opened her mouth, but no words came out.

Felipe looked up suddenly. Right into Grace's eyes.

'I guess *I* could go,' he said.

She wanted to hug and kiss him, but it all happened too fast.

'I *wasn't* alone,' Felipe said, his accent thicker than usual, which Grace had noticed before, usually when he was extra-tired or feeling emotional. 'I mean, until just . . . well . . . not long. Pretty much just a little while ago. A few weeks. I had a girlfriend. We were gonna get married. I gave her a ring and everything, and we had a little son. Twenty months. And then one day I get home from work, and there's this bag by my door. It has my toothbrush in it, and the spare shirts and underwear I kept at her house. And at the very bottom is the little box with the ring in it. The engagement ring I gave her. So I guess that's that.'

Felipe allowed a silence to fall, and . . . wow. It was a very silent silence.

'Did she say why?' Grace asked, reverently.

'I can't even get through to talk to her. I left a million messages. Finally I called her sister. And so her sister says there's another guy, and there's been another guy for *mucho tiempo*. A lot of time.'

More silence.

Rayleen seemed to have forgotten her irritation. She opened her mouth to speak, and the words came out soft and helpful, the way Grace wished Rayleen had spoken to *her*.

'Did you have any idea?'

'Yes and no,' Felipe said. 'I did and I didn't. I was so surprised. But now I look back and see some things. You know how it is. At least, I think you know. You see but you don't see. You see a thing. And you think it's a certain way. But you tell yourself, "No, that's crazy, you're wrong." And then you find out you're right. And part of you says, "Hell, I didn't know," and another part of you says, "Oh yeah you did."'

'What about *su hijo*?' Grace asked, her voice hushed with awe.

'What about *what*?' Billy asked, and then went back to shredding his thumbnail.

'His little boy,' Grace said. 'Don't bite your nails.'

'Well, I asked that,' Felipe said. 'I asked her sister. I said, "What about Diego? How am I supposed to see Diego?" I said, "After all, he's my son. My flesh and blood." Know what she said?'

Felipe's voice broke on the last sentence, and Grace found herself unsure if she wanted to know or not. She shook her head without thinking.

'She said, "Maybe he's your son, and maybe he isn't."'

Grace got up from her chair and ran across the room, throwing her arms around Felipe's neck.

'*Lo siento*, Felipe,' she said, in barely over a whisper. '*Lo siento para su hijo.*'

'*Gracias,*' Felipe breathed quietly.

'I have to go,' Billy said suddenly, from his perch by the door.

His panic must have hit him like a dam breaking, because Grace could hear how his words turned into the truth at nearly the exact same moment they rushed out of him.

She let go of Felipe and stepped back. Billy already had the door open.

'Oh, no. Billy. Can't you please try just a little longer? It's just getting to be a real meeting!'

'Sorry, baby girl. I can only do just so much.'

But he took a step into the room, not out of it. He took four or five steps, actually, toward Felipe, and stopped above Felipe's chair and looked down, and his eyes looked soft. Felipe looked up and smiled sadly.

'What does "*lo siento*" mean?' Billy asked quietly.

'It means she's sorry.'

Billy bent down and hugged Felipe around his shoulders, kind of quick and careful. Like he'd better not hug too long or too hard.

'*Lo siento,*' Billy said.

'*Gracias*, Billy.'

Then Billy raced out the door. Raced. Even Grace didn't manage to get places that fast, and she was a kid.

'I'll go next,' Jesse said.

Everybody looked up as if they'd forgotten Jesse talked.

'Don't look so surprised. I just thought I'd give you a chance to know me a little bit. Since I'm new here. And since I'll only be here a few months.'

Nobody argued, so he did.

'I grew up near here. Actually, I grew up about four blocks from here. Which is part of why I picked this apartment. So close to where I used to live. Lot of memories. Of course, it's changed a lot. And, then, the other reason I picked it is because I need to save as much money as I can. I'm on a six-month leave of absence, and my savings will only go just so far. They'll stretch, I think. But barely.

'Anyway, I live in Chapel Hill. North Carolina. I left LA to go to college there, and I never came back. The only reason I'm here now is because my mother is dying.'

Grace opened her mouth to speak. She had tons of questions. A whole brain full. She wanted to ask how soon Jesse's mother was going to die, and of what, and how close he was to her, and if it made him so sad he could hardly stand it. And if there was anything she could do to make him not so sad, even though she didn't figure there was, not with a big, awful, sad thing like that. But she never got to. Then again, she never had to. Jesse was a good talker. You didn't have to drag anything out of Jesse. He just opened the door and out it came. That was a new one as far as Grace was concerned.

'Funny thing about me and my mother. We never really got along. Never saw eye to eye. On just about anything.

We had a very volatile relationship.' Then, before Grace could even open her mouth to ask, he said, 'That means explosive.' As though he could read her mind. 'I think most everybody who knew us thought we didn't like each other. Maybe even that we hated each other. I tend to think of it more as a "fierce bond". If we didn't love each other a lot, there'd be no place for all that fire. It's love, and then it's the flipside of love. We happen to have a lot of both.

'So I guess people figure it's not as hard to lose your mother when you never got along anyway. But they're wrong. They're dead wrong. It's always hard to lose your mother. Always. If you loved her, if you hated her. If she smothered you, if she ignored you. It doesn't matter. She's your mother. Your *mother*. That's just a very tough bond to break.'

Grace opened her mouth to speak, and began to cry. Within seconds it morphed into sobbing. Full-on, uncontrollable sobbing.

It brought the meeting down, and fast.

Suddenly everyone was huddled around her, too close to her, on her, not letting her breathe. They wanted to know if she was OK – they asked over and over – but she knew she'd be more OK if they would step back and give her some air.

'I'm going over to see my kitty,' she said, and ran out.

She stood in the hall, sniffling and wiping her nose on her sleeve, and signal-knocked on Billy's door.

'I can't do any more outside time today, baby girl. I'm at my limit. I'm sorry. *Lo siento.*'

'I didn't come to say that. I need to come in. Could you open the door?'

He must have heard the sobs in her voice. He couldn't

very well have missed them. The door opened almost before she could finish her last sentence.

She shuffled past him and sat on his couch.

'Good meeting so far?' he asked.

That was just Billy's odd sense of humor. Instead of asking her what was wrong, he would make a wisecrack. But it was better than being surrounded and smothered.

Which, she suddenly realized, was why she'd come. It wasn't really to see her cat. Well, a little bit. Partly. Mostly it was to see her Billy.

She called for Mr Lafferty the Girl Cat with a little 'psst' sound, and the kitty came loping in from Billy's bedroom and jumped into her lap. Grace held the cat close and pressed one ear against her rumbly side.

She sniffled in as much as she could, so her nose wouldn't run on to poor Mr Lafferty the Girl Cat's fur.

Billy sat on the edge of the couch, about two feet away from them, and handed her a giant-size box of tissues. She pulled out three or four at once, and wiped her eyes on all of them at the same time, and blew her nose too loudly, with an embarrassing honking sound.

'I sure use a lot of your tissues.'

'I can live with it.'

'Maybe I should buy you another box.'

'With what? Are you sitting on a nest egg we don't know about? Holding out on us? You're really independently wealthy?'

'Oh. Right.'

She blew her nose again, this time using only three.

'Anything you care to shoot the breeze about?'

'In English, Billy.'

'Want to talk?'

Grace sighed.

'I just miss my mom, is all.'

'Oh,' Billy said.

'I know she's not a very good mom. At least, not right now. She used to be a pretty good mom, but that was a long time ago now. But even so, even though we don't get along or anything, and even though we had a big fight and I'm mad at her, and even though she loves drugs more than she loves me, I still miss her.'

'Hmm,' Billy said.

'Maybe you wouldn't understand.'

'Then again, maybe I would. I miss my mother every day. And she's the most dreadful woman who ever set her feet down on the planet Earth.'

Grace snorted laughter, in spite of herself.

'She couldn't be that bad.'

'Oh, no. She could be. And she is. You have to trust me on this. So. Meeting over?'

'I guess so. I mean, I'm the only one who even wants to have the meetings anyway, and I walked out.'

'Maybe they'll surprise you. Maybe they're over there spilling their guts about all the personal tragedies that resulted in their subsequent aloneness. Maybe you inspired them.'

'I'll go see,' Grace said.

She handed the cat to Billy and padded out of Billy's apartment and across the hallway. Once there, she pressed her ear quietly to the door.

They weren't spilling their guts.

Jesse was apologizing for upsetting her, saying he hadn't known he was saying anything that would make her cry.

She padded back across the hall and plunked down on Billy's couch again.

'I didn't think so,' she said.

Later, when she thought she'd heard everybody leave Rayleen's and go their separate ways, Grace headed back across the hall. And ran smack into Jesse.

Should've known that, she thought, silently kicking herself. Of course Jesse would hang back and try to be the last one out, so he could talk to Rayleen alone, because Jesse liked Rayleen, and any fool could see it.

Grace hadn't wanted to run into Jesse, because she knew he'd apologize for ever, and she didn't want his apologies. They'd probably only make her cry again.

'Oh, there you are, Grace,' he said. 'I thought I wasn't going to get a chance to apologize.'

See?

'You don't have to apologize,' she said, carefully not crying. 'You didn't do anything wrong. You just told the truth like you were supposed to. Just like what the meeting is for.'

'I didn't mean to upset you.'

'I know you didn't do it on purpose,' Grace said, irritation seeping through in her tone. 'You think I don't know that?'

Then she held still, waiting to see if he'd get mad back.

But he just patted her on the head and walked down the hall and up the stairs to his own apartment.

Grace watched him go and wondered suddenly how he was doing with the ghost of Mr Lafferty the Person. Or, if not a ghost, whatever it was that had scared off Emily, their old neighbor-for-a-split-second. On the one hand she wished she'd asked him, but on the other hand she was happy to be done with all the apology stuff, and she had no intention of pressing her luck.

She looked both ways in the hallway, as if spies could be lurking around any and every corner. Then she took an unplanned turn, padding along the hallway toward her own apartment and down the stairs.

She opened the door with her key.

The place was dark. Not pitch black, but no lights on. Nothing that felt alive or moving. She found her mom in her bedroom, sprawled on her back in bed, snoring.

She moved closer, first just watching. Then she reached out and tugged at the sleeve of her mom's shirt.

'Hey,' she said. Quietly, as if in conversation. The way people sometimes say 'hey' in place of hello.

Grace's mom's eyes flickered open for just a second or two.

'Hey,' she said back.

'You OK?'

'Ummmm. What're you doing here?'

'Just came to see if you're OK,' Grace said, something snagging and catching in her throat, nearly gagging her.

Grace's mom raised a hand, as if waving would be a good way to answer the question. But the hand didn't stay up long. Didn't really form into an actual wave, in fact. It just faded, and drooped, and landed on her belly again.

Grace waited, in case there was more, even though she wasn't sure what more she hoped there might be.

That's it, she said to herself, but not out loud. That's all there is. All you're going to get. You might as well go back to Rayleen's.

But she didn't. Not yet.

Instead she stroked her mother's hair, just three long strokes. Then she leaned in and whispered directly into her mom's ear.

'Love you, Mom.'

But she must've leaned in too close. Her breath on her mom's ear must've tickled, because her mom reached up and swatted at Grace, as if Grace were a mosquito or a fly. Smacked her right on the ear.

'Ow!' she shouted, louder than really necessary, and all out of proportion to how much it hurt. It had been an indignity, one which had hurt her on the inside, and the shout had been a way of letting it move through her.

Then, just as suddenly, it made her cry.

And the crying made her leave, made her run for the door, for the safety of Rayleen's, as though someone might see her crying if she stayed. Even though she knew, really, that nobody would have noticed. Not even her mom.

She knocked on Rayleen's door, still rubbing her ear.

Rayleen opened it and let her in. Grace noticed a couple of little lines in Rayleen's forehead that she didn't see too often, like Rayleen was holding her face tighter and scrunchier than usual.

'You hungry?' Rayleen asked.

'Kind of.'

'There's not much. It's going to have to be peanut butter.'

'Peanut butter's OK. Do we have any jelly?' Then she regretted her use of the word 'we'. Whatever was in Rayleen's refrigerator really belonged to Rayleen, not to both of them. Probably she'd just been very rude, and right when Rayleen was in a lousy mood, too. 'You, I mean. Do *you* have any jelly?'

Rayleen's head was still buried in the refrigerator.

'Strawberry jam,' she said.

Unfortunately for Grace, she didn't say whether they both had it, or if it only belonged to Rayleen.

'Perfect,' Grace said, even though she liked grape jelly much better.

Then, while Rayleen was making the sandwiches, Grace said, 'So, what do you think of Jesse?'

Grace heard the bottom of a jar slam down on the counter, startling her, but she didn't know if it was the peanut butter or the jam.

'You're going to have to stop this,' Rayleen said, in the voice that had almost made Grace cry earlier, at the meeting, and which almost made her cry again, now. What was it about this day? It seemed that hiding around every corner was something that could jump out and make her cry.

'Stop what? I didn't do anything!'

'Stop trying to fix me up with a man I don't even know.'

'I didn't! I didn't do anything!' Grace shouted, fighting hard with the tears. 'I just asked you what you thought about him. I would've asked you the same thing about that other neighbor, the spooky lady, only she didn't even stay long enough for you to meet her. Geez, Rayleen. I don't know what you're all upset about. He just likes you. What's so terrible about that? I didn't *tell* him to like you. He just *does*. It was all his idea.'

Rayleen set a sandwich on a paper plate in front of Grace, calmly, and without saying anything about anything.

Grace stared at it for a minute, noticing that she had been hungrier back when the sandwich idea first came up.

'Can I take my sandwich over to Billy's and eat it? It's nicer over there.'

'You can do anything you want,' Rayleen said, without much feeling.

Grace stopped at the door and looked back at Rayleen, who was washing the knife in the sink. Rayleen didn't look up or look back at Grace.

'You didn't used to be this grouchy,' Grace said, congratulating herself on what a brave thing it was to say.

'You didn't used to get all up in my private stuff,' Rayleen answered, still without looking up. 'Could be some connection there.'

'Cats don't like peanut butter and jelly sandwiches,' Grace told Mr Lafferty the Girl Cat.

It didn't seem to make much difference, though, because this particular cat was chewing and swallowing a piece of peanut butter and jelly sandwich all the time Grace was pointing that out.

'Rayleen is in a really sucky mood,' she said, this time to Billy.

'Yeah, I noticed that,' he said. 'What's up with that?'

'Not sure. I think it has something to do with Jesse. I don't think she likes him back.'

'Oh.'

'I just thought it would be . . . I mean, he likes her, and he's nice . . . and then at least one of you guys wouldn't have to be alone. You know. Like, one down, the rest of you to go.'

'I think it takes more than that for two people to get together.'

'What does it take?'

'I haven't the vaguest idea. I don't think anyone does. If

you ever figure that out, write a book about it. You'll be rich and famous overnight.'

'You're so weird, Billy.'

'Hey. Something I've been wanting to talk to you about. Here, hand me the cat, OK? This will be easier to say if I'm holding the cat.'

'Why?'

'I don't know. She just calms me down.'

'OK, whatever.'

Grace passed Mr Lafferty the Girl Cat to Billy, noticing that the cat was still trying to lick the last of the peanut butter off the roof of her mouth.

Billy pulled a big breath, so loudly that Grace could hear it.

'Tomorrow . . . when you go to school . . .'

'Tomorrow's Sunday.'

'Oh. Right. Monday, when you go to school . . . I thought I might try walking just a little tiny bit of the way with you and Rayleen.'

Grace opened her mouth to shriek, but Billy held up a hand to stop her. And he seemed firm about it. Much more than normal Billy-firm. He didn't want to hear any feedback.

'Don't say anything,' he said, 'because if you get all excited about this, then I'll just get more scared.'

Grace held still, against all of her impulses, for what seemed like an impossible length of time. Then, when she spoke, she was smart enough to whisper. Really whisper.

'Does this mean you're coming to my school?'

'One thing at a time, baby girl. One thing at a time.'

She threw herself at him, causing the cat to scoot away, and hugged him tightly around his neck.

'I knew you would,' she whispered, even more reverently. 'I knew you would say you couldn't, and it would really seem like you couldn't, but then when it came right down to it, I knew you would.'

'I only said I was going to walk part of the way to school with you on Monday.'

'Right,' Grace said, sitting back on her heels. 'Got it.'

'And you can't push me, and you can't judge me. Because, the first day, I might not get much farther than the front stairs.'

Grace could feel her own eyebrows scoot up.

'You're gonna do it every day?'

'Well,' Billy said, and then paused for a weirdly long time. 'I have to practice.'

'Is that why you came to Rayleen's today? To practice?'

'Well. Yeah. Partly. That and the fact that I didn't want the new neighbor guy to think I was a complete and utter freak.'

'What's so special about Jesse? What about the rest of us? What about what *we* think?'

'Oh, *please*. It's way too late for you guys. You already know I'm a complete and utter freak.'

'That's true,' Grace said. Then, after she'd thought the comment over, 'No offense.'

'None taken,' Billy said.

Billy

In a spectacular stroke of luck, when Jesse knocked on Billy's door the following evening, Billy was refining the choreography of Grace's school dance. Which meant he was dressed in his dance pants and a soft, oversized light blue sweater. And he was even wearing shoes.

Maybe our luck is changing, Billy thought, but not out loud.

He opened the door to find his handsome new neighbor standing with a shiny smile on his face, a bottle of red wine in one hand, and two wine glasses, held by their stems, in the other.

It filled Billy with an odd and hugely unfamiliar feeling. It was good, nonetheless. Though he couldn't have found the words in that moment, it was a sense of rightness. This is how life should go. You should be nicely dressed in your home when a gentleman knocks on the door to visit you, and he should be holding wine and smiling. And maybe he should say something like, 'Is it OK? Because I really should have called first.' And then you can say something like, 'Not at all. Do come in. I was just working on some choreography.'

Heaven-like, yet so completely forgotten. Such an ancient piece of history.

'How do you feel about neighbors who drop by unannounced?' Jesse asked, still smiling. 'Mild irritation? Irrational hatred? Homicidal rage?'

'Not at all. Do come in. I was just working on some choreography.'

Amazing. It was almost akin to a life.

'What are you choreographing?' Jesse asked, settling himself on Billy's couch. He set the bottle of wine and the glasses on the table. 'I wasn't sure if you'd have wine glasses. I didn't want to assume you would. Then again, I didn't want to assume you wouldn't. I wrestled with myself a lot about that.'

'I'm working on that dance for Grace to perform at her school.'

Billy stepped smoothly, aware of being witnessed, into his kitchen. He opened the cupboard and took down two of his own wine glasses. They were hand-blown, insanely fragile, with unique stems, no two quite identical. Syncopated, Billy thought. Syncopated for the more sophisticated.

He carried them back into the living room and set them on the coffee table in front of Jesse, who properly admired them.

'What about a corkscrew?'

Billy felt his face flush red. Right up to that moment, he'd been living the dream. Caught up in that image of 'this is my life, and it's just like everybody else's life'. Of course he had lovely wine glasses. Who doesn't, save a barbarian? But he had no corkscrew. So now Jesse knew he never used the glasses.

He didn't answer the question. But, apparently, he didn't have to. His red face and his silence had given him away.

'Next best thing,' Jesse said, standing and digging a hand down into his jeans pocket. He was wearing lightly faded blue jeans with a white button-down shirt and a tie. A tie! It made Billy proud that someone would put on a tie to come visit him. 'Swiss Army knife.'

'Were you a Boy Scout?'

'How did you know?'

'I was only kidding. Actually.'

'I *was*, though. I really was a Boy Scout. In fact, I pushed it all the way to Eagle Scout. You?'

Billy laughed. Blushed. 'Not nearly. Not even. I wasn't the scouting type. Camping is not my style. It has bugs.'

'It does indeed,' Jesse said, his words followed by the pop of the cork coming free. He held it up as if it were prize game he'd just shot. 'And bears. And mosquito bites itch unmercifully. Tell me about Grace and dancing. In fact, tell me about Grace in general. What's going on between that girl and her mother?'

'Oh,' Billy said. 'That.'

He sat on the couch, a foot or so from Jesse's knee, and accepted a glass of wine. It stirred something in him to hold the insubstantial glass by its stem. He took a sip of Jesse's wine, feeling the light warmth of it settle into his stomach. So many memories.

'This is lovely,' he said.

'Glad you like it. Had to make up somehow for my rudeness. Barging in like this with no invitation. And I don't know what you would normally drink.'

'Water,' Billy said, and it made his guest laugh. 'I would

normally drink water. For budgetary reasons,' he added, so Jesse would not think he was a barbarian. 'So, Grace. Her mom has a drug problem. As best I can figure, she had a couple of years in recovery and then fell off the wagon in a big way.'

'So who takes care of Grace?'

'We all do. Rayleen takes her to school, and Felipe picks her up and walks her home, and then she stays with me until Rayleen gets home from work, and then she's with Rayleen all evening and all night.'

Billy thought he saw a slight change in his guest on that last sentence, a brief flicker in Jesse's ever-present smile. Nothing worrisome. More as though a thought had pulled him briefly out of the conversation.

'Mrs Hinman upstairs even makes clothes for Grace on her sewing machine,' Billy added.

Jesse reached up and loosened his tie slightly.

'That's unusual,' he said.

'I suppose it is, in a place like this.'

'A place like what?'

'Well. You know.'

'Poor and run-down, you mean? No, I think it's unusual anywhere. But maybe a little *less* so in a place like this. The people with the least to give always give the most. Haven't you noticed that?'

'Hmm,' Billy said, because he did not want to admit that he hadn't spent enough time around actual human beings to gather many observations.

Mr Lafferty the Girl Cat sauntered into the room and rubbed against Jesse's legs. Jesse reached down and scratched the cat behind her ears.

'So these are all you?' Jesse asked.

At first Billy had no idea what Jesse was referring to. Then he realized Jesse was looking at his photos.

'Oh. Yes. That. My past life.'

'What kind of dancing?'

'Oh, you name it. Classical. Tap. Modern. Jazz. Even some ballet.'

'What made you leave it all behind?' Before Billy could even answer, though, Jesse said, 'No, sorry. Never mind. Too soon. That's for about two bottles of wine down the road, isn't it?'

'If not ten,' Billy said.

They sipped for a few moments in silence. In fact, it was so quiet that Billy was aware of the sound of Mr Lafferty the Girl Cat's purring. Meanwhile Billy dove down inside himself, chasing an elusive . . . something. There was something familiar about this. About Jesse, or drinking wine with Jesse, or the way he loosened his tie. Not that he thought he'd ever met Jesse before. It was not that kind of familiarity. But what kind was it? No matter how hard he chased it, it always managed to turn a corner and disappear, like the name of an actor that's just at the tip of your tongue.

'So what's the cat's name?' Jesse asked, startling him.

Billy wondered if he'd jumped enough to expose his pathologically flimsy nerves.

He laughed. 'I'm not sure you even want to know. First, before I tell you that, I have to tell you she's really not my cat. She's Grace's cat. And Grace named her.'

'Ah. Got it. I promise to take that into account.'

'Mr Lafferty the Girl Cat.'

'The whole thing?'

'Yes. The whole thing. It started out as just Mr Lafferty.

But then that got too confusing because there used to be a person by that name. So then she changed it to Mr Lafferty the Cat.'

'And then she found out it wasn't a boy cat.'

'Nice to know you're following along.'

'Wait a sec. Isn't Mr Lafferty your neighbor who killed himself in my apartment upstairs?'

'The one and only. This used to be his cat.'

Jesse set down his wine glass and picked up the cat. He held her under her arms, looking right into her face. The cat dangled amiably, still purring.

'So. Mr Lafferty the Girl Cat,' he said, addressing her earnestly. 'I do believe you have a story to tell. Care to talk about it?' After a silence, Jesse held the cat snugly to his chest. 'That reminds me,' he said, this time to Billy. 'I wanted to invite you to come to my apartment for the smudging ceremony. We're going to have a talk with whatever's left over of this Mr Lafferty. The person,' he added quickly, looking down at the cat. 'See if we can't make some kind of peace. The more neighbors who're willing to come, the better. After all. You knew him. I didn't. What was he like?'

'He was horrible. He was a bully. And a bigot. But he liked Grace a lot.'

'Good. I'll see if I can get Grace to come. There should be somebody there who isn't holding any hard feelings about him. I know you're not big on going out, I get that—'

'I'll come,' Billy said quickly. 'I can do that.'

Billy looked down at his wine glass, and, to his surprise, saw there was barely a sip left. When had he drunk it? He hadn't even been aware. But, now that he'd noticed it, he felt that old familiar feeling creep into his muscles. The warm tingling. It was just one glass of wine. But he had barely eaten. And he hadn't had wine in more than a decade.

He sat still a moment, watching Jesse pet the cat, and chasing that feeling again. Something ancient yet familiar. But why did it keep evading him?

'Oh, you need a refill, neighbor,' Jesse said.

He leaned forward, and the cat jumped off his lap and up on to Billy's. Jesse had to lean across Billy to some degree to fill his glass, which brought him closer. His blue-jeaned knee just barely brushed Billy's dance pants. And he smelled good. Fresh. A scent that could have been a hint of cologne, or maybe just his laundry detergent, or it could have been the way Jesse smelled all on his own.

Billy swallowed hard and grabbed on to the feeling that had evaded him.

Of course. Of course.

Attraction of the heart. Nothing base, though. Not that crass, purely physical attraction, but rather one of those romantic admirations that make your heart swell painfully. The kind that make all the colors in the world suddenly brighter, and have you smiling at strangers, and sending wishes of joy to people you hadn't noticed a moment before. Like love, only newer and less fully formed.

No wonder it took time to pin down. Now *that* was an ancient memory. No wonder he'd had a hard time recognizing it.

'There,' Jesse said, and sat back. He looked straight into Billy's eyes. 'Better.'

Billy glanced away and drank half the wine in one long gulp.

'I hate to have you thinking I came down here with any ulterior motives,' Jesse said, clearly changing the direction of events. 'I really just want to get to know my neighbors. But, while I'm here, I *was* hoping to ask you a couple of questions about Rayleen. If that doesn't seem too rude.'

A soft, wiggly line of pain etched its way down between Billy's ribs and settled in a spot between his stomach and groin. He stared into his wine glass for a moment, then drained it in one more long gulp.

It's not that he had ever thought otherwise. He wasn't surprised. It wasn't that. Still, there was something pathetic in that moment.

And that, Billy thought, is our life. Not that other lovely thing, where we answer the door in a nice outfit and tell the handsome man with the bottle of wine that we're happy to take a break from our choreography to visit. Nice try, he thought. No, *this* is our life. The one in which we realize we might be falling in love a split second before the beloved asks if we'll help fix him up with someone else.

Yeah. That one.

'You OK?' Jesse asked.

'Yes. Fine.'

'I just thought . . . well . . . you know her.'

'Yes and no,' Billy said. 'I do like Rayleen a lot. But just the other day Grace and I were talking about all the things we don't know about her.'

'You still know her better than I do.'

'True.'

'Maybe she just doesn't like me.'

'Don't be silly,' Billy said. 'How could anybody not like you?'

Then he flushed, and probably reddened, and looked down into his glass to have someplace to look.

'You're empty again,' Jesse said.

'I am.'

Billy held his glass out as far as his arm would reach. So Jesse could fill it without leaning in.

'Seems to me there's something very special about her,' Jesse said. 'But don't get me wrong. I'm not a stalker. If she's not interested, I don't intend to push. There's just a hint of something mixed in her signal. I think. I suppose I could be seeing what I want to see. I could be wrong. It's happened before.'

Billy breathed in deeply. He realized, in that instant, that he had a chance to potentially draw those two together. Maybe. Eventually. Or, with a few words, he could drive them apart. Definitely. Right now. For ever. All that power rested with him.

'I think there's some pain from her past,' Billy said. 'I shouldn't even talk about it, because I don't know. But she's an unusually good person. If I were you, I'd give her more time.'

Jesse reached over and patted Billy's knee, causing his whole body and brain to go numb as a style of evasion.

'Thank you, neighbor. I'll let you get back to what you were doing. When I've invited the other neighbors, I'll let you know when the smudging ceremony is set to take place. Then I'll offer something more like a formal invitation.'

'You don't have to go,' Billy wanted to say. That, or the more pathetically direct, 'Stay and talk to me.' But all he said was, 'Don't forget your wine glasses. And your Swiss Army corkscrew.'

Jesse laughed as he gathered them up.

'I had a sense about you,' he said. 'I'm a good judge of people. And you're what I call "good people". I knew that when I first laid eyes on you.'

Billy rose and walked him to the door. All three or four steps of the way. He said nothing.

'Thanks,' Jesse said, his voice soft. 'It meant a lot to me, what you said. More than you know.'

Then, before Billy could react, Jesse stepped in and embraced him. Billy stood stiffly, unable to even raise his arms to hug back.

'Back to your choreography. After all, what's more important than Grace's big performance? Maybe I'll go. Is everybody going?'

'I haven't asked everybody. *I'm* going to be there.'

As if it were a completely possible thing. As if he weren't out of his mind in even suggesting such a ridiculously unlikely event.

'Maybe I'll go,' Jesse said.

Then he let himself out.

'Goodnight, Billy,' he said, from two steps down the hall.

Billy opened his mouth to answer, but no words flowed. Apparently there were none left inside. So instead he just raised one hand in a weak, pathetic little wave.

Billy lay awake all night. Never closed his eyes once. Which is likely the only reason he received no visit from the wings.

*   *   *

'Don't hold my hand *too* tightly,' Billy said.

'Why not?' Grace asked. 'I'm the only thing keeping you from running away.'

Billy felt Rayleen take his other hand and squeeze it gently.

'Not quite,' she told Grace. 'I've got him, too.'

They stood in the hall, staring at the front door of the building. Through the glass inset of the door and out into the street. The street!

Billy was dressed in jeans and ridiculously white tennis shoes. He'd had them for a decade, but had never worn them. Not even in the house. Even the soles were still a perfectly untouched white, like a fresh snowfall before anybody wakes up to tramp around in it. He looked down at them disapprovingly, then out at the street again.

Billy felt something rise from his chest and into his throat, and he tried to swallow it back down. But, whatever it was, it remained unaffected by swallowing.

Rayleen asked, 'Got your keys?'

Her voice sounded tinny, with a slight echo. Far away. As if Billy were drifting away from the moment. Which he supposed he was.

'Of course I've got my keys. I only checked my pocket six times. God. Can you imagine what a disaster that would be? If I went outside and then got locked out?'

'Just checking,' Rayleen said. 'Ready?'

'Absolutely not.'

'Seriously? You're not going?'

'I didn't say I wasn't going. I said I wasn't ready. And I never will be. So let's just hurry up and do this thing before I change my mind.'

Rayleen swung the door inward, and a blast of morning air hit Billy in the face.

It reminded him of red wine. Scary. Distantly familiar. Too long forgotten. Nice.

Together, almost as one entity, they stepped out on to the stoop.

'You OK?' Grace asked, peering up at his face.

But Billy's throat had tightened and his chest had constricted, so it would have been impossible to answer. Instead he gestured forward with his chin.

They stepped out to the stairs and began to descend.

Five concrete steps. Only five. Billy began to calculate how many years it had been since he'd climbed them, either up or down, but he soon realized the answer wouldn't serve him well, and so changed the subject in his brain.

Over his head, he heard a bird chirping an excited song in a canopy of trees.

'They still have birds in LA?' he attempted to ask, but no sound emerged.

He tried to think, to remember. If birds sang in the trees outside his apartment, he would have heard them from inside. Had he? He couldn't remember positively, but he didn't think he had. Did that mean he was now alive in a way he had not been until this very moment?

Duh, as Grace would say.

He whipped his head around to see his building, now three buildings down the street from him. He had walked outside, on to the street, and three buildings away while pondering songbirds. But, now that he saw it back there, looking so distant, the panic found him, caught him, knocked the wind out of him. It felt like a vise crushing his chest. His face felt cold, yet he could feel beads of sweat break out on his brow.

He stopped dead.

Rayleen stopped with him, but Grace walked a couple more steps, hit the end of his arm and bounced back.

'What?' she asked.

But Billy couldn't speak.

'You need to go back?'

'Are you OK?' Rayleen asked.

He shook his head, and found the movement weirdly unsettling. As if he were only barely balanced, and any sudden moves could send him flying.

'You can go back,' Rayleen said. 'If you need to.'

'Just a little more, Billy,' Grace whined. 'Please? Just down to the corner.'

Billy shook his head again. More carefully this time.

'OK,' Grace said. 'Well, that's OK. You did good for your first time.'

They both let go of his hands at exactly the same time, apparently not thinking he might be a helium balloon, and they might be the only ballast pinning him to the earth. Without the warmth of their hands to ground him, standing on the street three doors down from the safety of his home was unimaginable. What had he been thinking?

He began to run.

It should only have taken a few seconds to reach his own front door again, but instead time stretched out, betraying him. He told himself it could only be an illusion, but it was such a vivid illusion, and so extreme. Still, in what seemed like ten or fifteen minutes, he arrived back at the front door of the building, twisted the knob violently, and tried to push his way through. Instead he bounced off again.

He tried again. It was locked.

A flare of panic struck him, a reaction similar to throwing a bucketful of grease on to a fire that had already been burning well enough to overcome him.

He steadied himself, and pulled in a big, manual breath.

'This door doesn't lock,' he said out loud, surprised by the return of speech. He must have been doing a good job of calming himself. 'We're just not turning the knob correctly.'

He tried the knob again. No, he realized. There's really only one correct method for turning a knob. And this door was locked.

He thought about trying to catch up with Rayleen and Grace, but that would involve moving in the wrong direction. He looked for them, to see if they were close enough to hear him if he yelled. But they were nowhere. They were gone. They must have turned a corner, but Billy didn't know which corner, or which way they would have turned.

The only way out of this would require getting the attention of one of his neighbors inside.

Not Jesse, he thought.

He pounded hard on the glass of the door with the backs of both fists at once.

'Felipe! I'm locked out! Can you come open the door?'

He waited. Nothing.

He looked up at the second floor. Was it Felipe's apartment that faced the street, the one whose windows he could see from the stoop? Or was that Jesse's? He didn't know, because he had never been upstairs.

'Mrs Hinman!' he screamed.

A few desperate seconds later he saw the third floor window pop open, and Mrs Hinman's head poke out.

'My goodness,' she said. 'What on earth is all that shouting about?'

'I'm locked out,' Billy said, and hearing his own words out loud forced a few hot tears to flow. He couldn't hold them in, no matter how hard he tried.

'Well, my goodness. There's no need to make such a fuss about it. Why didn't you take your key?'

'I did! I did take my key! To my apartment! This front door doesn't lock!'

'Well, of course it does, dear, or you wouldn't be locked out.'

'Since when? Since when does this front door lock?'

'Oh, ten years at least.'

Billy sat down hard on the concrete stoop, his back up against the door. He couldn't see Mrs Hinman from that position, which seemed like an improvement.

'Or at least eight or nine,' he heard her say.

All the fight had gone out of him. He pressed his back harder against the door, feeling drained and sick. He still needed to get in, but he only had just so much energy left to do anything about it.

'Can you come down and let me in?' he called, not sure if his volume would even reach her.

'I suppose I could, though the stairs are awfully hard on my knees.'

'Can you please hurry?'

'Now why on earth would you ask me to hurry when I just told you the stairs are hard on my knees?'

Billy squeezed his eyes closed, semi-resigned to being

stuck in hell. This is what happens when you go out. This or something else uncontrollable. You leave your safe environment and things just happen, and then what do you do? Well, there's really not much you can do. You're stuck. It's what you get.

The door behind Billy opened in suddenly, spilling him on to his back in the hallway. He looked up to see Jesse standing over him.

'You OK, neighbor?'

Damn.

'I got locked out,' he said, sounding pathetically child-like. Damn it. Damn it. Damn it. There were tears on his face, he was drowning in an obvious state of paralyzing panic, and his sneakers were too white. It was not the way he wanted to be seen. Damn. 'I went outside, and I didn't know they'd put a lock on this outside door, and I got locked out.'

Jesse reached a hand down to help him up.

Billy looked at the extended hand for too long before taking it. But in time he did bring himself to take it, and be helped to his feet. He could feel his own hand trembling as Jesse pulled on it, and he knew Jesse could feel it, too.

'You went out, though,' Jesse said. 'That was good.'

Oh, God. He knows. He knows everything.

'I have to practice,' Billy said in a shaky voice.

They walked down the hall together, toward Billy's apartment door. Jesse had a hand on Billy's shoulder. Apparently Jesse was smart enough to know a helium balloon when he saw one. He knew better than to let go.

Billy dug his keys out of his pocket with trembling hands and opened his door.

As he stepped back inside his familiar cocoon, every-thing drained away. Everything. His panic. His energy. His ability to think. Everything. It left him empty and hollow enough to echo, like a shell that washes up on the beach when the organism has vacated it through death.

He sat down hard on the couch and looked up at Jesse with dull eyes.

'I thought it was interesting,' Jesse said, 'when you said you were going to Grace's dance recital. I thought, Wow. If you're agoraphobic, that's a big statement to make.'

All is lost, Billy thought, though fortunately the thought was backed with little emotion. Jesse knows everything.

'I thought I could practice,' Billy said in barely over a whisper.

'You can,' Jesse said, sitting too close to him on the couch.

'Today was a glorious example.'

'Tomorrow will be better, because I'll make you a copy of the key to the outside door.'

The cat came meowing around, and Billy picked her up and held her tightly, enjoying her warmth, the softness of her fur, and the rumble of her purring. Unfortunately, though, it forced a few more tears to slip past the guards. But it was too late, anyway. It was too late to hide who he was from Jesse.

'I don't think one day will be time enough to recover.'

'OK. *Day after* tomorrow.'

'I don't think I can,' Billy said, his face buried in cat fur.

'Want some help?'

Billy looked up, half aware of a cat hair in his eye. 'What kind of help?'

'Want me to come along? It's better if you're not alone, right?'

'I wasn't alone. Actually. I was walking to school with Rayleen and Grace. But then I had to go back, and they kept walking.'

'So if I came along, I could make sure you got back OK.'

It was too much, really. It was simply all too much. On the one hand, it brought a swell of elation to think of taking a walk with Jesse every morning. But like that? With Jesse as a nursemaid to make sure he got home without falling apart? It was simply too many emotions at once, and Billy had no capacity left to process them.

'I'm so ashamed,' Billy said.

'Why? Why should you be ashamed? I had an uncle who had agoraphobia and a panic disorder. He never tried to go out. The whole time I knew him. You tried.'

'I tried,' Billy said, parroting emptily. 'I failed.'

'Big deal,' Jesse said. 'So what? Keep trying.'

Grace

Billy held Grace's hand as they walked up the stairs to Jesse's.

He was dressed nicely, Billy, in a white sweater and jeans, and Rayleen had given him a haircut, and then she'd blow-dried his hair so it looked soft and fluffy and shiny. He looked like a regular person, just like anybody else. And, also, he was walking up the stairs to Jesse's, just like anybody else. Maybe that little walk out of doors on Monday had done him good. Then again, four more school days had gone by, and Billy had ignored them all and stayed in. So, then again, maybe not.

'You're doing good going upstairs,' Grace said, because her first-grade teacher had taught her that you should always say something positive and nice about somebody before you criticize.

'Thanks,' he said. He was never too talky outside his own apartment.

'But you *are* going to try walking to my school again, right?'

'Oh,' Billy said. As if she were just waking him up in the

morning. 'Oh. Right. That. Yeah. Tomorrow. Tomorrow I will.'

'Tomorrow's Sunday. You missed the whole rest of the week. You know this has to be Saturday, because if this wasn't Saturday, then this wouldn't be the first day everybody could come to the smudging meeting all at the same time. Did you really not know that?'

'I guess I was doing my best not to think about it,' he said.

Grace had been all set to argue with him, but then she didn't, because she thought that was a very honest answer.

By now they were standing in the upstairs hall in front of what used to be Mr Lafferty's apartment, and it made Grace's tummy nervous, because, the last few times she'd been here, it had been weird, even if the last time did end on a great note with the arrival of the cat. Billy's hand got a little tighter on hers, too, and she didn't think it could be for the same reason, but she didn't know what reason it could be.

'Jesse is going to come along next time we walk,' he said.

'Why?'

'For moral support.'

'What's so immoral about it?'

'Not that kind of moral. Like morale. Like when you want someone's morale to be better, so you come along for moral support.'

'I have more trouble trying to understand you when you talk, Billy.'

'I know. It's a wonder you put up with me.'

'Yeah. OK. Fine. So bring Jesse. I like Jesse. Rayleen, though. Rayleen'll be pissed.'

'True,' Billy said. 'She will.'

The door flew open wide.

'Neighbors!' Jesse said.

Then he looked at Billy for a long time, and took hold of his shoulders, and turned him first one way, then the other. Like there were sides of Billy he just had to see.

'You cut your hair.'

'Rayleen cut it,' Billy said, sounding embarrassed.

'Looks nice. She did a nice job.'

'She kept saying she couldn't do it. Only Bella could do it. But I told her whatever she did would be better than leaving it the way it was. When I finally wore her down it turned out fine.'

'That's a lot of hair to lose after all those years.'

'Tell me about it. I feel weirdly light.'

'You should give it to that place—'

But Grace knew what he was going to say, so she jumped in and said it for him. 'That makes wigs for cancer people! Rayleen thought of that. She took his ponytail to work with her, so she could do that.'

'Should've known Rayleen would think of everything,' Jesse said.

The white sage made Grace's nose tickle, as though she might be about to sneeze. It was wrapped up into something like a stick, like the world's fattest cigar made out of sage leaves. But instead of being wrapped in one big solid leaf, like a cigar, it was wrapped in a criss-crossing of heavy blue and green threads that burned as the sage burned. Jesse held a lighter to the end of it for the longest time while Grace watched a curl of the smoke rise up to touch the ceiling of what had used to be Mr Lafferty's apartment.

Jesse had grouped them all around in a circle, with a

plate in the middle for the sage, if he needed to put it down. Next to the plate Jesse had set a copper bowl and a short, thick, carved wooden stick, both of which Grace had been watching, because she knew those two things fit into all this somewhere, but she didn't know where.

She looked around the circle, and around the apartment. Jesse didn't have a lot in the way of furniture, probably because he had come to LA on a plane, and was only staying a few months. But, even so, even without much stuff, the place was nice because he had all the drapes pulled back and the windows wide open. So there was light, and air. Nobody else's apartment had light and air. Grace knew they were afraid of unlocked doors, and each other, but what did they have against light and air?

Grace already felt she might miss Jesse some when he moved away again.

'Wait,' she said to Jesse. 'We can't start yet. Somebody's missing.'

She did a quick count in her head. Billy was here, and Jesse of course, and Rayleen, and Felipe, and of course Grace herself was here, too.

'Mrs Hinman! We have to wait for Mrs Hinman,' she said.

'She's not coming,' Jesse said. 'She says this is preposterous.'

'Oh,' Grace said, surprisingly disappointed that there should still be disagreements within the group. 'But it isn't. Preposterous. Right?'

'I guess it is if you think it is,' Jesse said.

It was one of those sentences that seemed to make sense to grown-ups, and Grace was wise enough not to question it.

Jesse put down his lighter and blew on the end of the sage stick, which glowed brightly red.

'The former Mr Lafferty,' Jesse said, like he was saying hello to him directly. Like Mr Lafferty was right here at the meeting, and not former at all. 'I didn't know you at all. These people I brought here today, they all did. They have some thoughts they want to get off their chests, I think. They feel like you were unkind to them, and I'm not saying you weren't. I see no reason they would lie. But now that I'm living here in your leftover energy, I want to tell them something they probably don't know – and maybe you didn't even know it, either. You were scared. Did you know you were mean because you were scared? Well, you were. I know what fear feels like, and that's what you left behind in this room. So we're going to clear this room of all the leftover fear, but we're going to remember just enough of it to remind us to live our lives and be less afraid. See there? Everything has a purpose, even if it's only a reminder of what not to do.'

Jesse stood in front of Billy, and Billy got this weird, shy smile on his face that Grace had never seen before, like he was embarrassed, but embarrassed in a way he sort of enjoyed. He also didn't look like he was just dying to run back to his own apartment, but maybe he was, and Grace just couldn't see it from the outside. Or maybe he wasn't, because maybe Jesse was giving him morale support.

Jesse blew on the end of the sage stick, sending a soft curl of smoke Billy's way. Jesse waved at the smoke with his hand so that it wafted all around Billy, from over his head to down below his knees. Billy didn't sneeze.

'I'm smudging each of you at the same time as the apartment,' Jesse said, 'in case there's any of his leftover energy in you. Which there probably is. Billy? Want to say anything to your former neighbor?'

Billy filled up his chest with air. It got big and puffed-out. Grace could see how big it got.

'Yes. I've decided I forgive you,' Billy said, and then looked surprised, almost as if somebody else had said it. He looked around a minute before saying anything more. 'I forgive you for yelling at me when all I did was look out the window at you, and I forgive you for all the terrible mean things you said when you came to my door that day. I really do. I'm not just saying that because I think I'm supposed to. All of a sudden I really do. You know why?' He looked around at different parts of the ceiling, like he was trying to decide which direction to talk in. 'Because I only had to deal with you twice, but you had to live with you every minute of every day, which is probably why you didn't live very long. So now I just feel lucky. And I feel bad for you. So, whatever you did or said to me, the hell with it. I'm seriously ready to let it go by.'

Billy brought his gaze down from the ceiling to Jesse, who smiled at him, and the smile made him get that weird shy look again.

Jesse could make people do things they never did, and be ways they'd never been before, Grace decided. Jesse was magic. Not magic magic, like more than just a real human person. Just better at making things happen than anybody else. At least, anybody else in Grace's world.

'Oh!' Grace said out loud, and everybody turned and looked at her. 'Sorry,' she said. 'Nothing. It was nothing. I just all of a sudden figured something out.'

Jesse wasn't afraid of everybody else. That was what she'd figured out. Grace had finally met somebody who wasn't afraid of people! That's what was so different about him. But she didn't say so out loud.

Meanwhile Jesse held out the little copper bowl on the palm of his hand and gave Billy the carved stick, and showed him how to hit the bowl one quick time on the side like it was a gong. Billy tried it, and this amazing tone filled the room, like a bell ringing out, high and clear, and lasting and lasting and lasting. It made something nice tingle inside Grace's middle.

Jesse moved on then, to Felipe, and smudged him with the little trails and curls of whitish smoke. Felipe looked serious, as though he had an important job to do.

'Well, I sort of thought I *didn't* forgive him,' Felipe said. 'Because it's hard to forgive somebody for hating you for such a bad reason. But maybe he was just scared of me, like Jesse says. Besides, if Billy will do it, I can try to do it.'

Felipe took the carved stick from Billy and hit the bowl, and the tone was much shorter and harder, and it hurt Grace's ears a little bit this time, but she still liked it.

Then Felipe handed the carved wooden stick to Grace.

Jesse blew on the sage again, and a cloud of smoke billowed out on to Grace and made her sneeze. It reminded her of Peter Lafferty, sneezing in this apartment because he was allergic to the cat. *Her* cat. It was already weird to think that Mr Lafferty the Girl Cat had ever been anybody else's cat besides hers.

'Bless you,' Jesse said.

'Thanks,' Grace replied. 'I sort of liked him OK. Not that I don't think he was mean. He was. But he did some nice stuff for me. So, at least somebody has something nice to say about you, Mr Lafferty. The person, I mean. At least it's not like you just died and nobody cares at all. Oh. And by the way. We're taking good care of the cat.'

Grace waited, expecting Rayleen to take her turn. But Jesse didn't move away. Just as she was starting to wonder why, Jesse held the bowl high on his palm.

'Oh. Right. Sorry.'

She gave it what she thought was a good hard tap with the stick, but it just made a pretty, but little, sound that faded away soon enough. Just the opposite of me, Grace thought. Quieter than you were expecting.

Jesse moved over then and stood in front of Rayleen, and looked right at her face. But Rayleen just kept looking at the glowing end of the tied-up sage. Jesse smudged her with waves of his hand in the smoke, but maybe for longer than anybody else. It seemed long to Grace.

'OK, that's good,' Rayleen said, but she didn't sound like she meant it was good. She sounded like she meant it was enough. 'I don't know a hell of a lot about forgiving people, to be real frank. I'm not set against it, I just haven't practiced much. I just more or less set things down and get on with it. I pretty much only came here for Grace's sake. And I can't stand here like Billy did and say I really mean it. But, like Felipe said, if Billy's willing to do it, I guess I can do it. Or at least I can try. He sure was an unhappy guy. I sure see Billy's point about that.'

She took the carved stick from Grace, and struck the bowl with the most enormous sound. It wobbled. It echoed. It hung around and around, and everybody just stood still and marveled at how long it took to fade. At least, Grace knew *she* marveled. And everybody else stood still, so she figured they marveled, too.

Grace wondered if Mrs Hinman could hear that last big tone from upstairs, and if it made her sorry she hadn't

come. After all, it sounded so beautiful, and not preposterous at all.

'We have to wait,' Grace said, hitching the straps of her
backpack higher on to her shoulders.

'For what?' Rayleen asked, sounding foggy.

Some mornings Rayleen could drink two or even three
cups of coffee and still sound like she'd just rolled out of
bed. Grace had noticed that. This seemed to be one
of those mornings.

'Billy is coming.'

'Oh. Good.'

A second later they heard footsteps trotting down the
stairs, and Jesse appeared, snapping his jacket as he jogged
along the hall. His scalp was shiny, like he'd just shaved it,
and his beard looked freshly trimmed.

'I'm ready,' he said.

'For what?' Rayleen asked.

Now she sounded a little defensive. And, also, Grace
noticed she ran her fingers through her hair to fluff it up
and straighten it out, which seemed weird. It did look
slightly on the uncombed side, which was unlike Rayleen,
but if she didn't mind Grace seeing it that way, and she
didn't like Jesse anyway, why fix it now?

'I'm going along,' Jesse said.

'Since when?'

'It's to help Billy,' Grace butted in to say. 'It's for morale
support for Billy.'

'Why aren't *we* moral support for Billy?' Rayleen asked.
'I thought that's why he went with *us*.'

Jesse walked up and stood close, maybe too close
for Rayleen's tastes, because she took a step backward.

'But that doesn't help if he can't make it all the way. Then you have to stay with Grace all the way to her school, and he comes home alone, and there's no one to make sure he doesn't get himself into some disaster like last time.'

Silence in the hallway. Grace wondered if Rayleen knew what disaster Billy had got into last time, which, if so, would still only make one of them who knew, at least so far.

'What happened last time?' Rayleen asked.

'You didn't know?'

Billy's voice. 'I didn't exactly tell them.'

Billy stepped out into the hallway. He was wearing a nice black sweatshirt and woven sandals and jeans, and looked the way people do when they're planning on relaxing, which Grace figured was at least worth trying for in Billy's case.

'Billy,' Rayleen said, like she was his mother and he was misbehaving. 'Why didn't you tell me something happened last time? What happened?'

'One. Because it was humiliating and I didn't want to talk about it. Two. I got locked out because I didn't know they'd put a lock on the front door since I first moved in. So Jesse's going to go with us and then walk me home. That's OK, isn't it?'

'Sure, whatever,' Rayleen said. 'Let's just go.'

So they did. But everything felt tense, and nobody said anything for blocks, except for Jesse, who was walking a couple of steps behind them with Billy, saying quiet things to Billy to calm him down, like the kinds of things people in Western movies say to their horses when they want them not to be so skittish, so nobody gets thrown.

Grace kept looking back, and Billy kept being back there, which was sort of a miracle all in itself.

'Jesse is magic,' Grace whispered, being sure Rayleen wouldn't hear.

'What did you say?' Rayleen muttered, still sounding asleep.

'Nothing.'

Grace turned again to see Jesse walking with one hand at the base of Billy's neck in the back. Like he was giving him a little mini-massage. It was interesting to watch, so Grace walked backwards a few steps and watched them.

'Loosen,' she heard Jesse say. 'Try to loosen up all through here.' Then he used both his hands on Billy's shoulders, feeling and rubbing. 'And all through here. Try to let all that go. OK, that's good, but I think you forgot to breathe again.'

Billy breathed in so hard Grace could hear the air going in.

'Better,' Jesse said, 'but if you can manage it, try for steadier. Not so feast and famine.'

Whatever that means, Grace thought. Just what she needed was two people who talked like Billy, so you couldn't understand a word they said.

She looked past them to see that they were three blocks away from home already.

'Billy!' she squealed. 'You came so far!'

Billy's eyes shot open wide, and he tried to turn his head, but Jesse used his hand at the back of Billy's head to keep him turned forward.

'No,' Jesse said, 'don't look back. It's like looking down when you're on a tightrope. Take another step forward. Keep concentrating on the step you're about to take.

Doesn't matter what's ahead or behind. Let it be all about the step you're on now.'

Rayleen put a hand on Grace's shoulder and turned her back around.

'They're doing fine,' Rayleen said, 'and besides, I don't want you to trip.'

So Grace just looked forward and walked forward, but she kept her ears tuned to Billy and Jesse in back of them. She listened to everything Jesse said, but never spoke another word to them, because she didn't want to be the one who made Billy look back and get scared.

What seemed like no more than two minutes later, Grace looked up and saw the school. They were on the same block as her school! She stopped and whipped around, and they were still back there. Billy was still back there!

'Billy, you did it!' she screamed. 'You walked to my school!'

Grace ran to him and hugged him around the waist.

'I have to go home now,' he said in a hoarse whisper, like he'd gotten laryngitis and lost his voice just since they'd started walking.

'You did so good, though!'

Grace felt Billy kiss the top of her head. Then he turned and ran. Flat-out ran. Grace had no idea Billy could run so fast. Must have been all that dancing he'd done for most of his life.

Jesse raised his hand in a little wave. 'Sorry I can't wait and walk back with you, Rayleen.' Then he took off after Billy.

'Jesse, you're magic!' Grace called after him.

She wasn't sure whether he'd heard her or not. But, after

it was way too late to take it back and not say it, Grace realized that Rayleen had definitely heard.

Grace stood a moment, extra close to Rayleen, and watched them run.

Then she said, 'I think I finally really believe it now. That Billy's coming to my school to watch me dance. It's like I thought I believed it before, only now I really do, and now I know that before I sort of really *didn't*, even though I thought I did. Do you really not like him? Because everybody else thinks he's great.'

'Are you kidding? I love Billy.' Then, before Grace could even straighten out Rayleen's thinking, she said, 'Oh. Jesse.'

'I don't mean it to be getting all up in your business. I just wondered. Because it seems like it would be hard not to like him.'

Rayleen sighed. Grace waited.

'He seems like a nice enough guy,' she said. 'I just don't want to be fixed up with anybody. Not even somebody nice.'

'I wasn't,' Grace shouted, stepping back and throwing both hands out, defensively, like a shield.

'I know,' Rayleen said. 'I'm sorry. I shouldn't have been so grouchy about it the other day. I apologize.'

'Yeah, you were really grouchy,' Grace said.

'Have you ever done anything wrong?'

'Um. Yeah. Lots.'

'Wouldn't you want someone to accept your apology?'

'Yeah. Got it. OK. I accept your apology. It hurt my feelings, though.'

Rayleen reached down and picked Grace up by her underarms for a hug, so that they were the same height, except that Grace's feet dangled and didn't touch the ground.

'I'm sorry I hurt your feelings,' she said. Then she kissed Grace on the cheek and set her down. 'Have a good day at school.'

Then Grace had to wipe a couple of stray tears out of her eyes, quick, before anyone from school could see.

Billy

Billy locked himself safely back into his apartment, feeling as though he'd run at least three marathons in as many days, without benefit of one single night's sleep in-between.

He washed his face, nursing the staticky exhaustion in his midsection. He changed back into his pajamas, pulled all the curtains closed, and tucked himself into bed, prepared to sleep the day away.

Not ten minutes later he was startled by a pounding on his door.

It didn't only scare him because of its suddenness. It was troublesome because nobody pounded any more. Grace and Rayleen signal-knocked, Felipe knocked gently, Jesse knocked like a gentleman, Mr Lafferty was dead, and Mrs Hinman didn't come around. And Grace's mom was still loaded. At least, so far as he knew.

'Who is it?' he called, his voice embarrassingly tremulous. He had no energy left for . . . well, anything.

'Rayleen,' Rayleen's voice said through the door.

Billy walked to the door, unlocked it and opened it wide.

'No signal-knock today.'

'Oh. Sorry. Right. I guess I forgot. So, is he gone?'

'Is who gone? Oh. You mean Jesse.'

'You bet I mean Jesse.'

'He's up in his own apartment. Why?'

But Rayleen just stood there, not offering anything in the way of answers.

'Care to come in?' Billy asked.

She did.

'You seem upset,' he said, because somebody had to say something.

'Do you really think he did that because he cares about you?' she asked, finally, settling herself on his big stuffed armchair.

Billy wondered if she had forgotten she was allergic to cats, or if she was just too upset to trifle with such an issue.

'I do,' Billy said. 'Absolutely.'

'You don't think he might've come along as a way of getting to me?'

'No. I don't. Because when he first volunteered to help me, he had no idea I hadn't been going out by myself.'

'Oh,' Rayleen said.

Billy watched an uncomfortable shift take place in her. She'd come in angry, and that anger had been serving her well, and providing a safe place for her to rest. Billy could see that, and feel it. Now he'd snatched it away, like pulling the sheets out from under her in her sleep. It was hard to watch her struggle to regain momentum.

He sat down on the very edge of the couch.

Rayleen dropped her face into her hands.

'I hope it won't upset you, what I'm about to say,' he said. 'But I'm having a hard time understanding why

you're so bent out of shape about this. I mean, if you don't
want to date him, why don't you just say no?'

A long silence. Rayleen did not remove her face from her
hands.

Finally she said, 'But what if "no" is the wrong answer?'

'Ah,' Billy said, placing his hands on his knees and lever-
ing to his feet. 'I'll just make a pot of coffee.'

When he arrived back in his own living room with the two
mugs of coffee, all prepared to ask Rayleen what she took
in hers, he found her curled into his big easy chair with her
knees to her chest, her arms wrapped around her knees,
her face buried.

She was crying.

'Hey,' he said quietly, sitting on the ottoman near her
knees. 'Hey, hey. What's wrong? You're scaring me. Don't
scare me. Don't forget *I'm* supposed to be the emotional
one.'

Rayleen's face emerged and she smiled sadly. Just a hint
of a little smile. Her make-up was slaughtered, mascara
smeared on to her cheeks.

'You don't have the monopoly,' she said.

'No, but I still do it better than anybody else. Tell me
what's wrong.'

'I just have issues with men, is all. I'm not trusting. It's a
very old leftover from when I was nine and got myself
thrown into the foster-care system. And that's all I'm going
to say about that, because . . . well, because that's all I'm
going to say about that. I don't talk about that time.'

Billy could hear the hoarseness forming in her throat.
Maybe from crying, but probably not. Probably from the
cat. He wondered if he should remind her, the way she and

Grace were nice enough to remind him when he was so upset he didn't realize he was standing out in the hall. Oh, but that was in the old days, wasn't it? This morning he'd stood by Grace's school, though not for long.

He set Rayleen's mug on the arm of her chair.

He sat quietly for a moment, warming his hands on his coffee cup. Not because they were cold, but because his own coffee, with his own cream, in his own mug, hadn't changed. Wasn't even in the process of changing. So he stayed as close to it as possible.

'You get along fine with Felipe and me,' he said, knowing he had to say something.

'You and Felipe aren't trying to get any closer.'

'True.'

'I don't think I can do this.'

'So don't.'

'But I keep thinking about what Jesse said. About Lafferty. How we should use him as a reminder to be less afraid. And I keep thinking . . . oh, my God, can you imagine ending up like Lafferty?'

'You couldn't. Don't even stress about that. It couldn't happen. You're not that mean.'

'But I'm that shut off from everybody.'

'No. That's not true. You're not. Look what you're doing for Grace.'

Rayleen laughed ruefully, then sniffled. Billy jumped up and brought her a box of tissues.

'I guess what I meant is, I *was* that shut off. Until she came along. And now I'm in this sort of no-man's-land in-between. And it's really uncomfortable.'

'I hear you,' Billy said.

'Oh. Right,' Rayleen said. 'Right. You do know. I forgot.

Here I am thinking you have no idea how scary this is. But I guess you do. I guess you know it's about as scary for me as walking down to Grace's school is for you. God, Billy. What do I do? What would you do if it were you?'

Just for a split second, Billy allowed himself to step into the imaginary role of the lucky human about to date Jesse. Then he stepped out again, in self-defense.

'Well, I just walked down to Grace's school. Does that answer the question? Look. Don't make it so all-or-nothing. Don't try to decide whether to marry him. Just go out for coffee with him. Just go out with him once. You know. Have a conversation. No more for now.'

'Oh. Yeah. OK. I could do that. Huh?'

Billy sipped his coffee, calming the live wire in his chest that wanted him to be alone. So much strain for one day. He didn't answer, thinking she had answered herself.

'Oh, wait. No. I can't do that,' Rayleen nearly shouted, sounding relieved. 'I have Grace in the evenings.'

Billy cocked one eyebrow at her.

'Right. Like you couldn't leave her with me for three hours to go on a date.'

'Shit,' Rayleen said, and dropped her face back into her hands.

'My God, Rayleen, you're as bad as I am. Look, if I can walk down to Grace's school, you can go on one date with one very nice guy.'

She looked up from her hands.

'You know what? That's actually true.'

'And here's another thing to consider. Jesse's really good at calming terrified people.'

Rayleen laughed. It was a wonderful sound. Natural and unforced. Light, like something that could float halfway to the ceiling. Clear, like Jesse's singing bowl when you struck it.

She leaned forward and threw her arms around Billy and held him tightly. Too tightly, but he didn't complain.

'You're so damn sweet, Billy,' she said.

'Thanks,' he said. 'You do know you're in an apartment with a cat, right?'

'Oh, shit,' Rayleen said. 'What was I thinking? I thought it was just the crying. I have to go. Can I take the coffee? I could use it. I'll bring the cup back.'

She kissed him on the cheek and hurried out.

Billy sighed and put himself to bed again.

He may or may not have dozed briefly. It was hard to tell.

Mrs Hinman came knocking at about half past noon.

It was a small knock, not much greater in volume than a mouse inside a wall. But she spoke to him through the door at the same time. Because she's a kindred spirit, Billy thought. She'd hate it just as much if someone came to *her* door unannounced.

'It's just Mrs Hinman from upstairs,' she said.

Billy sighed, rose, and pulled on his robe. He opened the door for her.

'Oh, I'm sorry,' she said. 'Did I wake you from a nap? My apologies. So long as you're up now, may I come in?'

I'm sensing an agenda, Billy thought. It just isn't natural for Mrs Hinman to seek out my company. And humbly, at that. Something must be up.

'Please do,' he said, standing back and opening the door widely.

It didn't pay to argue, he'd decided. You can bemoan the fact that your once-peaceful sanctuary has turned into an intersection on a busy human freeway, but there isn't much to be done. Just sigh, open the door, and let them talk until they seem done. It's easier that way.

Mrs Hinman limped into his living room carrying a folded garment of some sort.

Billy pointed to the chair, but she did not take the suggestion.

'I made this for Grace,' she said, unfolding the garment.

It appeared to be a wrap-around tunic, in Grace's favorite blue, with a sash to tie it around her waist.

'She'll like that,' Billy said.

'Do you really think so? Oh, I certainly hope . . . She didn't exactly pick it out. But it just seemed so . . . Grace. It can be worn as a dress, just by itself, or it can be worn over jeans, or especially I thought it might be nice if she made it into an outfit with tights. I thought it might be a good outfit for her dancing, maybe even something she could wear for her big performance, though I don't know. Maybe she has to wear a special costume for that. Do you know? Has she talked that over with you?'

'Sorry, no,' Billy said. 'She only talks to me about the dance aspects.'

'I'm knitting her a sweater, too, to take the place of that old one she wears nearly every day. It's in terrible condition. I don't know if you've noticed.'

'Hard not to notice,' Billy said. 'You can see her elbows right through it.'

A silence fell, during which Billy noted that she was still not sitting down, nor was she telling him why she was telling him all this.

'Why don't you bring it by after she's home from school?'

'Well, all right,' she said. 'I suppose I could.'

But she didn't move toward the door.

Just as the silence was becoming unbearably awkward, she said, 'I was hoping to have a little talk with you.'

'Got it,' Billy said. 'Have a seat. Would you like me to put on a pot of coffee?'

'Oh, no. Not for me, thank you. I go to bed very early. If I drink coffee after noon, it just keeps me awake.'

She still did not sit down.

'Have a seat, at least,' Billy said, feeling the strain of their combined discomfort.

'Hmm,' she said. 'I have a bit of an issue with that. My knees are going out on me. And sometimes when I sit down, it's very difficult and awkward to get up again.'

'I'd be more than happy to give you a hand up,' he said.

'Oh. All right,' she said, heading tentatively for his sofa. 'I don't much like to ask for help. I'm not very good at it. But I guess I didn't ask in this case. You volunteered, didn't you?'

She eased herself down carefully, causing Billy to wince from the conveyed sense of her pain. He sat on the other end of the couch.

'I wanted to ask you,' she said, 'about all your years of not going outside. I feel I need to understand that better.'

Billy instinctively sat back on the couch to distance himself from her. The cat came ambling into the room, and Mrs Hinman recoiled.

'Oh, dear,' she said. 'Can you take him away? I don't like cats at all.'

'She lives here, though,' Billy said, knowing, as it came

out of his mouth, that it sounded and felt more honest than his usual communications. He must have been too exhausted to guard that gate. 'I'll hold her, though, if that'll make you feel better.'

He snapped his fingers to the cat, and she came to him, and he scooped her up and pressed her to his chest.

'So, where were we?' Mrs Hinman asked, though Billy doubted she had forgotten. 'Oh, yes. About your not going out.'

'The thing is,' he said, 'that's more or less in the past. I'm working through that. I just went out this morning, in fact. I walked all the way down to Grace's school. That's ten blocks away.'

'Lovely,' she said. 'That's very good. But I still need to ask you about the time when you didn't go out at all.'

Billy took a deep breath, and geared up to do something he almost never did: speak rudely to someone.

'I think I'm going to choose not to talk about that,' he said. 'It's a little on the personal side, and it bothers me to be judged for something I've worked so hard to overcome. Now, if you'll excuse me . . .'

He rose to his feet, cat in one arm, and extended a hand to her.

'Please,' she said, purposely not looking at the hand. 'Please . . . let me try to ask this again. I've obviously made a mess of it, and offended you, and that was the last thing I wanted to do. Please let me say it again so you understand me better. My knees are going out, and I live up two flights of stairs. And one of these days pretty soon I just won't be able to get up and down them. Maybe I can do it for another year or two, or maybe it'll be the day after tomorrow. Probably closer to the latter, I'm afraid. And then, I've been thinking, what will I do? Will I die? I have to eat. How will I get food in to me? How will I get my mail, pay my bills? Take the trash out? And then I thought, well, that young man downstairs has been doing it for years, and he's still alive. So I thought you might be willing to give me some pointers. It's life or death for me, you see.'

Billy bent his knees and sat down on the couch again, closer to her this time.

'I'm not that young a man,' he said quietly. 'I'm thirty-seven.'

'That's young,' she said, more relaxed now. 'You just don't know how young it is. How do you get your groceries in?'

'I have them delivered. There are services in LA that will deliver anything to anybody. Trouble is, not all of them will come into neighborhoods like this. And even the ones that will, you have to pay them extra.'

'Sounds expensive.'

'It is. I have to eat a lot less to make up for it.'

'Oh, dear,' Mrs Hinman said. 'I'd hate to have to eat any less than I already do. I realize this is absolutely none of my business, and you're well within your rights to throw me out of here on my ear for asking . . .'

'My parents. My parents write me a small check every month. It goes into my bank account as a direct deposit.'

'Ah. So that answers two questions. Now I also know how you get out of going to the bank. I thought maybe you got one of those checks the government gives people who're too . . . nervous . . . to work.'

'I'm sure I'd qualify,' he said. 'But my parents have

spared me the indignity of having to find out. Or maybe it's their own indignity they're trying to avoid.'

'How do you take out your trash?'

'I tip the delivery men to do it.'

'Ah. But you must have needed the doctor.'

'No. I've been lucky. I've been healthy.'

'I'd need the doctor, though,' she said.

And Billy didn't – couldn't – argue. Instead he made a confession.

'It's not the doctor that'll get you. At least in my case. It's the dentist. I'm starting to get a little toothache. But I'm sure it'll get bigger. Even if you could find a doctor who makes house calls in this day and age, I bet you can't get a house call from a dentist.'

'Hmm,' she said. 'What about bills?'

'What bills? All the utilities are included in the rent. And the rent can be done by a monthly automatic withdrawal.'

'Not the phone.'

'I haven't got a phone. I used to have a phone. But it got expensive. And I had to keep a checking account, just for the phone. So now I order my food in person each time the delivery man comes.'

'Oh dear,' Mrs Hinman said, sounding more frightened again. 'I think I'd have to have a phone. Not that I ever call anyone. But what if there was an emergency?'

'I think there's one thing you're forgetting, Mrs Hinman,' he said, and watched her turn her eyes up to him in perceived helplessness. 'You have neighbors. Don't you think Felipe or Jesse or Rayleen would run to the supermarket for you? Don't you think you could just pound on the floor if there was an emergency, and someone would come running? Maybe somebody will even be willing to trade apartments with you, so you can stay independent a few years longer.'

Mrs Hinman wrung her spotted hands in her lap, creasing the blue tunic. 'Now why on earth would they want to do a thing like that for me?'

'Because we're neighbors?'

Mrs Hinman laughed doubtfully. 'We never were before,' she said. 'Not to the point where we looked after one another.'

'But now we are,' Billy said.

A long silence, during which Mrs Hinman seemed flummoxed by the concept of neighborliness.

'Well, I should let you get back to your nap,' she said, 'but I just can't tell you how much better I feel. I've been beside myself with worry, and now it all seems silly. I should've known Grace would care enough to make sure somebody looked after me. It's still a surprise that anybody else would, but I guess I'll get used to the idea. Listen. Don't tell the others we had this little talk, all right? It's very hard for me to say I need help, or even let anyone see that, so let's just keep this between you and me for now.'

'Fair enough,' he said.

He rose, and held out a hand to her, and she lumbered to her feet with a deep grunt, nearly pulling him over. He walked her to the door.

On her way out, Mrs Hinman said, 'Grace changed everything, didn't she?'

'That would be understating the case,' Billy replied.

'Go back to bed.'

'I will.'

'Thank you. More than I can say. You're a very nice young man.'

She waddled toward the stairway.

'Want help getting up the stairs?' he asked.

'Not yet. But thanks for asking. That time will come soon enough.'

Billy closed the door, set down the cat, and put himself back to bed.

Grace came bounding in at the usual three thirty.

'Oh, you're in your pajamas,' she said. 'I'm used to seeing you dressed now. Are you OK? I'm going to put my tap shoes on right away and work on my dancing. I really need more practice on those triple turns. What do you call them?'

'Buffalo turns,' Billy said.

'Do you think they named them after the animal or the city?'

'I don't know for a fact,' Billy said, feeling more bowled over than usual by her energy. 'But it seems like a tricky move for a bison. So I'll go with the city.'

'It's tricky for me, too,' she said, already lacing up her tap shoes. 'I keep ending up on the rug. If I could just get that down I'd have the whole routine pretty good.'

'Two more things I want you to work on.'

'Oh,' she said. 'There's always more, huh?'

'Only if you want to be good. Only if you want to shine.'

'OK. What?'

'I want you to relax your upper body more. So it doesn't seem like you're holding yourself so stiffly. And you need to smile.'

'I do?'

'Absolutely. It's de rigueur.'

'In English, Billy.'

'It's indispensable.'

'English!'

'You have to do it! But work on the turns first. I'm just going to make myself a nice bed here on the couch and watch you.'

Grace skated carefully across the rug into his bedroom and fetched the afghan off the end of his bed. She covered him up with it, and gave him a kiss on the forehead.

'Tell me if I look like I'm smiling,' she said.

Then the deeply satisfying sound of the tapping put Billy right to sleep.

'Rayleen is late,' Grace said, startling him awake.

'Maybe one of her clients was running behind,' he mumbled, trying to sound as if he'd never been asleep.

'I don't think so,' she said, sitting on the couch against his hip. 'I'm pretty sure I heard her come in at the usual time. But that was like twenty minutes ago.'

'Oh. Maybe she's talking to Jesse.'

'Why would she go talk to Jesse? She hates Jesse.'

'Hmm,' Billy said. 'Not sure. Everything changes.'

Grace raised her eyebrows and stared at him. 'Something happen that I don't know about?'

'I might've had a conversation with Rayleen about it.'

'You fixed it!' she shouted, excitedly. 'You're magic, Billy! You fixed it!'

'I didn't do a damn thing,' he said. 'She just needed to talk it out.'

'Oh, now I can't wait. Now I'm all excited, and I can't wait to see how it turns out. I have to dance now. I have to dance when I'm excited. Watch me. I'm going to do those Buffalo turns now. Watch me and see if I end up in the right place, and if I smile. Don't fall asleep this time.'

Billy sat up as a way of behaving more like a proper audience.

Grace shuffle-skated across the rug and took her position. But before she could even lift a tap shoe, someone knocked on the door.

'Rayleen's here!' she shouted, and ran for the door, skidding perilously.

She threw the door open wide, blocking Billy's view.

'Oh, it's not Rayleen!' he heard her shout. 'It's Jesse! Hi, Jesse!' Then, after a slight pause, 'Billy, he wants to talk to you!'

'I'm in my pajamas,' Billy said, but it didn't help.

Grace had already grabbed him by the elbow and begun dragging him to the door. He finger-combed his hair as best he could with his one free hand. This was not the way he wanted to be seen. But it was too late. He found himself standing in front of the open door, looking into Jesse's face, which was even more open and soft than usual.

Billy waited for Jesse to say something.

Instead Jesse threw his arms around Billy and held on tightly. Squeezed him. Billy felt tears at the backs of his eyes, as if tears were being squeezed out of him. Then Jesse let go just as suddenly.

'Gotta go,' he said. 'Gotta get ready. *Thank you.*'

Then he bounded up the stairs two at a time and disappeared.

'So what was that all about?' Grace asked, tugging on his pajama pants.

'Not sure.'

'He seemed happy.'

'He did.'

'You think it means he has a date with Rayleen?'

'It might.'

'I sure hope so. But you still have to watch my turns.'

Billy closed the door and sat on the couch, once again prepared to serve as an appreciative audience. Grace raised one foot and tapped it back down again. And someone knocked on the door.

'Damn it!' Billy shouted. 'It never stops. I just can't seem to get my old, quiet life back again.'

'You really sure you want it?' Grace asked as she shuffled to answer it. 'I don't think it's Rayleen. It wasn't the signal-knock.'

'Sometimes she forgets when she has a lot on her mind,' Billy said.

Grace threw the door wide, blocking his view again.

'It's Rayleen! Billy! She wants to talk to you!'

Billy sighed for what felt like the hundredth time that day. He could feel how little energy he had to get up and walk to the door. He did it anyway.

'I have to talk fast,' Rayleen said. 'I have to get ready. I'm taking you up on your offer to watch Grace. Here. Take this twenty.'

She pressed a bill into his hand.

'You don't have to pay me to look after Grace.'

'No. I know. It's not that. It's that I know your food supply is kind of tight, and I thought you guys could order a pizza on me.'

Wow, Billy thought. When Rayleen said she was going to talk fast, she wasn't kidding. He'd never heard so many words per second tumble from her lips.

In the background of his apartment, he heard Grace piping about the joys of pizza.

'Grace can come over to my place and order it on my phone,' Rayleen rushed on. 'If I'm already gone by then, she has the key. But here's a piece of advice. Don't tell her to get whatever she wants. Tell her she wants cheese and pepperoni, period. Otherwise it'll never fit into that twenty. Her bedtime is nine o'clock. So probably I'll be home by then, but if for some reason I'm not, maybe you could just put her to bed on your couch and I'll come get her in the morning. OK?'

But before he could even say whether it was OK or not, she had grabbed him into a bear hug and kissed him on the cheek.

'Gotta go,' she said. 'Thank you. I think.'

'You'll be fine,' he said as she disappeared into her own apartment.

Billy pulled a big, deep breath and shut the door. Grace looked up at him expectantly.

'Are they going out on a date?'

'Apparently.'

'Yea, yea, yea,' Grace sang, jumping up and down and swinging her arms over her head in a dance-like way. 'We get a pizza and they get a date, and I'm happy, and this is my Happy Grace Dance,' she sang, just before slipping and falling on her butt.

'And that last move was your Sad Grace Dance, right?'

'Got that right,' she said, still down and rubbing her butt. 'You're magic, Billy. Not magic magic, but like Jesse is magic. Because you make stuff happen. Like you made that date happen.'

'I didn't do anything. I just listened. She just needed to talk it out.'

'So? That's how you made it happen. It's still magic.'

*   *   *

'We studied the stars in school,' Grace said. 'Like space, and the solar system and black holes and stuff. It was freaky. It was really weird.'

They lay on their backs on Billy's tiny front patio, looking up at the stars. At least, the dozen or so that could be seen in spite of the smog and the city lights.

'What was weird about it?'

His exhaustion had mellowed him, making him feel deliciously sleepy and almost safe. He savored the feeling of the night air on his face, and his own lack of panic.

'Well, first of all, my teacher said space goes on forever. But that's impossible.'

'How do you know it's impossible?'

'It just is.'

'Maybe it's possible, but it's one of those things our brains aren't good at grasping. Look at it this way. You're in a space ship. And you're traveling out and out and out. Looking for the edge of space. For the place it stops.'

'Right. And there has to be one. Somewhere.'

'So what's on the other side? When you find the place where space stops, what's on the other side of it?'

They lay quietly, side by side, for a minute or so.

'Nothing,' Grace said, around the time he thought she might have dozed off.

'But that's all space is. Nothing. So if nothing ends, and there's nothing on the other side of it, then that's really just more space on the other side.'

'Aaagh!' Grace shouted. 'Billy, I think you broke my brain. OK, let's say space goes on forever, even though it doesn't really make any sense. My teacher said there're supposed to be billions of stars. Or trillions or something. So, look up there. Where are they all?'

'The city lights wash them out. If you're out in the desert or up in the mountains you can see a lot more.'

'I've never been out of the city. Have you? Have you ever been up in the mountains or out in the desert?'

'Yes,' Billy said. 'Both.' He could hear distant music. He'd heard it all along, he realized, but had only just then become conscious of it. It sounded Middle-Eastern. Someone was having a party somewhere. Everyone, everywhere was having a life. Even him. Even Billy. 'When I was dancing, I used to travel all around the country.'

A long silence. Billy listened to the music and felt warmer than he should have on a cool night like this.

Then Grace said, 'What *happened*, Billy? What *happened* to you?'

And he didn't even feel the urge to fight it. It was bound to find him sooner or later, and tonight seemed as good a night as any.

Still, they lay in silence for a long time.

'It's a little hard to explain,' he said at last. 'But I'll try. I'll try. I've just always had panic attacks. And I know you want me to tell you why, but I don't *know* why I have panic attacks and other people don't. I'm not sure if anybody knows that. I grew up in a weird, scary house, but other people did, too, and they don't all have panic attacks. But I've had them ever since I was . . . oh, I don't know . . . maybe even your age. Maybe first or second grade. But then they just kept getting worse. For years I could keep them away by dancing. Or keep them at bay, anyway. As long as I danced regularly. But then after a while I had to literally be in the very act of dancing to stop them. So I'd have panic attacks when I traveled, and on the way to the theater. And then during curtain calls. So I started going to fewer auditions. But when I was inside, I was always OK. So I just started staying inside. Like I told you before, it gets to be an addiction. You want to be OK right now, so you trade that for having a good life in the long run. It's a bad trade, but people do it all the time. That's all addiction really is. It's trading away the future so you can feel OK right now. That's what your mom is doing. And that's what got me. There's really quite a lot of it going around.'

Billy wondered if Grace had understood any of that. But she was a smart kid, so he figured she probably understood enough. As much as she needed to.

Billy heard her snore lightly, so he scooped her up and carried her in and laid her down on the couch, covering her with the afghan, which had never been put back on the bed.

He looked at the clock. Ten fifteen.

It brought a little pang of pain to his gut to think of Jesse and Rayleen out together, talking, or looking into each other's eyes, or whatever they were doing. But he brushed it away again. They had a right to find happiness, if indeed it was there for them. It benefitted Billy nothing if they failed.

Just as he was climbing under the covers, Grace spoke to him from the living room.

'Billy?'

'You OK?'

'Yeah. I just wanted to tell you something.'

'All right. What?'

'You can't tell anybody.'

'OK.'

'I'm going to be a dancer when I grow up.'

Billy breathed three times, consciously. As much as he could bring himself to believe in prayer, he prayed that the life would not wound her beyond repair.

'Why wouldn't you want anyone else to know that?'

'Because they wouldn't believe me. They'd think I was just being a stupid kid. But you believe me, right? You believe I can really do it, don't you?'

'Yes. I do. But, like I said last time you asked, you're going to have to work incredibly hard. But I believe you can, if you want it badly enough.'

'I do. I want it bad. And it'll all be because of you. You're the one who taught me to shine.'

'There's a lot more to it than I've taught you so far.'

'I know. But you're not done teaching me. Are you?'

'No,' Billy said. 'I'm not.'

Grace

'Someone is knocking on Rayleen's door,' Grace said. 'Billy, do you hear that?'

Grace paused her dance rehearsal to listen, standing balanced with one leg in the air. Her balance had gotten a lot better since she'd started with all the dancing. Still, she hoped she didn't look too much like one of those bird dogs you see in the movies and on TV, helping hunt pheasants. Or . . . then, on the other hand, those were really pretty dogs.

'Maybe we should go see who it is, so we can tell them Rayleen won't be home till five thirty.'

'I'll go along,' Billy said, lifting the cat up off his lap.

'Why? I can open a door, you know.'

'But we don't know who's on the other side.'

'Some protection you'll be,' she said as they approached the door nearly elbow to shoulder.

'Hey.'

He sounded hurt.

'Sorry.'

It was so natural to take those little shots at Billy, and he was around so much of the time, that Grace had to keep reminding herself that it was easy – too easy – to hurt his feelings.

Billy undid the locks and Grace opened the door, a team effort.

There was a lady at Rayleen's door, and Grace remembered her, but just for a second she couldn't remember from where. Then the lady turned around and smiled at her, and Grace's tummy did a little flip-flop. It was that lady from the county. The one who'd come already, once before, to check on her.

'Oh, there you are, Grace,' the lady said. 'Do you remember me?'

'Yeah.' Grace was surprised by how little her voice sounded. 'Just not your name.'

'Ms Katz.'

'Right. I wonder how I forgot that. Because I really like cats.'

'It's not spelled the same,' the lady said, still smiling that smile that didn't seem real. It looked more like something she might have put on earlier that morning with her make-up.

'Doesn't matter how it's spelled,' Grace said.

Out of the corner of her eye she saw Billy ripping at a thumbnail, but she wasn't sure how it would look to slap his hand in front of Ms Katz. She wasn't sure about any of the things you were or weren't supposed to do in front of a county lady, and that was just the problem. Somebody should have given her lessons, but they hadn't, and now it was too late.

'I don't think I've met you,' Ms Katz said, looking up at Billy.

Grace thought how it was a good thing Billy was dressed right now, and not in his raggedy old pajamas. Then again, he was almost always dressed these days, unless he was trying to take a nap, and Grace felt bad that she had only just now thought to notice.

'Billy . . . Feldman,' he said, and held out his hand for her to shake.

Too bad it was his right thumb he'd been chewing on, and now it had a little blood on it. Grace hoped Ms Katz wouldn't notice.

He opened the door wide and motioned the county lady into the apartment. Grace wished he wouldn't. But, then again, she sort of figured Billy wished he wouldn't, too, but probably he just figured he didn't have any other choice. Grace wondered if Billy knew what you did and didn't do in front of the county, or if he was just making it up as he went along, too. He looked scared.

Ms Katz sat down on Billy's couch and Mr Lafferty the Girl Cat jumped right into her lap.

'She likes you,' Grace said.

'That's nice,' Ms Katz said.

She ran one hand down Mr Lafferty's fur, and the cat did that little 'elevator butt' move that some cats do, raising her back end just as the hand got there. It made Grace like the county lady a little better, how she petted the cat instead of just shooing her away or something.

'That's my cat,' Grace said. 'She used to belong to Mr Lafferty upstairs, but then he shot himself, and now she's my cat.'

Out of the corner of her eye she saw Billy start back in on the same poor thumbnail.

'So she comes with you when Mr Feldman babysits?'

'Mr . . . who? Oh. Right. Billy. I always forget his name is Feldman. I just call him Billy. Or Billy Shine, if I need a last name. No. The cat doesn't come anywhere with me. She lives here.'

'Your cat lives here?'

'Yeah. My mom doesn't want me to even get one. Cat, I mean. But I already got her. But she lives here.'

Billy jumped to his feet.

'Coffee!' he shouted, and it came out way too loud, and then he looked embarrassed about it. 'Shall I make us a pot of coffee? I have real cream.'

'No, thank you,' Ms Katz said. 'I won't be here that long. So. Grace. Do *you* live here?'

Billy had started to sit again, but then when Ms Katz asked that question he just froze in mid-air, not standing, not sitting, his knees bent.

'Um. No,' Grace said, and Billy's spell broke, and he sat down. 'No. I don't live here. I just come here after school for two hours.' She watched Ms Katz nod and write notes to herself in a folder. 'Unless Rayleen has a date, which for the last week or two is almost every night. Then I'm here for a lot longer. But mostly I live at Rayleen's.'

A long silence. Long and also . . . not good. Grace ran back over what she'd just said in her mind, all fast and panicky, trying to figure out where she'd made a wrong turn. It had all seemed like reasonable stuff to say, but they were in a bad place now, and she could feel it. And somehow it was all her fault.

'You live with Ms Johnson? You're not living with your mother now at all?'

Grace's throat closed up, making it hard to talk.

'It's just for a little while,' she said. 'Just till she feels better.'

The words squeaked a little on their way out, and it was very embarrassing.

'From her back injury,' Ms Katz said. She didn't make it sound like a question.

'Her what?'

'Ms Johnson told me she'd had a back injury, and that's why she has to be on so many medications.'

'Right! The back injury! Yeah!'

Ms Katz sighed, and set down her folder, and looked right into Grace's face. Grace felt all the blood, and probably the color, drain out of her own face, leaving it tingling and cold.

'Here's where we run into problems, Grace,' Ms Katz said. She was talking that way grown-ups do when they want kids to know they care. 'I just had a talk with your mom. Well. I saw her. I asked about the injury. And she didn't seem to know what I was talking about.'

Grace glanced over at Billy, whose face was so white it looked like he might've died since she last checked. Nobody said anything for a scary-long time.

'The other problem,' Ms Katz said, being the only one who wanted to talk, 'is that I was told this was a baby-sitting arrangement. But if you're living here or at Ms Johnson's, that's a very different situation, because neither of your neighbors are registered as foster families. When will Ms Johnson be home?'

Grace opened her mouth to answer, but no sound came out.

'About five thirty,' Billy said. 'Unless one of her clients ran a little late.'

He sounded normal, and Grace marveled at how hard it must have been for him to say a normal, reasonable thing to the county at a time like this.

'All right,' Ms Katz said, gathering up her folders and swinging the strap of a briefcase over her shoulder. 'All right, that's fine. I have another visit to make, and I'll come back. Just tell her I'll come back.'

Billy rose to walk her to the door.

'Grace is thriving here,' he said.

He sounded desperate, and it reminded Grace that he was scared, and that they both were, and that they both had plenty of reasons to be.

Ms Katz smiled as if smiling made her sad, and started to say something, but Grace never gave her a chance. It was begging time, and she knew it. She got that from what Billy said, and it came through loud and clear.

Grace jumped up and begged.

'Please, you can't take me,' she said. 'You can't take me away from here. It's good here. I get to be near my mom so that way I'll know if she gets clean – I mean, better – and besides, I get to dance at my school, in, like, two months, and if you take me away now I won't get to do my dance, and it's the most important thing ever. And I'm a good dancer, too, and before I came over here to Billy's every day I didn't know how to dance at all, not even one little step, and I was all pudgy and everything was terrible. And now look at me. Here, I'll show you.'

She shuffled fast over to her plywood dance floor.

'I'm afraid I have to—'

But Grace refused to let her finish. There was too much on the line here to give up now.

'No, you have to see this,' she said. 'You have

to see me dance, so you'll know how important this is.'

She tapped her way into the center of the plywood.

'Now watch. You'll be impressed. You will.'

She closed her eyes. Pictured the first few steps. The way Billy had taught her to do. Counted to three. Started with a time step.

It was perfect. Billy was right. You start with something simple and perfect and it calms you down for the rest of the dance. But the Buffalo turns were coming up, and they had to be perfect, too. The whole future of the world depended on those turns being perfect.

Then it hit her, what she was forgetting. She relaxed her upper parts and felt her shoulders drop. And she smiled.

And the turns were perfect. The best she'd ever done.

She looked up at the county lady, who really was watching, and really did seem impressed. Maybe it was working! How could Ms Katz watch this, and then take her away from the very people who'd made it happen?

She ended her turns in the perfect place, right back in the center where she'd started them, and spun into her treble hops, counting them out in her head. And smiling!

One, two, three, four, five, six seven, hop . . . one, two, three, four, five, six seven, hop . . . one, two, three, four . . . one, two, three, four . . . one and a two, and a one and a two, and a one and a two, and a three and a stop!

She stood proudly, one leg still in the air, beaming. It was the best dancing she'd ever done. Ever. It needed to be, and so it was.

Ms Katz wedged her folders under one arm and applauded.

'Very nice,' she said. 'Excellent. You *are* a good dancer. You learned all that in just a couple of months?'

'Yeah,' Grace said, still puffing with exertion. 'I practice a lot.'

'Well, I think it's wonderful that Mr Feldman and your other neighbors have been so helpful to you. And I really wish it changed the legal facts. But . . . Just tell Ms Johnson I'll come back after six.'

And with that she let herself out.

'You have to get up,' Billy said. 'You have to dance.'

'I can't dance at a time like this,' Grace said.

She was sitting slumped on the couch, holding her cat tightly. Maybe too tightly. But the nicest thing about Mr Lafferty the Girl Cat was how she never complained. Grace figured it was because there were worse things in the world than being held too tightly. Mr Lafferty the Girl Cat had a point about that.

'You have to dance *especially* at a time like this. That's the whole point. The dancing will bring you back into the moment. It's the dance that will save you.'

'What time is it?'

Billy leaned way back to look at his kitchen clock. 'Ten after six.'

'Nothing will save me.'

'You don't get to say that until you try.'

Grace sighed. She set the cat down on the couch and pulled to her feet, only to find that nothing but Mr Lafferty the Girl Cat warm fur and comforting purring had been standing between her and the panic. She felt suddenly as if there were no air to breathe.

She looked up at Billy, who was lacing up his own tap shoes.

'I think I'm having a panic attack,' she said.

He leaped to his feet and ran to her, one of his tap shoes still untied.

'No!' he shouted. 'Undo! No. You're not. Don't even give it a name. Don't even give it so much power. Cancel,' he said, waving his hands around Grace's head as if he could erase her thoughts. 'Unthink that one, right now. Come on. I'm going to dance with you.'

He took her hand and pulled her into the middle of the kitchen, all four of their tap shoes echoing in rhythm. He bent down quickly to tie his other laces.

'Billy. You said we can't dance in the kitchen.'

'I can only *hope* your mother will come up here to yell at us,' he said. 'I could use a word with her.'

Grace smiled a little in spite of herself. She still wasn't really used to hearing him say stuff like that.

'Now line up with me,' he said. 'No, a little farther away. We have to make room for each other in the turns. Now I want you to see how all the anxiety flies away when you dance.'

So, having nothing to lose the way she figured it, Grace ran through the dance with him, half watching him from the corner of her eye. She wasn't perfect this time, and she forgot to smile, but it was so interesting to see how their movements matched and timed, and then all of a sudden she was in the present, dancing, just like Billy said she would be, and feeling like things would work out somehow. Because . . . well, because they just would.

'You're the best dancer,' she said, after the turns.

'I'm not ten per cent of what I used to be.'

'You must've been good.'

'Yeah. That's me,' he said, apparently not even needing

to count out his treble hops. 'A "must've been". That's like a has-been or an also-ran, only worse.'

'Didn't understand a word of that.'

'Doesn't matter,' he said, and then they did their grand finish.

And then they heard the knock on Rayleen's door.

Grace sniffled in Rayleen's arms, nested with her on Billy's couch. Billy handed her tissues.

'At least I got her to give us another month,' Rayleen said to Grace, sounding falsely upbeat, yet sounding at the same time as if her heart was breaking. And just when she needed to sound strong, Billy thought.

'But that's not enough *time*!' Grace wailed. 'My dance for school is in more than a month! So if they come take me away in a month, then I'll miss the dance at school, and then even if it's OK in the long run, and you get to turn into a foster mom and come back and get me it'll still be too late for my big dance!'

Billy reached over and wiped tears off her face, accidentally streaking the tissue with traces of blood from his bitten nail beds.

'But at least that's another month for your mom to get clean,' he said, 'and if she does, then there's no problem. So we have to work on that. We have to think what we can do to help her get clean.'

'We have to get Yolanda,' Grace said, seeming to calm down somewhat.

'We could try to—'

'No,' Grace said. 'We can't try to do anything. It has to be Yolanda. Because Mom won't talk to you guys because she's so mad at you, and I can't be going down there again, because we said she can't see me till she gets clean.'

'Again?'

'At all. At all, I meant.'

'This might be worth an exception,' Rayleen said.

Her voice sounded flat and deadly calm to Billy, like the glassy surface of the ocean when the wind suddenly stops blowing. Like the sailing ships that lie stranded until it blows again. She also sounded as though her throat had begun to close up.

'No,' Grace said. 'It was a promise, and a promise is a promise. Besides. We all tried, and it didn't get us anywhere. It has to be Yolanda. Yolanda is scary. Not always, but she can be when she needs to be. She's one of those scary sponsors.'

The dead calm struck again, and none of their ships moved. Not a flapping sail among them.

'I have to get out of here,' Rayleen said. 'Or I won't be able to breathe. Grace, run home . . . I mean, run over to my apartment and call Yolanda while I talk to Billy. You still have her number, right?'

'I don't know where I put it,' Grace said, wiggling down off Rayleen's lap, 'but I think I can remember it by heart.'

She ran out the door and disappeared.

Rayleen looked up at Billy, utter defeat and panic some-how coexisting in her eyes. Billy would never have guessed that the two could occupy the same moment, not to mention the same eyes.

'Just when everything was going so well,' she said.

'Yeah, watch out for that. Sometimes I think that's God waiting to drop the other shoe.'

'God doesn't wear shoes,' she said, and Billy had no idea if she was serious or not. He couldn't imagine her joking at a time like this. 'I have to get out of Cat Land here. My throat is closing up. Come over to . . . no, Grace is over there. I need to talk to you alone. Walk to the end of the hall with me.'

Billy followed her out of his door and down the dingy hall, his heart drumming. At the back end of the hall was one depressingly small window. Billy wondered if he had even known it was there. It was crusted over with dirt, but through it Billy could vaguely see the dead branches of a once-flowering tree scrape lightly in the wind.

Rayleen lost her balance – or so it seemed – and pitched forward on to the hardwood. Billy grabbed to catch her, but missed. Only when she stayed down, curled up with her back against the water-stained wall, did Billy understand that her knees might just have gone out from under her.

Shades of me, he thought. Did other people react so violently to the overwhelm of their emotion? News to him. He'd lived his life quite sure he was the only one.

Billy sat close to her and pressed his back against the wall in a pathetic grab for emotional stability. It didn't help, of course.

'I didn't lie to Grace,' Rayleen said, her voice sounding unnatural and unfamiliar. 'I told her everything Katz said. No, that's not true. I didn't. Everything I told her that Katz said was true. I didn't lie about what Katz said. I just left some stuff out. There were a few things I couldn't bring myself to tell Grace.'

'Just say it,' Billy said. 'The faster the better. This is scaring me.'

'It should.'

'Just say it.'

'Grace thinks I can go out and apply to be a foster mom and get her right back again. But probably not.'

The news hit a blankness in Billy, as though it had landed nowhere, hitting nothing. He did not reply.

'I talked to Katz a lot about it. I can go through the paperwork. But it takes a long time. Meanwhile, if there are plenty of foster placements open, Grace'll already have been assigned to one. Or, if they're short on homes when my paperwork goes through, I'll probably be matched with a black girl who's been waiting a lot longer than Grace. There's a very small chance it could work. But it doesn't look good. Once she gets into the system we've probably lost her. We have no legally recognized relationship. It's not like we're blood relatives. We have no standing to get her back. Not even to inquire about her welfare.'

Billy tried his mouth to see if it would work. It did – surprisingly well – but seemingly detached and independent of the rest of him.

'You would think the bond she has with us would . . .'

But then he realized he wasn't sure what he thought it would do. Or why. After all, this was the county of Los Angeles, not a single wise and caring decision-maker.

'Yeah, you'd think the bond with a parent would be pretty unbreakable, too, but they break those all the time.

Katz said there's *some* consideration for a familiar environment. But it doesn't hold up well against time waited and "other suitability factors". Her term. I think it's racial, but I didn't ask.'

They sat in silence for a time. How long a time, Billy wasn't sure. Could have been a minute. Could have been fifteen.

'Maybe I'll just take her,' Rayleen said. 'Just take her and go.'

Billy glanced over at her, but Rayleen would not return his glance.

'You're not serious, right?'

'I might be.'

'They'll catch you. And they'll put Grace in foster care and you in jail, and then the chances of your getting her back go from slim to none.'

Rayleen chewed on the inside of her lip for a moment in silence. Billy had no way of gauging what was going on inside her head.

'You're right,' she said. 'It's crazy.'

Billy breathed for what felt like the first time in a long time.

'But maybe we just won't get caught,' Rayleen said.

Billy felt an odd tingling along his scalp.

'Look,' he said. 'I hate to say this, and please don't take it the wrong way, but you won't be able to blend in. Black woman, white kid. People won't just assume she's yours when they see you. I'm sorry, but . . .'

'No. You're right. Don't be sorry. I was talking crazy. I don't know what I was thinking there. It was a crazy thought.'

Grace's huge voice suddenly broke through. 'Hey!' she

called from Rayleen's doorway. 'Good news! Yolanda says she'll come kick some addict butt!'

Rayleen looked into Billy's eyes as if they'd been friends all their lives.

'Can you make an addict not be an addict by kicking her butt?' she whispered.

'I don't know,' Billy whispered back. 'But let's hope so. Because right now it's looking like our only shot.'

After an entirely sleepless night, Billy's morning coffee looked and smelled and sounded even better than usual. He made just enough for one full mug, to help assure that he wouldn't run out toward the end of the month.

While it was percolating, and while Billy was watching it drip, he heard a rough pounding on the door of the basement apartment downstairs.

A brief silence.

Then, 'Open up, Sleeping Beauty, it's your damn sponsor.'

A moment later he heard the creak of the door swinging open. It clarified something at the back of his mind, something he hadn't entirely known was there. Some part of him had always wondered if Grace's mom really could hear them when they knocked on the door. And now he knew.

He stood chewing at his nails nervously, then slapped his own hand away. The way Grace would, if she were there with him, instead of at Rayleen's. Only more gently.

He took the coffee into the living room and drank it, slumped on the couch, watching, through the thin veil of his curtains, as cars rolled by on the street out front.

It would be time to walk Grace to school again in less than half an hour.

Billy sat up straight and made a sudden decision.

He marched into the kitchen and started a fresh pot of coffee, a full pot. While it was brewing he checked his cream supply. He shook, and frowned at, the carton for a long time. Until he realized he was letting too much cold out of the refrigerator. But when he closed the fridge door, the carton of cream was still there in his hand, feeling cold and precious, even though there was no arguing that his supply was barely adequate to last until the next delivery.

Some things you just have to do. So you do them.

Billy tied on his robe.

Pot of coffee in one hand, cream tucked in the crook of his arm, he made his way out of his apartment and down the basement stairs.

He knocked.

The door flew open roughly and there stood Yolanda. Billy remembered her well from one of Grace's meetings. In fact, he would never forget her.

'Yeah?' she asked.

Billy resisted the urge to run away.

'I'm one of Grace's neighbors.'

'Right. I remember you. The nervous one. What smells so good? Oh. It's you. You're holding coffee.'

'It's early, and I thought you might want some.'

'Well, aren't you a doll. Come in.'

Billy stepped cautiously into the apartment for the first time ever, heart hammering, glancing nervously about to see where Grace's mom might be. He found her sitting on the couch, smoking a cigarette and glaring at him. When their eyes met briefly, she flew to her feet and marched into the bedroom, slamming the door behind her.

'She hates me,' he said, setting the coffee and cream down on the revoltingly dirty kitchen counter.

'Yeah,' Yolanda said. 'She does. You think you're exaggerating to be funny, but not so much. Let me get a clean mug. You're a lifesaver with this. It's early and she doesn't have shit. No coffee, no milk, no food. Amazing she hasn't starved to death. I think she stumbles down to a fast food place every couple days. Oh, here's a . . . no, I was looking for a *clean* mug. OK. I'll just wash one myself. Anyway, you're a doll. Should I wash two mugs? Are you joining me?'

'I've had mine,' he said.

Yolanda yelled suddenly, causing Billy to jump.

'Eileen? You want coffee?'

No sound.

Yolanda marched over to the bedroom door, opened it and stuck her head in. Then she pulled back and closed Eileen in the bedroom by herself again.

'Two mugs. She'll have some.'

Time for the ultimate sacrifice, Billy thought.

'Cream?'

He held up the precious carton.

'No thanks, hon. I take mine black. I think Eileen goes black but with sugar. And I think I saw some sugar some-wheres . . .' She swung open a cabinet door. Inside was a box of sugar, a bottle of syrup, and nothing else. 'Yup. Know why she still has sugar? Because she has nothing to put sugar in. Or on. So is that really the whole reason why you came by here, just to make my morning a little nicer with a pot of coffee?'

Billy pulled the cream back, holding it protectively in the crook of his arm.

'I guess I wanted to make the point that we appreciate your being here. We're all very concerned about what's going to happen to Grace. And I guess maybe part of me was wondering how it's going so far.'

Yolanda laughed a braying, spitting laugh.

'Honey, I been here like ten minutes. I haven't completely changed her life yet, if that's what you mean.'

Billy felt his face flush hot. He backed toward the door.

'Sorry,' he said. 'I'll just leave you alone to . . . do . . . what you do.'

'Look, didn't mean to be harsh there, but shit takes time, you know?'

'Right, of course, I'm sorry.'

Billy opened the door and scooted through it, out into the hall. He tried to pull the door closed behind him, but it stopped suddenly. Next thing he knew, Yolanda was standing in the hall beside him.

'Look, Ace, it's like this. First thing I gotta do is toss every inch of her apartment and flush everything she's got. Then I gotta go to work. Then I gotta come back here and see if that stopped her, or if she figured out how to get more. On the plus side, she hasn't got a dime. On the minus side, addicts have ways of getting what they need. So we'll see. So how bout I come by your place later, bring you back your coffee pot, and let you know how we're going so far? I see that you're concerned, which is nice. You live on the first floor?'

'Yes, right across the hall from Rayleen.'

'OK, then. Just give this thing time to run its course.'

Billy scooted back up the stairs to his own apartment,

put the cream away in the fridge, and sat on the couch, consciously breathing, until his heart rate returned to normal.

'I'm serious,' Grace said. 'I'm having a panic attack. I'm seriously having a panic attack here.'

They were three or four blocks from home when she said it. Grace had been holding Rayleen's hand, but she stopped cold on the sidewalk and pulled free. Jesse ran a few steps to her and got down on one knee, leaving Billy on his own and unguarded in the big world.

Billy went to Grace's side and knelt down close to Jesse.

'Erase that,' he said to Grace. 'Remember how we erase that?'

'Dancing,' Grace said. Breathless. 'But I don't have my tap shoes out here.'

'This is *so* my fault. I never should have told you I get panic attacks.'

'You didn't,' Grace said. 'You get panic attacks?'

She looked into his face curiously. At least for the moment, she seemed effectively distracted.

'That night on my patio. When we were looking at the stars and you asked what happened to me.'

'But you never answered me, Billy.'

'I did, actually,' he said, putting a hand on her shoulder the way Jesse always did for him. 'But maybe you were asleep by then. How did you even know to call it that if you didn't hear it from me?'

'I don't know. Maybe I heard it somewhere, but I think that's just what it feels like. It's like I was just walking down the street and looking at this block like every day, because I lived here every day of my life, and then all of a sudden I thought how I might never see it again after next month, and then I got all panic-like and couldn't breathe.'

'I'm going to help you erase it.'

'How? I can't dance out here on the sidewalk.'

'Why can't you?'

'I don't have my *shoes*!' she shouted, and a man watering his hedges turned to stare at them.

'So? You don't think there's any other type of dance besides tap? There's all manner of dancing, Grace. I'll show you a couple of new dance steps and you can dance all the way to school.'

'People will stare at me.'

'So? Let them stare.'

'Will you dance with me?'

Billy swallowed hard. Oh dear God, he thought. People will stare at me.

He looked over to see Jesse watching him, waiting for his answer.

'Yes. I will. Now let's get started. I'm going to show you a really basic Latin salsa move. You just do it on a six-count. One, two, three . . . four, five six.' He stepped his feet forward and back in an exaggerated motion, bucked his torso back at the end, swung his bent arms in a Latin rhythm. 'Don't forget to use plenty of arms with this. Try it.'

Grace copied his moves, counting it out under her breath.

'Arms,' Billy said.

'Right. Arms.'

'Smile,' Billy said.

'Right. Smile. OK, so how long do I stand here in the street doing this?'

'Don't be a smartass,' Billy said, still synchronizing the

step with her. 'I'm getting there. Now, all you have to do is take very long steps forward and very short steps backward. And we'll be moving.'

And then they were moving.

They salsa-danced slowly along the front yard of the man still watering his hedge. He had stopped to watch them, an arc of water from his hose flying off into nowhere. As they reached the far edge of his property line, he held the hose in the crook of his elbow and clapped for them.

'*Muy bonita!*' he called, sounding not the least bit sarcastic. '*Miradas buenas!*'

Billy could tell the phrases were compliments, but was curious to know specifically which ones.

'What did he say?' Billy whispered down to Grace.

'Well . . . *bonita* means pretty. And *bueno*—'

'*Bueno* I know. See? He's not laughing at us. He likes it. Your first applause.'

'Rayleen applauds for me. And the county lady did, too.'

'Your first *public* applause. How does it feel?'

'Weird. Weirder than I thought it would. I guess I didn't picture I'd be salsa-dancing down the street at the time.'

About a block later, Billy glanced over his shoulder. Rayleen and Jesse were walking side by side behind them, about ten steps back.

They were holding hands.

It was after six, not long after Grace had gone to Rayleen's for the night, when Yolanda appeared at Billy's door.

He opened wide and invited her in, even though she scared him.

He took the coffee pot from her and walked it to his

sink, blankly pondering how many times he would have to wash it before he could forgive it for having spent time in that filthy, horrible apartment.

When he got back to the living room, Yolanda was sitting on his couch, petting the cat.

'So this is Grace's cat, huh? I sure keep getting an earful about this cat. From both sides. So let me not waste your time. It's like this. I got no idea. She's walking and talking, and she says she didn't use while I was at work, because she couldn't, because I found all her stashes. So I don't know. Maybe tomorrow she'll get sick of being clean, or the day after, and she'll find a way. Or maybe I got through to her with what I said about Grace, how Grace was about to get thrown into the system. That was the main point, I guess, at least for right now, to clean her up enough to tell her that. But I doubt it'll do the trick, and I'll tell you why not.'

In the pause that followed, Billy sat on the very edge of the other end of the sofa, his face feeling bloodless and cold.

'It's because she doesn't think that would be any worse,' Yolanda said. 'She thinks you guys are the devil, and whoever they give Grace to in foster care would be a better deal than what she's got now.'

Billy noticed Yolanda chewed gum with a snapping motion. An irritating habit in his opinion.

He tested his voice by clearing his throat.

'But we adore Grace,' he said quietly, and it – his voice – worked fairly well. 'And she loves us. And she's thriving here.'

'Addict logic,' Yolanda said, not missing a beat. 'Life viewed through resentment. It's possible it's still mostly the drugs talking, and a couple days down the road we'll hear from the real Eileen. You know, I sponsored her for over two years, and she had good recovery. There's a reasonable person in there someplace. It's just been a while since I got to see it.'

'What was she taking? What did you find?'

'Oxy, mostly. A little hydrocodone.'

'I'm not familiar.'

'Thank God. Don't familiarize yourself. Very heavy-duty painkillers. Big abuse potential. Oxycontin is the stuff they call hillbilly heroin. It'll string you out fast for a legal prescription medication.'

'Oh, she has it legally?'

'No, *she* doesn't. But doctors give it, anyway. They just mostly know better than to give it to *her*. No, she's getting this on the street. If I knew where, that'd be helpful. But I don't. Could be anywhere. It's not exactly what you'd call a rare commodity.'

They sat in silence for a long moment. Too long, by Billy's internal clock.

'Grace thinks Rayleen will be able to get her right back again if the county takes her away,' Billy said dully.

'Somebody ought to tell her the damn truth, then. Once she's in the system, she's gone. Oh, her mom could get her back. But she'd have to prove she was clean over a long haul. At least a year, most likely. It's not a speedy process. Girl deserves to know the truth. It's her future. Maybe not right now, though, because maybe we still got a shot. But if we know they're coming for her, she ought to know what she's getting into.'

'So you think we still have a chance,' Billy said, reaching

into that figurative pool of stinking garbage, and grabbing the one treasure worth salvaging.

Yolanda twisted her long hair around one finger. A nervous habit, maybe.

'I got one little trick up my sleeve. I got five vacation days to draw on. So I'm gonna be here on the day this county lady is supposed to come back, plus two days on either side. I'm gonna be sitting down there making sure she's clean.'

'That's great!' Billy piped, startling himself with his own volume.

'Eh,' Yolanda said. 'It's weaker than you think. I can't sit on her if she tries to go out and buy. I can try to talk her out of it, but I can't tie her up. Not legally. Alls I can do is hope she'd be too ashamed to do that right in front of me. Plus it's got another weak spot. Well, a couple, actually. First off, the county lady said she'd give it another month. But maybe she means twenty-six days or maybe she means thirty-five days. You never know with them, and that's on purpose, I'm sure. She didn't exactly help us out by making an appointment. But let's say she shows up right in that nice little window when I'm with Eileen. So she's all clean, and that's good, and nobody throws Grace in the system. Great, right? You think the county's gonna leave it at that? You think this lady's too stupid to know an addict might be clean one day and loaded the next? You think this is the first she ever met one? No, she'll be back to check. Regular. So all this effort, and I don't really know what we're getting. Just maybe a few more weeks. Unless Eileen gets her ass back in the program and sticks, this is all for nothing. Unless she gets with it again, there's really only one way this can go.'

Billy sat still for a long time, just breathing. He held a question in there somewhere, struggling its way up through his roiling middle, but he couldn't yet gather the strength to ask it.

'Sorry,' Yolanda said, and rose to leave.

'Wait,' Billy said. 'I just want to ask you one more thing. What are the odds? I mean, not in this specific case, because obviously nobody knows that, but what I meant was . . . what are the odds in general, do you think? What percentage of addicts really get clean and stay that way? Do you know?'

Yolanda paused a minute with her hand on the door.

'Bout three in a hundred,' she said.

Then she let herself out.

It was nearly two in the morning, though Billy didn't know its place in clock time until later, after he was awake.

At the very bottom of a dream cycle, he stood uncertainly and looked about himself, seeing nothing but wings on every side. Wide, white, richly feathered. And absolutely still.

It unnerved him, that they should be so still. He felt taunted.

'Flap!' he screamed at the wings, when he could no longer bear the suspense.

The wings remained still.

Billy lost his temper with them.

'Flap, damn you! You know you want to! You know you're going to! Get it the hell over with and flap already!'

The wings continued to hang in motionless suspension. But something made a rapping noise.

'Billy!' the wings said, distantly.

No. It wasn't the wings speaking at all. It was Grace.

Billy opened his eyes. He lay still a moment, staring at the cracked off-white plaster of his ceiling in the dim light, trying to clear his head and return from the dream.

'Billy!'

This time he knew. It was clearly not a dream in any way. It was Grace's hissing voice, a loud stage whisper through his door.

He tied on his robe and stumbled his way to the door to let her in.

'What are you doing up?' he asked, looking down at her.

She stood on the cold hardwood of the hallway, wearing a new-looking blue nightshirt and shifting from one bare foot to the other.

'What's wrong?' she asked. 'Why were you shouting?'

'Oh. Was I? It was nothing. Just a bad dream. You can go back to bed now. Everything's fine.'

'No, it isn't! Why would you even say that, Billy? You shouldn't say everything's fine when it isn't!'

She pushed past him and into his living room and hoisted herself up on to his couch. Billy closed the door and sighed.

'Don't you even want somebody to be with you until you're done being all scared, and you're ready to go back to sleep? When I have a bad dream, I run get in bed with Rayleen, and she strokes my forehead, and she asks me what the dream was about, and then she says, "Poor Grace, never mind, Grace, it was just a dream, and dreams can't hurt you." Don't you want somebody to do that for you?'

Tears sprang to Billy's eyes, but he held them in as best he could. Yes, he did want that. Had all his life. He had just never known it existed until that very moment.

'OK,' he said, and sat down with her on the couch.

'What did you dream?'

'I dreamed there were these wings all around me, these really huge white wings.'

'Like bird wings?'

'Not like any bird wings I ever saw.'

'Like angel wings?'

'I don't know. I never saw an angel. I don't think so. Because I think if they were angel wings they'd be comforting. These aren't comforting. I dream about them all the time, but usually they flap. And it's very disturbing, the way they flap. This is the first time they ever held still.'

'Oh,' Grace said. 'Then why were you yelling at them to flap?'

'Oh. You heard that. Well. Because . . . I'm not sure. I can't really explain it. It's like you know something bad is going to happen, and the suspense is too much. It's almost better to just get it over with. But I'm not sure if you know what I mean. Maybe you just had to be there.'

'Doesn't matter,' Grace said. 'Dreams are like that. They're not usually very understandable.'

Grace pulled up to her knees on the couch and stroked Billy's forehead.

'Poor Billy, it was just a dream, Billy. Never mind about that dream because dreams can't hurt you.'

'Thank you,' he said, fighting tears again.

'You're welcome. I think I'm gonna go back to bed. Can I sleep on your couch? Oh, no, wait. Rayleen would get scared cause I was gone. I better get back.'

'I'll be OK,' Billy said.

'I know you will, cause dreams can't hurt you.'

She padded across his rug to the door, opened it wide, then stood still with both hands on the knob.

'I just want to tell you something,' she said. 'I just want to tell you I'll always find you. You might not be able to find me, but I know how to find you. So, wherever I go, if I do, which I hope I don't, but if I do, and Rayleen can't get me back again . . . cause, you know, I keep saying she can, but every time I say it everybody looks a little green and funny, so if maybe that doesn't work out, just remember I'll always find you, even if I have to grow up to be eighteen first. Cause you're my very best friend.'

She pulled the door closed behind her with a small muffled thump.

Billy stayed up the rest of the night, watching TV, all the lights on. Because he knew the wings were out there. And that they'd wait for him. And that they would – or would not – flap.

Grace

It was about a quarter after seven in the evening, and Grace was sitting cross-legged on Rayleen's rug, watching TV. She liked to watch from close up. It made her feel more a part of the world she was watching, as if she could get into somebody else's life for real. She was watching that show she liked the best, the one with the four grown-up guys trying to raise one little boy, who always managed to run the household, even though he was only about three feet tall. It was a funny show, and usually she laughed out loud, but something was off that night. In fact, she missed most of the lines by going away someplace in her head, but then later, when something brought her back – like when she heard Rayleen laugh behind her – she couldn't quite figure where she'd been.

She turned around to see Jesse and Rayleen holding hands on the couch, but their hands came apart again the minute she looked at them.

'You can hold hands in front of me, you know. It doesn't have to be this big secret.'

Rayleen looked over at Jesse and he looked back. Like

they were picking who had to talk next, but without making any sound.

'It's just . . .' Rayleen began.

But she didn't make it far before she sort of . . . ran out of gas.

'That I'm a kid.'

'No. It's just that this is so new.'

'So? At least somebody's story is turning out right.'

'But we don't know how it's going to turn out. That's just the thing. When it's new, you want to kind of keep it to yourself until—'

But Grace held up a hand to cut her off.

'Wait! I think I hear Yolanda!'

Grace ran to the door and pressed her ear to it, then ran to the kitchen and lay on the floor, one ear against the cool linoleum.

'I can't hear anything,' she said.

She looked up to see Rayleen holding a hand down to her.

'She'll come up, honey,' Rayleen said. 'She always does.'

'But that takes *time*!' Grace whined.

'I know. Come on. We'll wait together.'

Grace took the hand and pulled up to her feet, and walked with Rayleen to the living room, where she sat on the couch between Jesse and Rayleen.

'It's day after tomorrow,' Grace said, 'and I just keep getting more scared.'

'Actually,' Rayleen said, 'day after tomorrow is just when Yolanda takes her first vacation day. Then we've got a couple days after that before Ms Katz comes. And who knows? Maybe she'll be late.'

'Or early,' Grace said.

'Don't get yourself so upset that you throw up again today, OK? I mean, if you can possibly help it.'

'Sorry,' Grace said. 'I'll try. But it's hard.'

By the time Yolanda knocked on the door, it was nearly an hour later, and Grace had thrown up twice.

Yolanda actually came in and sat down, didn't just stand in the hall and shake her head like she usually did, and Grace didn't know if that was a good sign or a bad sign.

Grace watched Yolanda press her hands on to her knees and lean forward. Everything was taking too long.

'Oh, my God, Yolanda, if you don't talk right now I'm going to explode!'

The words burst out of Grace, stumbling all over each other to get free.

'Sorry,' Yolanda said. 'It's just that . . . I always hate to get people's hopes up too much. If it was bad news, well that would be bad, but at least I would know it was a true thing. But this seems more like good news, but I'm not positive it's a true thing. At least, one of those true things you can count on. So that's why I was going slow. Anyway. I get here today and she's clean. Just clean. Just on her own like that. First time in a week I get here and find her sitting up looking at me. She knows the county lady'll be back soon, and I guess that put the fear of God in her.'

'I thought she didn't care about that,' Grace said, not sure whether to be elated or angry, or even what other options might be available to her in that moment.

'Me, too. When I first brought it up she didn't seem like she did. But back then it was all sort of theoretical, I think.'

'In English, Yolanda,' Grace said, knowing it sounded grumpy, but not caring enough to fix it.

'It was more just this *idea* of a county lady. Like just something you talk about. Now it's gonna happen for real, and she knows it. So . . . next two or three days are really key. If I could switch around and get my days off now, I'd do it, but it's too late. I already traded with somebody. But, if she feels the pressure and stays with it. You know. After a few days maybe I can really talk to her. Like I used to. Maybe get somewheres. Anyway. I'll come back tomorrow. I don't know what else I can do.'

Grace felt rooted to the spot, like a copy of Grace cast in cement instead of the real thing. She heard Rayleen walking Yolanda to the door, and they were saying something, but she didn't even look up.

A minute later she felt Jesse's hand on her shoulder.

'Hey, little one,' he said. 'Don't look so down. It was good news. Remember?'

'I know,' she said. 'I know. But before I was just all down about it, but now I'm scared, and that feels even worse. Because, like Yolanda said, you feel like it's not really real. You have no idea how many times I thought she was clean. Before. But then it didn't last. I can't get happy about it. Not yet. I can't. I'm too scared, and I feel like I'll jinx it. I don't want to go to school tomorrow. Rayleen, can I stay home from school?'

Grace looked up to see that the door was closed and Yolanda was gone.

'Wouldn't that be worse?' Rayleen asked, sitting close beside her. 'Just staying home and worrying?'

'I'm afraid I'll throw up in school.'

Rayleen sighed.

'Maybe I can help,' Jesse said. 'I can do some reiki on

your upset stomach. It's an energy work that helps the body heal itself.'

'But you won't be there when I'm in school tomorrow.'

'But I can teach you how to do it for yourself.'

Jesse rubbed his hands together to get them warm, and maybe also to fill them with some kind of energy, and then he put them *near* Grace's tummy but not *on* it. That seemed odd to Grace, that he didn't actually touch her tummy. And she said so.

'Is that cause I'm a kid, and men aren't supposed to touch kids?'

'No, that's how it's done.'

'But you're not touching the spot that hurts.'

'But the energy is. It jumps the gap.'

So Grace waited, and felt, and tried to believe it.

'I do feel a *little* something,' she said, because it was either true or very close to true. Or maybe because she really wanted it to be. 'But maybe you always feel something when somebody's hand is that close.'

'Right,' Jesse said. 'You feel their energy.'

'But it doesn't always help.'

'Because it isn't always reiki. It isn't always a healing energy. Why don't you just try closing your eyes and feeling what's going on in your stomach?'

'OK,' Grace said.

That meant she was talking too much, and Grace knew it, but she decided not to waste time feeling hurt about it. It felt like too much trouble.

After a while she decided she probably was a little more settled inside, but maybe only because she thought she was supposed to be. But then she decided if it felt better it didn't matter why.

'But that's just my upset stomach,' she said. 'Maybe you should be doing what's really the trouble. Maybe you should do my brain or something, because my stomach is only upset because I'm nervous.'

'Your brain has nothing to do with it,' he said.

His voice was very calming. Grace liked his voice a lot.

'It doesn't?'

'Very little. The emotions that are making you sick live in your gut.'

'They do?'

'That's why you feel them there. Just close your eyes and don't think for a minute.'

So Grace tried to do that.

'Was that a minute?' she asked, about a minute later.

'That was seven,' Jesse said in that calm voice she liked so much. 'Let me show you how to do this on your own at school tomorrow.'

And he did.

And then Grace agreed that it was probably best to go to school in the morning, and not just stay home all day, throwing up and worrying. After all, at the end of a whole day doing that, where would she be? Just facing a few more days that looked and felt exactly the same.

It must have been a good thing to decide, because Jesse and Rayleen both liked it a lot.

On the way home from school the following day, walking side by side with Felipe and learning the Spanish words for 'luck' and 'happiness', Grace saw her. Ms Katz. Which was neither *suerte* nor *felicidad* in Grace's opinion.

It was just one block down from their apartment house. Ms Katz drove by in a silver car. A little silver Honda or

something. Not the kind of car you'd really notice or anything, and Grace had no idea why she'd even looked
inside. But she had. And it was Ms Katz. There was
no mistaking her. Grace's stomach knew her when it saw
her.

'She came early,' Grace said to Felipe, rubbing her hands
together to heal her poor tummy if she could. 'That county
lady. She came early.'

'Oh. Why are you holding your stomach like that? Are
you sick?'

'I'm trying not to be.'

'Maybe it's good she came early. Your mom was clean
yesterday. So maybe it's good.'

'How do I find out, though, Felipe? I have to know how
it went! I can't wait for Yolanda to come, that's in *hours*! I'll
die!'

'I guess you could go ask her.'

'No, I can't. She can't see me until she gets thirty days.
You go ask her, OK, Felipe? Please?'

'I don't know, *mi amiga*. She hates me so much.'

'Oh, my God, I have to know. Please, Felipe?'

'OK, *mi amiga*. OK. No guarantees, cause I don't even
know if she'll talk to me. But I'll try.'

'Why are you holding your stomach like that?' Billy asked.
'Are you about to be sick?'

'No, I'm trying *not* to be,' Grace said, impatiently. 'It's
reiki. Jesse taught it to me. Otherwise I'm just going to
explode because Felipe is taking too long.'

'I think that's good, though. Maybe it means she's talking to him.' Then his voice changed. 'Grace Eileen
Ferguson! Are you biting your nails?'

Grace woke up as if from a dream, and looked down to see that she had torn into her right thumbnail.

'Geez, Billy. I'm getting more like you every day. I think you're rubbing off on me, and not so much in a good way. Oh, my God, here he comes! I hear him walking!'

She ran to the door and threw it open wide, and Felipe came in.

'She wouldn't talk to me,' he said.

Grace's hands automatically found their reiki position again.

'Not at all?'

'Not really. But I told her it was for you, not for me. I told her you were really scared about how it went with the county lady, so she said if I waited she would write you a note. So here's the note.'

Felipe held a folded scrap of bright yellow paper in Grace's direction. She recognized it as torn off the message pad her mom kept by the phone. Grace had thought for more than a year now that it was silly to keep a message pad by the phone, since nobody ever called them any more. Not even Yolanda. Yolanda always said it wasn't a sponsor's job to go chasing after her mom, that her mom had Yolanda's number, and if she didn't use it that must mean she didn't want help.

'What does it say?' Grace asked, afraid to touch it.

'I dunno. I figured it was private.'

'Oh,' Grace said. 'Right.'

She took the note from him. It didn't burn her. It didn't bite.

'Here, I'll read it out loud,' she said. Because Billy looked like his tummy could use some reiki, too. ' "Dear Grace, I was clean when the lady came from the county today. I've been clean for two days. I did it for you, baby. Twenty-eight more days and then I get you back. Love, Mom."'

A long silence.

'That's good, right?' Billy asked.

'Well. Yeah. Sure.'

'You don't look happy,' Felipe said.

'I'm scared to believe it,' Grace said.

'But the county lady was here, and she didn't take you,' Billy said.

He was trying to improve the mood of the room. Grace could tell. But he was also right, she suddenly realized. Whatever happened in the next twenty-eight days, there was still the point that Ms Katz had come and gone and Grace was still here.

She'd expected to be elated if that happened. She'd pictured it so many times. And in her fantasies she'd danced, and sung happy sentences of joy, instead of just saying them. Now, in real life, she just felt a little unsteady, and needed to sit down.

Yolanda came to Rayleen's door at the usual time.

Jesse got up and answered it, because Rayleen was taking a bath.

'So,' Yolanda said before she even got through the door. 'Want to hear the good news first?'

'The county lady came early, and my mom was clean, and so she's not taking me away,' Grace yelled.

She hadn't meant to yell it. She'd meant to say the words in a normal voice, but then they got away from her and ran wild.

'Oh. You know already. OK. Did you hear about the follow-up visits?'

'The whats?'

'Oh. OK. You didn't.'

Yolanda took her by the hand and walked her over to the couch, and sat down, and sat Grace down. Grace figured you'd have to be stupid not to know that all those things added up to bad news. Her stomach iced over, and she didn't know if reiki would help for that, and she got overwhelmed and didn't try.

'OK, Grace, it's like this. Ms Katz is going to be coming back between two and four times a month to check on your mom. To make sure she stays with it.'

'Two to four a *month*?'

Grace's mouth felt numb when she said it. The words sounded fine coming out, but she couldn't feel herself saying them.

'She's not stupid. She knows you gotta keep a good eye on an addict.'

'Oh,' Grace said, because she couldn't think of anything else.

'But, hey. We got through the first one. So that's good, right?'

'Right,' Grace said. 'Good. That's good. I'm going to go see my friend Billy. And my kitty.'

Just as she got to the door, she turned back to look at Yolanda, who didn't look very happy.

'Now you don't have to waste any vacation days,' Grace said. 'Hey. I just thought. Now you can come to my school when I dance. Remember I asked you, but you said you'd be all out of vacation days by then? Well, now you won't.'

'Yeah,' Yolanda said, like she was thinking about something else. 'OK.'

'You'll come? Really?'

'Yeah. I really will.'

'Good. Thanks. If my mom does what she said in the note, she can even come, too. But we'll see.'

She padded across the hall and signal-knocked on Billy's door.

'It's only me, Billy, let me in, OK?'

Billy opened the door.

'What's up, baby girl? Are they going out on a date?'

'No. I don't know. I don't know what they're doing. I just want to come in.'

'OK. Come in.'

'You look nice,' she said when she sat down on his couch. 'I'm sorry I always forget to say that. Every time I see you now you look really nice, in nice clothes and with your hair brushed and all, and I should have already said so a long time ago.'

Mr Lafferty the Girl Cat jumped up on the couch, and Grace held her close.

'What's wrong, baby girl?'

'That county lady is going to come two times or maybe even four times *every month* to check on my mom.'

'Oh,' Billy said. He sat close to her on the couch. 'For how long?'

'Like . . . I don't know. Like for ever. Or until she catches her loaded, I guess.'

'Oh,' Billy said.

'Yeah. Oh.'

They sat that way for a long time. Grace was watching it get dark through Billy's thin front curtain. It got dark a lot later these days. Grace had noticed that. The days just kept going by.

Billy's voice made her jump.

'So, are you just going to be unhappy every day? Because something could go wrong next time, even though it didn't this time?'

'What choice do I have, Billy?'

'I think that's the one thing we do have a choice about,' Billy said. 'Ms Katz came today, and your mom was clean, and I didn't see you spend even one minute being happy about it.'

'Hmm,' Grace said.

It made a weird sort of sense. Ms Katz could take her away any time now. In a week, or two weeks, or next month. But she also could have today, and she didn't. Grace could be gone right now, but she wasn't.

'OK, you're right,' she said. 'Yea, yea, Grace didn't get taken away today. Every day I'm here I'll say that little cheer. Hey, that even rhymes. Yea, yea, Grace didn't get taken away today. Every day I'm here I'll say that little cheer. See? Even that second part rhymes.'

'It doesn't scan, though,' Billy said.

'What's scan?'

'Nothing. Sorry. I shouldn't criticize. It's a great cheer. Very good attitude.'

'No, really. Tell me what scan is.'

'When it works out right rhythm-wise.'

'Oh. Right. That. Like a real poem. I could fix it with more yeas. Yea, yea, yea, yea, Grace dint get taken away today. I have to sort of say "dint" instead of didn't. But then it works pretty good. Billy. Teach me another kind of dancing, OK?'

'What kind?'

'I don't know. Anything. I just want to dance, and I'm getting over-rehearsed on my tap dance for school, you said so yourself. So let's do something different.'

So Billy, because of his being Billy and all, taught her a waltz.

You did it to the count of three, facing each other and holding hands, which was kind of nice because it was something they could do together. And then, after a few steps, he taught her how to step back and twirl. He held one of her hands above her head and she twirled. And then she made Billy step back and twirl, even though that's the girl's part, and even though Grace had to reach up high and he had to duck down low. It made them both laugh.

So that was a good day.

It was twenty-three days later. Twenty-three once-daily 'Grace dint get taken away today' cheers later. Exactly. Billy had been counting.

Someone signal-knocked at his door in the middle of the day. Grace should have been at school, Rayleen should have been at work, and nobody else even knew about the signal-knock. Billy hurried to the door and opened it.

It was Rayleen.

'Hey,' he said. 'What are you doing home in the middle of the day?'

'It's Jesse's mother,' she said. 'She took a bad turn. They took her from the nursing home to the hospital. It looks like it won't be long now. Can I come in? I need to talk to you. It's important.'

He stood back from the doorway, and she came in.

'Coffee?'

'No. Thanks. I have to talk fast so my throat won't close up. I stayed way too long last time. Took me days to get over it. So, really quick. Jesse wants me to be with him. You know. When his mother's dying. So I'm going.'

'Oh. Good. So you want to know if Grace can be here tonight?'

'Maybe not just tonight. I have no idea how long it'll be. Could be days.'

It struck Billy hard that Jesse was away. He wouldn't walk with them to school in the morning. The best part of Billy's day. How would he feel when Jesse left permanently? He put the thought away again, knowing he couldn't take it on just then.

'It's fine. She can be here as long as she needs to be. But. Oh. You'll be gone, too. For days. So . . . how's she going to get to school in the morning?'

'Right. That's what I need to talk about. I was hoping . . . you.'

'Me?'

'I was hoping.'

'Just me? Alone?' His voice rose alarmingly.

'Well. You and Grace.'

'Not on the way home it wouldn't be.'

Billy felt panic rising up through his words, feeding on itself.

'But you're doing so much better. You've been walking with us every morning. It must be starting to feel a little more natural by now.'

'Oh, yes,' Billy said. 'Very. It feels very natural. Probably because I never have to do it all alone any more.'

'OK. Look. Bottom line, I think I need to go with Jesse. But I know this is asking a lot of you. I knew it would be. So I already called Felipe. He says he'll do it if there's really no other way. But he doesn't get off work until after one in the morning. So it's really going to cut into his sleep. But if the two of you could work it out . . . Maybe he could go with you tomorrow, and the day after you could try it by yourself?'

Billy forced himself to take a deep breath.

'I don't know,' he said, 'but we'll work it out somehow. You just go. We'll work it out.'

Rayleen stepped in and threw her arms around him. Billy felt the warmth of her lips on his cheek. It didn't move off a second later, either. The lips remained pressed to his face for what felt like an extended time. And much later, even after she'd hurried out the door, the warmth was still there to be felt.

'Here, take this up to Felipe,' Billy said to Grace. 'He'll need it.'

Grace took the mug from his hands, holding it carefully in both of hers.

'Poor Felipe. He doesn't get to bed until after two. No cream? Why didn't you put cream in it?'

'Because Felipe doesn't take cream. He takes it black.'

'You sure?'

'Positive.'

'Wait,' she said, paused in his doorway. 'When did you ever have coffee with Felipe?'

'One day while you were at school. Run get him now, OK? We have to go.'

Truthfully, Billy realized, they were right on time and there was no need to hurry. It was only his stress that drove the moment.

A few minutes later she led Felipe down the stairs, both hands on his elbow. Felipe was holding the mug of coffee with one hand and rubbing both eyes with the other, feeling his way down the steps without looking.

When Grace led him up to the doorway, he looked up at Billy and smiled sleepily, then yawned.

'OK. I'm here, my friend. Ready when you are.'

His accent was thicker than usual, probably owing to his being mostly asleep.

Then he gave Billy a quick, one-armed hug. It almost made up for the lack of Jesse. To the extent that anything could ever make up for the lack of Jesse.

He stood shoulder to shoulder with Felipe, watching Grace walk through the school yard.

'So, that's really something, then,' Felipe said.

'What is?'

'Oh. Sorry. I guess when I'm sleepy, I think out loud. I was thinking how when I first met you, you didn't even go across the hall. And now here you are standing in front of Grace's school.'

'Don't remind me,' Billy said. 'Six days left until Grace's big day. And the hardest part of all is actually going inside the school. And I haven't even tried it once.'

Billy sighed, and they turned and began the long walk home together.

'You'll be fine,' Felipe said. 'Look at all you did so far.'

'If Jesse's there, I'll be fine. But he might not be.'

'What's so special about Jesse?' Felipe asked. 'No, you know what? Never mind. I sort of know. I can't quite put my finger on it, but I know what you mean. When people are having trouble, he's the guy. Maybe he'll be back on time.'

'I sure hope so. Sorry to get you up so early.'

'My own fault,' Felipe said. 'I stayed up extra-late last night. I knew it was a mistake. I knew I'd pay big for it. But I did it anyway. You see . . . I sorta met a girl.'

'Really? That's great.'

'Well, not really, I didn't. Well, I mean . . . I did. She's a girl. And I met her. But I don't know much yet. You know. I just met her. But she came on as prep cook at my work. Clara, her name is. So we ended up going up on the roof of the restaurant and talking till three. Crazy, I know. But she's so different from my last girlfriend. All quiet and shy. My last girlfriend was really pretty, too pretty, and she knew it. She knew what she had, and she never let me forget it. You know? So, listen. What did Jesse do that helped you when he walked with you? Anything special? Or was it just Jesse being Jesse?'

'Well. Let's see. A little bit of both, I guess. He used to put one hand on my shoulder. But you don't have to do that if you don't want. It might look weird. But I think Jesse doesn't care much what people think.'

A moment later Billy felt Felipe's hand settle firmly on to his shoulder.

'Thanks,' Billy said.

'When I was a kid I was scared of the dark,' Felipe said. 'Who knows why people are scared of things, right? If you are you just are. And my dad was kinda strict about stuff like that. You know. Being all independent and making him proud by doing everything just right. I was always supposed to be a man. You know? But when you're five it's kinda hard. So I'd just pretend I wasn't scared. But it's easier if you don't have to pretend. That much I know. I know how it feels to be scared.'

Billy heard the rumble of a car engine, beefy and rough

and with no appreciable muffler. His blood turned to ice when it slowed beside them.

He looked over to see a tough-looking Hispanic man leaning out the open driver's window. The man made kissing noises at them.

Felipe's hand dropped to his side.

'*Maricones!*' the man shouted cheerfully. '*Es tan en amor, maricones!*'

He stepped on the gas, and apparently the brake at the same time, and the tires spun with a screaming sound. The acrid smell of burning rubber filled Billy's nostrils. Then the car blessedly sped away, the driver flipping his middle finger at them as he drove.

'Sorry,' Billy said quietly.

'No, don't be sorry. I should be sorry to you. I don't know why I took my hand away. I was just being your friend, anyway. I shoulda told that guy to bite me. Screw him. Screw 'em all.'

Felipe put his hand back on Billy's shoulder, more firmly and more affectionately this time, and they began to walk again.

'See now why I hate to go outside so much?'

'Yeah. I guess I do. But you gotta do it anyway, right? I mean, it's life. You gotta do life. Right?'

'Not really,' Billy said. 'You don't have to. Lots of people don't do life any more. They just stop at some point. And once you stop, it's really hard to get started again. But then, once you get started again, it's kind of hard to stop. What did that guy say to us?'

'You don't want to know.'

They walked in silence for a block or two, that reassuring hand resting on Billy's shoulder.

Then Billy said, 'I can take her myself tomorrow.'

'Really?'

'Really. I have no idea how. But I will. You stay after work and talk to Clara. I'll make it work somehow. I just will.'

'I'm holding your hand,' Grace said.

As if he wouldn't know.

They stood in the open doorway of their building, the spring morning hitting Billy in the face. The same kind of morning as yesterday, he reminded himself. And dozens of days before that. Except it wasn't. Because today he had to walk home alone. He swallowed hard against the pounding in his chest and temples, for no reason he could have explained.

'You have to do this,' Grace said. 'You told Felipe to stay up extra late, and now you have to get me to school.'

She tugged gently forward on his hand, gripping it tightly in both of hers.

'Yes,' Billy said. 'The inevitability of the moment is not lost on me.'

'You're so weird, Billy. Come on. Stop thinking about it and just do it.'

She pulled him forward, and he willed his feet to keep moving, to build some momentum. Next thing he knew he was down the stairs and out on to the sidewalk.

'I'd close my eyes,' he said, 'but I'd probably trip or something.'

'You can close your eyes. I can lead you like you were a blind guy. I could be the guide dog.'

'I'm not sure it would help.'

'Try it.'

Billy closed his eyes and took four steps blind. And immediately pictured angry men in passing cars, muggers at the end of the block. All manner of miscreants, none of whom Grace would know enough to warn him about.

He opened his eyes again.

'That doesn't help.'

'Right,' Grace said. 'I was just thinking you can't close your eyes on the way home, anyway.'

'Oh, thank you so much for reminding me of the way home.'

He stalled on the sidewalk. Grace tugged at his hand but could not restart him.

'I think I'm getting just a wee tiny bit panicky,' he said.

'I'm going to let go of your hand, but don't you dare run home.'

She let go, and Billy remained rooted. He glanced over his shoulder.

'Don't look back!' she shouted. 'You know better than to do that. What if Jesse were here? What would he tell you?'

'Not to look back, I think.'

'You don't *think*, you *know*.'

'Are your hands cold? Why are you rubbing your hands together like that?'

'I'm going to do reiki on you.'

'Right out here in front of everybody?'

'Got a better plan?'

So Billy stood a moment while Grace held her hands close to his belly, but not touching. He glanced around to see if anyone was watching. It didn't seem to help much, but then, he figured, he wasn't really cooperating. Instead of releasing his anxiety, he was drowning in fresh anxiety over receiving reiki in public from a ten-year-old.

'Let's walk some more,' he said.

She grabbed his hand and pulled.

He walked two blocks on sheer willpower, and then stalled again.

'You have to do this, Billy. I can't go the rest of the way alone. I'm not allowed.'

He opened his mouth to answer but found his voice disabled.

'OK, there's just one more thing we can do. We'll have to dance to school.'

Billy dug deeper in a desperate attempt to get his voice back.

'I can't,' he said.

'You said it would work for me, and you were right. Now come on. Latin salsa.'

'I can't. People will stare at me.'

'So? Let 'em stare. That's what you said to me.'

'I wish you wouldn't always parrot back what I've said to you. It's irritating.'

'Why? Because it's true stuff?'

'Something like that.'

'Come on. Latin salsa. Right now. Unless you want to waltz.'

'I don't think the waltz would work well in a straight line. It more takes you around in a circle.'

'Then start salsa dancing, Billy.'

Freshly out of options, he did as he was told.

Wonderful, he thought as they danced down the street together. The only thing worse than being out in public: being out in public behaving strangely and drawing attention. He reminded himself that he had done this before, with far less anxiety. But he didn't even ask himself what the difference might have been. It was obvious. Jesse.

An older couple came out on to their porch to watch them go by. Four cars slowed down. One driver shook his head slightly before accelerating again. He heard someone call out, 'Hey, Frankie, come 'ere an' see this,' but could not tell from which direction.

And then they arrived at Grace's school. And Billy had to admit, though not out loud, that the blocks had flown by.

He leaned down and kissed Grace on the forehead.

'You just gonna run?' she asked.

He nodded, having misplaced his voice yet again.

'OK. See you after school. You can tell me how it went.'

Billy nodded one more time, and then took off sprinting.

He built up to a speed he could not recall having ever accomplished before. The houses and apartment buildings streaking by him seemed to stretch out, as if he were altering time by racing through it. The rasp of his own labored breathing sounded artificial and far away. Then the world began to whiten, and it dawned on him suddenly that he was probably in the middle of a steep oxygen deficit, and that if he didn't slow down he might pass out. But he couldn't bring himself to slow down.

And then, somewhere in that moment, he had an imagining. It wasn't a hallucination. He didn't literally see it. It just came into his head, with a strong picture.

Wings.

They did not flap at him, nor did they taunt him by

holding still. They surrounded him. Wrapped themselves around him like a warm blanket.

Billy slowed to a trot, and trotted the rest of the way home.

'Oh, boy, you're here. Thank goodness,' Grace said. 'I was worrying about you all day at school. So I guess you got home OK. So how did it go?'

'It was all right,' Billy said. 'I just ran.'

'That's it? That's all you're gonna tell me about it?'

'At least for now,' he said.

Billy woke from a dreamless sleep to hear Grace whisper his name from her bed on the living room couch.

'Billy? Are you awake?'

'Sort of,' he said.

'Did I wake you?'

'Sort of.'

'Oh. Sorry. I'm having trouble sleeping. You know tomorrow is Wednesday.'

'Right.'

'And then Thursday and Friday, and then the weekend, and then the big day. It just gets harder and harder to sleep every night.'

'Are you nervous about the dance? You know it backwards and forwards.'

'A little bit. Just because it's big and exciting. Not because I think I won't be good. Mostly I'm nervous waiting to see if my mom really is coming, and if she really is about to have thirty days clean. Just think. I could go back and live with her again. But then the closer it gets to that, the more I get scared.'

'Yolanda says she's really doing it.'

'Right. I know. That's why I get scared. Cause I always say I won't get my hopes up, but then I do. I just can't stop. Cause I really do want to live with her again.'

Billy said nothing, absorbing the emotional resonance of Grace going home.

As if she could hear him thinking, she said, 'I'll still come visit you all the time, you know.'

'I know.'

'I'm also worried that it'll get harder and harder to sleep every night. And what if Sunday night I don't sleep at all? I'll have to do my big dance and I'll be all tired.'

'If Jesse's back, I bet he could do reiki on your sleeplessness.'

'But what if he isn't? And that's another thing. What if Jesse's mom is still dying on Monday? Maybe he won't come to my school to watch me dance. Maybe Rayleen won't even come.'

'You're getting yourself too upset to sleep. Here. Try this. Close your eyes and picture something with me. Picture big, white, feathery wings. All wrapped around you. Taking care of you.'

A long silence.

'Wings? Like the ones you have nightmares about?'

'Except not scary. Because . . . I mean . . . you can turn things like that around. Remember how I used to be scared of cats? But then I got to know one. There are all manner of things that scare us at some point in our lives, but then later we find out they really never meant to hurt us anyway.'

'What made you think of that, Billy?'

'Just try it. Please.'

A long silence. It lasted. And it lasted.

Finally, a good five minutes later, he got up and checked on her, quietly. She had fallen back asleep.

Grace

It was Friday, last school day before the big event.

Billy had danced her to school every morning, and every morning more and more people had looked out their windows or stepped out on to their porch to watch them go by. Like people knew to expect them by now. Like it was the morning performance of some big show, and everybody wanted to get a good seat. Except they mostly stood.

On Thursday they'd done the tango, and people really seemed to like that.

And Billy seemed OK.

But then it was Friday, and Grace had the big idea to waltz to school. Because it was fun when they waltzed in Billy's living room, and it had made them laugh.

Billy said again what he'd said the first time, that the waltz takes you more around in a circle. Not so much to school. But Grace was sure they could just take longer steps in the school direction, like they did with the Latin salsa. And she was in one of those moods that involved not letting anything drop.

They were about halfway to school when it happened.

Billy had just spun her around in a twirl, and that nice Spanish-speaking family in the blue house were all watching and clapping, and Grace thought it would be nice to spin Billy, too. She thought the family would like that.

So she reached up high, and he ducked down low, and he spun wildly, really getting into it, lots of forward motion, and then he got his foot caught on a big slab of concrete where the sidewalk was uneven. Grace saw it happen, but there wasn't much she could do. It just all happened so fast.

He went down like the trees she'd seen in movies about lumber cutting. You know, right after somebody says 'timber'. He built up speed on the way down and landed right on his face. Literally. He put his palms down, but it just wasn't enough to stop his face. Grace could hear the sound all the air made when it rushed out of him. She heard the sound of gasps from the nice family.

'Oh, my God! Billy!'

Grace helped him turn over and sit up. There was a lot of blood coming from his nose. A scary lot.

'It's fine,' he said. 'I'm fine.'

But he definitely said it in that way that people say they're fine when they're not fine in any way. And by then the family had run out to help them. A nice older man, short and thick, a grandpa type of guy, who brought a handful of tissues, and a woman who might have been his daughter even though she was definitely grown to maybe middle age, and a girl who was a teenager.

Everybody was talking at once, but mostly in Spanish. It was too much Spanish for Grace, but she did get the part where they kept asking if he was OK.

Billy took the tissues, and held them gently to his nose

to try to stop the bleeding, but it was too much bleeding, and those tissues got swamped right away. He kept saying he was OK, but they kept asking in Spanish, and Billy kept answering in English, and Grace could see that nobody was getting anywhere with that system.

So she said, '*Esta bueno.* Billy *esta bueno.*'

But then she wondered why she even said it when she knew it was just a big lie.

The lady, who Grace didn't even see leave, came back with a clean dish towel, and Billy held that to his nose.

'I have to get home,' he said to Grace.

'I know,' she said.

'You can't go on alone. You have to come back with me.'

'I know.'

'You can wake up Felipe. He'll walk you.'

'Maybe I should stay home with you today.'

'It's fine. It'll stop bleeding. Ask if they want their towel back.'

'I don't know how to say "Do you want your towel back?" in Spanish.'

'OK. Whatever. Help me up, OK?'

He was still using both hands to hold the towel to his nose, which left no hand to grab him by, so Grace took him by the elbow and pulled. But he didn't budge. But then the nice grandfather guy took the other elbow and they got him on his feet, even though he swayed hard partway up, and Grace thought he might pass out or something. She couldn't figure out if he was really hurt that badly, or if looking at tons of his own blood made him feel a little faint, but she figured it was something she could sort out later on.

Billy stood swaying on the sidewalk for a minute, all by

himself. Then he held the towel out to the woman, questioningly. As if she might want to take it from him. As soon as he did, a bunch more blood ran down his lip, and he had to wipe it away.

'No, no,' the woman said, waving off the idea. 'Is your.'

'Thank you,' Billy said.

'*Gracias*,' Grace said. '*Muchas gracias.*'

And they headed off in the direction of home. But then Billy swayed again, so the old grandfather took him by the elbow and walked with them.

Grace could tell Billy was embarrassed and wishing the old man wouldn't be so helpful. But he was, and there was no way Billy was going to fix that.

The old guy walked them all the way to their front door.

'*Gracias*,' Billy said.

'Go wake up Felipe,' he said to her.

He was lying propped up on his couch, still holding the towel to his face. The cat was sniffing all around him, like she was worried and wanting to know what was wrong.

'Why? Do you need him?'

'No. You do. To get to school.'

'I'm late anyway.'

'So? Be late. But you have to go.'

'I'm not leaving you, Billy. You need me. Here. Let me get you some ice.'

'Don't you have a big rehearsal today?'

'Nope,' she shouted from the kitchen. 'Tuesdays and Thursdays. Yesterday was our last rehearsal.'

She scooped two double handfuls of ice cubes into a paper napkin and ran them back to Billy. He pulled the towel away, slowly. Like he was scared what would happen when he did. Nothing happened. It didn't bleed any more. It had finally, finally stopped.

'Oh, my God. Billy. You look terrible!'

Somehow it had seemed like a reasonable thing to say. At the time. She couldn't have imagined he would take it too personally. Wouldn't most anybody look bad after falling flat on their nose?

'What does it look like?' he asked quietly.

Grace hated to tell him. The bridge of his nose was swelling up, but that wasn't the worst of it. His eyes were both going black all the way around. And he had veiny red blood showing inside the corner of one of his eyes. It was horrible. It was hard even to look at him.

'I'll bring you a mirror. Where's a mirror?'

'I don't have one.'

'You *don't have* one? Who doesn't have a mirror?'

'Me,' he said.

He touched the ice to his nose and yelped.

'Have you got any aspirins to take?'

'I doubt it. If I do, they're probably years old.'

'I bet Rayleen has aspirins. I'll go look.'

She ran across the hall and opened the door with her key. She took two aspirin from the bottle in Rayleen's medicine cabinet. Then she thought better of that, and took another two. On the way out of the bathroom, she grabbed Rayleen's hand mirror as an afterthought. Then she locked up fast and ran them back over to Billy.

'Here, I brought you four aspirins,' she said.

She quietly set the mirror upside-down on the coffee table, hoping Billy wouldn't notice. She'd begun to doubt whether it was good thinking, presenting him with a mirror.

'Let me see,' he said, pointing to it.

'You sure?'

'Let me see.'

Grace handed him the mirror and stepped back. Billy raised the mirror and stared into it for a long time. Grace wondered what he was thinking, and wished he would hurry up and say.

'Oh, dear God,' he whispered, after a long pause. 'How did I get to be so old?'

'I think I should check to see if it's broken,' Felipe said. 'But I gotta warn you. This is gonna hurt like a sonofabitch.'

'Are you going to the hospital if it's broken?' Grace asked.

'No,' Billy said. 'If it's broken it'll just have to heal itself.'

'Maybe you shouldn't even hurt him, then,' Grace told Felipe.

'It'll heal bad,' Felipe said. 'I had a cousin got his nose broke in a towing accident. And he wouldn't do nothing. He was stubborn like you – no offense – but prob'ly for different reasons. Anyway, it still looks real bad. It healed with a hook, and a big knot. That's never gonna go away, either.'

'I guess you should check it.'

'OK, now grab hold of my hand and squeeze it really hard. I'm gonna take my other hand and put it on the bridge of your nose and just wiggle it a little bit to see if the part that shouldn't oughta move moves.'

Grace closed her eyes, because she couldn't bring herself to watch. She heard Billy yelp. Then she heard nothing, so she opened her eyes. It was all over, thank God.

'It's not broken,' Felipe said. 'Come on, Grace. Let's get you to school.'

'I need to stay here with Billy.'

'I'll come back and stay with Billy. You need to go to school.'

Part of Grace had been worried that if she didn't show up to school that day, and with no explanation, then her teacher might think she wasn't showing up Monday, either. And Felipe would be good to Billy while she was away.

But then she thought of a really good reason to argue.

'But I can do reiki on his nose all day. And you can't.'

And that was when Grace heard it. That smooth, nice, calming voice that she liked so much. That everybody liked so much.

'Or I could stay with him and do the reiki,' it said.

Grace whipped around to see that the door to Billy's apartment was still standing wide open. And in the open doorway she saw Jesse and Rayleen.

Grace literally shrieked with pleasure, and from the corner of her eye she saw Billy stick his fingers in his ears.

'You're back! I thought you might not get back on time! But you got back!'

She threw herself wildly at Rayleen, startled by how much she had missed her. She nearly bowled Rayleen over when they made contact.

'I'm so glad you're back!' she shrieked.

Somewhere at the bottom of her mind, she wondered briefly if her mom was downstairs, really clean and awake, sitting up and listening to all this, and, if so, how it made her feel. But her curiosity about Jesse's mother knocked the thought away again.

She ran at Jesse, and he picked her up so she was just his

height, and she rubbed his beard as if it were some kind of lucky charm.

'Jesse,' she said, her voice hushed with respect. 'Did your mother die?'

'She did.'

'That's terrible. I'm really sorry.'

'It wasn't that terrible,' he said. 'It was freeing in a way I probably couldn't explain. Besides, she was in a great deal of pain. So it was something of a blessing.'

'So . . . then . . . is it sort of a little bit OK that I was hoping that, if she had to die at all, she'd die soon enough so you and Rayleen could come see me dance on Monday? Because I felt really bad about that.'

'I think it's OK,' Jesse said, setting her back on her feet again. 'I also think you should let Felipe take you to school now. I'll stay here and take care of Billy.'

'OK,' Grace said. 'That's good enough. If Jesse's here to take care of Billy, then I think it's OK if I go.'

And she marched off with Felipe, satisfied that all would be well in her absence.

It wasn't until they were nearly halfway to school that Grace noticed she had a good bit of Billy's blood on one of the sleeves of her sweater.

'Tell me what happened, neighbor,' Jesse said, leaning over him and touching the ice pack gently to first one of Billy's eyes and then the other. 'Somebody on the street do this to you?'

Rayleen had already gone home, in search of better, non-cat air to breathe. It made Billy edgy to be so completely alone with Jesse, but of course he didn't say it.

'No,' he said in barely over a whisper. He had entered into a state of utter surrender. 'I did it to myself.'

'But not on purpose.'

'No. I was dancing Grace to school, and I tripped on a big crack in the sidewalk.'

'The dangers of crack,' Jesse said.

Billy surprised himself by laughing. Or, actually, something between a snort of laughter and a cry of pain. It wasn't only his nose he'd hit, it was his ribs, too. But he hadn't shared that with anybody yet. For some reason he wanted that to be his little secret. At least until the more obvious wounds had been assimilated.

'Well, good,' Jesse said. 'Good to know it was only you,

and not on purpose. Now I don't have to kick anybody's ass for hurting my friend Billy. Not even yours. So, what else did you bang up? Your ribs?'

Oh, my God, Billy thought. He really is magic. He'd heard Grace say so, but had assumed she was speaking figuratively.

'How in God's name did you know that?'

'It wasn't hard. I could hear how much it hurt you to try to laugh. Now come on. Let's see.'

He moved to lift Billy's sweater, and Billy exploded.

'No!' he shouted. 'No,' he said again, gathering calm around himself like an old blanket. 'I'm sorry. I didn't mean to yell. But no. I don't want to be seen like this.'

Jesse took his hands back, and they sat in silence for a moment.

'OK, fine. Here,' Billy said, and raised the sweater himself.

Jesse looked, and Billy looked at the same time. He hadn't looked yet. There had always been somebody around, somebody who was already too worried. It was bad. Worse than he thought. A road map in black and blue. His head ached imagining how it would look in the morning, or in three days. Well. His head ached anyway.

Meanwhile Jesse's hands moved in the direction of his naked, unguarded torso.

'I just want to feel around and see if anything's broken.'

'No,' Billy said. But this time he was careful to keep it to a whisper. 'No, please don't touch me. I mean, putting your hand on my shoulder is one thing. But not that. I couldn't bear it. I love you and I just couldn't bear it.'

He could feel a tingling sensation along his scalp, a sort of tangible feedback from the words he had just spoken.

He noticed his eyes were squeezed shut, but could not remember closing them. He heard Jesse's hands rubbing together, and he waited for something to happen, but nothing did. Except that, in a few moments, he felt a sort of warm tingling in the area of his damaged midsection.

'Are you doing reiki on my ribs?' he asked, eyes still shut.

'I am. Is that OK?'

'Yes. It's fine. Thank you.'

He received the blessing in silence for what might have been several minutes.

'It seems to be helping not just with the pain in my ribs. It seems to be helping a little with the anxiety. Not like it isn't there any more. More like it isn't stuck. Like a chunk of it wants to move up and out of me.'

'Let it,' Jesse said.

Oh, God. That voice.

'I don't know if I can go on Monday,' Billy said.

He still did not open his eyes.

'But you have to,' Jesse said. 'You have to, for Grace. And you know that. So I know you will. Because you promised her, and she's depending on it.'

'But what if I can't?'

'I think you have to anyway.'

'Literally can't.'

'Not sure there's any such thing,' Jesse said.

'See, this is why I was by myself all those years. Because as soon as you let people in, they start depending on you. And then, if you can't be everything they think you should be, you've let them down. It's easier not to have anybody around at all.'

'Too late, though. You got Grace already. Like it or not.

So, look. Try this on for size. Let's say I'm magic like Grace thinks, and I can wave my wand and make Grace disappear from your life. Retroactively. Like she never existed for you. Then you don't have to go to her school on Monday. Want me to do it?'

He tried it on. Amazingly. He was in so deep, feeling so desperate, that he actually tried it on for size. Disappearing Grace.

'No,' Billy said. 'Don't disappear her.' He sighed. Jesse was right. He was stranded. 'I can't stand to be seen in public looking like this.'

'Hat and sunglasses.'

'I don't own a hat or sunglasses.'

'I do.'

'And there's another thing. I haven't been inside a school since I was in school. And it was the most dreadful, most traumatic era of my entire life, and I just have to add here: that's a tough competition to win. And I think I'm going to freak out when I get inside. I think I never should have shot off my mouth and said I could do this. I thought I could learn to walk her to school, but now look what happened. Look what happens when you go out in the world.'

'Yes,' Jesse said. 'I see. The world gave you a bloody nose. It'll do that from time to time.'

His eyes still closed, Billy felt the energy from Jesse's hands move to his forehead, eyes and nose.

'So how do I get back up?'

'With help from your friends. There's an upside to having people depend on you. Life turns around, and then you get to depend on *them*. You get to say, "I'm in over my head and I need your help."'

'I could never say that to anybody.'

'You already did,' Jesse said.

Grace came over three times on Saturday, once on Sunday morning, and then again on Sunday evening, when she brought Billy homemade chicken soup.

'Did Rayleen make this?' he asked.

'No. Jesse made it,' she said, scooping up the cat. 'So . . . I came to ask you a question that I keep wanting to ask you, but then I get scared. You're still coming tomorrow, right? Even after what happened?'

'Seems like I have to find a way,' he said, quietly, from the kitchen, where he had gone to get a soup spoon.

'That doesn't feel like a definite, definite yes.'

He took a spoonful of the soup, which was intensely good. On top of everything else, Jesse was a good cook. Amazing. It bordered on the unfair.

'I'm going to tell you the most honest thing I can possibly tell you. I feel like I can't. Like I just don't have it in me. But I promised you I would. So I'm going to see if it's possible to do something even though it's impossible. Jesse says he'll help, but I'm not sure what he can do.'

'Jesse can do it. Jesse can do anything. So, here's how it's gonna go. The assembly is last period. So you guys'll get there a little before two. You have to go to the office and get a visitor pass. And then you just go into the auditorium. First there's going to be this really stupid little play. See, not all the kids can do a talent, so they had to find a part for everybody. So then after the play this kid named Fred is gonna play the trumpet, and then Becky sings a song, and then me. I'm the big finish, which I think is a good sign. Saving the best for last, and all that.

And then school's over and I can go home with you guys. I know you'll be there, Billy. I just know you will.'

'Thanks for the vote of confidence. Are you going to sleep tonight?'

'I hope. Jesse said he'd teach me a meditation for relaxing. Are you going to sleep?'

'I doubt it,' Billy said.

And, of course, he didn't.

At noon on Monday, Jesse came to his door. It hurt to get up to answer it, but Billy did anyway. He was already clean, dressed and ready to go. Too ready. Too early.

'Grab some water to take these with,' Jesse said.

He dumped about twelve capsules from his hand into Billy's. Billy stared at them as if they might identify themselves verbally.

'Not drugs,' Jesse said on their behalf. 'Herbs. But pretty strong ones. Valerian root and kava kava. In large dosages. They should have a calming effect. They might make you a little drowsy.'

Billy barked a short laugh, and it hurt his ribs.

'Right. In public, in a school, relaxed enough to doze. That'll be the day.'

'They can't hurt.'

'True. Thank you.'

'You might want to go across the hall in about an hour. Rayleen wants to put some make-up on your black eyes and bruises. So you'll feel more presentable.'

'Well, it's a nice thought, but I don't think we're the same shade.'

'She made a special trip to the drugstore yesterday to

buy foundation and concealer in a shade she thought would be a good match for you.'

'Oh. Then I'm incredibly sorry I just made that rude comment.'

'Don't be. Don't waste any energy on anything but what's in front of you.'

'Good advice,' Billy said, feeling even more sobered by the terror of the day.

He swallowed all twelve of the capsules standing at his kitchen sink.

Billy sat at Rayleen's kitchen table, awkwardly unsure of where to look as she tenderly applied make-up to his nose and around his eyes. Now and then he winced, and she apologized. And he had to tell her over and over again to stop apologizing.

'Where's Jesse?' he asked.

'Helping Mrs Hinman down the stairs. Then he's going to bring the car around.'

'Mrs Hinman's coming? But she can't . . . Wait. Car? Jesse has a car?'

'Sure. How'd you think he was getting back and forth to see his mother?'

'But he flew out here.'

'And then he bought a cheap used car to get around while he was here.'

Billy wanted to ask what Jesse'd do with the car when he flew home. But he didn't want to introduce the idea of Jesse flying away. Not to Rayleen. Not to himself.

'There,' Rayleen said. 'Not bad if I do say so myself. Here. Take a look at yourself in the mirror.'

Billy accepted the mirror, and, for the second time in

three days, regarded his own face. She'd done a great job on the bruises. They had all but disappeared. Of course she couldn't fix the swelling of his nose or the broken blood vessel in his eye. It was hard to focus off that, but he tried. He tried to just take in his face.

'Much less beaten-up-looking,' he said. 'Still older.'

'None of us are getting younger.'

'But you got older one day at a time. I took on twelve years all in one sitting.'

Jesse held the door of the school open for him. Billy walked into the tiny hallway, his vision darkened by the loan of Jesse's sunglasses. He felt Jesse's shoulder pressed against his on the right, Felipe's shoulder on the left. He felt their arms hooked through his, as if holding him up, transporting the wounded. In Jesse's other hand Billy saw a single long-stemmed red rose. Billy assumed he'd brought it for Grace, but hadn't asked. He glanced over his shoulder to be sure Rayleen and Mrs Hinman were still back there. Rayleen pointed toward the office as if she knew exactly where to find it. Maybe she did.

'Everything is so tiny,' Billy whispered to Jesse.

'Is it freaking you out?'

'Very much so. It makes me claustrophobic. Like I'm in a doll house. It reminds me of my school days. And I really thought I'd managed to forget them.'

'Are you breathing?'

'Not very much, no.'

'I'd recommend it.'

Rayleen held the office door open, and they massed in. A young black woman with close-shaved hair looked up from behind a desk.

'We're here to see Grace Ferguson's dance performance,' Jesse said.

The woman looked baffled for a moment. She looked them over, stopping to pay particular attention to Billy. Or was that his imagination? No. He didn't think it was.

'All five of you?'

'All five of us,' Jesse said, without missing a beat.

'And you would be . . .'

'Her neighbors.'

'Ah. I see. You know her mother is already here, and with a family friend.'

'Good,' Jesse said.

Billy admired Jesse's ability to answer only the question in front of him, and not the subtext of the situation.

'Well, OK, then,' the woman said. She pulled open a drawer while sneaking another glance at Billy. 'Five more visitor's passes. That makes seven just for Grace. I think that's a new record.'

'She's an unusually popular girl,' Jesse said.

Billy struggled with the clip on his visitor's pass as an excuse not to look at the lockers and water fountains and classroom doors. When he looked up, he saw the sign for the auditorium, and his heart jumped.

'Was it just me?' he asked. 'Or was that office lady looking at me funny?'

'Oh, no,' Rayleen said. 'It wasn't just you. I think it was the sunglasses. And the fact that you look nervous. But it doesn't matter now.'

They stopped in front of the auditorium. Billy could hear the din of hundreds of grade-schoolers inside. Jesse opened Billy's hand and pressed something into his palm.

When he examined his hand, he saw two little foam cylinders.

'Earplugs,' Jesse said. 'It's going to be noisy in there.'

'It's noisy out here.'

'Here, I'll show you how to put them in.'

Jesse tugged gently on the outside of his ears, one at a time, and slid the compressed cylinders into place.

'They'll expand,' he said. 'You'll still hear, but it should muffle things.'

Then he swung the door to the auditorium wide, and the sound of kids' voices hit Billy, a solid wall of noise. He couldn't imagine what it must sound like unmuffled. But the earplugs created a sense of distance, which felt almost like dreaminess. As if he were dreaming the sound. And maybe the herbs were making him just a tiny bit sleepy. So he decided to pretend he was dreaming about a grade-school auditorium.

They sat together in a roped-off area of seats, the first two rows in the center section. Billy glanced around briefly and found himself eye to eye with Grace's mom. She was sitting with Yolanda, one row forward and five or six seats over. She glared at Billy and then made a point of looking away.

'Eileen is shooting daggers at me,' he whispered to Rayleen and Jesse, wondering if the earplugs made him talk too loudly without knowing it.

'Oh,' Rayleen said. 'To be expected, I guess.'

Silence. If you could call the din of three hundred noisy kids silence.

Then Rayleen said, 'Did I ever tell you that was my mother's name? Eileen?'

Jesse said, 'Yes,' and Billy said, 'No,' at exactly the same time.

'I meant Billy, actually. And my dad's name was Ray. Ray and Eileen.'

'Oh,' Billy said.

'So . . .'

'So . . . Oh! Right. Ray and Eileen. Rayleen.'

A grown-up took the stage and demanded quiet, so the show could begin. And, amazingly, the kids shut up. Not on a dime, but in a matter of tens of seconds. So it was a quieter dream after that.

'How long is this whole thing?' he whispered in Jesse's ear. 'Is this play part an hour all in itself?'

'The whole assembly is fifty minutes. Including Grace's dance.'

'My God, it's been more than fifty minutes already. Hasn't it?'

Jesse peered at his watch.

'It's been nine minutes,' he whispered.

'Oh, dear God.'

A moment later Billy glanced down to see Jesse's hand close to, but not touching, his panicky gut. Billy breathed deeply and received all the healing he could gather.

When Grace walked out on the stage, all five of them applauded. And Billy could see Eileen and Yolanda clapping as well. He pulled out the earplugs and took off Jesse's sunglasses, so he wouldn't miss – or even muffle – a thing.

She was wearing the blue tunic Mrs Hinman had made for her, over black tights. Billy hadn't even known Grace owned black tights. Someone must have bought them for her for this occasion.

He leaned over Felipe and touched Mrs Hinman on the shoulder.

'Told you she'd love it,' he whispered.

And Mrs Hinman's face lit up.

Grace took a position properly back from the edge of the stage, and the world stood still.

'Oh, my God, she looks so beautiful,' Billy breathed out loud.

Rayleen had wound flowers into Grace's hair, and every ounce of Grace-spirit glowed from the inside out. If she was nervous, if she hadn't slept, you'd never have known it.

'She's a natural,' he breathed quietly. Reverently. 'I was wrong about that.'

How could I have made that mistake? he wondered. Maybe because he'd never taught anyone before, never witnessed the first few months of anyone's lessons except his own. And maybe everybody goes through an awkward stage, one that's recognizable only from the outside.

She hadn't even begun dancing yet. The music hadn't even started. It didn't matter. He'd seen her do the dance a hundred times. That much he knew she could do. Now he was watching her take the stage. Take the audience.

'She's a natural,' he said again.

The music started, the song Billy had picked out. Grace tilted her head ever so slightly, as if listening. And she smiled. And she danced.

And she was perfect.

Her time step was perfect. Her Buffalo turns were perfect. Her arms were perfect. Her upper body looked relaxed. She never once stopped smiling. And it was a real smile, too. Not a stage smile. Even her smile was a natural.

He counted out the treble hops with her, biting down hard on his own molars with tension, as if he could drive her motions. But he couldn't, nor did she need him to.

The trebles were perfect.

Her finish was brilliant. Crisp and clean. She even threw her arms wide, as if inviting, receiving, the acclaim she so deserved, had worked so hard for.

One beat of silence. The audience needed a split second to catch up to the performer. Then the applause. Billy leapt to his feet to applaud. His four neighbors followed, Mrs Hinman leaning on Felipe and struggling. Then Eileen and Yolanda jumped to their feet. Grace took a bow from the waist. The applause continued. Intensified, if anything. Other parents were standing now, and Grace's smile had turned into a beam.

'She was born for this,' Billy said out loud.

Jesse cocked his arm back and sailed the red rose, end over end, on to the stage.

Grace ran to it, picked it up, and curtsied, cradling it in the crook of her arm. Curtsied! He had never taught her that. He had never told her how to hold a long-stemmed rose. Had she seen these things in a movie, or on TV? Or did they just spring from her in some natural way?

The din set in again as the kids behind him began to shuffle out of the auditorium, but Billy paid it no mind.

Grace trotted down the stairs from the stage and headed right for him, and he met her halfway. He didn't even bother to look around and see if Jesse, or any other form of moral support, remained close by.

She stood at his feet, beaming up into his face, between the stage and the front row, asking a question with her eyes. Well, not *a* question. *The* question. And not even, 'Are you proud of me?' Because that went without saying. More, 'Exactly *how* proud of me?'

He took her face between his hands.

'I was good,' she said breathlessly.

'Oh, my God. Grace. You were . . .'

But he should have been faster. He should have spit it right out. Because, before he could even tell her what she was, what she had been, the face disappeared from between his hands. It was yanked away.

Eileen had Grace by the elbow and had taken her back.

'You see this?' Eileen said to Billy, all bluster and anger.

She held up a bright orange plastic disc, like a little key fob on a chain. It had some gold writing on it, but Billy couldn't make it out.

'You know what this is?' she spat.

Billy shook his head blankly.

'It's a thirty-day chip. It means I have thirty days clean. It means I have no drugs in my house, I have no drugs in my bloodstream, and it means that if any of you come near my daughter – and I mean within a hundred feet of my daughter – I'm going to call the police and have you arrested for kidnapping. That's what it means.'

She pivoted abruptly and towed Grace down the aisle to the door. Grace looked back over her shoulder and offered a plaintive wave goodbye. Billy waved back.

'Sorry,' Yolanda said, startling him. 'Sorry. She actually didn't warn me she was about to do that. I'll try to talk to her.'

And she trotted down the aisle to catch up.

Billy woke suddenly from his dream-turned-nightmare and found himself in public, in a school, in a tragedy. He spun around looking for Jesse, who, it turned out, had been standing just behind Billy's left shoulder, and nearly knocked him down.

'I need to go home,' Billy said. 'It's an emergency. I'm totally panicking. I'm in over my head. You have to help me.'

'I wish you'd talk to me,' Grace's mom said.

Grace was sitting on the floor about two feet from the TV, cross-legged, with her elbows on her knees and her chin on her fists, staring at that cartoon show she didn't much like. But it didn't matter that she didn't like it, because she wasn't paying any attention to it anyway.

'Want to play a game of checkers?' Grace's mom asked.

'No, thanks.'

'You used to love it when we played checkers.'

'I just don't feel like it, is all.'

'Want to walk down to the boulevard and get an ice cream? Can't very well say you're not in the mood for that.'

'Yeah, I can. I'm not in the mood for that.'

Grace's mom stepped between Grace and the TV set, and turned off the show. She stood looking down at Grace, and Grace had to crane her neck back painfully to even see her mom's face hovering up there, high above her.

'I'm having a little trouble,' her mom said, 'with how you haven't even said you're happy to be home. Or that you're proud of me for my thirty days. I worked hard for those thirty days. And you're so bent out of shape about some neighbors and a cat that you don't even seem to have noticed. You haven't even told me I did a good thing.'

Grace sighed.

'That part was good,' she said.

Her mom threw up her hands, literally, and stomped away.

Yolanda came by the following day after work. About six thirty. And she brought a pizza. Pepperoni and double cheese.

'Thanks,' Grace said, and took one slice.

'Whoa,' Yolanda said, more or less to Grace's mom, because Grace had walked away by then. 'She been like this ever since—'

'No,' Grace's mom said. 'Sometimes she's even worse.'

'How bout a family chat?'

'I don't want to hear it again,' Grace's mom said.

'I'll chat,' Grace said.

Grace sat on one end of the couch with her pizza, and Yolanda sat at the other end. Grace's mom stayed at the kitchen table, lit a cigarette, and looked the other way.

'I hate it when you smoke in the house,' Grace said.

'I know you do,' her mom said. 'But you don't always get your way.'

'I don't ever get my way,' Grace said.

'Hey, hey, whoa,' Yolanda said. 'Chatting, not bickering. Useful chatting. Eileen, Grace just told you how she felt about something, and you totally blew her off. You want to do that one over?'

Grace's mom sighed.

'I know I used to smoke outside. And I know you liked that better. But now I feel like I have to watch you every minute. I feel like if I turn my back for even that long you'll go running to see one of the neighbors.'

'So? Would that be such a terrible thing?'

'Whoa, whoa, Grace,' Yolanda said. 'Useful chatting. If your mom promises to go back to smoking outside, do you promise not to go anywhere while she's gone?'

Grace sighed. Sniffled.

'Yeah, OK.'

'Listen to her,' Grace's mom said. 'She sounds like a wrung-out dishrag. We used to be great together. We used to be all we needed, just me and Grace against the world. Now she's moping around like a sick puppy because I won't let her see those awful people.'

'They're not awful people!' Grace shouted.

'Eileen! Foul!' Yolanda barked. 'Do that one over.'

'OK. Fine. I'm sorry. Because I won't let her see her friends. She used to be happy with me. Without all those other people. And now look at her. She looks like she just lost her best friend.'

'I did,' Grace said.

Grace's mom turned her back and smoked more ferociously.

'Yeah, she looks bad,' Yolanda said. 'She was really coming alive for a while there. And now she looks like a plant you forgot to water. Every time I look over at her, I expect to see a dead leaf fall off. Don't you want her to thrive?'

'I want her to thrive with *me*,' Grace's mom said, her back still turned.

'That's selfish.'

'F—. Screw you, Yolanda.'

'Oh, so that's how it's gonna be. Now listen here, little missy. Yeah. It used to be just the two of you, how lovely. But then you took a powder. And that wasn't Grace's fault. Now she has new people in her life, and it's a damn good thing, because without them, she'd either be dead or in the system. You wouldn't get her back for a year, minimum. She's here because some people took over for you. You can't undo that. She bonded with them, and you can't subtract them no matter how hard you try.'

'Watch me,' Grace's mom said, stamping out her cigarette on a plate left over from dinner.

'OK, let me put it another way. You can subtract them from Grace's life, even though that sucks and it's not fair in any way. And I can't stop you. But you can't subtract them from Grace.'

'She'll get over it,' Grace's mom said. Quietly. Almost as if she might be crying a little, but Grace couldn't tell for sure.

'Well, let's see,' Yolanda said. 'Grace? Are you ever gonna get over it?'

'No.'

'She says she's never gonna get over it, Eileen.'

'People always say that. But then they do.'

'You're breaking your daughter's heart. I strongly advise you to consider a compromise.'

'I don't want to compromise.'

'Nobody ever does,' Yolanda said. She picked up another slice of pizza on her way out the door. 'Call me if you need me, Grace.'

'She doesn't need you!' Grace's mom shouted. 'She just needs *me*!'

Yolanda tilted her head a little, and raised one eyebrow in a funny way.

'Call me if you need me, Grace,' she said again.

"K,' Grace said.

Then Yolanda let herself out, and Grace snagged three more pieces of the pizza and locked herself in her room for the night.

When Grace woke in the morning, the sky was barely light. She lay still a minute on her back under the covers, watching the tiny bit of light bleed through the curtains over her bed. In her head, she replayed Monday's dance, right up to the part where her mom grabbed her elbow and snatched her away.

Grace threw the covers back and jumped out of bed, tiptoeing barefoot to her mom's bedroom door. She peered in, barely breathing. Her mom did not wake up.

She tiptoed over to the yellow message pad by the phone, slowly and quietly tore off one sheet, and wrote a message on it in her best block printing.

YOU NEVER TOLD ME WHAT I WAS. YOU STARTED TO TELL ME. DO YOU REMEMBER WHAT YOU WERE GOING TO SAY?
LOVE, GRACE

She unlocked the door silently, stopping to be sure nothing stirred in her mom's room, then vaulted upstairs, folded the note in half, and slipped it under Billy's door.

'Hi, Billy, hi, kitty,' she whispered through the door. 'I love you.'

Then she ran back home and jumped into bed before her mom could possibly have time to wake up.

When Grace woke the following morning, her mom was already in the kitchen making oatmeal, which was disappointing. Not the oatmeal – Grace liked oatmeal – but the not having any time to sneak away. After all, she'd only promised not to sneak away while her mom was outside smoking. She hadn't said a word about six o'clock in the morning.

Grace padded to the kitchen table and sat down, frowning, and her mom quick stubbed out a cigarette.

'I thought you were only going to smoke outside.'

'You were sleeping, so I thought it'd be OK. I thought that was just when you were around.'

'Well, I'm around now, and it stinks in here, and I hate it.'

Grace's mom sighed.

'Fine. Tomorrow I'll take my morning cigarette outside.'

'Thank you.'

Grace knew her mom was trying extra hard now. Cooking three meals a day, vacuuming the rug, picking her up right on time from school. And Grace knew why, too. She was trying to do every single mom-thing right to make up for the one really important thing she still refused to do.

'I don't want to go to school today,' Grace said. 'I feel sick.'

'What's wrong with you?'

'I'm sick to my stomach.'

Grace's mom put a warm hand on her forehead.

'You don't have a fever.'

'I didn't say I did. I said I was sick to my stomach. Will you go to the store today and get me ginger ale?'

'Yeah. OK. After breakfast. I guess I could.'

'Good. I'm going back to bed.'

Grace lay in bed and listened to her mom washing the dishes from the breakfast nobody had bothered to eat. Then she heard their apartment door open.

'I'll be back in, like, ten minutes, Grace.'

Was her mom really going to walk out the door without extracting a promise from her to stay put? And, if so, was it a trap? Would Grace stick her head out into the hall only to be ambushed by an angry mom?

Grace heard the door slam shut again, and the deadbolts turning from the outside with her mom's keys. She held still, barely breathing, then slunk out of bed and crept to the window, where she watched her mom's legs disappear down the block.

Grace ran to the door, threw it open, and bolted up the stairs to Billy's door.

She almost knocked. For one breathless, excited moment, she almost knocked on his door. But then she remembered what her mom had said about getting him arrested. In which case he would die. Seriously. Even if Jesse and Rayleen figured out how to get him out a day or two later, it was Billy, and Billy would still die.

She ran her finger carefully under the bottom of his door and touched the corner of an envelope. She pressed down on it and pulled, and it slid out into the hall at her feet. She grabbed it and ran back to bed, careful to lock the same deadbolts she had unlocked when leaving.

She lay in bed, fingers trembling a little, and tore open the note.

Yes, I remember. You were the shiniest thing I've ever seen. That's what I was going to say. That you were the shiniest thing I've ever seen.
  Love, Billy

When Grace's mom got home, Grace heard her rattling around in the kitchen, and she could even hear the fizz of the ginger ale when her mom took the cap off the bottle.

A minute later, her mom stood in the bedroom doorway, smiling sadly.

'I'm sorry if this whole thing is making you so miserable you have an upset stomach,' she said. 'So . . . I was just thinking . . . maybe a little bit of a compromise *is* in order.'

'What kind?' she asked, too hopeful.

'Never mind. It'll be a surprise. You'll see.'

The pounding on his door nearly stopped Billy's heart. He instinctively looked down at himself. He was still in bed. He was wearing his rattiest pajamas. He ran a hand through his hair. He hadn't brushed it for days.

'Who is it?'

'Eileen Ferguson.'

She didn't sound any happier. Her tone filled Billy's sore gut with nails and ice.

'What do you want?'

'I came for Grace's cat.'

Billy lay frozen for several seconds, then got up and made his way to the door. He breathed deeply three times before opening it.

She looked startled to see him. She actually took one step back. He must look a fright, he realized, with his black eyes turning yellow, and no make-up to hide the truth. But he didn't have time to care about that now.

'You're taking the cat?'

'It's Grace's cat.'

'Well. Yes. But she's become accustomed to a certain

standard of living. Are you going to take care of her?'

'Grace will take care of the cat.'

'Grace has no idea how. She's never so much as fed her.'

'She'll figure it out.'

Billy pulled a big, deep breath and thought about Jesse, and how he'd handle a situation like this.

'I am responsible for the cat,' Billy said evenly. 'I can't just hand you the cat. There's more to the cat than just handing her over. She needs her litter box, and her litter. And the little scoop you use to clean it. And she needs her food and water dish, and her wet food, and her dry food, and her brush. And unless I get to instruct Grace in her proper care and feeding, the cat leaves this apartment over my dead body.'

Billy's heart pounded as he waited for her reply, and it made him feel weak, as though he needed to sit down. He had no strength for a confrontation.

'Tell you what,' Eileen said, brushing back her hair the way she tended to do when angry. 'You give me the cat. I'll take her downstairs to Grace—'

'Why isn't Grace in school?'

'None of your business. I'll give the cat to Grace. And you put all that other stuff out in the hall. And I'll come get it in . . . about . . . an hour. And that'll give you time to write out a note for Grace about feeding and stuff.'

Billy blinked too many times, too quickly.

It had never occurred to him that he might have to give up the cat.

He called her with the special 'psst' sound he used to announce the serving of wet cat food, and she came running. He scooped her up, turned her on to her back, and buried his face in the soft fur of her belly.

'Bye, kid,' he whispered. 'Take care of yourself.'

He handed her over to Eileen, but the cat panicked and leapt down again. He picked her up and tried again. But she refused to be held by Grace's mom.

'She doesn't like you,' Billy said.

'That's a load of horseshit.'

'She probably feels your anger. It scares her.'

'Just give her to me. I'll hold tighter this time.'

'No,' Billy said. 'Send Grace.'

'I'm not—'

'Stand right here and supervise if you want. But I either hand the cat to Grace or she doesn't leave this apartment.'

Billy looked right into her eyes. She glared back at him, as if considering a suitable response – one that might or might not involve fisticuffs. Then she turned and stomped off down the stairs.

A minute later she stomped back up with Grace by her side. Billy's heart fell to see Grace. She looked terrible. Downhearted and downright sick. Well, she must be sick, literally sick, or she wouldn't be home from school.

She padded up to his open doorway in her bare feet, looking up at him with her face open and soft.

'Please, Mom,' Grace said, her voice breaking Billy's heart. 'I'm worried Billy'll be too lonely without the cat. Please?'

'Just take the cat,' her mom said. 'You're always complaining how I won't let you keep your cat and I won't let you see your friends. Take the damn cat.'

Billy bent down and placed the cat in her waiting arms

'Take her,' he said. 'It's OK.'

'I'm sorry,' she whispered. 'You sure you won't be too lonely without the cat?'

'I'll be OK.'

Then Grace's mom grabbed her by the elbow and pulled her along the hall and down the stairs.

Billy closed the door and gathered up everything that belonged to Mr Lafferty the Girl Cat, attaching sticky notes to each item to indicate when it was to be used and how. Then he stacked it all in the hallway outside his door. As a final afterthought, he dragged out the plywood dance floor, managing to lever it up at a sharp angle to get it through the door.

Then he put himself back to bed, listening as it was all dragged and carried away.

It was lonely without the cat.

Twelve lonely days later, Rayleen announced that Jesse would be flying home soon.

'He's going to come over in a minute to talk to you himself,' she said, settling comfortably on his couch. She'd begun to stay for long visits since the cat moved out. 'But I just wanted to talk to you alone for a minute first.'

Billy sighed, and waited, and let the information filter down into his gut. It was hardly unexpected. That was the best he could say for it. And he knew it must be a much greater hell for Rayleen, who was, after all, his girlfriend.

'Well,' Billy said, in his best attempt at circumspection, 'it's not like we didn't know it would happen. Sooner or later. Is he leaving you with the car?'

A long silence. A silence freighted with some important subtext, but Billy could not imagine what it was. After all, it was just an old junker of a car.

'I'm going with him,' Rayleen said.

And they sat.

'We've been talking about it for a while now,' she said. 'But I didn't know if I could bring myself to abandon Grace. But now we can't see Grace anyway . . . And, look, I feel really bad about leaving you, too. It's not that I don't get that this probably feels like an abandonment to you, too. But—'

'But I'm a grown man,' Billy said. 'I may not do the world's best job at it, but I'm an adult. And it would be lunacy for you to stay here just for me. Absolute lunacy.'

'Thank you,' Rayleen said, 'I really appreciate you taking it this way. It's just that . . . I just keep thinking maybe this is the last train to happy. And I better get on.'

'You better,' Billy said.

'I'm sorry.'

'Don't be,' Billy said. 'Just go be happy. Just get on the damn train.'

Later on that same lonely day, Jesse came over by himself, to say a proper goodbye. He held a paper grocery sack in one hand.

'I brought you three presents,' he said, in that voice Billy could no longer recall how to live without. 'Well, two and a half. They're not new. They're hand-me-down presents, because I'm almost out of savings. I need to go home and get back to work.'

He handed Billy the bag.

Inside Billy found a pair of red-silk pajamas, which he realized with a jolt must have been Jesse's, and the partially burned sage stick.

'That's not an invitation to live in pajamas twenty-four seven,' Jesse said.

'I'll try not to take it as such. Thank you. Is the sage stick the half?'

In which case one whole present was still missing, but it might seem ungrateful to say so.

'Oh. The car,' Jesse said. 'We're leaving the car. I was going to leave it to you, but we talked it over and decided it would be more of a burden to you than anything else. You'd have to go to the DMV and get it in your name, and get your license back, and pay for insurance. So I signed it over to Felipe, with the understanding that it's really for the three of you. You and Felipe and Mrs Hinman. So I guess that's a third of a present. He promised to drive the two of you to the grocery store at least once a week.'

'That'll be nice for Mrs Hinman.'

'That's what we thought,' Jesse said. 'I think it's hard for her to walk.'

'It is.'

'We thought it'd be nice for you, too. That delivery service can't be cheap.'

'It costs almost as much as the groceries,' Billy said.

'Something to remember us by.'

And then he stepped in and embraced Billy. And it hurt so much that Billy almost couldn't embrace him back. And not because of his ribs, either, though they still ached some. But in time he did manage to fulfill his side of the hug.

'I don't know what I'm going to do without you guys.'

He'd been trying not to say it. But sooner or later it had been bound to break through.

'You won't be without us,' Jesse said. 'We'll just be a lot farther away. And you'll have to start checking your mail-box again.'

'I can do that,' Billy said.

*   *   *

Three lonely days later, they were gone.

In the four lonely days that followed, Billy and Felipe and Felipe's shy girlfriend Clara and the building super, Casper, moved Mrs Hinman downstairs into Rayleen's old apartment, which seemed to make her happy.

And seeing Mrs Hinman happy made Billy feel just the tiniest bit less lonely. But like everything else, good and bad, the feeling passed along on its own.

In the lonely weeks that followed, Billy now and then heard unfamiliar voices in the hallway as two new couples moved in.

Once he stuck his head out into the hall and said hello to one of the couples, a young Hispanic boy and girl who didn't look a day over seventeen. But it seemed to alarm them. So he gave up on that and went back to being lonely.

Two lonely months later, Billy found another bright yellow note tucked under his door.

It said, in Grace's careful block printing:

MR LAFFERTY THE GIRL CAT MISSES YOU. AND SO
DO I.
LOVE, GRACE

The words had been written inside a border, a little pen drawing. At first Billy took it to be a stylized heart, even though the top lobes were too pointy, and the series of loops all around it didn't seem to fit the heart motif. Later he realized it was a pair of wings, the loops depicting feathers.

He wrote a note back.

Remember how you said you'd always find me? Well, don't ever forget that. Please.
Love, Billy

But it sat under his door for more than a month, and Grace never seemed to manage to get away to retrieve it. So in time he took it back and threw it away.

Three lonely months after that, Felipe came to his door, and sat with him, and talked to him, and announced that he was moving in with Clara.

'It's just that her apartment is so much nicer than mine. Bigger, and in a better neighborhood. And with both of us paying one rent, we'll have a lot more money. Maybe even enough to get married. She's putting herself through cooking school, did I tell you? She's gonna be a chef. Not a lot of lady chefs. 'Specially not a lot of Chicana ones. That's a big deal, you know?'

They sat for a time.

Billy made a pot of coffee.

'I'm not trying to take the car. I know it belongs to all of us. If you want, I'll leave the car.'

'What would I do with the car? I don't even have a license.'

'We won't be so far away. It's like a fifteen-minute drive. I'll come back once a week and take you and Mrs Hinman to the store. I won't let you down on that.'

'I know you won't.'

He poured Felipe a mug of black coffee, and poured himself a mug with more than an inch of room for cream. He took more cream in his coffee now that he didn't have to have his groceries delivered. A lot more.

'It's not that I don't feel bad leaving you here,' Felipe said. 'I do. It's just that . . .'

'It's just that this might be the last train to happy. And you want to make sure to get on it.'

Felipe chewed that over for a moment.

'I guess. I wasn't thinking of it like a train. But something like that. Yeah.'

'And you should,' Billy said. 'You should get on the damn train.'

A lonely month after that, Billy bumped into Grace and her mom in the hallway on his way out to check the mail. They must have been coming in from school.

He was wearing his red-silk Jesse-pajamas, and his hair was uncombed.

Grace's eyes lit up to see him. But they still didn't look anything like Grace's eyes before. When she was thriving.

'Billy!' she shouted.

'Stop talking to him,' Grace's mother said, and steered her down the basement stairs by the arm.

Billy peered over the railing, and Grace looked up at him and waved sadly, and he waved back.

He locked himself into his apartment, made coffee, then realized he had never checked the mail, and had to do it all over again.

It was worth it, though, because he'd gotten a letter from Rayleen.

She said, among other things, that they had a foster kid

now, that his name was Jamal, and he was only four, and his mom had just died from an overdose. But she said Jesse was working his famous Jesse magic on him.

'I don't doubt that,' Billy said, out loud to his lonely apartment.

And, also, as both Jesse and Rayleen always did, she enclosed a letter to Grace, for Billy to pass along. If. If he ever saw her.

'Well. I saw her,' he said out loud.

He wrote a letter back to Rayleen.

'Dear Rayleen,' it said, among other things. 'You're a natural. This is the role you were born to play.'

Four lonely months after that, Mrs Hinman passed away.

Billy hadn't seen her in a day or two, but hadn't thought much about it, because sometimes he saw her every day, but oftentimes he did not.

Then Felipe came over to drive them to the grocery store, and knocked on her door, but never got an answer. Felipe jimmied the lock on her mailbox and found about three days' worth of mail, including her Social Security check, which she was notoriously careful about retrieving promptly on the third of every month.

Felipe called the super, Casper, on his cell phone, and Casper came over and unlocked the door. Neither Billy nor Felipe went in.

A minute later Casper came out and said she was in bed, just as if she were sleeping, and that it looked like she had died peacefully in her sleep.

'Well, that's something,' Felipe said.

And Casper said, 'Yeah, we all gotta go sometime.'

'Least she had somebody to take care of her right up to the end.'

'Yeah,' Casper said. 'When did you guys get so close, anyway?'

But Billy didn't like to talk to Casper, and Felipe chose not to offer the obvious answer.

Later, after Casper left to notify the proper authorities, Felipe asked if there was anything Billy thought they should do.

'No friends or relatives,' Billy said.

'So no memorial,' Felipe answered.

'Unless we have one ourselves.'

So they did, even though they had no idea what they were doing, figuring the intention was more important than the style in a case like this.

Then one morning Billy looked out his window, and it struck him that it was nearly spring again, and that all those lonely days and weeks and months had added up to a lonely year.

'So what did you think, Billy Boy?' he asked out loud. 'That just this once they'd break with tradition and add up to something else?'

Grace

Grace heard Yolanda let herself in with her spare key. It was the key that used to belong to Grace, only now Grace's mom figured Grace wouldn't need a key any more, since she never went anywhere by herself.

Grace was lying on her belly on the plywood dance floor – because it was cleaner than the rug – doing homework. The Lewis and Clark expedition and Sacagawea. Grace was writing an essay about how the woman didn't get enough credit in the history books. Like what's new?

Yolanda came and stood over her.

'History?' Yolanda asked.

'Yup.'

'I used to like history.'

'I hate it.'

'Don't you ever dance any more?'

'Not so much, no. I got tired of doing that same dance over and over. I asked my mom if I could take lessons, but she says we can't afford it. Are you here to go to the meeting with us? For her one-year anniversary? You're pretty early. It's not for, like, two hours.'

Yolanda squatted down and put a hand on Grace's back. 'We need to do her fifth step first.'

'Which one is that?'

'Grace. I can't believe, after all the meetings you go to, you don't know the steps.'

'Nobody said I had to *listen*.'

'The fourth step is the one everybody hates . . .'

'Oh, right. The inventory. The one where you have to write out all your character defects. Oh, wait, I know. Then the fifth step is the one where you have to tell them all to your sponsor or somebody.'

'And that's the one thing I absolutely *insist* on as a sponsor. Any sponsee of mine has to finish her fourth step in the first year.'

'Oh, well, that explains a lot,' Grace said. 'Good thing she didn't put it off till the last minute or anything.'

'Well, you know your mom.'

'I can hear you guys!' Grace's mom yelled from her bedroom.

Yolanda rolled her eyes ceilingward.

'Stay here, don't come in the bedroom. *Muchos* privacy required for this one.'

Grace ratcheted her voice into a scrunched-down whisper.

'Are you going to tell her it's a character defect to not let me see my friends?'

'I can't really tell her too much,' Yolanda whispered back. 'She kinda has to tell me. But if it comes up, I won't be shy about sharing my opinion.'

They came out of the bedroom after seven thirty, past the time they should have left to get a good seat at the birth-

day meeting. Grace's mom was being too quiet, and looking mostly at the carpet, so Grace figured it must've been a
tough deal in there.

Yolanda elbowed Grace's mom in the ribs twice, but
nothing happened, so she said, 'Grace. Your mom has
something she wants to say to you.'

Grace sat up cross-legged on her old dance floor and
pulled the cat close.

Grace expected her mom to come sit with her, but she
never did. She just stood by the kitchen counter, running
her finger along the edge where that one tile was missing.

'Shouldn't I wait and do all the amends together when
we get to the ninth step?'

'Eileen,' Yolanda said. 'Your daughter is right here in
front of you. Make the damn amends.'

Grace's mom sighed dramatically.

'OK. Fine. Grace. It came up while I was doing the steps
with Yolanda that it was kind of mean and selfish of me to
take you away from those people.'

'You can say names, Mom. You don't have to keep calling them "those people".'

'Well, what difference does it make, Grace?'

But Yolanda shot her a tough sponsor look.

'OK. Fine. To take you away from Billy and Rayleen and
the others.'

Grace waited. But it didn't sound like there was more.

'And?'

'And . . . I know it was very hard on you, and it made
you droopy and sad.'

'So . . .'

'So I'm telling you I'm sorry.'

'But you're not changing your mind.'

'I'm telling you I'm sorry.'

'But you're not. You're not sorry. If you were sorry, you'd stop doing it.'

'Oh, my God,' Grace's mom said, turning to Yolanda for support. 'You see what I put up with here?'

'Don't come crying to me,' Yolanda said. 'I'm with Grace. Sorry doesn't mean shit. Not if you don't plan to stop doing the thing you're so sorry about. There has to be more to amends than just a word. Anybody can say a damn word.'

Grace's mom squeezed her eyes closed, like the way she did when she was counting to ten to keep from losing her temper. Then she opened them and said, 'It's never enough, is it? Whatever I manage to do, it's just never enough.'

'Well, that's recovery for you,' Yolanda said, not sounding too sympathetic. 'We better get to this meeting. You just edgy cause it's your year? Lot of people get edgy when they come up on a year.'

'Maybe,' Grace's mom said. 'I *have* been feeling a little squirrelly lately.'

Grace was hoping they'd talk more on the way to the meeting, but nobody did.

Grace was on her way to the coffee and literature table in the back to see if they had cookies this week or if nobody bothered to bring them, and while she was pushing and 'excuse-me-ing' her way through all the people, she banged right into the big tire of a wheelchair.

'Oh, my God,' she said. 'Curtis Schoenfeld.'

'Hey, Grace,' he said, like he wished he didn't have to talk to her at all.

'Where'd you go? I've been coming to meetings with my mom again for like a year and I never once saw you. Did you move away?'

'No,' he said, wheeling himself away from her. 'We didn't move.'

She thought about walking along with him and talking some more, but he didn't seem to want to talk, and besides, she reminded herself, he *was* a giant stinkhead, and he didn't seem to have gone in a very non-stinky direction since she last saw him. So instead she just snagged three peanut butter cookies and sat in the back and waited for the meeting to start, which wasn't a very long wait, because they'd gotten there a little late, practically when the meeting started.

She decided to listen better to the steps this time, even though she really didn't wake up and decide that until the reader got to four.

'Four. Made a searching and fearless moral inventory of ourselves.'

The man who was reading the steps had a deep, honey voice that reminded her a little of Jesse, and made her lonely for him.

'Five. Admitted to God, to ourselves, and to another human being the exact nature of our wrongs.'

Well, at least she *admitted* it, Grace thought.

'Six. Were entirely ready to have God remove all these defects of character.'

So maybe she just wasn't entirely ready yet, and maybe that was OK, because she was only at step five so far.

'Seven. Humbly asked Him to remove our shortcomings.'

Grace didn't tend to think of her mom together with words like humble. Then again, she'd looked pretty humble when she'd come out of the bedroom with Yolanda.

Maybe she just needed time to get through more of the steps. It sounded like just admitting a defect wasn't the same as having it taken away. That was a whole two steps down the road.

At four steps a year, that would be . . .

But something interrupted her thoughts. The reading of the steps and traditions was over, and the group leader asked if anyone was in their first thirty days of recovery, so he could give them a welcome chip. And Grace could never have guessed who would raise their hands. *Both* of Curtis Schoenfeld's parents, that's who! Both of them! So that's why she hadn't seen him for this whole year!

Grace looked around to see where Curtis was sitting, and she saw him right away, but he wouldn't look at her. Poor Curtis. Grace hoped his parents would get it right this time, and not put him through what she went through with her mom. There wasn't a stinkhead on the planet Grace would wish that on.

The first lady who shared was an anniversary person, like her mom. There were two that night. This lady, who had eleven years, and then her mom with one. So Grace knew her mom would go second.

But, for some reason, even though she usually didn't listen very well in the meetings, Grace listened to the Eleven Year Lady. Maybe because she was talking about positive stuff, different ways to look to things, not just going over and over all the drugs she took. Or maybe it was because Grace could tell her mom was listening, and that something her mom was hearing was making her look . . . humble.

Accepting things. That's what the talk was about. About

how insane it is to try to pretend something isn't a certain way, or that you can make it another way, just because you don't like it. And how that seems to be the one thing that makes addicts use drugs, and pretty much ruins everybody's lives. This thing about refusing to just accept the way things are when you can't change them anyway.

Then it was her mom's turn to talk, but she didn't seem to have much of anything to say. She said her name was Eileen, and that she was an addict, but then she just kept tripping over her own words. Finally she said she couldn't really say anything because she didn't know anything. She said she used to think she knew a lot, but she just got it now, how wrong that was, and how she didn't know a damn thing.

Grace snuck a little glance over at Curtis Schoenfeld to see if he was laughing at her mom for not knowing a damn thing, but he didn't look like he was even listening. Besides, at least her mom had a year clean, so probably he wouldn't dare.

After the meeting, Grace distinctly heard Yolanda tell her mom she'd done a good share. She gave Grace's mom a pat on the shoulder and said that.

'Good share.'

Everyone was milling around and talking, and Grace squeezed her way through to Yolanda and said, 'What was good about it? She said she didn't know anything.'

'Right,' Yolanda said. 'That was the good part.'

'OK, that makes no sense at all. How can it be good to know nothing?'

'It's not. But if you know nothing, it's good to know that you know nothing.'

'Oh,' Grace said. 'Yeah, I guess.'

'Because as long as you think you know everything, nothing changes.'

'Oh,' Grace said again.

'You sound tired.'

'I am. It's late.'

'OK, I'll go round up your mom and drive you guys home.'

On the way to the door, Grace smacked right into Curtis again. Literally. Banged her shins running into his chair.

'Ow,' she said. 'I hope your mom and dad stay with it this time.'

'Seriously?' He still wouldn't look at her.

'Of course seriously. I hated it when my mom was out using. I wouldn't wish that on anybody. Not even you.'

Then they walked to Yolanda's car together, Yolanda and Grace and Grace's mom.

Yolanda said, 'I thought you hated Curtis.'

'I do. He's a giant stinkhead.'

'You were pretty nice to the giant stinkhead.'

'Yeah. Well. No point me being a giant stinkhead, too.'

It was nearly the end of June, the morning when Billy heard a soft knock on his door.

Nobody knocked on Billy's door any more. No one. He had gotten his wish about that. Felipe still came once a week to take him to the grocery store, but at such a set time that Billy always waited for him in the hall. And no delivery person had come by here in ages.

'Who's there?' he called through the door, trying not to sound edgy. Not realizing, until his words fed back to him, how badly he had failed.

Such a soft knock. Filled with something like trepidation, or even humility. If Billy had to venture a guess, he'd say the spooky, incredibly young couple upstairs needed something. Probably something he didn't have anyway.

'Eileen Ferguson.'

'Oh,' Billy said, realizing deeply within himself how desperately he did not want to open the door for her. 'What do you want from me?'

'I was hoping I could come in and talk.'

Her voice sounded lifeless and droopy, and it hit Billy hard that something might have happened to Grace.

He ran to the door and threw it wide.

'What's wrong? Where's Grace? Is she all right?'

'She's fine. She's downstairs.'

'Oh,' Billy said, his heart still hammering. 'All right. You want to come in. All right. Come in. I guess. Should I make a pot of coffee?'

'Oh, my God, that would be great. I could *so* use some coffee. It's near the end of the month and I'm out.'

She did not follow Billy into the kitchen. She just sat on the couch while Billy started the coffee. In his head, he tried on a dozen different ways to ask why she was there, but did not succeed in asking any of them.

'Black with sugar, right?'

'How do you know how I take my coffee?'

'Long story.'

Then he couldn't decide whether to stand there and watch the coffee drip or go back out and sit with Eileen. And the decision locked him up so completely that he knew he had to break in one direction or another. So he rejoined her in his living room.

She did not speak.

'So, how's Grace?'

'Medium,' Eileen said. 'Still a little droopy.'

'Is she still dancing?'

'No. She says she got sick of doing that same dance over and over. She asked me if she could take lessons, but I said no. Because we don't have the money. Seriously, we don't. But all the time I was saying it I knew she could get lessons for free if I would let her, and I just felt like such a total shit.'

On the word 'shit', tears began to leak from Eileen, despite an obvious effort on her part to prevent them. Billy brought her a box of tissues. He'd had them for nearly a year. A box of tissues didn't fly away, not like it had used to. Nobody came over to Billy's and cried any more.

'I'm not sure how much you know about twelve-step programs,' she said.

'Really nothing.'

'You have to make amends to the people you hurt.'

'Oh. I would think you'd want to make amends to Grace, not me.'

'I already made amends to Grace. Why? It didn't hurt you when I took her?'

'Oh, no. It did. Quite a lot. Still does.'

'Then why would you say Grace and not you?'

'Oh,' Billy said. 'I don't know. Good question. I guess because I care more about Grace than I care about me.'

After that conversation-stopper, a long silence reigned.

Finally Billy popped up and said, 'Let me just go get us that coffee, and then you can do whatever this thing is you came to do.'

He noticed, as he handed her the mug, that his hands were shaking. Eileen must have noticed it, too.

He sat across from her, and nothing happened for a truly excruciating length of time. Billy sat stock-still, weirdly aware of the slant of morning light through his thin curtains, and the way tiny dust motes danced in it, performing in front of his nose.

'It was mostly humiliation,' Eileen said, startling him.

Billy did not dare speak.

'You know that feeling, like you're a total fraud, and the

world is going to find out, and then everybody's going to judge you?'

'Yes,' Billy said. 'I do.'

'That's how I felt when you guys took Grace away from me.'

'Oh,' Billy said. 'I can see that must have been hard. I'd say we didn't mean for you to feel that way, but I'm not sure that would be the whole truth. I think everybody knew it would be terrible for you, and we hoped the pain would inspire you to go back to being Grace's mom.'

'You mean you really were trying to get her back with me?'

'Oh, yes. It was mostly Grace's idea.'

'You see, I never believed that,' Eileen said, picking up volume and emotion.

'I know you didn't. But it's the truth.'

'Why would Grace want you guys to say she couldn't see me at all?'

'Because she thought if you lost the most important thing in the world to you, it might wake you up. She thought it might drive you to get better. She wanted you to get better. Didn't Rayleen tell you that?'

'I'm not sure. Maybe. Probably. Honestly? If she did, and maybe she did, I don't think I would've really heard it. At the time. I would've just thought, Losing Grace'll make me worse, not better, so that's stupid.'

They sat for a painful length of time. Dust motes swirled.

'I'm still humiliated in front of you,' she said.

Billy laughed out loud.

'Me? No one is humiliated in front of me. How could you be?'

'Because I was such a horrible parent, and you saw it. And I know you're judging me for it.'

'Look. Eileen. I don't judge. I don't have the right to judge. I don't have that kind of standing. I'm an agoraphobic with an anxiety disorder and a strong tendency toward panic attacks. I spent twelve years of my life refusing to even go out on my front patio, or out in the hall to get the mail. Nobody is so low that they think I'm looking down on them. There is simply no space underneath me.'

They sat in silence for another painful length of time, during which Eileen drained her mug of sweet coffee.

'OK,' she said, rising suddenly to her feet. 'I'm glad we had this little talk. It was good.'

She headed for the door, so Billy ran ahead and unlocked it. And she walked out. Just like that. No further thoughts. No formal goodbye. And, Billy couldn't help noticing, no real amends. He didn't know much about twelve-step programs and how they handled amends, but he knew enough English to know the definition of the word.

It usually involved mentioning that you were sorry. That or better. That or actually doing something to make it right again.

It might have been two or three minutes later that he began to hear it, or it might have been five or ten. A sound. A very familiar, yet ancient, yet exhilarating, memory.

It was Grace. Shrieking with joy. Billy had no idea what she was feeling so joyful about, but it filled his chest nearly to breaking with emotion. He had heard nothing from Grace through his floor of late. For well over a year, Grace seemed to have forgotten that to be Grace was, by its very nature, a noisy proposition.

He heard the door to the basement apartment fly open, and a shriek big enough to fill the emptiness of the entire building.

'Billy! Billy, open your door!'

He ran to the door, undid the locks, and threw it wide. Just in time, too. Grace was literally off the ground, launching herself in his direction. She landed squarely in his arms, pushing a great 'oof' out of him, and nearly sending them both flying on to his rug.

Then she jumped down and looked up into his face, eagerly, her eyes fully alive. Just the way he remembered them.

'When do we dance?' she fairly shrieked, hurting Billy's ears in the most gratifying way.

Grace

'Whoa!' Grace shouted. 'Wow, wow, wow!'

They stood in a stretch of sandy dirt at the side of the road, Grace keeping one hand on the car for balance. Felipe cut the engine and the headlights, and then it was dark. Real darkness, which Grace had never seen. She hadn't known she'd never seen real darkness, but she knew it in that moment. Just fake city-dark.

And she'd never seen the stars. Not for real.

'That's amazing!' she shrieked.

'Ouch. My ear,' Billy said.

'Sorry.'

Grace pried her gaze away from the stars and looked around. Nothing. Not as far as her eyes could see. No buildings, no other people, no streetlights, no nothing. Just a dark road, her friend Billy, and her friends Felipe and Clara, who had driven them more than an hour out into the desert surrounding LA. Until they found this beautiful nothing.

They stood beside the car together, Grace and Billy, in this brand-new blackness, their necks craned back.

'That's so amazing,' she said again. More quietly this time.

'What, you didn't believe me?'

'I believed you. You said there'd be more stars and I listened. But I didn't know there'd be *this* many more. And I didn't picture it right. You didn't tell me they'd be all around us, like a dome. Like we're in a globe. It makes me really see how the world is round. I mean, I know it is, cause we learned that and all, but it never *seemed* like it is until now.'

Billy lifted her by the waist and set her on the hood of the car, and she leaned back against the cool windshield, wondering why the desert gets cold at night if it's known for being so hot and all.

Billy sat next to her on the hood. On the driver's side. And they looked up. Together. Grace held her hands out and made a ring, like the lens of a camera, to see if she could count the stars in just that tiny circle of sky. But even the stars through her lens-hands seemed infinite. So she set her hands in her lap again and took it in as a flabbergasting whole, breathing in deeply and then sighing.

'What's that?' she asked after a while, pointing. There was a tiny, tiny light in the sky, moving. Not a plane. Something way, way farther away. 'Is that a space ship?'

'I doubt it. Where are you looking?'

'Right there.'

'I don't see anything.'

'Right where I'm pointing. It's real little, though.'

'Your eyes are probably better than mine.'

'It looks like it's about a billion miles away. But it's moving.'

'Fast?'

'No. Kind of slow.'

'Maybe it's a satellite.'

'Oh. Maybe. But don't they go right around the Earth? Kind of near it?'

'As distance goes, yes, that would be fair to say.'

'So if that's a satellite, and satellites are in the orbit-thingy around the Earth . . . wow. Makes you wonder what else is even farther out there. You know. If we could see it.'

'Now you see what your teacher was trying to tell you.'

'Don't break my brain again, Billy. I just got it all put back together.'

They lay side by side in silence for a time. Then Grace started to glance over her shoulder at Felipe and Clara, who were still in the front seat of the car. But she stopped herself, deciding that might be embarrassing. Depending on what they were doing.

She elbowed Billy lightly.

'Hey. Are they making out back there?'

Billy looked over his shoulder.

'No. Just looking into each other's eyes.'

Felipe's voice came through. 'We can hear you in here, you know.'

'*Lo siento*, Felipe,' Grace said. '*Lo siento*, Clara.'

'*Esta bien*,' Clara called back.

They sat in silence a while longer.

'You seem pretty relaxed,' she said to Billy.

'*Pretty* relaxed. For me. I'll be a lot more relaxed when we get home, of course. Don't forget I've gone to the supermarket every week. For more than a year.'

'Is this the first place you've been that's not the supermarket?'

'No. I went to the dentist.'

'You did? When?'

'Not too long after . . . Pretty early on in that year when I didn't see you.'

'Yuck. Dentist.'

'I didn't have too much choice.'

'So how does it feel to be so far from home?'

Billy didn't answer for a time. Grace was beginning to wonder if he maybe never would.

Then he said, 'Remember the time when we were out on my patio watching the stars? I was just now thinking . . . these are the same stars.'

'No way! There are so many more!'

'No. Same amount. We're just seeing more.'

'Oh. Right. So they're the same stars. That doesn't really answer my question.'

'I meant it to. I was just thinking, if I'm under the same stars, then I can't be too far from home. From a larger perspective, I mean.'

Grace wasn't positive she knew what the word perspective meant, but she got the general idea.

'Hey. That's good. For *Billy*.' They gazed a while longer, and then Grace said, 'You still want to get home as fast as we can, though, huh?'

'More than you know.'

'How does it make you feel? I don't mean being so far from home, I mean looking at all the stars there really are. How does it make you feel?'

'Hmm,' he said. 'Like the world is big again. No. Not again. Like I only thought it had gotten small while I was inside, but now I see it was big the whole time, just waiting out there. Waiting for me to come back. How does it make *you* feel?'

'Kind of excited. But I don't know how to say why.'

'And insignificant,' he said.

'In English, Billy.'

'Like I'm not important.'

'You are to me.'

'Thanks. Can we go home now? I'm running out of brave.'

Grace sighed theatrically.

'Oh, *OK*. I guess that's about all I can expect from you for one time, isn't it?'

'I don't know why you put up with me.'

'It's not easy,' she said, and jumped off the hood, silently wishing the stars goodnight. Reminding herself that when she got home, they'd all still be there. Whether she could see them from home or not.

THE END

READING GROUP GUIDE
for
DON'T LET ME GO

Dear Reader,

Are you in a reading group? Or would you just like to linger a little longer on the novel now that you've turned the last page?

Catherine Ryan Hyde has prepared some questions which we hope you will enjoy.

1) Rayleen has her reasons for distrusting the child protective system, and they become clearer as the story unfolds. What would you do if you saw Grace sitting outside on those stairs alone? Would you call the authorities immediately, or move closer and see if there was something more personal you could do to help? Do you feel the societal safety net for children is a fair option for a child in need?

2) Have you ever known someone like Billy, who fears the world—the outdoors, people, anything unfamiliar? Did you understand, or find it impossible to be patient? Can you find a place in you that feels the same, but to a much smaller degree? Or do you approach the world with more confidence, like Jesse?

3) How did you feel when Grace made her observation (before meeting Jesse) that all the people she knew were afraid of other people? Does this seem to match with your experience? What are your observations about our fear of strangers, or even others we don't know well enough to trust?

4) Do you agree that Billy's compulsion to stay indoors in a comfortable environment is an addiction similar to the drug addiction battled by Grace's mom? Have you ever been addicted to anything, even something fairly small and benign, like shopping, or the Internet? Does it help you understand the compulsions of others, or does it seem very different?

5) Do you feel that children like Grace are best off with their moms, even when their moms are well short of ideal?

6) It's said that it takes a village to raise a child. This set of neighbors seemed an unlikely village. Do you feel they got the job done? Were you more critical of their unsuitability and failings in the child-rearing department, or more supportive of their willingness to try? Would you be willing to do what they did for a child who lived close to you?

7) Have you known someone like Jesse? What do you think is 'magic' about them? Is it just, as Grace feels, that they approach others without fear? Or is there more to it than that? Why do you feel that some people have such a talent for inspiring and influencing those around them?

8) Billy ventured out quite a bit by the end of the story – for Billy. Were you proud of him? Or still impatient? Did it feel like a big victory, or too little too late?

9) In your imagination, will Grace go on to become a professional dancer? Why do you think so, or think not?

If you would like more information about Catherine or her novels, visit her at: www.catherineryanhyde.com

Here's a teaser from
Catherine Ryan Hyde's wonderful novel

The Hardest Part of Love

Chapter One

1996

The Headlight Zone

Hayden Reese picked his way on foot in the dark, straight uphill into national forest territory, his Jenny dangling heavy on his right shoulder. Still supple she felt, and almost warm. His only little bit of comfort.

In his left hand, the shovel.

Here and there he'd take hold with his right, grasp the smooth, red, strangely burnished trunk or limb of a manzanita for balance, for pull, gently pressing the fistful of shovel handle to her smooth flank to keep her from tumbling. The sun would be coming all too soon.

He'd kept this trail clear by his own maintenance and concern, hiking by day with a sheathed trail saw hanging on one side of his belt, a strong hinged clipper for smaller branches on the other. He knew this trail the way he'd known his Jenny, could navigate it in the dark, knowing by memory when to grasp, when to duck his head.

What few things Hayden knew, he knew. The rest was a mystery, pure and simple.

As he grasped and ducked he cursed himself, and his burning chest, and promised himself he'd quit smoking again, this time for real, and touched his shirt pocket, wondering if he'd remembered to bring the pack along. It both comforted and disgusted him to feel it there. He'd lean on them now, because he needed to; then, in a day or a week, he'd reclaim his stolen wind.

He reached the saddle of the ridge, the clearing he'd created and maintained, and gently spread her on her side on the cool ground and sat for a moment before going to work. Sat by her side and fired up what he hoped would be one of the last, and set the shovel across his knees, hating the finality of the whole deal. And touched one hand to her cooling side, wishing the sun was up so he could enjoy her smooth blue coat with his eyes and not just his hand. He drew hard on the cigarette tucked deep between his first fingers, watching the red tip glow, hating the way the hot smoke soothed him going down.

Maybe his eyes had adjusted to the dark, or maybe that odd moment of predawn had found them, because Hayden noticed he could nearly make out the silhouettes of buckbrush, the gnarled shapes and nature-sanded smoothness of the manzanita branches. He felt his thinking change about Jenny. He did not wish to see her, not now. Not like this. And the dawn would bring the heat of the day, the enemy, tormentor of men with shovels. No. It wasn't dawn. Couldn't be. Still long too early for that. But it would be, sometime. He had better get started.

For one brief moment he allowed himself to think about Laurel, let himself feel the need, a touch or a word from her to fill the ache of this moment. Hayden told no one, not even Laurel, when he ached, but he often ached for his ache to be seen, to be known by her. To be cooled and settled.

He put the urge away again but it left an echo, the blank, unfilled shock of a craving deferred.

He set about to dig in the hard ground.

Hayden stared down at his hands, at black dirt still packed underneath the nails, ground deep into the calluses of his palms. He didn't mind dirt, not as such. He minded the lack of sleep, the sandy eyes and dicey stomach from staying up the night, challenging the dry soil inch by inch. He minded that Laurel would come soon to start the cinnamon rolls in the half dark, in the barely-morning light, and what if she reached for him or allowed him to reach for her? What, then, would he do with all this dirt?

More even than this, he minded his Jenny in the ground, lost to him. Minded it so much he could not permit his mind to complete that revolution, to spin its gears around to the new, real, entirely changed day. He needed instead to stay mired a few more moments in that foggy no-man's-land, like the moment between sleep and waking when a vivid dream slides away, one unlikely image at a time.

He sat in the dawn in the cab of his old pickup and waited for her to unlock the diner's back door, thinking, Where will I wash my hands, in case I get to touch her? It was a good moment to cry, or would have been, anyway. Only for one thing, though. Hayden didn't cry. Never had, as long as he could remember. Didn't figure at this late date he ever would.

Even Hayden's mother, whom he hadn't seen since he was nineteen, had told him the story time and time again, along with anyone else who would listen. Maybe when you were in diapers, she would say. But after that, nothing. Not even if you hurt yourself bad. Which was usually. Not even when you broke both your legs that time. And it's a funny thing, she would add, because you were always the most deep-down oddly emotional boy anybody'd ever met. Just no tears.

He sat looking out across the long valley, smoking a cigarette, sighting along the endless line of electrical towers. They always looked like headless lattice giants to him. Long legs slightly spread, short arms extended, strands of wires dangling from their fingers and dipping slightly between towers, traveling off into infinity. Every year some fool kids tried to climb them. A combination of rural boredom and some strange rite of new manhood Hayden wished he didn't understand. This year some poor kid paid the price, which was going to happen sooner or later. Rumor had it his watch was still up there somewhere, half melted and fused forever to that unremorseful steel. Even the crystal melted. Hayden didn't know which tower, and he damn sure wasn't going up to look, but it was possible. He knew such a thing could happen.

He looked in his rearview mirror to see the sun just cresting the mountain ridge, the highway clear in that still air, and an animal worrying over something right on the centerline. An odd sight. And it felt good to be distracted, to wonder over somebody else's problem for a change.

A cat, he decided. Moving a kitten across the highway. Hurry, Hayden thought. It's a mean highway. It's a headlight zone. One of those flat two-lane stretches in the middle of nowhere on which motorists are instructed to run their headlights by day. Only way anybody can think to cut the fatalities. Nobody wants to just do nothing, but how much can you do? People die on highways. It's what happens.

Hayden stepped out of his old pickup and watched the

lights of a big rig bear down from the east. Move, cat, he thought, but it wasn't a cat with a kitten, it was a possum. Mother and baby. Which was too bad. A cat he could pick up and move. But possums. Vicious little bastards when threatened. Razor-sharp little teeth.

The rig roared down, and Hayden watched, a bit detached. Somewhat confused. They would move. Of course they would move. Momma possum held her tiny one, eyes barely open, in her teeth, but it squirmed free. Hayden moved closer. Not squirmed, he saw. Convulsed. Something wrong with the baby. Maybe it had been hit already. It seemed to stiffen into little seizures that made it impossible to handle.

Momma possum seemed to know the truck was coming. Death, motherhood – Hayden knew it must be hard to decide. When the headlights fell full across her she abandoned her young and ran. It was late, nearly too late, really, but Hayden stepped into the road and picked it up. It weighed a few ounces at most; it was soft. He jumped back, not even thinking it might bite him. Thinking more about his near miss with the semi. The deep, shocking blare of the truck's air horn pressed into his ears; the wind of the passing monster flapped his big shirt about. The driver flipped Hayden the finger out the window as he blew by.

Hayden only smiled.

The baby possum did not try to bite him. It stiffened into another convulsion in his palm, tiny eyes closed, feeling soft and looking ratlike but innocent. He put it in his shirt pocket, where it seized against his chest. He wanted to return it to the mother but couldn't see where she had gone.

He wondered if it could feel his heart beat.

Old Dr Meecham, the veterinarian, lived over his store-front office. Hayden leaned on his truck horn until Meecham came to the window to ask what the hell gives.

'Oh, you,' he said. The lights came on upstairs and in time he shuffled down.

A hard glare of full morning assaulted Hayden's eyes from the east, over the flat valley landscape; the day's heat already more than threatened. They stood outside, boots in the dirt, two big men hovering over a few ounces of sudden trouble. Meecham wore a shock of pure white hair still tumbled from his pillow.

'Momma abandoned it, huh? That'll happen,' the doc said. 'Born wrong somehow. They know to let it go.'

Hayden didn't bother to say this lady was loath to let go, like Hayden himself with his Jenny, Meecham being a logical sort of a fellow. Some of us, Hayden considered, aren't fortunate enough to possess that cool luxury.

'Some kind of seizures. Want me to put it out of its misery.' Meecham told this as a fact, didn't ask it.

'No, I want you to fix it.'

'Not everything's fixable, Hayden.'

Don't I know it, he thought. 'You're the veterinarian. You're the one supposed to know how.'

'Well, leave it here. I'll see what can be done. Might cost.'

Everything costs, Hayden told himself, money being the least of it. 'I'm prepared to cover it.'

'Don't get your hopes too high. Sure you want it saved? Just what we need around here, another possum.'

'Do what you can, Doc.'

'Be under somebody's wheels on the highway

tomorrow. Born roadkill they are. Just the way of the world, Hayden.'

'You do what you can,' Hayden said, one carefully formed word after another, trying to keep the reasonableness from draining out of his voice.

He walked back to his truck, scuffing his boot toes in the dirt, thinking he must've missed Laurel's arrival at the shop by now, that quiet, untouched moment before life wakes up and shuffles around, disturbing their chances. He said inside himself, That little mass of fur will never grasp the sacrifice.

'How's that good-looking bluetick hound of yours?' Meecham called to his back.

Hayden drove away and did not answer.

When he arrived back at the diner her station wagon was there, along with the car that belonged to the morning waitress.

He stuck his head in the back door and just stood that way a minute, watching Laurel roll the big flat sheet of dough for this morning's cinnamon rolls.

He was that late.

He wondered what might be about to transpire, and whether or not it would hurt. It seemed more or less an even draw, like flipping a coin. Or so the past had taught him.

She addressed him, never once looking up. 'Not like you to sleep in.'

'I haven't slept yet.'

She looked up, as if to confirm or deny that information with her own two eyes; she seemed convinced once she saw his face. He wanted to tell her about Jenny, but it seemed like the morning had already set off in the wrong direction, almost before he'd opened his mouth. So he just stepped inside and watched her work. Watched the place where her apron tied snug at the belt line of her jeans, a pleasingly narrow waist, and the way her hair, kind of brown but red, a dark brown with deep red highlights, had already begun to come apart from the simple way she'd pinned it up this morning. It was better, anyway, apart, mussed looking. It reminded him of other mussed moments, and made his stomach hurt.

He wished she would say something, or that he would.

He moved closer, around her side of the wood table, and slid one arm around her waist, heavy to breaking with his need to do that, but just then the swinging door to the front flew open and the waitress carne through. Laurel ducked away from him, he wasn't entirely sure why. He was never entirely sure if they were a secret or not. If they were anything or not.

They waited for the waitress to bustle around and take what she needed and go again. Hayden stood close enough to Laurel to smell her, not perfume exactly but something like it, that blend of soap and shampoo and Laurel that wouldn't come out the same on any other woman, or in his head on a lonely night. It just could not be reproduced.

'This is not a great time,' she said when the girl had gone. 'Jack'll be in any minute. Anyway, we need to talk.'

The words collected in his stomach, gained weight, and settled hard. And then he saw it. Looked down at her hands gone back to slicing cinnamon rolls from the coil of dough, and there it was, half covered with flour, but there all the same. He grabbed her left hand hard and held it close under his face, in case it was only an illusion, and proximity might break it apart, make it go away. But it was still her wedding band. It wouldn't leave him alone all that easy. He felt dizzy, like he might pass out, but in the end was not nearly so fortunate.

'You couldn't have told me about this?'

'I'm trying to tell you about it right now. Could you let go my hand, please? You're hurting me.'

'Oh. Sorry.' He dropped her hand and dropped his own hands to his sides, and looked up to see Jack standing in the doorway, watching them. 'I was just leaving,' Hayden said.

At the doorway Jack did not step out of his way. They stood like that a moment, nearly nose to nose, maintaining eye contact in the manner that any animal will know to do in such a bind. Jack was good looking, which didn't help, with that shiny kind of pretty-boy looks. He had a fifteen-year age advantage on Hayden, but Hayden had a couple of inches and maybe fifty pounds of bulk on Jack. Just for that moment Hayden wouldn't have minded throwing all that into the fray, just to see what would prove more important than what. Wouldn't have minded a bit.

'Guys,' Laurel said, which broke up those thoughts and knocked Hayden onto a different train of action.

'You're in my way, Jack,' he said, and Jack took one step to the side to let him pass. Just as he did, Jack bumped Hayden's shoulder hard with his own, but Hayden just kept walking, at least until it was time to drive.

It was too soon to go back to Meecham's, Hayden knew. Yet he went back there all the same. Where else would he go? Home, to an empty cabin? To no Laurel, no Jenny, no buffer for this roiling disarray spilling around inside him, where it could do harm to himself or others? Better to use himself in some way. If only this had been a working day. If only this had not fallen on his day off from the hardware store, but so it did.

Meecham's assistant was nowhere to be seen. Meecham himself came out from the back examination room, wiping his hands on his lab smock and shaking his head.

'Gone, Hayden. Sorry.' He didn't say it so much like he felt deeply sorry, more like he was sorry to have to tell Hayden something Hayden didn't care to know.

'Seizures killed it?'

'Well, I—'

'What exactly killed it?'

'Can't save everything, Hayden.'

Now it began to rise in him, that hard disdain for being gently tutored in something he knew better than anybody. Meecham stood close up on the other side of the front counter now, and Hayden wanted him to stand farther back. Much farther. To where nobody could get hurt.

'In other words, Doc, you decided not to save it, so you just put it down.'

Meecham seemed to see, or read, or smell the anger in Hayden, packed into and driven in front of those words, and he peered into Hayden's face with a frightened curiosity. He did not stand back. He should've stood back.

'It died, Hayden.'

'You put it down.'

'It died.'

'Fine. Give its body over to me, I'll drive it to the vet in the city, we'll see what it died from.'

'Can't do that. Against county law. Animal dies in this county, remains gotta go in for rabies testing.'

'It wasn't even alive long enough to have late-stage rabies convulsions. You damn well know that. You said yourself it was just born wrong.'

'County law.'

'Okay. Keep what you need to test, give me what's left over.'

Meecham's look had become more frightened, then leveled off, now turned stony with indignation and enough stubbornness, he seemed to feel, to match Hayden's. 'Won't be nothing left over. They got to take a bunch of cross sections of that brain. Look. Hayden. We've known each other for a while now—'

'You killed it.'

'All right, goddamnit. Yes. I put it down. For Christ's sake, Hayden. It was born wrong. It wasn't a hound dog. It wasn't your momma. It was a possum. A god damn fucking possum. Get a grip, man.'

While Hayden's fist arced, he felt it like a lung full of hot smoke or a private touch from Laurel, soothing deep in his belly, the delivery of something sweet and sorely needed. He threw his upper body half over the counter and caught the doc square on the jaw, fist to face, knucklebones to jawbone, and the jaw gave, and so did the fist.

It was not the first jaw Hayden had ever broken, and he knew the feel of it well, the sickening feel of give, and the sound. Not a clean crack like what one might expect, but an unsettling crunch, the sound of boots on icy crusts of snow on a school day morning in Hayden's long-lost youth.

It was also not Hayden's first boxer's fracture, and he knew the feel of that as well, the bowing of the outer bone of his hand, then that sudden point of bright pain where it decides to let go.

The vet tumbled to his own linoleum floor.

Hayden came around to the doc's side of the counter, and the old man rolled onto his belly to protect himself, but it was for no purpose. Hayden had finished being angry.

He picked up the doc's phone and called the local ambulance service. Could've called 911 to dispatch them, but it seemed like a lot of histrionics for a simple case of two broken bones.

While he waited on a ringing line he spoke to Meecham. 'Okay down there, Doc? I'm gonna call somebody to come by, take you to the hospital. You just hold steady where you are, okay?'

No intelligible sounds came back to him, just a muffled grumble.

'Morning, Della,' he said into the phone. 'Hayden Reese . . . Good, how're you? I'm over at Doc Meecham's, and I think he'd like it fine if the ambulance came and scooped him up and took him into the city . . .

'Just a broken jaw, I think, but he's in some pain.' He glanced down at his right hand, noted the early stages of swelling and blackening.

'Me, no, I'm fine, Della. I'm just going to swing by the doctor here in town. You could do me a good favor, though. Once you got that ambulance on its way, could;

you give Scott a call for me? Tell him to meet me by the doctor's office? . . .

'Yeah, I'll wait for him . . . .

'Thanks, Della.'

Read the complete book – *The Hardest Part of Love* is available now

The Hardest Part of Love

CATHERINE RYAN HYDE

Any idiot can fall in love. No special talent required for that. The trick is to love somebody who might actually do you some good. That's the part hardly anybody gets right.

Hayden briefly has it all: a wife and daughter he adores and a baby on the way. But when his son dies at birth, a deep anger emerges, robbing Hayden of everything.

Years on, Hayden is living in self-imposed exile. He's just lost his beloved dog and is now losing Laurel, the only woman he's loved since . . .

But just as Hayden's rage rises again, a young figure from the past emerges, forcing him to re-visit his long-buried childhood . . .

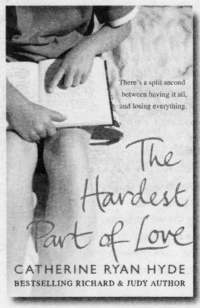

'Ryan Hyde spins her tale so effortlessly that the reader closes the book with a quiet sense of elation' *San Francisco Chronicle*

Originally published as *Electric God*

When I Found You

CATHERINE RYAN HYDE

When Nathan McCann
discovers a newborn baby
boy half buried in the woods,
he assumes he's found a tiny
dead body. But then the baby
moves and in one remarkable
moment, Nathan's life is
changed forever.

The baby is sent to grow up
with his grandmother, but
Nathan is compelled to pay
her a visit. He asks for one
simple promise – that one
day she will introduce the
boy to Nathan and tell him,
'This is the man who found
you in the woods.'

Years pass and Nathan
assumes that the old lady
has not kept her promise,
until one day an angry,
troubled boy arrives on his
doorstep with a suitcase . . .

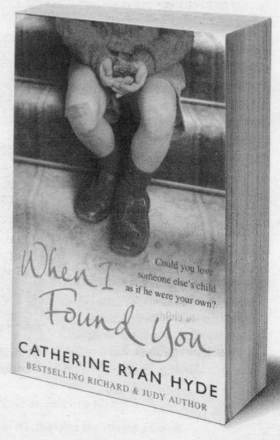

Could you love
someone else's child
as if he were your own?

When I
Found You

CATHERINE RYAN HYDE
BESTSELLING RICHARD & JUDY AUTHOR

Second Hand Heart

CATHERINE RYAN HYDE

'Thanks for the heart,' she said.

It was a surprisingly simple statement in the midst of all that life and death and indebtedness.

One girl

Vida is nineteen, very ill, and has spent her short life preparing for death. But a new chance brings its own story, because for Vida to live, someone had to die.

One man

Richard has just lost his beloved wife in a car accident. He hasnt even begun to address his grief, but feels compelled to meet the girl who inherited his wife's heart.

Someone else's heart

In hospital Vida sees Richard and immediately falls in love. Of course he dismisses her as a foolish child. But is she? Can two people be bound by a second hand heart?

'An extraordinary and unforgettable novel' *Susan Lewis*